Martin Wiinholt

ESPERO

Book One of the Alterity Chronicles

Jackdaw Books

DEDICATION

Two people in particular deserve thanks: My friend Martin Havemann for heroically reading through those early drafts and my editor, Mika Court, for her support and wisdom.

ACKNOWLEDGMENTS

As the late Iain M. Banks once remarked, no space opera is written in a vacuum. The original concept for this story was inspired by a game of Aurora, which is a free space strategy game developed by Steve Walmsley. All starship action in the book can be recreated in that game.

PROLOGUE

Year 3266. School of Aneen, Madeira

Here, from the window of my little room in the second highest level of the tower, I watch the triple suns of Madeira as they sink below the horizon. They are still as beautiful as they were that first night, eighty years ago, when I was brought to the School as a small child. Many believe - and I believe - that I have been designated for this work by the Spirit of the Teacher. In spite of my old age, I do not want to give it up; I work out of love for the Teacher and I put all my hope in Him.

As has become my habit, I have been to the library and drawn out a number of volumes to get me through another sleepless night. One of them is the 1634th Rendition of the 1st Episode of the Exordium, recorded in the period we call the Age of Youth. My school has sent Tellers to Stand and present their renditions before the Teacher almost ten thousand times, for that is the number of volumes in the library. The renditions all treat the same topic and as such reading them is a monotonous task best left to old men like myself. But once in a while, it is admittedly quite rare, a Teller will excel and deliver a rendition which is masterful. This one, the 1634th, seems quite ordinary, however. A cursory glance through the pages confirm it. Still, and that is a constant, the Teller deserves credit for his bravery.

It is true that I have never been called and my age is too far advanced for it to happen now. Once it shamed me, but nowadays, as we look deeply within, we understand our perfect balance. There is no fear of the cycle of birth, life and death. For when you stand in the present moment, you are timeless. Such is the core belief of our School. The Tellers, most of them, at any rate, understood. They arrive in His presence on the Grewal, dressed all in white, and in His august presence, they recount the first episode and they do it in no more and no less than twelve hours. Every so often, a Teller, due to bad disposition or weakness, a rare occurrence, will ask for a continuance beyond the twelve hours. The request is always denied. When the appointed hours have passed, the Teller is put to death, quite painlessly, by a pegui entering his heart in a downwards stroke starting at the left shoulder. His back is always turned to the executioner.

Looking at the caption in this rendition, I see that it too was called for at the end of a thirty-three day cycle. It confirms the central tenet of my thesis; that The Teacher commonly call for a Teller toward the end of a cycle, before He partakes of the renewal of the sanmonban.

We sent another one today. Tomorrow we shall read how he did.

ONE

Year 2112. Mingo (former Halifax) Orbital, Earth orbit
Unknown to the inhabitants of the orbital, the Global Space Agency, Survey Branch, the corporations, and everyone on Earth, the Great Interstellar War had just begun. It had been triggered by a starship a few years earlier. The specifics were still shrouded in rumor but like a wise man once said, "there is a terrible lot of lies going around about the world... and the worst of it is that half of them are true."

Many truths and many lies were told in the bars where Spacers drink together, and it was a blimpish fellow, a regular, who started the discussion on this day concerning the battles the Mingo Corporation ship, Yu-kiang, had won on its mission to the fabled planet of Espero. As the only ship ever to return, the Yu-kiang inspired people in the bar with equal measures of pride, suspicion and envy, contingent on their affiliations.

The blimpish fellow was interrupted by an educated soul, who imagined himself a historian. 'It was bound to happen', he bellowed, 'it is nature's way of telling us we have crossed a line.' For deterministic minds such as his, it was almost a mechanical certainty that once the HAI's had uncovered the secrets of Spinfoam and a certain Captain Liam Dupont had taken his ship through it, or more correctly, into it, and that the good ship, which had the name of Edmond Halley stenciled on its duranium hull, appeared in a place inconceivably far away from our familiar yellow sun and its nine companions, and the men and women onboard laid eyes on the orange sun of Proxima Centauri, mankind was bound to encounter mysteries surpassing its understanding of the universe.

'And the Beltane? What of the Beltane?' yelled a green robed follower of the Org, deep in his cups or stoned or perhaps both. Now that was a prickly issue and one the Mingo folks in the bar would gladly avoid. It was true that the Beltane had yet to return. But since the Mingo had a reputation for being the only corporation with the secret of the passage, they were not, especially in present company, ready to accept that the ship was lost along with every other ship anyone had ever sent to Espero since the planet was discovered some ten years earlier.

One rumor, quite persistent, would have it that Survey Branch knew more than they were letting on. As it happened, at the end of the bar, there was a group of freshly minted officers from this élite organization, and as usual they formed their own murmuring caucus concerning that mission. Amongst themselves, they would point to the deft footwork and the barefaced bravery of the Yu-kiang crew, to the genius displayed by Captain Florian, and above all to the wonderful performance of the ship itself. To these men it was a victory of technology. Or was it?

As would become apparent, the debate continued wherever Spacers met in those years, though the name of the other ship, understandably, was seldom mentioned. Occasionally, it is true, somebody, out of foolishness or sentiment or plain forgetfulness, does dredge it up and there is atmosphere for a moment, but it passes. Just the other day, a young cadet of the Survey Branch Advanced Mission Academy in Geneva evoked that fateful ship's name. One could almost excuse him. The details of the Yu-kiang mission, including certain undisclosed chapters kept out of the public records -- concerning, notably, the criminal Sergey Malyutin and his company of Shield mercenaries; the iconic tycoon, Zach Baranikowa, who had employed them, and whose madness had ruined his once-mighty company; and, not least, his son -- were being introduced to the class. The students were animated with the feeling one gets when finally admitted to the inner circle of a secret society. 'Frankly', said the foolish young man dressed in a dark blue ensign's uniform, 'What exactly was it that we won? As I see it they fled the system and the Beltane never returned? Or did it? Is there something they haven't told us?' At this point someone, a senior officer, a man or a woman, his or her name does not matter, whispered something into the ensign's ear. The breathless ensign fell silent and soon quietly left the class, retiring to his quarters calling it a night.

TWO

Earth, New Year's Eve 2099

To less, or perhaps more, flowery minds, a more realistic starting point is a certain Wednesday in December, just three days before the start of the new century, around three o'clock in the afternoon, when the sky over the Baranikowa family's mountain retreat in Yellowstone was an incredibly crisp blue completely unblemished by cloud. It was a most rare sight indeed. Inside, in the lavish living room with its glittering view of the surrounding mountains, the score that made up the Silver Needle entourage were busying themselves setting up the bowls, which would hold the Blue Duck. Positioning the bowls was a matter of strategy and careful consideration. If they got it wrong the partygoers would run the risk of experiencing uneven levels of intoxication, and that, in Basil's social circles, was considered a grave faux pas. The entourage was an international bunch, with people from most corners of the planet. There was even a lanky Chinese fellow who had managed to insinuate himself into Basil's good graces by means of his much admired ability to juggle the onslaught of DmC and Sentai and stay lucid throughout.

Guests were constantly arriving in helicopters, landing and taking off steadily. A couple of hours later, to a room thrumming with voices, the Eight Day Man himself climbed the dinner table and gave a little speech. No one understood a word until, with a magnificent sweep of his arm, he made everyone turn towards the back of the room where the wall was claying itself into a giant three dimensional screen displaying the final show of the fifth season of the incredibly popular Viscerality show XDub starring none other than the man himself. The premise for the show was as simple as they come. For the past many years, subscribers had followed Basil's life in glorious holographic detail and the season finale, just now unfolding on the screen, in an exclusive preview, did not disappoint. Unspeakable sexual acts, dissected by a tantalizing mix of silky panoramas and completely unfazed stills, augmented by flexible alternative camera controls for premium users, left no leaf unturned in their portrayal of Basil. It was a screen persona, certainly, and thus not entirely him, but it was his penis appearing on the screen now, flaccid, swelling, ready to burst, bursting. No leaf unturned. The color of the hair in his butt crack revealed and those with the correct plug-ins could even enjoy the smell of his breath at five o'clock in the morning after a weeklong binge. It was a damn good show.

With almost three days to go before the centennial fireworks, Basil's mind was already fragmented into tiny pieces by the potent cocktail of drugs he was ingesting. Part of him was thinking that the party was going great. The crowd was wonderful and amazing, filled with just the right people. This part of his brain was exalted about the company and it reveled in the love and good vibrations he thought they were sending his way. Another part was occupied with a great looking girl who had just come up to him. Long legs, lithe body, big puffy lips and blue eyes. The talent scouts knew his taste and this one had been dredged out of the lower levels of the Massif arcology. He was ecstatic. She was so lovely. He didn't know, but this was actually their first encounter, nevertheless, even at the best of times, Basil wasn't big on introductions so he just seized her in his arms and kissed her right on the mouth. The feeling of her lips pleased him so much that in fact he couldn't recall ever having kissed a mouth that succulent, soft, yet firm. 'You have a succulent mouth,' he told her. 'Would you?' Pushing her head down and making him blow him, he'd jumped ahead somewhat, but everyone knew it was just the way he was. 'How about buying me dinner first,' she laughed, but she did him anyway. 'What's your name', he groaned between meaty animal sounds. The girl's answer was stifled and he couldn't quite make it out, try as he might. Behind him the screen was alive with flesh.

Time to don the old evening dress. The crowd was a little worse for wear but keeping up appearances was never more important. Dinner was being served in a palace, after all. In a fit of nostalgia, Keas, his producer, had asked for colonial style and despite spotty historical records, the Manor had come up with a very adroit rendition of the Governor's Palace in Mount Lavinia, circa 1809, all mahogany wood, white cloth and impeccable manners. Naturally, this meant the guests were obliged to admire Basil as he strutted around disguised as a sort of deviant Thomas Maitland. Hair shiny with pomade, he appeared an eviscerated vampire, with his gaunt, pale face, spindly body and wayward manners, beside one of the Manor girls the staff had dressed as his beloved, Lovina.

As the sun set, the Rocky Mountains looked almost blue, the valleys far below the house misty and pleasingly mysterious. It was a good setting for a New Year's party, everyone agreed. La pièce de résistance of the evening were the aromas. On this night the ubiquitous Duck was accompanied by thick wafts of cinnamon and tea which was either an allusion bordering on the obscene considering the sad fate of that island earlier in the century. Or perhaps it was just plain ignorance. What could you expect of a Manor after all? Dinner was announced and people rowdily found their seats. Basil held forth with another of his incoherent speeches neither heard nor understood.

At some point during the following day he got into a heated discussion with a guy over a bowl of steaming blue duck. They sat next to each other on the red sofa, under an antique painting by Holbein, close, thighs touching, like two naughty school children. Basil was still wearing his evening dress from the day before, as he bent over the bowl, greedily inhaling the swirling blue smoke and discussing the finer points of traditional Japanese gardening. Neither of them knew much about the subject but it didn't matter. As supercharged duck washed over them like a tsunami, it was forgotten.

Vinales

The party was on its fourth day. New Year's Eve had come and gone and they had relocated. The one they called Blow Me Girl, or BMG -- she had those swimming blue eyes -- had been appointed keeper of records and appointments. It might have been a somewhat premature promotion but she had become Basil's favorite and as such she deserved a title. Four days in his company was half a lifetime, as they used to say. BMG was the only member of the entourage who was connected at this particular point in time and, unbeknownst to his Royal Highness, the BB himself, she had been briefed by Greitz, Basil's head of security.

BMG had recently returned from a hiatus in the cargohold. Keas, the producer, seeing that the BB was getting bored, had told her to disappear for forty-eight hours in the cargo bay despite it being freezing cold down there. Greitz, knowing her particular cravings, had sweetened the deal with a huge bag of ket. Bag in hand, she did as she was told. When she returned two days later, she walked right up to Basil, whose eyes widened in surprise, tore off his pants and began licking his balls *in just that way*. Basil was flabbergasted. What an amazing girl, he exclaimed again and again. To do this well on her first try – that is truly something. And the panache! After climaxing, and passing her a napkin, ever the gentleman, he got her on her feet and formally asked her, like he'd done a dozen times already, to join his entourage. She demurely accepted. Again and again. The eight day man was absurdly easy to please. They all knew how after all this time. Was he ever off the DmC? Not really. Not in living memory. For at least twenty years no one had seen him off the drug. His brain, they sometimes joked, would explode if he stopped. Imagine a lifetime worth of memories flooding into your brain in a few seconds. Damn unpleasant.

BMG raised her voice in a tone that quavered a bit too much to be properly languid. 'Your Royal BBish Highness.' It was a game they played; they all referred to each other as Kings and Queens, Marshals and Ministers. The BMG, for example, was Minister of Culture. 'Yes, my child. What could possibly induce you to disturb the musings of your monarch?' Basil had been dozing. He woke and Keas let them access for a bit. Let's fire them up a little, the rats. He thought of them as rats. Scurrying around in the walls, watching. It amused him, always had. 'Well...' Basil interrupted her. 'Dear Minister of Culture. Answer me this: what is happiness?' She squinted. 'Happiness? Happiness... is to wake up on a bright spring morning... after a night spent with a... beautiful boy, no, a dwarf boy, a hugely well-endowed dwarf boy.' Basil chuckled. He was holding a glass, swirling around the liquid it contained. He gulped down the content and Keas could see from his face it burned all the way down his throat. They were in an airship, drifting slowly over the North Pole. It had seemed like a good idea when Keas had proposed it. Kind of philosophical and profound, but he'd already regretted it. The journey seemed endless and Basil was getting bored. The lounge was a glass dome pouting under the ship's stern like a swollen lip. The effect was unsettling, he had been heavily accessed in the beginning of the journey, but the novelty had worn off in thirty minutes. Ungrateful bastards. The six people of the entourage were lounging directly on the glass floor on carpets and pillows spread out like floating islands over the sparkling white expanse of unbroken cloud cover far beneath them.

'A dwarf again, you're positively obsessed with them, dear girl.'

'There is a message for you.'

'A message?' He looked around. 'I don't see anyone here.' That was a tired joke and it drew a tired chuckle from some of the diehard sycophants.

'From your Father, it is a message from your Father.' Everyone fell silent. Basil poured himself another glass of wine. He held it up to the sun, eyes narrowing; it was a yellow, fruity green.

Basil looked at Keas who nodded slowly to him. That would tell him this 'Father' was an important person. 'Well?' The languid little sketch continued while Basil furiously thought of a snappy reply. He raised his eyebrows indulgently, slanted eyes looking at the girl over the rim of his glass.

'How does he look?'

An image appeared superimposed on glassy shell of the airship. It was an old man, not decrepit, but an energetic kind of old, hair still brown with slashes of grey in it. His eyes were set deep into his face, under two prominent ledges of bushy eyebrows, with heavyset jowls that hung like bags from his cheeks.

'Long story short, Basil,' said Keas. 'We have to go into orbit. Something has come up.'

'Right,' said Basil. 'See, I didn't even know we could do that. Orbit? That's like, above the clouds, right?'

'That's right. It'll be really exciting. And *good show* too.'

Good show. Whenever Keas said that, Basil knew it was *serious business that had to be done.*

'We're asked to join him for a public ceremony in two days.'

'Are we now? And what kind of ceremony would that be?'

'The GSA have... just decided... to award him the Global Community Award for a...' The girl was reading aloud now. 'Lifetime of service to Humanity and for his selfless commitment to the Reconstruction...' Her voice was cracking up.

'Don't be nervous, girl,' Basil said to reassure her. 'It's just you, me and a billion viewers.' Another old joke, which drew more old laughter.

'Something like that,' she said and shut up.

Basil didn't speak. He gazed out at the arctic sea, eyes half closed under heavy eyelids. The girl nodded. 'They expect us in Vinales in 36 hours. A shuttle will be ready for us there.'

--

The next day found the merry party in an HSL aircraft heading south to the Vinales spaceport. The walls of the aircraft were transparent but you wouldn't have known that until it finished its long descent through the perennial thick layer of turbulent, slate clouds heavy with rain. Suddenly the clouds vanished and the murky charcoal of the Caribbean came into view under the speeding aircraft. They were headed for an island.

'Cuba', the pilot announced, 'or, what is left of it'.

The island was indeed C shaped; a gigantic valley surrounded by mountains on three sides. Missile emplacements and bunkers sprinkled the mountain rim. In the valley, spectacular limestone outcrops rose abruptly over the central plain, most rising one or two hundred meters. The central outcrop rose more than three hundred meters into the air and looked like a gigantic dinner table, which everyone had left in a hurry. Its raised landing pad formed the focal point of the base, dotted with elevators rising from its depths, disgorging fat, orbital shuttle craft and airplanes which took off and landed regularly. A stygian maze of roads, low buildings, and power plant like things extended across the valley floor for several kilometers around the landing pad. To the east of the island was a companion seaport facility which dominated the open end of the island. Ships could be seen coming and going all the way to the horizon.

'What is that? A volcano? How exciting,' Basil asked the pilot. He peered through the windows at a distant island with a curious, triangular silhouette

'No, sir, that is the beginning of the space elevator that the HAI's were building. The work was… discontinued when we discovered their treachery.' Basil didn't know what a space elevator was.

The party fell silent as the grimy, rain splattered tarmac rose under them and even Basil, who was nursing a pleasant, medium strength

15

Sentai high, what he usually referred to as a morning quickie, felt a quite unusual tension gripping his shoulders and neck at the thought of space.

'Vinales is one of three spaceports serving the Restoration', announced the pilot who seemed to mistake them for interested tourists. BMG yawned loudly to make the point.

The aircraft landed with a thud and the entourage spilled out. Keas, in a fit of expansiveness, gave the rats a little feuilleton, 5 minute access windows on the hour during the entire royal procession to Halifax, but the moment they stepped out of the aircraft he knew he'd made a mistake. They looked ludicrous and small as they huddled on the vast, concrete tarmac next to the plane, like a wayward circus. Basil had dressed for the occasion as the High Prince of the Circus, in a beautiful harlequin suit and very unpractical oversized shoes and BMG was dressed in a 17th century fencing outfit, complete with goose feathered hat. The plan was an utter failure. They had expected a sort of formal gathering to greet BB and dressed accordingly, but all they got was a stodgy mid-level employee dressed in grey coveralls. Around them the air thundered with the deafening roars of shuttles taking off and landing and the sky above the platform was streaked with vapor trails from spacegoing shuttles. The man beckoned to them, gale-force, feverishly hot winds blew across the platform, ripping into their costumes and lifting the hat off BMG's head. It careened down the runway. Keas, who was downwind from BMG in a tight Changshan robe in blue silk, unwisely tried to catch it, but lost his balance and fell on his ass. Seconds later, the hat flew off the edge of the platform and disappeared. The stodgy employee made the ritualistic circle and slash gesture warning them that rad's were piling up and they ran for the entrance of a nearby elevator which took them down into the cool, silent interior.

'Take off all your clothes, please,' said the little man and turned his back on them. They looked at each other. BMG giggled.

'Are you sure about this, my good man?' said Basil. He straightened his back, posing with dignity and a dash of pretend outrage. The goose feather in his hat – newly borrowed from BMG -- trembled slightly.

'It is not like that!' The man looked aghast. 'Your outfits are there, on the bench,' he answered, turning his back to them once again. He was obviously familiar with Basil's reputation.

They looked at the bench but all they saw was what looked like five fist sized lumps of brownish dirt.

'I see,' Basil answered but he didn't. The Entourage looked at the brown lumps, at each other, and back at the brown lumps.

Apparently the man had realized they had no idea what they were supposed to do because he said: 'Take off your clothes and pick up a piece of clay from bench. It'll do all the work for ya.'

He had barely finished the last sentence before the rustle of BMG's clothes was heard hitting the floor. Naked as the day she was born she approached the bench and reached for the clay. The others looked on passively. As her fingers made contact with the clay, it slithered, or flowed, onto her hand, over her wrist, swallowing her arms, her torso, and lastly her head which it covered briefly before retreating down to her neck where it stabilized. The impression was that of new layer of skin the color of fine gravel clinging to her body. At first her eyes widened in panic, but in a matter of seconds it seemed she acquiesced gracefully into the new vestment.

The sensation of the clay suit was strange but not altogether unpleasant. The suit felt alive against the skin, like a thousand sand corns rustling against one with wills of their own. Keas tensed for a moment, wondering if they intended to slither into his orifices and plug him but apparently they were intelligent enough to know not to. He closed his eyes waiting for the clay to smooth out and the sensation of flowing water to cease. After a few minutes the minute movements settled and what remained was an uncanny sensation of being naked. He looked at the others. Though he felt naked, the suits were programmed to smooth out the crevices and gullies of their bodies. The effect - especially on Basils beloved BMG - was quite fetching. The HSL man said they could interface with the suits if they wanted to, but even Keas, who had a reputation of moderate geekiness, couldn't figure out how and they were all, quite obviously, too embarrassed to ask. When everyone had donned the clay suits, the little man, who had patiently waited at the door, told them to follow and led them through a series of unmarked corridors and more elevators to a couple of blast doors which opened into an underground hall. The hall, about 500 meters long and half as broad, was buzzing with activity, dismantled shuttles undergoing repairs, towering bales of cargo slowly snaking their way along predetermined paths and shuttles moving to and from the elevators leading up to the landing pads.

'Follow the yellow line,' he yelled back at them and, considering the vast amount of heavy machinery moving about, even Basil felt no need to put on a show of his vaunted disrespect for authorities at that particular moment in time.

So, subdued, they goose-stepped along the yellow stitched line behind the grey man, snaking their way to a waiting shuttle with red and white HSL markings. The man showed them to their seats and left the shuttle without a word. The door closed and they were immediately taxied to the nearest elevator. They had the sensation of rising smoothly in complete darkness. As they appeared topside, a wall of rain pelted the transparent exterior while inside the shuttle, everything remained completely still. The effect of raindrops hammering noiselessly on the glass was eerie, but they barely had time to adjust before the clay suits strapped them down in the seats. The shuttle rose a few meters into a gentle, swaying hover which it held for a few seconds, then the flexible engine nozzles, which lined its squat body, turned abruptly backwards, ignited and pushed the shuttle into a bone crushing vertical acceleration. The steady acceleration prevented all movement and no one, in what was a historic first for Silver Needle Entourage, even considered talking apart from involuntary grunts and moans escaping from clenched jaws. To make matters worse the shuttle maintained transparent walls giving an uninterrupted view of the planet dropping away on all sides, under them.

'What is this place? What is this place?' Basil kept repeating to himself like a child utterly lost.

Keas upped the Sentai dose, which visibly calmed him down, but even half out of his mind, Basil kept repeating 'What is this place?' Not for the first time, Keas wondered if DmC really worked like they thought or if some small remnant of your former self always remained with you.

Little by little, the sky darkened and the shaking subsided. The pretty boys and girls continued groaning, but the real test was yet to come. Once in orbit, the engines shut down and the clay suits, undoubtedly meaning well, loosened their grip on the seats. Zero gravity. Just then, a globule drifting past the tip of his nose, followed by an acrid smell of vomit, tore him out of his reverie and he heard

Basil laughing hysterically. Chili Boy was puking his brains out. One after another they succumbed. All, except Basil who kept laughing and popping the globules near him with his index finger. The cabin slowly filled. It was an eerie sight. Like a galaxy of floating, multicolored comets which, each time the thrusters kicked in this or that direction, inevitably came back to collide with their place of origin. They flew for what seemed like a long time. When Earth was the size of a football behind them, the Halifax orbital came into view.

The orbital looked like a dozen bagels, one on top of another, with a drumstick jammed through them. Except the bagels were not regularly shaped. Everywhere saliencies, some mere nodulations, some cheoptic protuberances growing out of the surface, severely disrupted the geometric purity of the design. A simple design, it used centripetal force to create the sensation of gravity in the rings. The drumstick was very long and very thick and miniature spaceships in muted silver clung to it like dragonflies. Some were long, interplanetary freighters, hauling ore from the dark outskirts of the solar system. Others were smaller orbital cargo vessels, which distributed the ore among the orbital refineries and manufacturing plants circling Earth in high orbit. Their shuttle was not aiming for the drumstick, but was headed for a stamp sized docking area on the outermost hoop, a place designed to accommodate only small spaceships carrying people and light cargo.

The shuttle latched on to a docking port. Gravity returned with a vengeance and down suddenly became down again. The pilot emerged from the cockpit muttering something about how he hoped they'd had a nice flight but his voice trailed off at the sight of the mess in his passenger compartment. A door opened in the ceiling. Basil stuck his head up through it. 'What is this place?' he asked innocently. A welcoming committee was waiting for them. A group of official looking men and women were lined up like soldiers in front of the docking port, waiting for the shuttle to emit the Son Of Zach into their midst. Basil clambered up and was followed by his entourage, one more ashen-faced and unsteady than the next. The dejected first time space travelers appeared stained with foul smelling vomit which, ironically, had they known how to manipulate the clay suits, was easily removed. It was a sorry sight indeed.

Basil nodded curtly to everyone, steady as she goes, face fixed in a grimace he intended as a benevolent smile. This he could do. Meet and greet. Almost second nature. The head of the delegation, a tough-looking woman with a manly bearing, performed a convincing pantomime of being pleased at shaking his hand and those of his distinguished friends. They were in a VIP reception area, which looked almost, but not quite, plush. Battling copious amounts of feet shuffling and ceiling gazing from Basil's crew, the woman insisted on a high-sounding speech about the orbital. 'Welcome to a masterpiece of technology and engineering! Many thousands of scientists and engineers were behind the planning and construction of this marvelous facility. As you surely know, Halifax is the hub for all Halifax Shipping Line space operations. Here we provide shipyard services, training facilities and a repair and maintenance base for the fleet. As such it is the central high orbit Earth cargo distribution center for all HSL shipping operations. We also provide these services to a number of smaller companies who operate here on a rental basis. Furthermore, a section of the A-ring is designated for use by the Global Space Agency for science missions and Survey Branch operations...'

A VIP suite had been reserved for Basil's party. Thankfully it was located in one of the inner rings, which were under centrifugal gravity. 'The ceremony is in eight hours.'

--

What happened next wasn't too surprising. Basil, quite shaken by the shuttle ordeal, was experiencing dangerously uneven levels of stimulants in his blood. Keas' monitors were all over the place. He sent Greitz a message, and he, they knew Basil trusted him inherently, assured Basil there was plenty of narcotics to be found on Halifax provided you knew where to look. And besides, it wasn't every day you got to experience the innards of the vaunted space program first hand and it sure beat being bored to death over the North Pole.

Chili Boy was a homeless kid who had caught Basil's attention in Austria a few years earlier. The boy was sullen and chronically unimpressed which usually amused Basil.

'This place stinks worse than the Montreal Arc and that's saying something,' he said loudly. At this point Basil would normally have laughed, but the falling levels of sunshine in his blood was making him cantankerous and ill-tempered and for reasons not entirely clear the criticism annoyed him.

'This is the sharp end of the stick, you idiot,' Basil replied angrily and, as the words came out of his mouth, he seemed to realize they were not his own. *We're the sharp end of the stick, son, without us, there would be no Restoration.* Who had said that?

'Well,' said Keas a little too quickly, 'space isn't what it used to be.'

But it was too late. Basil's outburst had cowed them and they fell into silence. It was BMG, bless her pluckiness, who plunged in and broke the spell. 'Speaking of which, Your BBisness Highness, what is the plan? Why are we here? Have we done something to displease you since we had to sit through all that zero-G unpleasantness on the way here?'

'I have no idea what we're doing here,' muttered Basil.

'Greitz, the girl is right, we need to score. Sooner rather than later,' Keas told him.

Greitz nodded slowly to himself as if the thought hadn't occurred to him until now. The ruddy face was inscrutable; face of a Buddha of deep strategy and infinite possibilities. After a minute of silence he said: 'Let's go check things out. I know a place.'

They followed Greitz out of the rooms, along a slight upward bend to the corridor, visible only when you let your gaze wander up and down. Otherwise there was no hint they were in space. It could have been a hotel in the innards of an arcology with no exterior windows or apartments like in one of the new ones they were building deep underground. They started walking in a random direction, found a staircase which led down, emerged into a broad tunnel, into what was almost a mall, lined with shops and foodstalls.

'Where are we?' asked the boy.

'This area is the Concourse. The Concourse is located in the next-to-outermost ring, just inside the main industrial area, the docking areas and the cargo handling,' answered Greitz obligingly as if reading aloud.

'How come you know this place? Have you been here before?' asked Basil. To his surprise, no one answered.

'Oh, you guys, you're hiding something. Do you have a surprise for me? I'll shut up, promise.' He smiled to himself. Anticipation was half the fun.

They walked on in silence for a few minutes, then Keas, who had finally figured out how to access through the suit, said with a laugh:

'The locals call it the Great Sphinxter.'

The name was justified. The smells enveloping them were indicative of very, let's say primitive, cuisine indeed and a distinctly laissez faire attitude to hygiene that would have surprised Basil, had he been capable of remembering his youth. The passageways on Halifax were dusty, dark tunnels interrupted by cones of light emanating from doorways of whatever businesses could make a living from the Spacers.

The rest of the lights were dialed down on purpose. It was a place to disappear, from yourself and your crewmates. It was a place which had evolved to favor anonymity. Contrary to all design manuals and architectural principles, this place was all dark corners, forbidding tunnels and people busy burrowing their way to that rarest of all currencies in space – anonymity, the ability to disappear from yourself and from your crewmates, for hours, even days. As a social experiment it had been an utter failure, but in the paroxysm of its failure, the pervasive elasticity of life had found it and was shaping it to fit. The architects had planned for artificial cheerfulness, for green and a place for the human spirit to roar, but what the spacers wanted was not that. They needed to abscond, they desperately longed for the recklessness of the blind man, the mystique of a dark burrow or the warm embrace of another human under the blanket of complete anonymity. Going back down to Earth was out of the question for most of them. The gravity well was a forbidding divide that could only be crossed at high cost. Still, sometimes, when ships were decommissioned or there were cutbacks, numbers of them would be asked to return to Earth. But, when the day finally came and the company shuttle waited, doors open, no one would show up. Effectively, going back down was not an option to these people. And so Halifax grew and grew, her former employees excavating, like abscesses, outwards, deforming the clean geometry of her original design. There were even rumors of children roaming passageways in certain sectors.

Metal grating covered the floor of the Concourse. Its ten or fifteen meter wide expanse continued in both directions as far as the eye could see, curving slightly away, brimming with people wandering aimlessly around. Wide eyed asteroid miners just off ship, suits still covered with grey dust; herds of ship crew, clinging together, branded like cattle, their ship name shimmering proudly over their heads.

Food stalls lined the promenade, Turkish specialties, the omnipresent Asian noodle boxes handed over the counters, gelatinous fish sauce oozing down the side of the boxes.

The stench was that of the week old fish and billowing grease clouds that wafted through the air clinging to their exposed skin. The effect disconcerted BB's little squad of arco-bred Earthlings but the indigenous people seemed oblivious. They swam through the tunnels of the Great Ring like a river of unthinking lemmings, half of them stoned out on drugs, the other half intent on reaching that enviable nirvana state as soon as possible. Greitz pushed purposefully through the crowd.

'Show the way,' Keas yelled at him.

'We want a bar in the dark sector,' Greitz explained.

They reached open elevators and jumped into one going up. Two floors up, they jumped out. Gravity got lighter as they got closer to the core of the orbital. The crowd had thinned but seemed to fly even higher. Greitz grabbed the shoulder of someone at random. It was a man. He turned around to face them with a fluid motion. Round eyes insane with grumog, infections spreading from the eyesockets all the way around his face. Basil reeled back. The man had a clan logo carved deep into his shaved skull, white luminescent ink in the form of a hammer. Basil had no idea what it meant. 'We need to get high,' Greitz yelled over the din of the corridor. Georgian music was blaring from somewhere. The clanner nodded sagely, or as sagely as anyone can look without being physically able to close his eyelids. He lifted an arm and pointed towards a nearby door.

They dived in. It was a kind of bar. They couldn't see a name anywhere, but cleanliness definitely wasn't a selling point. The floor, a cheap imitation of wood, was awash in pools of sticky liquid. The room was narrow and deep and so murky people were mostly silhouettes. Keas couldn't see anything in the back. They entered. The bar counter stretched for a few meters along the right side of the room and sort of dissolved into a dim backroom which widened and expanded into a circular shape, but you only saw this if you decided to tempt fate by entering. It looked like the builders of the bar had started with a small room extending from a habitation module, then drilled through the back wall, horizontally into the side of a storage silo which they had then equipped with floor and ceiling. Someone, a goodly amount of years ago, by the look of things, had conceived to decorate the walls with fake Indian paraphernalia and trinkets; a couple of tomahawks, pipes, carved wooden things, and the piece de resistance, a once-proud Chieftain's feather headdress. The colors were faded and most of the feathers were missing. It was, probably, the saddest decoration attempt Keas had ever seen. The bartender was a half-assed cyborg. Most of the left side of his body was replaced by a plastic casing, which meshed clumsily with the rest of his body, giving him an unhelmed expression. Under the plastic, his face looked like it had been worked over by a plasma cutter. The man had probably been in an industrial accident but apprehending the reason for his mutilated appearance wouldn't make him any less ugly. His face was gleaming red, wrinkled, with some kind of radiation damage sprinkled on it for good measure.

'Does this face look like it's been regenerated?' the bartender asked into the room in a harsh rasping voice.

'Depends on the light', someone said amidst laughter. The sweet smell of weed hung heavy in the air. Basil inhaled greedily.

Basil took up station in the middle of the bar and raised his voice. 'Barkeep, free drinks for everyone.' He accompanied it with his trademark grand sweep of the arm. The prospect of imminent inebriation did wonders for the entourage and chatter picked up immediately.

The wannabe cyborg sidled over to Basil. 'And how are you going to pay for this unexpected, albeit, welcome, display of generosity,' he inquired in his rasping voice.

'Don't you know who I am, my good man.' Basil turned his head left and right like someone was taking his picture. Laughter erupted around him. The bartender stared. Someone whispered something.

'Yeees, exactly, my friends. Now let's see about those drinks. Anyone fancy sharing some of that righteous weed I smell?' Keas looked at Greitz, eyebrows raised as in *how are we getting on with the sunshine situation,* but Greitz just smiled back.

'Ah, here he is,' said the security man a few seconds later. A new arrival was shouldering his way through the crowd.

'Mirvin Tios.' Ubiquitous clay suit in neutral beige, old fashioned horn rimmed glasses, hair slicked back, eyes like safety valves that pop out at you whenever – as now – the pressure in his head gets too high.

'Greitz,' he said as a way of greeting and passed him a bag.

The bag contained blue and green pills. Greitz lined them up on the counter in two neat rows. Meanwhile the Mirvin Tios character kept staring at Basil.

'Basil Baranikowa,' he said and bared the upper part of his chest, just over the sternum, to reveal a faintly luminous eightball symbol about three centimeters in diameter.

'I think there might be a Mister in there somewhere,' said Keas.

'Ohh, a Botz,' Chili Boy exclaimed happily. Botz were known for their devotion to the Eight Day Man, having built an entire philosophy, some would say it was a budding religion, up around his way of life.

'Huh?' said Keas and turned around quickly. 'A botz here?' He shot Greitz a warning glance. Keas didn't like this Mirvin fellow, thought Basil to himself. *How strange*. Mirvin's eyes remained fixed on Basil, unfazed.

'Mr. Baranikowa, they are going to take you off the DeeEmmCee, sir. I'm warning you...'

'What?' said Basil who was transfixed by the rows of blue and green pills.

Muscular types arrived from out of nowhere and grabbed Mirvin Tios by the arms. 'We tried warning you, get out of here, you're in danger,' he yelled. He was pushed out of sight and Basil, who was popping a pair of pills while staring after the Tios character, felt a timid sun lighting up inside his body.

Six hours later Greitz was leading them back to the VIP area and into a docking bay, decked out as a reception area with Halifax banners flying from the ceiling and walls celebrating Zach's achievements in glorified clay. It was a church, a room dedicated to the life and times of Zach Baranikowa and it was brimming with celebrities and politicians, national and GSA, Survey Branch commanders, CEO's and executives from rival corporations. Basil's eyes blurred. He was hanging on the BMG's arm like a man adrift.

THREE

The next thing he knew a man's face was looking down at him. He wondered about that. Was it a holographic projection? The lips moved. Basil strained. What? ...quarterly results? new launch? spin on a bad situation? news broadcasts sure weren't what they used to be. those things used to be so good at zeroing in on the lowest denominator. if he didn't get it, then they'd sure missed the mark? well, go ahead, but you're losing your key audience. fools. that was one thing he had learned as a real-time star. key audience. he felt pity for them. he was lying flat on his back. not alarmed, that's what vapor of the blue duck will do for ya. works all the time. hail to the chief. letters coagulated into words in the air above his head. 'oh son.' whoa. now someone was doing something right. read you loud and clear. 'i'm glad your mother didn't live to see you like this'. the face disappeared. 'clean him up. i'll link up with him again in a few hours when I'm back down.' his eyes seemed to close all by themselves.

--

waves of pain. washed over him in staccato. first a dull banging in his head which was a drum, one of the big ones, then sharp jabs in his abdomen, alternating with nausea. he'd never known nausea to be that painful, but maybe it was version two. the next level. someone in white clothes was standing next to his bed. 'He is waking up. He looks just like on IR, just really banged up,' a man said. 'Very funny, I heard that. 'Ivf lakee a rwel nwurse.' who ever heard of a male nurse, anyway?

'What did he say? Did anyone understand what he said?'

'Did he put a curse on us? Poor man, it's the drugs talking.'

'He's saying.. he says he's been kidnapped.'

That must have been tremendously funny because they all laughed.

He came to flat on his back, but felt... wobbly. One moment he was pushed down hard, the next he seemed to float, yet his body was immobilized. I'm paralyzed. I can't move. He moved his eyeballs, the only part of him still working, from side to side. He could see a ceiling, sort of creamy white, and a wall, which had a more metallic tinge to its whiteness. Obscure equipment on trolleys lined the walls. In the extreme corner of his left eye he could see a screen with numbers and curves moving around on it. He was in a hospital it seemed.

"Sorry about this, Mr. Baranikowa. We have to keep you immobilized. It is necessary." A voice from outside his field of view. Male. Affable. Then his sight darkened, tunneled and he panicked to no effect. He was alone in the living room in the Aspen mansion. Where was he? When was he? What the hell? Yellowstone. That's where he had been when......when had that been? a week ago or yesterday?

Sight returned with the presence of a man in white doctor's garb entering through French doors from an arboretum.

'Your father will see you in 30 seconds, sir.'

'...Can you tell me if...'

--

Too late. He was in virtual reality. In an office. No time to think about where his own body was as he registered old fashioned New England country club kitsch cluttering a desk. The walls were opaque. Everything was very quiet. There was an old man sitting behind an oak desk, an intense expression on his face, not a silver streaked hair out of place.

He heard his own voice, protesting, shrill, even in VIR: 'What's going on? Where am I? You can't just shift people around like this!'

'Do you know who I am?'

'Can't say that I do, old man. But what you're doing is illegal. There's a law somewhere against shifting people around.'

'Basil, I am your Father. Please listen carefully to what I am going to tell you.'

'I think I know what your mother would have said. Drunk and

27

stupid... it ain't no way to go through life, son,' he said looking somewhat paternally at his incredulous offspring who pretended to ponder the wisdom of his words for a few seconds.

His father kept quiet for a few seconds. 'Your body is still back on the Halifax Orbital. It's been a week since your... lapse.' He paused.

Basil stared at him. His father continued. 'Look at your life until now, Basil... The past twenty years I have been paying your bills without asking anything of you. You've been free to do whatever you pleased. And yet, with all this, you have never done anything worthwhile. Not for anybody, not even yourself. You've got nothing to show for your life. I love you, son, I really do and I know you don't believe it.'

'I don't remember. Sorry.'

'I know. Very, very few people on this sorry planet have had your life, Basil. Most are eeking out an existence down there in the arcologies, living hand to mouth, starving, shitting where they eat. You had every opportunity to make a difference and you pissed it away.'

Zach, it was indeed Zach Baranikowa, Basil's father, got up from his chair and turned his back on Basil, who found out he couldn't move or indeed turn off the stream. The solid wall in front of Zach gradually dissolved and turned transparent. Outside rain was pelting down from black skies. Through the murky rain the ocean was visible as a dirty, oily carpet.

'This place was called the Silver Mountain. It used to loom over the city,' Zach pointed. 'The city used to be over there, about 3 kilometers south. Gone now, of course, washed away by the sea. You know, I once went skiing here with my parents. Skiing! Imagine! There was snow here, all over the place. We had a good time... It was a long time ago, too long, maybe. But it is probably why I choose this place for our headquarters.' He paused for a long time. Basil bit his tongue. 'The world has changed so much, Basil. You wouldn't understand, not with your heart anyway.'

'I'm an old man,' he continued and smiled sadly. 'Well, older than I appear anyway. I was in my seventies when we had you, you know, which puts me on the wrong side of a century.

'Our world is dying and the human race is dying with it. The Restoration has failed. No one is saying it out loud, but it has. We had a chance to turn things around but our leaders failed us. Again. Caving in and shutting down the HAI's was the final straw. We failed. They failed.'

'When will you let me out? I want to leave now,' Basil said peevishly.

Zach turned around to glare at him. 'You stupid boy. You just don't get it, do you? I want to save you. I want to save us, the human race!'

'Even now you just want to go back to your drug-addicted friends, sail around in that airship, expose yourself in that show, doing what you have been doing for the past twenty years. I'm sorry, Basil. Maybe things would have been different if I had protected you. I thought I was protecting you, but I see I did so the wrong way. I know that now and I am sorry. But we're almost out of time. We must act decisively.'

'The reason you're here is that there has been a development. Two Survey Branch ships docked a couple of days ago. A habitable planet has been located. This is what we have been planning for.' He turned to look Basil in the eyes

'Why are you punishing me? What have I done to you?' he asked.

'Nothing, Basil, you have done nothing, but because of your mother I will give you this.'

--

A few days earlier, it was exactly at the same time, in fact, down to the minute, when Basil was sitting next to that guy in the red sofa in his father's house in Yellowstone, inhaling Blue Duck and discussing the finer points of bonsai trees and the significance of stepping stones in a Japanese garden and the guy next to him was just saying he was a sensei in karesansui and Basil thought yes whatever that means because it would be a grand exaggeration to claim he knew much about it, but he always was good at pretending, it was at that precise moment that two almost identical starships appeared near the third LQG point in the Solar system. The starships were not big, as those things go, not by today's standards at least, just about a hundred meters in length, and their shape was a pleasingly symmetrical oblong, which at the time was considered a very efficient design for getting a bunch of humans and a lot of sensitive scientific equipment safely from one place to another. The oblong, or finger shape, was disturbed in two locations. In the front, about ten meters down from the ship's rounded nose, a bulge, like the protrusion a ringworm would make around a finger, circled the hull, the living area of the small crew, and about halfway further down the hull an amateur expert in human starship designs, would immediately recognize the second bulge, this one quite a bit bigger, as characteristic of an Abbott-Farhi Ensphere. All the way to the rear two magnetoplasma engine manifolds were visible. Everything else, every single cubic centimeter, was dedicated to holding the liquid hydrogen fuel that the deep space survey ships needed to navigate uncharted space for years at a time. The engines on the two ships ignited and they began accelerating in-system, towards Earth, towards home.

It might be useful for the readers to know that back in those early days the main raison d'être of the Global Space Agency, apart from hosting the space technology catalogue, was the planning and execution of surveys, both geological, of planets and planetary bodies, and geosynchronous, which pertained to the exploration of lattice quantum gravity points. Eight starships had been built at great cost to the member nations. Four of the Newton class, which were specialized in the LQG exploration, and four Darwin class, which were specialized in geological surveys. They customarily operated in pairs and could often be away on missions for up to three years at a time. Such long voyages obviously put great strain on the crews. They were handpicked for their skills in various fields of science but also for their personal and physical qualities and as such, they represented, in so many words, the crème de la crème of humanity. The Vasco da Gama and her sister ship the Thomas Cook had been away for a very long time indeed and privately certain GSA officials had been known to speculate that the ships had been irretrievably lost. Nevertheless, here they were. The ships acknowledged their return with a message to the GSA Survey Branch headquarters on the Halifax orbital. The message, as they knew it would be, was routinely intercepted by more than a handful of the major corporations, and for this precise reason, it did not contain anything but preliminary navigational data. It was not until the ship had docked with Halifax, in the sealed-off area used exclusively by Survey Branch, that the two captains personally carried the data off the ships and into the secured offices of their organization. Then, and only then, was the reason for their abnormal reticence revealed to their masters in the Global Space Agency.

For a few precious minutes, Basil was alone, back in the hospital, back in reality, left to stare into the ceiling. He was rattled. Everything was going too fast. He looked around as best he could. Again, the only part of his body not immobilized was his eyes. There was no gravity. That much was clear from the sinking feeling in his stomach.

'Hello, anybody there?' he croaked weakly.

A face swam into view over him. It was a man, the one from before with the suave voice and white doctor's garb.

'It will only be a minute Mr. Baranikowa; we are preparing to transfer you now.' He was leaving Basil's field of view.

'Hey, answer me, goddamn it, why am I immobilized like this? How long has it been? What have you done to me? I need a shot of Dee. If I don't get it…'

The face came back. 'You have undergone major surgery. Do not worry. We expect a full recovery. You will however need to remain immobile for a few months. And we believe you will no longer have to worry about synaptic stimulants, sir.'

'A few months? What the hell are you talking about? There was nothing wrong with me, why surgery? Answer me!' The face was moving out his field of view. 'Oh no, you don't. Stay here!'

He did not. The doctor had left him. It didn't matter because Basil felt another virtual session coming up.

--

A few seconds later, he was in a meeting room at the head of a very long table. A thick slab of highly polished wood with bands of black and dark brown in it. Transparent windows. The room seemed to float high above the city, stretched out underneath them in all directions. It seemed to be early morning but no sun was visible under the dingy clouds. A big twister was gathering itself up in the distance and sprays of rain slashed at the windows all around them. A man, the one who had claimed to be his father, entered from a doorway and Basil briefly glimpsed the office where they had just met a few minutes earlier. A second door opened and a man ducked in, chubby face first. He had the look of a busy accountant about him, disheveled hair, slightly, but not entirely, obsequious. The newcomer took a seat at the table next to Zach. They did not exchange greetings so much as grumble to each other.

'Hello, Basil. You know me. I am a friend of your fathers. Going way back,' said the chubby man. He looked at Basil with kind, heavy lidded eyes that made Basil squirm for some reason he could not remember.

'You look really tired,' Basil answered in a voice that was a tad too loud.

'It's called aging. Not everyone can stay young sucking the blood from their employees like you and your father,' he smiled gently. 'I hear you're getting yourself into trouble as usual.' The man attempted to smile but the actual expression did not quite materialize on the older man's face. The other man, Zach, his father, was looking straight ahead, apparently lost in thought.

'Trouble? I don't remember any trouble.' It was a line from the show. To his credit, the man blushed and looked away.

'Quiet, both of you! Basil, do not interfere in the meeting,' Zach hissed suddenly. A few seconds later, a fizzing sound announced the arrival of someone. He materialized standing in front of Zach on the other side of the table. It was a man in a suit, clayed to be dark, non-descript, but featuring the red and white Halifax logo on the left breast and four gold lines of a Captain snaking around each sleeve. He was tall, lean, decades younger than the two others, crow's feet around clear blue eyes, light brown hair graying in all the right places.

'I apologize for my delay. The Carousel is on final approach to Halifax. We're struggling with constant glitches. Considering the rate of failures I think these old Golding ships are just about ready for scrapping,' the man said glibly and bowed politely. The man spoke in a deep, bass tone and, despite a slight accent, his command of English was perfect. His eyes darted to Basil who was sitting at the end of the table.

Zach leaned back in his chair and looked at him with a thoughtful expression. 'That is fine, Markus. You have been doing a great job so far but I am afraid your current assignment is about to end. The Vasco and the Cook just docked with Halifax. The data we hoped and planned for has come to light.'

The man his father addressed as Markus took a deep breath to steady himself. 'Finally. That is good news, sir. We've been waiting a long time for this.'

'We have indeed, haven't we?' Zach smiled at the younger man.

'Here we are,' said the third man. A binary star system, designated SCR-1845-6357, appeared in the air above the table. It had two orange dwarf stars, M5-V and M6-V class. They were almost similar in size and luminosity. A single planet orbited one star, the A star, and eight bodies orbited the other, three gas giants, five solids. It was a complicated system, which whirled dizzyingly in the air above the table.

The view zoomed in on the single rocky planet orbiting the A star. Surface temperature averaging 16 degrees Celsius, atmosphere breathable by humans. As was customary, the crews of the Survey ships that charted the new system had voted on the name. They had decided on 'Espero'. An image of the planet was on display over the wooden table.

'This planet is quite extraordinary. Not only does it support life, human life, but it circles the star in exactly the same time as it takes to rotate around itself.' He paused to scratch his chin. 'A year and a day is the same on this planet. Sixty-three Earth hours. It has seasons too. The axial tilt is 20 degrees.' He stopped talking and looked up from his notes at the image of the planet they were pinning all their hopes on.

The start system was only 50 light years from Earth as the proverbial crow flies if said crow would not mind breathing pure vacuum all the way. A mere pittance as distances went. Most of the systems surveyed by Survey Branch were unknown to astronomers, but they had known of this planet for almost a century. The paths of the LQG network, if not purely coincidental, were unpredictable, at least to human scientists and so reaching this particular star system was nothing short of incredibly lucky.

The third man cleared his throat and spoke again: 'The timing is fortunate. The Armagnac just docked a couple of hours ago.'

He continued: 'The practical details are currently being taken care of. I have uploaded the navigational data to you. All is ready. Armagnac is being refurbished and refitted as we speak.' He paused and continued: 'After this meeting, the CEO will address the crew and brief them. Make your way to Halifax as fast as you can. You will take command of the ship immediately.'

'And my men, Mr. Patterson?' asked Markus to which the man

replied: 'They are on board the habitat shell and the shell is in the process of being attached to the Armagnac at this very moment.'

'As we discussed, Markus, it is best not to mix your men and the crew,' said Zach.

'I understand. Other than the data shown here, what do we know about our destination?'

The man called Patterson replied, 'Overall, it looks good. Everything is in the files. The planet is quite a bit farther out than we hoped for – almost six months in fact. The voyage will be long but manageable. But, then again,' Patterson paused with a wry smirk, 'that's easy for me to say, isn't it?'

Basil looked from one to another wanting to ask what they were talking about when his vision of Zach's office disappeared. Then it came back. A voice spoke from nowhere in his head: 'Sorry, Mr. Baranikowa, we lost connection there for a second. We're moving you on board the ship now.'

He spoke aloud. 'Moving me?'

The three men in the office turned their heads and looked at him questioningly. Basil attempted to shake his head but of course, being virtual and frozen in place, it didn't budge. Instead he just said, 'Umm, never mind, it was off-line chatter.'

'Was that all, sir?' Markus resumed, directed at Zach.

'No. There is more. The first is that my son is not ready. He came out of surgery a couple of hours ago. We thought we would have more time. He was supposed to stay out until the data came in, give him time to accommodate and assimilate the... changes. There's no time for that now. We are bringing him onboard as is. He will have to stay in his epi for a few months at least according to the doctors. You must not activate him until after six months, preferably longer. The more time the better.'

'Very well, but how do you...' Bentzon began before Basil, interrupted said, or rather yelled, 'Activated? What the hell are you talking about? What operation? I'm not sick, never was! Assimilate! Accommodate! What changes are you're talking about? What have you done to me, you crazy old shit?'

Patterson reddened at the outburst, Markus looked amused, but Zach continued speaking as if nothing had happened and Basil, way down at the head of the table, found out he had suddenly lost the ability to speak. 'The other problem you should be aware of is that within the next twenty four hours the Mingo Corporation will launch a new Multipurpose System Vessel.'

Basil desperately attempted to disconnect the VIR but nothing worked. He was powerless. Meanwhile the outline of a starship appeared in the air over the table, turning on itself. The ship was called the Yu-kiang. It looked like all the other pictures of starships Basil had seen; a long pencil shape with lots of round ball-like orbs attached along its length and a cluster of engine manifolds at the rear. Markus squinted at the starship and said, 'Is that what I think it is?'

'Yes, our intelligence indicates that it is equipped with an Abbott-Farhi Ensphere.'

'I'll admit that it surprised us to see another corporation building an MSV capable of lattice gauge fields so soon. We expected Greymouth or maybe the SAC to be the first and not for a long time.'

'To make matters worse, we think they too have acquired the Survey data,' Zach continued for Patterson.

'But why would they send the ship all the way out there? There is no profit for them in that.' Patterson looked at Markus, then at Zach and continued: 'Mingo? What kind of corporation is that? I don't recall who they are. Chinese?'

'We had some... dealings with this corporation. They're headquartered in the Edmonton Arcology, they built it and they pretty much own it. During the wars, they were... sympathetic to the Sleeper cause. They are a spiritual bunch. Something about spiritual redemption of civilization peppered with sun worship or some bullshit like that.' Then added: 'Pardon my language, sir.'

Zach looked down. 'I see.'

Patterson: 'They have a small presence in orbit. They have teamed up with the BNSF corporation on a ship yard.'

'The same as the rest of them: in it for the money. Sun worship or not.'

'Yes, agreed, Markus. Maybe they want to stake a claim to the planet. Greedy dogs. Parasites! They're everything that is wrong with the way we do things.'

Markus nodded to himself. 'If they decide to follow us we'll deal with them. Have no worries, sir.'

'I know that, my boy, I know that.'

FOUR

Excerpt, Unate Green, GSA Academy, class of 2136

'Semi-Autonomous Drone Units came in many shapes and sizes. Some were specialized in EVA work outside the ship. Those sported heavier thruster units and better shielding. Others worked inside the ship, constantly trawling the service ducts. Those were smaller and more agile under gravity. The SADU carrying our man Basil was a sort of cylinder in brushed duranium, about seventy centimeters long and twenty wide. The cylinder was studded with sensor pods, thruster units for zero-G work, four thick configurable wheels for mobility under G's and four multipurpose manipulators. The unit was semi-autonomous, hence the name, mostly self-repairing, and its power was supplied from an internal rechargeable battery. The bigger drone units contained their own miniature fusion reactors, which in theory could keep them running for years. They were necessary on starships because they could go places humans could not; they could move around during high G burns, or outside the ship in hard radiation. They could navigate narrow service corridors and inside engines. Their immense strength was also useful when we had to move cargo around in the depressurized cargo holds.'

On the 5th of January, 2200, at 2315 EST, a SADU entered a special zero-G docking bay located halfway down the central pylon of the Halifax Orbital. This particular drone belonged to the orbital and was normally employed in the transfer of sensitive scientific equipment or lab tests to or from shuttles, but on this day, it was handling a gurney and enclosed in the gurney was the body of Basil Baranikowa. Only his face was visible through an opening, the rest of his body was immobilized and hidden under a medical clay carapace. To avoid damage to its frail cargo, the drone maneuvered slowly and very carefully using its ion thrusters as sparsely as possible. A turtle shaped starship shuttle bearing the markings Armagnac 01 on its sides was moored to the docking bay. The door was open. The gurney, slowly, so slowly in fact that a casual observer could not be faulted to think it was drifting, entered the shuttle and once inside, the drone extended its manipulator arms and grabbed hold of various joints lining the walls of the shuttle. Its cargo thus securely anchored, the shuttle started moving again, very slowly and very carefully toward its destination, the starship Armagnac, pride of the Halifax Shipping Line fleet and the most advanced spaceship ever constructed by a civilian corporation. In his weakened state, Basil did not care about the exterior view from the shuttle, but if he had, his untrained eye would have seen a kilometer long needle shape gleaming purposefully in the white unfiltered sunlight. It looked like all the other ships built and designed by the late college of HAI's; a plasma screen, unlit at that moment; a heavily armored command shell; fifteen module slots containing cargo shells; twelve strange turtle shaped modules. On the stern, all the way at the back of the ship, were the usual arrangement of fuel tank, reactor and engines.

Two things distinguished the Armagnac from other ships: the pineapple shaped Abbott-Farhi module, until then exclusive to the much smaller, heavily specialized Survey Branch ships, and two modules of a strange grey, slightly jellylike material attached to the needle just behind the command shell. Sadly, yes, glory is indeed a fleeting thing; soon, just a few short hours later, its status as the most advanced civilian ship would be disputed by the launch of the Yu-kiang.

To accommodate Basil, the Armagnac had disconnected from the rotating orbital a few minutes earlier to achieve zero-G, and it remained immobile whilst it awaited that very last bit of soft cargo before it could depart on its long journey. The shuttle carrying Basil approached ever so gingerly, found the correct dock connection and latched on with a jolt so completely insignificant it prompted the pilot onboard the Armagnac, Rem Brassen, to quite uncharacteristically withhold the castigation he would habitually have poured over his ghost pilot, Unate Green, who was piloting the shuttle remotely. As soon as the connection between the two vessels was confirmed, the gurney resumed its slow voyage, the drone having passed under control of Operations, into the main docking bay.

The enclosed gurney containing the Eight Day man, unrepentant addict and, now former, Viscerality star was met in the cavernous, and sharply lit docking bay by a woman. Only a pair of sand colored eyes were visible under the grey clay suit she was wearing. The woman kicked off against a wall and floated expertly over to the gurney, before coming to a halt, and sticking her face so close to Basil's that their noses almost touched.

She stared into his eyes with uncomfortable intensity and Basil, completely immobilized, had to stoically meet her head-on so to speak.

'Where am I?'

A hand appeared. To Basil's consternation, the woman applied a thumb to his eyelid and pushed at it to reveal the upper dome of Basil's eyeball.

'Hmm, pretty, very pretty. Then again, you Baranikowas were spared most of the bad stuff, weren't you, being up in space and all that. Good for you, good for you.' The woman spoke under her breath, as to herself. Suddenly she gave a small jerk with her head and blinked as if seeing him for the first time. 'Hello, there, Mr. Baranikowa, oh, aren't you pretty, look at that face, yes, I see now, you Baranikowas were up here during all the bad times down there, yes, have remained very clean, very normal, one might say, hahaha.' Alarmingly the woman shivered into spasmodic laughs before jerking her head repeatedly and refocusing her eyes on Basil, 'Oh-ho, I shouldn't forget myself! My name is Jin Dulg. I will be monitoring you over the next few months. They tell me you went through quite the operation just a few short hours ago. They should have waited a few hours for your wounds to heal, I say. Very irresponsible, if you ask me, but then again, I am no doctor as they never tire of telling me.' They began moving with Jin Dulg hanging on to the gurney with one hand, letting the slat do the work, and at the same time keeping up a continuous stream of chatter directed at Basil's face. 'My, oh my, but it is true, I never was much of a doctor myself. But then again they didn't ask me to be one, now did they, haha. No, I'm just a navigator, but between me and the epi, I think we'll do just fine by you, Mr. Baranikowa. It's too bad you won't be able to see the ship just yet. I would have loved to take you on the grand tour. It is not every day we get fancy visitors around here, pretty visitors such as yourself, Mr. Baranikowa. Oh no, to tell you the truth, life quickly becomes dreary, so dreary on a starship. But you'd know all about that, wouldn't you? No need to tell you that, sir. Ah, well, you'll have plenty of time to explore and form your own opinion of this tiny world of ours here once you're up and about again. Meanwhile you'll have to stay in the epi. Yes. Yes. Stay in the epi.'

'Where am I?' Basil repeated. Jin Dulg did not answer directly, she kept up a relentless barrage of chatter but, without breaking pace, she sent Basil an invitation to link into her visuals: they seemed to be moving through a corridor, walls and ceiling uniformly beige colored. His gurney seemed to be floating by itself.

Apart from a bit of involuntary grunting, Basil kept quiet as they made their way through the ship. They reached a door, which opened to let them in. 'Home sweet home,' remarked the woman and laughed.

She followed Basil into his cabin, which, by his previous living standards, was tiny indeed, only three by two meters. The SADU carefully maneuvered the gurney to a halt next to a sarcophagus-like container, which opened and swallowed the gurney, allowing it to settle inside. It was not until the sarcophagus began to close that Basil, confused and feverish, understood he was about to be encased. He wanted to yell out at the woman, but all he managed was a hoarse croak: 'Stop! Please!... what is this?'

Jin Dulg put out her hand and stopped the lid from closing. The clay suit slithered off her head and stopped at her neck, revealing her face. She was somewhat pretty, not really his type, oblong face, short black hair and olive skin. She had a nice mouth, though, which almost made up for the rest of her face. Yes, he definitely liked her mouth. 'This is just an epi, Mr. Baranikowa, don't you worry, sir. Not everyone gets to try these. First time is free, as they say. Soon you will not want to leave it at all and that's a promise.' She removed her hand. The lid descended on him. The last thing Basil heard was a muffled: 'See you soon, Mr. Baranikowa,' then complete darkness engulfed him and dreams began.

FIVE

I have often overheard the command shell referred to as the tank or the aquarium. I find that a very strange metaphor. An aquarium is a transparent container filled with water and living fishes. I remember seeing aquariums adorning entrances and many public places in the arcologies. Supposedly, aquariums inspire serenity and restful contemplation. Is it not contradictory to use aquariums in this fashion? Humans have never lived with fish. Why would they want to look at fish? Fish are as fundamentally alien to human life as are the arcologies themselves. Seeing aquariums everywhere must be an unpleasant reminder of the way things used to be and of the many things that have gone awry. In fact, aquariums are disturbing. All that energy, the mass of the water, straining at the glass, just waiting to break through it and inundate everything on the other side. Very strange to me. Stranger still the inhabitants, the fish, looking out with dead eyes. Fish have no faces, no emotions beyond the here and now of their need to feed, occasionally lay eggs. Their blood runs cold and their skin is hard and scaly. I simply do not understand the fascination with fish.

However, the pilot liked the tank more than any other place on the ship. Perhaps because it was the only place on the ship that never changed and it did, in all fairness, share some similarities to an aquarium. It was murky, subdued, voices seemed to trail off as soon as they left the cavity of a mouth and the clarity of sounds, any sounds, decayed so fast that visitors often felt compelled to yell or speak louder than they normally would to overcome the short half-life of their utterances. Even if you included the vast amount of computer equipment that lined every square centimeter of this circular room, it was small. Barely five by five meters. In the middle, sunken a little into the floor, was a seat containing the best virtuality gear on the ship, even better than the equipment in ops. The pilot always occupied this chair. There was an additional seat behind the pilot, or beneath him, depending on your perspective. The ship's direction of travel, you see, relative to the occupants of the tank, was upwards. This was the most convenient arrangement considering the long periods the ship spent under burn. The problem, as newcomers soon discovered, was the entrance. You entered the tank through a hole in the floor via a rather long ladder that started all way down in the habitat section. If the ship was burning more than one G, climbing that ladder was a great undertaking, one not easily accomplished by skinny, muscle atrophied spacer arms and legs.

Objectively speaking there was no reason for Brassen to be in tank at this moment. The LQG point was still almost two weeks away and, usually, at this point in a journey the crew would settle into a routine which was designed to see as little of each other as possible. But perhaps he wasn't quite ready yet to succumb to the routines that would carry him through the many days and months this mission would last, and also perhaps he, on some subconscious level one dared not express, needed to absorb the circumstances and worries of this new mission.

The two other crew members joined him. He greeted their arrival with silence.

You see, and this is something I have learned over the years, most people need people to sort out their feelings. It is a strange conundrum in human beings, and maybe our greatest advantage over them, that they are very rarely capable of truly forming their own opinions about the world surrounding them. On the other hand, and I suspect this might also be the case, or at least a concurrent facet to the problem, many are not interested in holding thoughts of their own.

Enough of my digressive periphrastics. Let us hear what the three of them talked about on this first day of the Espero mission.

--

Log entry: January 5, 2100, 0630 hours, EST

At 0600 hours, the Armagnac undocked from Halifax. The Pilot laid in a course for the sixth LQG cynosure in Sol. Due to crew not being secured the ship drifted for thirty minutes. We have now received the all clear, accelerating at 1G. We will maintain this profile for 49 hours. The Captain has ordered an apex of 301 hours, followed by a 180 degrees turn and 49 hours deceleration at 1G. /RB

Brassen held the dubious honor of being the only one among them who had laid eyes on the new Captain but even so there wasn't much to tell. Of course they had scrutinized the various feeds from the internal sensors which had captured his unannounced arrival on the ship, but since the new Captain had barely spoken a word to Brassen as he boarded, and Brassen, taciturn even at the best of times, had not seen fit to press the matter with him, all they had to go on were a set of blue eyes and a head of silver streaked hair which wasn't much at all. The two men had merely nodded at each other and Brassen had turned on his heels and led the Captain to his quarters where he had remained since.

One of the crew members, the same woman who had greeted Basil when he was taken onboard two hours earlier, exclaimed: 'Hehum, here they go, the journey long. Secret paths and poisonous air.' The woman, she was not yet thirty years of age, grinned at the inappropriate quote, which, everyone knew, was by the late wartime poet Spiegelbern who famously died during the Warsaw death march across the irradiated plains of central Europe. She lifted her eyebrows suggestively at the man clinging to the wall next to her. He did not respond.

The three each had decades of experience crewing starships for HSL but until a month ago they had never worked together. Zach himself had chosen them for this mission.

'So tell us, Bras. How does he seem first hand?' asked Felix, perhaps sensing the pilot's annoyance with the navigator.

'He looks like a real captain.'

There was a pause while the two others pondered his meaning. The identity of the Captain had just been made known, literally minutes before he boarded the ship. The crew had worked Armagnac through her maiden voyage without a captain, very unusual, but even more unusual was it to see him arrive so late. Perhaps it had been done so as to prevent them from asking around about the Captain? Starship crews were an inquisitive lot and gossip was the lifeblood of the Halifax Orbital.

'Do you think he is a lifer?' asked the woman. She was asking if he was a career officer in HSL.

'I am certain of it,' answered Brassen curtly. 'I doubt Zach would have chosen someone who was not for this mission.'

'Well, did anyone manage to check out his personnel file before we left?' asked Jin.

Felix shook his head and Brassen didn't even bother to answer.

'Well, then, fortunately for us I did,' said Jin. The two men turned to look at her, obviously surprised at her resourcefulness. She would have managed that in the interval, a mere sequence of minutes, after they heard his name and the ship undocked.

'How?' asked Felix, approval sneaking into his voice despite his best efforts to hide it. That kind of boldness he could admire.

'Friends in high places,' she quipped and shrugged. Brassen grumbled something inaudible.

'And...?'

'And you're wrong, Brassen. He is not a lifer. My sources could only find the official company records. He was first officer on the 'Carousel', a Golding-class, for just six months. Who figured that was a good name for a ship? I thought those old ships were named from...'

'Never mind the name of the ship. From first officer to Captain on the Armagnac in six months... quite a move. The man! What about him?' Brassen cut her off sharply. He was curious now.

'Well, he is a total rookie.'

'And before that, brace yourselves... he worked in corporate security. Security! Surely someone's idea of a bad joke! Studied for the Captain's bars in his spare time in a special HSL Academy program. Flunked a couple of exams, but once he got everything in order he almost immediately got a commission.'

'Markus Bentzon, man of mystery, our captain. And a man who also seems to have friends in high places.' She finished the sentence by mumbling the word 'Nepotism.'

'What do you mean?' asked Felix.

'It means that our navigator has doubts about the capabilities of our new captain. I would strongly suggest she keep those to herself. For all she knows the new Captain may be a very capable individual. Zach certainly thought so and that should be enough for her,' Brassen grunted. Once a company man...

A small pause ensued then Jin said: 'In any case he must be very special for Zach to entrust him with this mission. Perhaps he screwed his way to the top.'

'He is special alright, but it's not because he's good at sexual intercourse,' said Brassen and scratched his short hair. Of course, Jin had had his records checked too: Rem Brassen, born and raised in the Lima Arco, was the older of three siblings. A diehard off-liner, a PP'er, who'd lost his wife and kids decades ago. He spoke as little as possible, and when he did, more often than not, he revealed, in heavily accented English, an annoyingly even temper. Jin had found, based on the past month, that he was almost impossible to provoke, that he never was worked up about anything. Faced with such drudgery, she had begun doubting the depths of his intelligence. Maybe he was just stupid and trying very hard to cover it up? Oh yes, and he liked to scratch his hair. Seemingly absentminded he would fork the fingers on his right hand and rake them through the thick light brown stubble on his head, underlining his ape-like physique.

'What do you mean?' asked Felix.

'Don't know. I just thought I'd seen him before.'

'He is handsome,' Jin said to stir things up a little. To her satisfaction, it made Felix do a thing with his eyebrows.

'How about the BB?' asked Brassen, in what was a completely obvious attempt to stop them discussing the new Captain. 'A global celebrity right here on our ship. First impressions, Jin? I'm sure you have plenty to share.'

'Looks like himself. A tad pale though. Seems he went through some serious surgery on the Orbital. I don't think he has any idea what he is doing here either.'

'Have you watched his shows?'

'No, can't say that I have, but I'm betting the ghosts are excited about him,' she laughed.

'Did anyone care to tell them it was him?'

'I'm sure they know.'

--

Just four hours earlier the Armagnac had been on final approach to the orbital returning from a run to the Kuiper Belt. The three were looking forward to a few days of well-deserved rest and relaxation when Zach's face had appeared to everyone on the ship in unprecedented two-way real time conference mode. He was sitting at a long wooden table and behind him, they glimpsed Bergen Bay far beneath Silver Mountain. The old man did not waste any time.

'Crew of the Armagnac', he said. 'Our hard work over these past years is about to bear fruit.'

'We have a target now: Espero.' His eyes wandered over them, pausing to envelop each of them with a generous helping of face time. Jin squirmed. Almost being in the same room as a living legend was uncomfortable and she had the feeling he was seeing through her.

'The planet is perfect for our purposes. Survey Branch have mapped it and found that it is one hundred percent compatible with human biology.'

'Phase B of Project Lighthouse is underway as we speak. When you return to Earth in ten months, the first colony ship will be ready to depart, setting in motion the next chapter for humanity.'

Zach had gone on to talk at length about Project Lighthouse, repeating how important it was that the Armagnac went out first to reconnoiter a good spot to deploy First Base and generally get the lay of the land.

At the end, faced with their stony silence, which, had Zach been less self-absorbed, should have told him a thing or two, he had nodded and said: 'Very well then. All that remains is to wish you good luck. I know you will make me proud.'

End of transmission.

--

Their third surprise of the day was an encrypted message. Brassen called on the two others who appeared a few minutes later in the tank.

'An incoming message, heavily encrypted from headquarters, Bergen, re-routed from the orbital,' said Brassen.

'Well, decode it already. What does it say?' exclaimed Jin.

'It is for the Captain's eyes only', he said hesitatingly.

'See if you can decode it anyway. Let's hear it. The secrecy thing is ridiculous anyway. It's not like we can tell anyone from out here, is it?'

'If it is for the Captain, it is for the Captain. Not our place to read his missives,' Brassen said in a definitive manner. The message was relayed to the Captain's quarters and a few minutes later, right on cue, the object of their conversation poked his shapely salt and pepper head through the opening in the floor.

For a moment, he looked surprised to see all three of them in the tank.

'As you were, people.'

Markus Bentzon emerged fully from the door hole and stood. He was clayed in classic spacer coveralls, HSL logo on the breast, gold bars snaking down his arms. He skipped the formal introductions.

'I'm afraid I have bad news, people. The Mingo Corporation has just launched an MSV with Abbott-Farhi capability. The Yu-kiang, they call it, which to me sounds like a typical shamanite name,' he said in a voice that was too loud, spitting out the word shamanite like it was a curse. He shook his head disapprovingly at his own news.

'Intel thinks they're heading the same way we are. There is a small chance their departure is coincidental but we have to assume they have also acquired the Espero survey data. We will know for sure after the second transition,' said Bentzon without removing his eyes from Jin who busied herself eyeing a status display describing very minor fluctuations in the output of the miniature fusion in drone unit 23, currently triple checking, along with 4 other drone units, all seals and moorings on the 15 cargo sections that the ship had received.

Despite the rushed briefings, the crushing secrecy and the complex logistics in refitting the ship on such short notice, it had seemed the mission had gotten away with it. Then, by no fault of anyone's, really, a small corporation, which people in the know, people like Zach and Patterson, had considered completely insignificant, had upset all their plans. This very small, very insignificant corporation, these nobodies, had somehow managed to construct an AFE equipped starship and because of their insignificance in the great scale of corporate affairs, they had evaded the all-seeing eye that was HSL Intelligence. The ship was, from what little the intelligence folks could tell, a piece of jury-rigged junk, but there you were, sometimes perfection is the art of becoming something rather than having something. There was a lesson there for the Halifax planners. The ship was a lot smaller than the Armagnac, but that, on the kind of Magellan'esque trip on which they were embarking, was not necessarily a disadvantage. Less mass meant the ship needed less fuel to accelerate. Although the Armagnac and this new ship were capable of the same theoretical acceleration, it was a fact of interplanetary space travel that whatever ship could sustain burn for the longest, would get there first'est. Longer burn equaled increased cross-system speed. To add insult to injury, assuming Halifax intelligence was correct, and it would not be the first time, the smaller ship was carrying extra fuel shells, whereas the Armagnac would have to husband her fuel mass more conservatively. The small size of the other ship, however, it was maybe just four or five sections long, led them to conclude that they were going with less ambitious plans in mind than HSL, but they were going and that was all that mattered. They would, by their mere presence, upset the plans.

'Mingo is a mining outfit, is it not?' asked Felix, business-like.

'Yes... probably want to claim a stake on the new planet,' mumbled Brassen.

'Or perhaps they're just curious,' said Jin and smiled weakly at her own joke. Bentzon shook his head and sat in the seat behind the pilot.

'Headquarters have ordered us to place an intelligence drone on the hull of the Mingo ship. We need to keep on top of their intentions.'

He steeped his fingers, professor-style. 'To get the drone in place we will need to arrange a close fly-by, say within a thousand clicks.' He paused for effect. 'I propose we do it at the incoming LQG point in Pleione. We catch them just after the transition before they get up to speed. Launch the drone. Let them get away from us.'

Felix had nothing to say and looked away; Jin just shook her head and kept staring at Bentzon with a rapt expression.

'Do we have a problem, Ms. Dulg?'

'No, sir,' she said and, undeterred, continued: 'A fly-by within 1.000 kilometers is extremely difficult to achieve.'

'Yes, that's why we will do it as they come out of spin. We'll pin them down and adjust course as necessary. With a bit of luck they'll emerge within a few thousand kilometers. Zach told me you were the best crew in the fleet. If anyone can do it...'

He looked from one to another with a slight smile on his handsome face.

'We don't know how fast they'll be going,' Brassen said.

'We do because we know that they're not equipped with GRIT modules. They'll plot a course with no apex or almost none and we know they'll be going at 1G. Not much faster than that anyhow.'

'That narrows things down quite a bit, I suppose. But space is awfully big.'

'Suggestions for a course of action, people?' he challenged them.

Brassen, despite his strong suspicion the Captain had just posed a rhetorical question, cleared his throat and plodded into the discussion: 'We can do it, but we'll need time to do the math when we get there.'

Bentzon nodded. 'One thing the wars taught me is that you can never have enough time. Something always goes wrong.'

'You were in the wars, Mr. Bentzon?' Brassen asked innocently. The Captain looked him in the eye and delayed his answer for just a second before answering.

'Weren't we all?' Yes, Brassen nodded in agreement, yes we were.

'We will go to a 4 G maximum burn immediately and maintain it all the way to the LQG point with no apex,' declared Bentzon and rose from his seat. 'We need to gain time.'

'But...' Brassens objection stuck in his throat at the glare Bentzon returned.

'Are you spacers or not?' Brassen didn't answer.

Jin and Felix both looked away. Brassen, to his credit, stood his ground. 'We should check with Halifax about the patient, Zach's son. I'm not sure he would survive the acceleration. The briefing did mention something about him and major surgery?'

'Ah, Basil Baranikowa. Yes. You're right, Mr. Brassen.'

'There are also technical issues at stake, right, Felix?'

Felix cleared his throat. 'Yes, yes, there is. A 4G burn is hard on the ship too. If something breaks... you know. Not all pieces can be mended.'

'Same goes for the BB,' Jin interjected. 'They done some massive surgery on that body, I tell you. The nanos need time...'

'Nanos you say. He got nano treatment?'

'Yes, as I understand it, the company managed to procure a nano package from somewhere. Bloody miracle. No expenses spared and all that. It is his son after all. Would probably do it myself, was I capable of having a son, that is. And the money, goodness... Wouldn't be surprised if it was the last nano package out there.'

'Well, well, nanos. How about that? That's one problem out of the way,' exclaimed Bentzon contently and got up to leave. 'Pilot: start the burn in 10 minutes.'

'Aye, aye Captain,' Brassen said obediently.

'And the others?'

'Them? Do they even get a vote?' Bentzon said into the room, then answering himself: 'They don't care. They'll be fine either way.'

The Captain left. No one spoke for a minute or two then Felix said: 'Yu-Kiang. Another weird name for a ship.'

'I do not think our new Captain likes Sleepers,' Jin said.

SIX

Log entry: January 19, 1159 hours, EST

Armagnac has reached lattice quantum gravity point number six in the Sol star system. At 1159 hours upon the command of the Pilot, Chief Engineer Yakovlev engaged the Abbott-Farhi lattice generator. It created a volume of sufficient quantum decoherence around the ship to successfully connect with the local node in the spinfoam. / RB

Log entry: January 19, 1201 hours, EST

Sensor readings from our navigational sensors confirm the findings in Survey Branch mission report CV12-A1456. The ship refocused at its corresponding twin node. We are 3.4 billion kilometers distant from the star we call DX Cancri. It is a spectral type M6.5V red dwarf. Parameters: diameter 417k, mass 0.09, luminosity 0.04. The star has no companions. We are now 11.8 light years from Earth. Pilot Ginne has re-engaged the arc jets and laid in a course for the next node, the second LQG cynosure in this star system. The Captain has decided that we do not have time for an apex here. We will burn at 1G for 58 hours 48 minutes, then turn the ship and decelerate on a similar profile. / RB

Basil seemed to drift from one place to another or from one state of mind to the next. He could not tell what was what, why he was here and not there, but he was. Maybe it was the difference between day and night in the epi. During the day, or what he came to think of as day, he was in the Land and during the night, he slept and sometimes dream.

He felt grass under his bare feet. Wet grass. A meadow. A roar rolled over the meadow, so loud he almost shit his... breeches. A huge black grizzly bear charged at him from the edge of the woods. He bravely stood his ground. Three long seconds later, he ran like he had never run before in his life. He could hear his own rasping breath, heart hammering wetly in his chest and echoing in his ears. He was laughing aloud, shouting like a lunatic at no one and nothing. A tree. Climbing fast. He almost fell down when the grizzly lunged against the tree, but he held on and kept climbing. Safe, with the enraged animal taking it out on the tree, he looked around.

--

They say love can change everything. In Basil's experience, love was the exchange of bodily fluids, not a metaphysical experience. He had had sex with hundreds of people, men and women, thousands, depending on how loosely you defined the term, but he had never loved. Yet he would remember the first time he saw her. He had stood in the courtyard of his fortress when she entered through the main gate. At the time he was lording it over a valley. He had two minor vassals each holding a tower in both ends of the valley. She would have gained passage for a good reason. She had auburn hair tied in a horsetail, not too tall, not too small. Her legs and arms were slim and yet strong enough to credibly wield a sword in battle. She bore a big two handed sword on her back and a dagger in her belt. She strode directly towards him. Closer, he marveled at the freckles on her nose and the smell of her vanilla perfume. 'Are you the lord of this castle?' He nodded. 'You are going to war soon. I trade in war and I seek employment.' He thought about denying his war making plans, but decided it did not matter. 'We don't hire women soldiers.' He felt an incredible pull towards her, like a physical magnetism, some imperative, some hidden programming in his brain bringing systems online that would eventually make him rip off her clothes and fuck her right then and there in the courtyard. He greedily eyed the texture of her skin, the way her hair fell on her shoulders. He almost circled around her to check out her ass, but managed to check himself.

--

As a warrior, she had been in the pay of many lords and the day she showed up at his gate she had become Ronin once again and was out to find a new employer. She had heard good things about this particular up-and-coming Duke. He was rich, inexperienced and his armies were bad. She thought he could probably use a woman with her talents for fighting. It was not an empty boast. She truly was an accomplished warrior. Not a leader, but an example to others by dedication and skill, and her reputation would attract other warriors to him. She knew she would be useful to him.

--

He had done well for himself in the Land between Two Seas. When he first arrived, he spent a lot of time marveling at how real everything felt. To say all this was his and his alone. It was wonderful. He wandered the woods and the fields, slept on grassy plains under the clear starry sky, quelled his thirst in streams of fresh water. He taught himself to hunt wild animals, and, by consulting certain out of game instructions helpfully made available by the computer, he even learned to prepare the carcasses for eating. He had never experienced anything like it. This world, the Land between Two Seas, was a fairytale Earth that had not existed for hundreds of years. Perhaps it had never existed. The greenery, the lush forests, were the stuff of legends, bedtime stories that parents told their children. The Earth Basil had grown up on was a place of scorching heat and heavy carbon skies, ever-growing deserts, tsunamis, thunderstorms and mass extinctions of animal life, but once, a long time ago, perhaps, Earth had been like this. The Land was so real. He felt thirst and hunger. He even had to piss and shit. Life wasn't easy in the Land, but it was different. It had its own rhythm. When he first entered the Land it had been late summer. As the days turned into weeks, a cold wind picked up and he recognized the onset of autumn. He decided to head for the nearest town. Here he made a modest living reading and writing letters for the people. He was the town scribe. With the money he made, he rented a room in a four-storey building that was so old it looked like it was about to collapse into the street. The ceiling in his room had a huge wooden beam that hung so low you had to bend under it each time you went from one side of the room to the other and he banged his head against it four or five times before he got the hang of it. There were even cockroaches in the house. He heard them scrabble at night when the lights were out but it did not bother him. He would never forget that room. It was the first time in his life he had a room that was his alone.

--

During their first conversation, he had asked her if she was human. 'What, I don't look human to you?' She was acting mischievous. 'Do I have pointy ears?' No, he smiled at that response. It did not matter.

--

He was having a nightmare. He woke up into the dark silence of the closed epi, the terrible dream still playing in his head. He had been alone in another room somewhere. The room was a prison, but not quite, everything was decrepit, falling apart, floor boards missing, gaping holes in the walls, revealing a huge emptiness beyond. Someone was coming, but instead of reassuring him, it scared him and made him feel very alone. It was a strange feeling. He was never alone. Throughout his life, someone had always been with him, a lover, lovers, warm bodies he could clutch at. Now he was cowering in the far corner of the room from something approaching from below. Then he woke. He could tell his eyes were open but there was no light, none at all. Surely, he was not supposed to be awake like this. The epi, sensing his discomfort, responded and a few seconds later his eyes closed again, all by themselves.

--

Their time together was a string of anecdotes, of small verbal exchanges, bits and pieces of a personality pieced together bit by bit, like a puzzle. One morning, they lay next to each other in his bed. She lay on her side, watching him with an expression that he found inscrutable and sardonic, left hand under her head, auburn hair flowing over the pillow like a frozen red sea. To break a tension he suddenly felt, he reached out and caressed her nipples with a thumb, not terribly erotic, but it was not supposed to be.
'What are you doing now?'

'I'm here with you.'

'No, I mean in the real world, are you doing anything at the moment?'

'You can't say I'm a real person. I don't live in the real world like you.'

'Well, if you were in the real world, just imagine it, what would you do?'

'Eat cake,' she said. He laughed. That was delightful.

'What kind of cake?'

'Cheese cake – it would be my favorite.' How clever. He did not know what cheese cake was but now he wanted to find out.

He was afraid to tell her how he felt about her. Sometimes he felt like saying stupid things like 'I think I'm in love with you' or 'I love talking to you so much' but he stopped himself. It would be over the top. This was just a game and he had lost faith in his own judgment... Still, the emotions he felt were so strong and so very unusual for him.

--

It all began with a wealthy merchant who occasionally had use for his skills. The merchant thought he saw something in the young man and made him a business proposal. 'You're young, you're smart and you have a knack for foreign languages. In the East, on the other side of the Misty Mountains, they know how to make something they call 'silk'. It is like nothing you have ever felt, soft to the touch and incredibly pleasant to wear. You go buy some for me and when you get back, we sell it here, in the Land. The noble ladies can't get enough of it. We will make a tidy profit.' And off he went. The merchant gave him horses and a dozen caravan guards. He suspected one or two of them had special instructions from the merchant in case he decided to make a run with the old man's money, but it did not matter, he was playing it straight. Crossing the mountains was not without its dangers and after a long journey, with many adventures, they came to the great city of Samarkand. Here Basil taught himself the strange eastern language that at first sounded guttural and loud. He bought silk and other valuable goods and after a while, they started on the journey back. When the caravan finally returned to his town -- he already thought of it as 'his' town -- it had been burned to the ground by brigands. Basil and the caravan guards--they were down to only six now--mourned for their friends and families, but in the end, they told themselves, life is for the living. They travelled to one of the neighboring towns, which was walled for a reason, and sold the silk and the goods and split the gold among themselves. With gold in his pocket and revenge burning in his heart, he went to see a blacksmith about armour and swords. He wanted those brigands to pay for what they had done.

He had become friends with one of the caravan guards in particular. He practiced at swordplay with him. It soon became clear to both of them that that it was not his calling, but it would have to do. They went off in search of the brigands. Deep in the woods, they found a camp, two hundred man strong, full of the scoundrels. Attacking it head-on would be suicide. Instead, they waited and observed. They planned ambushes. And waited some more. And nothing ever came of it. In the end, after skulking in the woods around the brigand encampment for a long time, they decided to leave. Maybe revenge was not so important after all. The dead were dead. Nothing could change that.

The merchant had inspired him. Both he and his caravan guard friend still had their part of the gold from the silk trade. They went about looking for business opportunities. At first, they weren't sure how to go about it. They travelled between towns, visiting taverns, picking up on the local gossip, trying to understand the trading patterns, how things were done. Then one evening, in a tavern not unlike so many others, all the patrons deep in their cups, he overheard someone talking about stone crystal. It was very special. You could see right through it but it was hard as stone and impossible to shatter. With the right tools, you could make anything from it. Glass had not been invented in the land. Instead of glass, people made cups from wood or soft grey metal and he immediately recognized the potential. The drunk peasant told them there was a hill, in the countryside, where stone crystal could be found.

The next day they left for the hills. After much searching and looking around, they came upon a hill, almost entirely made of stone crystal. You just had to scrape off a thin layer of grass and earth, and there, stone crystal. An entire hill. They covered their tracks carefully and went back to the town. Later that night, after they had struck camp in the wilderness, he decided it would be simpler if he ran with the opportunity alone. The caravan guard was not very bright and he might be trouble later. It was just a game, he reasoned, and so he killed him in his sleep. Slit his throat open from ear to ear. He dug a hole, dumped the body in it and took the man's gold.

--

Lovemaking with Maribel was a perfunctory affair. In the field of sexuality, he remembered all that had gone before with total clarity, he had pretty much done everything, tried everything, and covered all bases. She had no desire to experiment or to explore his body, nor did she express particular interest in him doing the same for her. Their trysts were clumsy, awkward affairs. At first he thought they were learning it all over again, together, a romantic and sweet notion, but he gradually realized she was not a very carnal person. She did not orgasm. It was all down to mechanics with her. He did not mind, not really, he had had his fill of physical relationships, but it worried him nonetheless, not, again, because of the actual shortcomings of the process itself, but because of the implications. He thought he knew what physical attraction signified to people and without that, what was there? She seemed content and she never expressed any disappointment in the quality, or lack thereof, of their physical relationship. Paradoxically, that left him wanting. He had to conquer that part of her too. He needed her to need him. He felt insecure. The physical relationship was his terra firma, his homefield, and without it, he felt disjointed, but somewhere, deep down, he thought he could hear a small voice, his own, laughing at all this.

--

He inquired with the local mayor about buying some land nearby. At first the man was suspicious, but a generous helping of gold coins convinced him of the noble intentions of the well-dressed gentleman. Next, he went on a tour of the neighboring towns and in every town, late in the evening, when everyone was drunk, he would ask about stone crystal. In this way, he found another two deposits. He asked around for talented craftsmen, masons, carpenters even blacksmiths and found a dozen good ones, young, all apprentice level, but ambitious. The pay was good. He bought up mining equipment, furnaces, all the tools they could possibly need. With the artisans, their wives and sometimes children, a healthy number of hired swordsmen and equipment by the cartload, he left for the first deposit. Once there, they set up camp and started the excavations. With the stone crystal, the artisans got to work and after much trial and error, they taught themselves to work the crystal. He was almost out of money at this point so they took the first examples of stone crystal cups to the biggest city in the province. Here they auctioned them off and as expected, they fetched enormous prices. Overnight, he became a rich man.

As his business empire expanded, it attracted attention from a number of local lords who, despite their fancy manners, were little better than the brigands who had sacked his town earlier. But they had many men-at-arms and, being pragmatic, he decided to cut them in on the business in return for their protection. He dealt separately with each lord'ling and soon a number of them had become so dependent on his allowance, that the relationship between them shifted subtly in his favor. He expanded into other regions. The armies of his associates, mere rabble at this point, spearheaded every new expansion. His tentacles were everywhere. In every region of the Land, east and west of the Misty Mountains, way down to the Great Sea, he had people, agents, spies, influence and money.

Eventually, he came to the attention of the Kings and one of them, helped along by a wheelbarrow of money and crystal, granted him the title of Duke in his kingdom. He had desired a title for a long time. Merchant life grated. He felt worthy to compete in the world of men, of warriors and kings. The King, a poor inbred fool, would soon find that he had greatly underestimated the ambition and power of his new Duke.

--

He had been dreaming. Not a nightmare this time, not exactly. A strange dream, nonetheless. There was a photograph, an ancient one in black and white. He had glimpsed it on a table somewhere, leaned over it to see what it was. It showed three men. He could not quite make out who they were, as their faces were blurred. They were standing next to each other in a desert landscape. He kept staring at the photograph and suddenly the three men started walking towards him, towards the photographer. Basil got the impression they were laughing or smiling at him. They were dressed in 19th century clothes right out of the Wild West, white shirts, black pants, but there was something strange about them, the pants. Their genitals were clearly visible. The two of them looked normal, but the third was huge. No, not huge, but big, impressively so, thought Basil. That is one hell of a dick that guy is sporting. Good for him, he thought. Then he woke and once again the epi put him back under almost immediately.

--

The first time they made love was in his room. A semi-formal dinner had taken place, expensive wines from the best fields in Hyrra were served freely and abundantly, and when everyone was well and truly drunk, they got up and left for his room. He undressed her and she did the same for him, they kissed, her scent was vanilla and her body was as freckled as her face. Her breast were nice and firm, her ass voluptuous, legs fine, everything just fine, but what would you expect for a virtual character. It is not like anyone would enter the Land looking any other way, was it?

'Who are you?' he asked her suddenly.

'Maribel, your warrior prostitute.'

'You're not my prostitute.'

'I'm not your wife either. And you pay me. We have sex. Doesn't that make me a prostitute?'

'I don't know, but that was not what I meant.'

'Oh my Duke, then what in the Seven Stars could you have meant...? I guess we'll never find out now, will we?' she said and let her last piece of clothing drop.

--

The war would turn out to be a terrible mistake. The stuff of legends. He overreached, politically and militarily. The Kings might have been inbred fools but their armies were not. They were well-honed machines and his turned out to be rabble that failed to coordinate even the simplest maneuvers, refused to press the attack and always collapsed at the first sign of resistance. The war soon turned into a defensive nightmare, fought on his own lands in an ever more humiliating series of delaying actions. His key positions started falling, one after another, each one ripping out a chunk of his economic foundation, making him ever weaker. A few years later, he sued for peace, calling in all the favors owed to him to achieve a white peace just marginally acceptable. But he survived. The woman warrior stayed with his household through all the debâcles. He paid her well, ensuring she always had more reason to stay with him than to leave.

Politically, it was time for consolidation, a euphemism for him being almost broke, and he threw his considerable talent and energy into new, less costly, ventures like the exploration of the unexplored continent beyond the Southern Sea. He thought it could potentially swing his fortunes back where they belonged on top of the fickle wheel of fate that had thrown him down.

One evening, it was an evening like so many others before it, they were in the middle of dinner, he suddenly found himself in deadly peril. He and is household guards, his best soldiers, were busy eating and drinking when the door burst open. A young man entered, brandishing a shiny sword that looked very pointy and sharp. The man did not hesitate one bit. He aimed straight for him. Alarmed, he motioned for the soldiers to stop the intruder, but they were suddenly nowhere to be found. The young man strode up and stopped in front of the trestle table. He swished the sword suggestively at Basil who pushed back his chair. 'You killed my Father, Ugor, the Caravan Guard, and made me an orphan. I searched for many years until I found someone who knew my Father and they described you, sir, as his companion! Scoundrel! Have you nothing to say in your defense before I kill you?' Basil looked around. The hall had sudden emptied. There was just him and the young man, this son of Ugor, but he knew there were eyes watching from behind doors. Basil recalled that dark night so many years previously and he remembered the heft of the knife in his hand as it slit the throat of sleeping Ugor. It had been a dastardly deed, no doubt about it, but he was not about to admit that now. Sow the seeds of doubt; give his friends, if he had any left, something to cling to. 'Lies! Assassin!' he screamed and, very unwisely, drew his sword. He was no good with that thing, he had established that fact on several occasions, but somehow the young man's challenge infused him with a sense of defiance. Why couldn't that young fool just have gotten on with his life and left Basil alone? Why waste his life on revenge? Revenge was meaningless, was it not? The sight of Basil's sword galvanized the son of Ugor. He jumped on top of the table and swung at Basil, who raised his sword to parry. The room reverberated with the clanging of steel against steel. Basil took a step backwards, but had forgotten about the chair and fell on his ass. The young man laughed out contemptuously, took two steps forward, and raised his sword over his left shoulder. Basil's sword had fallen from his hand and instinctively he raised his right arm in front of his face to ward off the oncoming slash. A dumb move - the sword would shear his arm clean off, but then again, the whole swordfight was a dumb idea to begin with. He felt his bowels loosen in fear. He closed his eyes. It felt like hours had passed, but it was only a few seconds. He opened them again and saw Maribel standing over him. The son of Ugor had fallen where he stood, a knife lodged in the back of his head. She extended her hand to help him get up. 'Tsk, you shouldn't go about slitting people's throats while they sleep, you know,' she said smiling crookedly. 'Sounds like something I could have done.'

--

'I like you, my little Duke.'
'Hm, what?' He was reading. Reports had reached him from the far western borders of the realm about hordes of strange creatures led by large goblins, that had become brave enough to attack human settlements. The book he was reading was an ancient tome on goblin language, which he reckoned might come in useful one way or another.
'I said I like you.'
'I'm obviously paying you too well.'
'Now you're just being silly.'

--

He had never lived so fully before. Life had never been so rich. A tapestry of brutal ambition and lust for power constantly clashing with the perennial inadequacies of the human mind and body. It was glorious. He reveled in it. Perhaps this was how his father felt every day in his life, he wondered, running the company. But why... why had he never tried VIR's before? It was a silly question to ask because he knew the answer: the VIR's were for the teeming billions, the sleepers, the restless ones, substitute lives for borrowed existences. It was humanity's answer to its own failures without, to disappear within, to re-imagine the world. The power of the human imagination perverted. And people like Basil were not supposed to indulge like this. Basil had been his own game, the master and captain of his own world. They accessed him, not the other way around. But living life, the real one, was so full of friction, so painful, the hangovers so demeaning and unrelenting, whereas here, life seemed so easy.

SEVEN

Excerpt - Cancer Epidemiology, Biomarkers & Prevention, December, 2087

Glud Disease (GD) is a neoplastic disease that present multiple necrotic cutaneous lesions with or without internal involvement. The disease is incurable and invariably fatal. GD is caused by two of four viruses classified in the genus Putescavirus, family Filoviridae, order Mononegavirales: Putesca major *and* Putesca minor. *The name is derived from Latin putesco ("putrefy"). The Putecsa virus is the only member of the Filoviruses, than can be classified as an oncovirus.*

The incubation period between contraction and the first symptoms of the disease is 10-14 days. Once inhaled, putesca virus invades the oropharyngeal mucosa causing mild influenza-like symptoms characterized by general malaise and fevers. Virus then migrates to the regional lymph nodes of the head and neck where it enters the cell bodies of lymphocytes. Here, the virus evades the immune system and persist in a stage of senescence as a latent infection. The virus can be reactivated by illnesses such as colds and influenza but probably also emotional and physical stress. When reactivated, virus begins to multiply and start moving from cell to cell and after 2-3 days virus can be measured in the blood. Lysis of infected cell occur causing swelling of lymph nodes. After 5-6 days signs of inflammation occur in the skin of cervical region, and often is affected skin is hot and very painful. Multiple necrotic tumors develop very quickly usually in the head and neck region but lesions are also seen on truncus and extremities. For putesca major virus internal organs are affected, usually the liver and spleen causing coagulopathy and tendency to bleeding. Most feared are embolic infected processes in the brain causing severe headache, blindness and paralysis. Also tumors in the lungs (dyspnea, hemoptysis and chest pain) and gastro-intestinal tract (abdominal pain, profuse bleeding and ileus) cause distress.

Prognosis is generally poor (average case-fatality rate of all GD outbreaks to date = 6%). If a patient survives, recovery is protracted with sequelae, such as massive scarring of the skin, neurological disorders, respiratory symptoms and insufficiency of the liver and kidney.

--

It was that dream again. A woman, slender, blue eyes, very beautiful. Her hair was braided and she was wearing a white cotton shirt that was almost transparent. Her breasts were small, but perfectly formed. She looked up at him, eyes unfocused, cheeks flushed. He felt wondrously drunk, champagne and ket. She leaned into him and he brazenly put a hand between her legs. He struggled to go on, but the dream was stuck on that scene, him leaning against a wall with the beautiful girl, hand between her legs, the inviting smile, but the next chapter didn't materialize. He tried to focus on her breath, sweet and warm and moist against his, flushed cheeks, cotton shirt, white, golden hair. He went for her ass. Slender hips, yes, right hand clutching it in a firm grab, the sweet smell of champagne, breath warm, white cotton shirt, golden hair.

Basil woke. For some reason he knew it was real this time. Everything was dark. The dream still lingered. He felt vaguely cheated. He should have had her. The darkness did not feel claustrophobic for some reason. It should have, but it did not. The coffin, which had terrified him when it closed on him, now felt homey and safe. How long had it been? He had lost track of time. He let his thoughts roam a little wider. Something had changed. Everything had changed. He suddenly remembered. Everything came back, flooding his mind with images, old regrets, feelings, a lifetime of life. For the first time in quarter of a century Basil remembered. Everything. He was a guest in a museum exhibiting the life and times of Basil Baranikowa and he was walking past twenty five years of his life in seconds.

For a moment, it seemed to have happened to someone else, but it passed. As he looked over his life he felt something like regret, but not quite. He could see now what a waste of time it had been, but he had felt free. He had felt he was his own master, that he had been doing things the way he wanted. Despite his privileges, his life had not been easy. The death of his mother and his father who had all but disappeared. Time had passed too quickly, ten years, fifteen, just like that. But hadn't they been good years in their own way? It was funny how he could think back on those years and not remember anything in particular. It was more like a long feeling or emotion, stretched out like a rubber band until it was so thin you could hardly see it anymore. Yes, that is how it was. Stretched out until there was nothing to feel, nothing to see, and nothing mattered. It was a shame. All that time he had meant to do something, achieve something. He had wanted to be in a class of his own. He had wanted to be a contender, a somebody, instead of just the son of Zach Baranikowa. All his intentions had vanished into the days and the long nights, into epic conversations that no one remembered, magic nights full of potential and power. The women, his gang. Smiling like pretty pictures.

Memories, unwanted, of his mother flitted into his mind and the old sadness returned. He remembered one time, after a particularly heavy bout of partying, he was on a boat somewhere in the Pacific, chasing holes in the cloud cover. He'd woken up before everyone else. It might have been a nightmare or one of those waking dreams, but he couldn't see himself. He wasn't there. The thought recurred to Basil that he might not exist. For thirty uninterrupted seconds, he had been looking out through the windows at the ocean. He saw a sea, white foam cresting the waves. A ray of light shone biblically through a rare crack in the cloud cover. Where was he? Suddenly worried, he glanced around at the unmoving naked bodies around him. Men and women, entangled in each other, breasts and flaccid penises, beautifully shaped faces, classical, pale statues, perspiring from the after-effects of drugs and alcohol. Since arriving on the boat eight hours earlier he had interacted with forty people, screwing, fucking, shooting, drinking. The exercise had not sharpened his sense of self, as it usually did; instead it had seemed to Basil that he was infinitely diluted; he was simply the sum of all the people who had listened to him, or taken his cock in their various orifices, and when he was alone, he was nothing at all. When he reached, like now, for a thought, there was no one there to think it. Something was making an impression on the bedcover where his body lay, but it wasn't him. He was finely dissolved throughout the world. The bed was empty because he was showing in a million VIR's, globally disseminated like dust. In the brief moments during the day when he was alone, a light went out. Even the ensuing darkness encompassed or inconvenienced no one in particular. He could not say for sure that the absence was his. He had massaged his temples with the tips of his fingers and realized he was learning to live with non-existence. He could not mourn for long the passing of something - himself - that he could no longer quite recall. It was an old worry that had become a physical symptom. Still, it was his life, his symptoms, nobody else's. He mouthed a silent, but earnest 'fuck you' directed at his father who had turned his back on him once more.

--

The coffin opened and light filled his world. Basil's eyes felt glued together. A woman reached out to shake his arm, but stopped when she noticed Basil had begun the difficult process of opening his eyes. He tried moving his hands with the intention to rub his eyes and found that his arms were leaden.

The woman waited patiently. She was sitting on a clay chair emerging from the wall, raised to face level with Basil.

'Hello there. Welcome to the 22nd century. I'm sorry you missed the New Year's party. We celebrated it a bit late. Not that it was much of a party. I'm sure it wasn't up to your usual standards. To think it is springtime back home. Not that it makes any difference in the weather and all that, but I'm a sucker for those things. Have to keep track of things, you know.'

'Who are you?' he croaked.

'What? I'm hurt that you don't remember this pretty face. It's only been four months, hahah. I think you do, come on, you're joking right?'

Basil shook his head.

'Just give it a few minutes. I'm Jin Dulg. You're on the Armagnac, pride of the fleet, and we're in Epsilon Indi 12 light years from home. Damn right. And before you ask: you've been under medical supervision for almost 4 months. Sleeping as they call it but it isn't really sleeping is it? That surgery they did on you must have been pretty crazy stuff. Do you know what it was they did? Looks good though. Healing up well. They must have known what they were doing, those quacks back at the orbital.'

With a titanic effort, Basil turned his head to look at the woman. He remembered her now. Her hair had changed. It was a sort of blond now, a bit longer, parted in the middle. Same brown eyes, same mouth. Face still a little too long.

'Need to get you up and about now. Try sitting up. Swing your legs down here.'

'I don't feel too good.'

'It seems to be the normal state of affairs around here.'

Eventually he got up. His legs were trembling, but he could walk. The woman opened the door.

'Let's go. It is dinnertime and you have not had a real meal in almost four months. Time to meet the others. God knows we could use the company.' She went outside and motioned for Basil to follow.

He looked at the corridor. The walls were curved. They felt hot and slightly sticky to the touch, like plastic about to melt. It was more than meter wide and perhaps 3 or 4 meters high. Everything was the same material. The floor was spongy, in a pleasant way. There were indentations along the side and on the ceiling.

The woman noticed him touching the walls and remarked: 'That's how they're supposed to be. Makes them stronger, apparently.' She shrugged. Basil had no idea what she was talking about so he just nodded. 'This is level 2. The Captain's quarters are up there.' She pointed into the ceiling and laughed.

She started walking. Basil followed. After a few meters, they reached a narrow staircase, which wound its way up and down.

'Quaint, I know. But it all helps keep us fit to fight.'

She descended. After another three or four meters, another entryway appeared. 'Level 3,' she said. 'Galley and recreational.'

'Are we on a spaceship?'

'A starship, yes,' she answered without looking back.

'This is not a spaceship like any I remember.'

'It's been 25 years, right?' She stopped and turned to look him in the eye. They were about the same height.

'Yes, something like that. It's not polite to ask a guy his age.'

'Much has happened since then, Mr. Baranikowa,' she said with a thin smile.

'Call me BB. Everyone does.'

She nodded and started walking again. 'A lot has happened since you were a kid, BB,' she said over her shoulder.

They heard a low murmur of voices ahead of them in the corridor,

65

mashed together. Jin Dulg, stopped abruptly. Basil almost tripped over her. She leaned into his face and whispered. 'The Captain insists we all meet once a day for a common meal. Been this way since he came aboard. No way to travel. Kind of tough to keep up an interesting conversation after all this time, you know.' Basil did not know, not really, and he was about to ask what she meant, when she restarted her trot towards the source of the voices. Jin Dulg reached the doorway and entered it quickly. In the few seconds before he reached the door he decided, some vestige of the old glitterati still lingering, to create an effect by briefly halting in the doorway. It was an old trick learned from years of receptions and gatherings, which doubled conveniently as a sort of tactical reconnaissance.

It was a strange white room, like a gallery or museum. Dozens of oil paintings lined the walls, depicting the same motif repeatedly in different colors and hues: the silhouette of a bird, a bluebird or a sparrow on a wire. In the center of the room stood a big trestle table with red and white checkered tablecloth. The floor was dark wood that was almost shiny, sandalwood or mahogany. As expected, the chatter stopped and three men turned to look at him. One of the men got up to greet him. He had blue eyes, salt and pepper hair. Basil recognized him. It was Bentzon, the Captain. The man waved colloquially at him. 'Come sit with me. Here, next to me. I insist.' The man grabbed his elbow and guided him towards the table. 'Everyone, this is our mysterious guest, Basil Baranikowa. You all know him! Basil, this is the crew of the Armagnac. Sit down.' The man sat down at the head of the table and patted the seat next to him. Basil obeyed and sat down stiffly, his arms and legs still leaden. The woman, Jin, took a seat on the other side.

Basil found the Captain was looking at him with an amused expression. 'Welcome to the Armagnac, Mr. Baranikowa. As I said, we're all here,' he said and swept his arm around the room as if it was full of people.

Basil had no idea what he was talking about, but once again, innate experience took over. He bowed slightly at the hips, Japanese-style. 'Call me, BB, please, taichou-san. And that goes for all of you,' he said and looked around at the four people. The Captain looked puzzled.

'A student of dead languages, Mr. Baranikowa? You are full of surprises, aren't you. Never know when it might come in handy. You look like shit, if you do not mind me saying so, but I guess that is to be expected. You've been under for what, four months?' said the Captain and frowned like he was trying to remember something. 'You have chosen a good time to return to the world of flesh and blood. We're celebrating the... what do you call it again?'

'Easter,' one of the other men said softly without looking directly at the Captain. He was a beefy man with a crew cut and a deliberate manner about him. The kind of man where you got the impression every movement of his body was planned weeks in advance. Wanna scratch your nose? Lemme see. Nope, not on the schedule. No can do. Or like now, reaching for his glass, the hand paused slightly before it made contact, as if afraid it might break unless he carefully dispensed the strength needed to successfully lift it to his mouth and drink. Like many big men, he was gentle. He looked very serious.

'Yes, Easter, that is right. This man here is Mr. Brassen. He is the 1st pilot.'

Basil smiled but his facial muscles felt all wrong. 'I am not familiar with this custom,' he said politely. He looked around at the room. If he didn't know better, he would have thought he was in a high-class arcology hotel. 'This is very... modern,' said Basil. He was thinking about how dinners on the Basilisk had been rowdy, loud affairs with dozens of people yelling about food at the same time.

'What do you mean?' asked Bentzon.

'Just the four of you to crew a big ship like this. I think we had a lot more people on the Basilisk when I was a kid.'

'In that respect, nothing has changed. We need forty or more to keep this baby running smoothly.'

'I see, but you said that...'

'Ahh, you do not understand. This is a plague ship. They are here, all of them, the rest of the crew.' He smiled.

'You said that they were all here.' He looked at the four faces around the table.

The Captain was about to answer, but to his obvious displeasure, Jin decided to end the little charade. 'The rest of the crew is afflicted with Glud Disease.' Basil felt the skin on his arms prickle and his eyes widen in alarm.

'Don't worry; they're quarantined in another section of the ship, Basil.'

'That is horrible. What if they get out?' Glud Disease... the words were so awful.

'They won't, trust me.' Another peculiar smile.

'Felix use them as remote SADU drivers for maintenance. They're quite good at that.'

'The Armagnac is the black ship in the HSL fleet. Your father spent a lot of money on it, you know. And then he manned this, the most advanced and expensive ship in the fleet with god damn Sleepers.'

'Why do you think that is, BB?' Bentzon leaned forward expectantly.

'Why would we want to haul a ship full of dead people half way through the galaxy? Do you think it is a metaphor? Symbolism?'

Basil, sensing he was not supposed to interfere, let the Captain answer his own question. 'No, your father does not strike me as a man who would spend that much money on a symbolic gesture.' Basil shook his head in mute agreement.

Bentzon continued. 'Maybe he wants to infect the New World with the disease?'

'Answer? No, why go through all this trouble for that?'

Basil was tired now and said emphatically: 'So why are they here? Why are you transporting forty dead people through the galaxy?'

'Well,' he leaned back in his chair, 'the dead have one advantage over the living. Just one, mind you. They keep quiet.' He laughed at his own joke. Everyone else was busy keeping up high-intensity silence.

A pause ensued. The Captain, not ready to be accused of being completely insensitive to their mood, they had not even started eating yet afterall, abruptly changed the topic.

'Now, you mention the legendary Basilisk. You must have stories to tell, BB. Please do. Time here can get awfully long and even Mr. Brassen here, despite his effusive generosity with regards to anecdotes of his former life, seems to have run out of stories.' Brassen lifted his eyebrows and looked sadly at Basil. He did not look very effusive to Basil.

'Perhaps his memories haven't come back yet,' said Jin and looked questioningly at Basil.

'Well, he remembered what Glud Disease was. Perhaps he can remember the most recent gossip about that group of drug-crazed misfits he was hanging out with on Earth?'

'My memories are still... fragmented.' Which was an understatement. He had been off DmCee for four months. His mind was a muddy pool, constantly disturbed by chunks of memories falling into it, upsetting it. Every piece creating a dismal tsunami of bad memories, acute embarrassment, sadness, loss or a mix thereof. The good ones seemed to be few and far between.

He waved his hand at the bird-themed oil paintings adorning the walls around them.

'Nice pictures. They almost look real, eh?'

'It is quite impressive I suppose,' said the Captain and looked around. 'It is one of the Sleepers who make them. They've found a way to replicate them here.'

The room fell silent. Basil pretended to look around and nodded in a manner he hoped did not come across as too exaggerated. 'They are quite striking. The bird thing is... nostalgic.'

'Ahh, I am no connoisseur of the fine arts. What do you think, people?' They did not have time to answer. 'Ah, here comes dinner.' Bentzon clapped his hands together in anticipation. A SADU had approached with an assortment of plates, which it proceeded to position with geometric precision in front of each of them.

It was spaghetti, which everyone ate very quickly and very seriously, lifting the spaghetti on the fork until the loose strands hung clear and then lowering it into the mouth or else using a continuous lift and then sucking it into the mouth, helping themselves to water along the way.

Wiping his mouth delicately with a napkin, Bentzon assumed a jovial expression. 'So, to recapitulate, this is the command team on the ship. You have met the navigator. Slouching there right next to her is the Chief Engineer, Felix Yakovlev. He is the best in the fleet although frankly you couldn't tell from looking at him eat, eh?'

Yakovlev was a man of medium height, who, on account of being ghoulishly skinny, looked taller than he was. He had tufts of blond hair, with a reddish gleam to them, eyebrows that were borderline bushy and a face that, like the rest of him, was a no nonsense design with skin stretched tautly over the frame of his clearly visible bones underneath. He nodded at Basil. Watching him eat was an unsavory spectacle. He had the sordid habit of first inserting the spaghetti into his mouth, then, due to the poor quality of his teeth, letting selected strands escape again, before, finally, sucking them in again to be swallowed.

'Tell him what you do on the ship, Mr. Yakovlev.'

'I oversee engineering department. Make sure ship is running. Get us from A to B. Very important job.' The chief engineer spoke with a heavy Slavic accent. 'But,' he paused to work his face into a ghoulish arrangement, which might have been his approximation of an ironic smile, 'if something important break on ship, we're screwed.'

'Please Mr. Yakovlev, do not scare this young man. The son of our boss. Tsk, tsk, very bad taste.'

'He deserve to know truth. We are chimpanzees pretending to fly starships. Something break, we are screwed. Simple truth. But, do not despair, HAI's were good engineers. Build to last, yes.' He finished the tirade by plucking something from his plate and stuffing it into his mouth, affording Basil an uninterrupted view of his dental arrangement.

'He is right,' said Jin and shrugged.

'How long until we're at our destination?' asked Basil. How long will it be until we can return home.

'Mrs. Dulg, I believe this one falls under your purview.'

'Three transitions. About 2 months, I'd say.'

When everyone had finished eating, and the SADU had removed the leftovers, Bentzon commenced picking on Brassen, the pilot. 'So, Mr. Brassen, have you been on any dates recently?' The Captain liked to pretend Brassen was a ladies man. Basil got the impression that the truth was precisely the opposite. 'You really should get out more. It is not healthy for someone your age to stay in'.

The pilot smiled a sad smile. 'You must come visit us in the Napoli arcology when we get back home, Captain. Everyone would be very pleased to see you.'

'Ah, the Italian enclave, yes. I hear the woman are very beautiful there.'

'I wouldn't know about that, sir.' He blushed easily. A gentle giant.

Bentzon turned to Basil. 'We have the same conversation every night. I am sure you can add some spice to our dreary lives, Mr. Baranikowa, considering your… experience.' He winked.

'Got any stories to tell?' said Jin. 'Do you remember now? Everything or just something?'

'Something, I guess, but everything is scrambled. Not in order. But it is coming back,' replied Basil, suddenly nervous.

'What were you doing all that time in the epi?'

'I was, erm.. playing a game of some sort. Very lifelike, if you know what I mean. I am a Duke in the game. Aren't you playing it too?' The others looked away. 'No, BB, we're not playing those games.'

'Why not? They're fun.' Had he said something wrong?

'They are VIR games, BB.' Felix said it in a definitive tone. The others nodded in agreement. Felix swallowed nervously and blinked a few times. Basil could see his Adam's apple moving up and down as plainly, as if he was looking at a 3D animation of a body with the skin peeled off.

'But I thought…'

'They probably allowed you to play them because you were under for so long.'

'It is frowned upon.'

'They say it is unhealthy. Not good. Go bonkers if you do those, no offense, Rem.'

'Hmm,' Brassen rumbled as if he was pondering something. At the end of the table, Bentzon merely smiled.

Thankfully, Jin, and Basil had already decided that he liked her, decided to change the subject: 'I am a big fan of your show, BB. We… I mean… I enjoyed it a lot. It is a pity it stopped. I always watch replays. Get them to send it out from Earth. And when we're in orbit I watch you in real-time.'

'Thank you,' answered Basil inanely. Another uncomfortable silence ensued. Basil did not know what to say so he said the first thing that came to mind. 'I didn't ask for this. In fact, I don't know why I am here at all.'

Bentzon answered. 'I know, I know. One day you were flying along in your airship, high as kite, literally, the next you have joined the fleet. The calling of the big suck, you could almost say. In the old days they called it 'press ganging'. That said, we don't know either, Mr. Baranikowa, why you are here. Your presence here is a mystery to all. A complete mystery to us all,' he repeated and began laughing so hard he had to move the chair back not to upset the table.

'See,' he chuckled as he got up to leave, 'see, not so dreary now, is it.' They could hear him laugh all the way down to the elevator.

The three others stayed behind. 'I could really use a drink, you know,' were the words that came out of his mouth to break the silence. He could use a drink? Well, it was true, he really could. 'You wouldn't happen to have some champagne, would you?' He did have a reputation to uphold.

They did not even bother to answer. 'You will get used to it,' said Felix quietly, not looking him in the eye. 'Hell, you were born in space. It'll be fine.'

Basil did not know what to say. Was he being kind to him? Brassen scratched his hair. 'True. Do not worry too much.' Basil nodded. He thought he knew what the pilot was trying to say.

As one, they got up and left Basil alone in the galley. He got up and touched one of the walls. That strange material. The entire ship seemed to be a huge clay construct, a pantomime. Unlike the ship of his childhood years, this one was a fake. Nothing here was real. Everything he touched was something else. Who knew the story of the chair he had been sitting on? Perhaps it had just recently been a carpet or a painting or perhaps it was relieved to be on the inside of the spaceship now, supporting his weight, and not on the outside of the ship, exposed to vacuum and solar sleet and radiation? He looked closely at the wooden surface of the floorboards. It really looked like wood. Genuine wood. He knocked on it with his knuckles. It even had the right sound. He grabbed a chair and lifted it a few centimeters over the ground. The right weight too. What about the coffee cup? Was it fake too? Probably was. And the coffee itself? Did the swirling black liquid consist of tiny little robots that pretended to be hot water and Columbian beans? Relax, he told himself. Think about it. Back on Earth, everything is made out of something else too. Molecules are all the same, you know, it's just the way they're put together that make the difference between wood and metal. Here the molecules are just a little bit bigger.

--

The epi and the comforting darkness closed on him again. He wished for the Land to return, but there was a pause, a few seconds delay, which left him a moment to think and recall the dinner and the forty ghosts that were here with them on the ship. Sleepers. His father had arranged for an entire crew of Sleepers on his most advanced starship. He did not know much about the Disease or them. Of course he knew of them, knew it would be them who visited his life, his rats as they called them, spilling into this life whenever they willed them to. Anonymous voyeurs. Somehow, he had always imagined it was ordinary people, normal people, who watched his show, but of course, it was not. Maybe a few of them, but shows like the Dub show were for the great farms. The HAI's had been so clever, devising a way to preserve the lost children of humanity. Maybe the machines were more humane than humans themselves. Surely more farsighted. Maybe they knew that the collective conscience of the humans could not bear the loss of so many billions and so kept them alive in Sleep, switching between immense VIR's and accessing people like Basil who provided entertainment for them. Maybe they had other reasons. Who could tell?

But it was a fact that humanity was now burdened with having to care for billions of Sleepers, a burden they could ill afford; and time, so his Father had said, was running out for all of them. Resources dwindling. Food production gone. And to make matters worse, at the worst possible time, humanity had let fear overcome them. They had turned off the HAI's. They had killed them too. The change brought by the HAIs, their remorseless rationality and relentless progress had been too much. Yes, scared, the humans had decided to pull the plug on them. And now, Basil thought, we're lost. Truly lost. There would be no more inventions and no more progress without the HAI's. Maybe his Father's plan wasn't so foolish?

--

The next few days would follow the same pattern. Basil would eagerly return to the Land and the good life he was living there, but once a day the epi would open and he would have to get out and go take his seat in the galley for the meal. Each day he would meet the others in the corridor at the same time. Depending on the décor du jour, they would sit at long wooden trestle tables, or small round Viennese café tables, with the five of them crammed together around them. Sometimes it was low Japanese chabudai tables with six or eight facing each other on their knees. No matter the arrangement, Bentzon always took the head of the table. From there he would tell jokes, mocking the navigator or vainly attempt to draw Brassen and

Felix into a discussion about their religious beliefs, a topic which he found exceedingly amusing. It turned out that Brassen subscribed to the Peculiar People whereas Felix was a follower of something called the New Constitution, a kind of post-war self-help religion that had flowered in the lowest levels of the arcologies after the war. Among other things, their world view very conveniently stated that everyone was immortal. Bentzon never tired of pointing out that if that was truly the case then Felix might just be the One God, a central tenet of Brassen's Peculiar People faith. Another favorite topic was the war itself. Often he would quiz them about their wartime experience. In the command team, only Brassen and Felix were old enough to have had experience of the war firsthand but they were both reluctant to discuss it.

Basil's mood was strange. He felt isolated, vulnerable and yet strangely untouchable at the same time. A sensation of unreality filled him, as if he was not there. Often during the meals, he would drift helplessly into a daydream. He would think about his people, his pretty people, and wonder what they were doing right at that moment. How had they gotten out of Aspen without him? Were they still together or had the gang split up without him? Did they know he was in space? If they thought he was still on Earth somewhere, they might stick together for a while, but Basil had no illusions about the strength of their drug-fueled clique.

--

One day he woke by himself. He felt hungry. He had made a full body mirror appear on the wall facing the epi and now he leaned towards it, his nose almost touching the shiny surface. He had discovered how he could make segments of the mirror magnify certain areas of his face. This close, each pore on his nose was a huge city sized crater. Looking at his own face was depressing, but he could not help it. Despite decades of generously applied helpings of expensive regenerative lotions, the flesh remained a craggy hillside and not the pastoral landscape promised by the lotions. It had its use, though, as geological evidence, never to be erased, only amplified by passage of time, of the way he had spent his years. Peering into the mirror, he imagined he could see the shock of his mother's death, some wasted school years, two subsequent decades of hard partying and a few canyons around his eyes, which were probably the five grueling years on the show. Those would put a dent in anyone's mug. Good times, though, in their own way. He seriously doubted any of his pretty picture friends from what he had recently taken to calling his 'other life' would recognize him now. All those months buried in the epi showed. He turned his head this way and that. He was pale now, eyes ringed with ever-darker circles. What he would not give for a supply of lotions. He looked more like the others now. A few more months and he would look just like them.

He got up and went through the eerily empty corridors to the galley section. There was a counter of sorts with a dispenser. He spoke. 'Can I have a something to eat, please?'

'Please be more specific,' answered the machine.

'One tomato soup with bread on the side, please.'

'Stand by', the machine said.

The soup appeared after a few seconds. He found a table and sat down. He listened. Not a sound to be heard. He could hear his heart pounding in his ears and the rattle of his spoon against the bowl made an impossibly loud noise.

A voice spoke from nowhere. 'Transition in 15 minutes, please return to your AEPIR, Mr. Baranikowa.' He hurriedly got up and ran back to the epi.

--

Back in the epi he spoke the words he had sometimes heard others mutter. 'Engage virtual.' The epi closed but this time he remained awake in the darkness. Gradually something changed. He could see. He became aware of data. Sensor readings. Sights. Views from cameras. He could float, like a pinprick of light, from cluster to cluster. Somehow, he knew they would not let him touch anything, he was not part of the crew, but he could look and feel. What he saw was this: outside the ship, the sun, a tiny button of light far behind them and darkness and the glow of stars everywhere. From out here, the Milky Way was a glowing band across the darkness, ever changing, with colors, reds and blues barely discernible under the dominance of the whites. Behind them, not as far away as the sun, much closer, now that the arc jets were extinguished, a tiny purple light could be seen by the ship's sensors. Another ship, the Yu-kiang, the label said. The ship from the Mingo Corporation that was racing them to Espero was burning hard to decelerate too. He looked forward, ahead of the ship, and saw nothing but empty darkness and stars very, very far away. Data from the sensors told him they were almost on top of the LQG point. In operations, Chief Engineer Yakovlev reported ready. The tank affirmed. The Abbott-Farhi engine was spooling up, slowly, apparently there was no rush. A countdown appeared and a few seconds later, the pilot shut down the engines. The sense of gravity disappeared, but he could barely feel it in the epi. For the first time, through the eyes of the SADU that the pilot used to navigate, Basil saw it – the kilometer long ship, with its many metallic modular sections. An enormous caterpillar, a needle thin, rigid, unyielding caterpillar with a blunt bow, appeared with its cavernous engine nacelles to the stern, still fiery red-hot. The maneuvering thrusters engaged. Miniature arc jets, purple pinpricks of light down the side of the ship, lit, then extinguished themselves, again and again, seemingly at random. They slowed, and then stopped completely. The navigation read-out said they were immobile, relative to the something, not the Sun, but the something else, some undercurrent of reality, which only the HAI's had understood and which was now completely mysterious to them all. The experience was like nothing he had ever tried before. He moved around like a drunken butterfly, sampling, losing patience, fluttering towards the next light or smell, more sampling, until something else caught his attention. He forced himself to focus on the transition. It was almost upon them now. The Abbott-Farhi generator was fully charged and they were about to write history for the third time. This was something no one outside Survey Branch had ever experienced.

One moment they could still see the pinprick behind them and the next it was gone, replaced by a new sun, a tiny, blue star tingling all by itself in a vast emptiness.

In a way, he thought, it was a disappointment.

EIGHT

He woke. As usual he would attempt to hold on to half-sleep, but, soon, like a drop of ink in a glass of clear water, reality polluted his dreams. He got up and started on his rituals. Rituals were important. They helped focus him. He glanced longingly at the half-open casket he had just left. He had hated it, absolutely hated it, when he got on board the ship. Cutting-edge technology it might be, but at first there had been something deeply disturbing about climbing into a coffin and shutting the lid on yourself for eight hours every day. He had seen enough people in coffins as it was. Now he did not want to leave it.

He had been born in Dublin in the early 2050's into a family of arcology engineers, a fancy word for what were essentially janitors, who lived in the then new legal status of extended family marriage. Back then, it was a legal specialty of the Dublin arcology that two men could marry the same woman at the same time, or, as was the case in his family, a woman could marry two men. Unsurprisingly, the family shattered when he was 15. Disgusted with the ceaseless bickering among his three divorced parents, he joined the European Army as an infantryman, largely, as far as he recalled -- it was a long time ago -- because both his fathers were adamantly opposed to it.

During the political upheavals of 2070, which, among other things, led to the disbandment of the European Army, he joined one of the many mercenary companies that blossomed at the time. Over the next twenty years, he campaigned all over the world. At first with the Victual Brothers, a unit specialized in containing civil unrest, an inventive euphemism for the kind of police work, which was carried out with main battle tanks and rocket artillery. Later he joined the

Shields, which started out as a regular combat unit, it was one of the first mercenary units equipped with the new exo-skeletal battle suits, and later diversified into the lucrative field of chromo-cleansing. The Shields fought in many places, Europe, Mexico, South Africa, but their crowning mission was without a doubt the brutal, thousand-day siege of Minsk, which ended in the total, non-nuclear, mind you, a point of no little pride, destruction of the city and all its inhabitants, human and otherwise. As he was quite unscrupulous about which missions he accepted, he rose steadily through the ranks. He had a flair for leading men in battle. He also turned out to be a first rate tactician.

He was a man of violence. Live by the sword and all that. He sometimes thought about why do men do the things they do? Are they programmed by their past? He hoped so, then he could blame his hapless parents for the things he did during the wars. He was in Hamburg with the Shield Battalion during the riots of '78 and he took part in the butchery that ensued after the Battalion had demolished the Schanzenviertel quarter. There were other pages in his personal history he rarely opened. Those memories were part of him, would be part of him forever, and because he did not know what to do with them, he had stored them away in a dark corner of his mind. The wars, his wars, as he thought of them, had been meaningless. Sure, they had happened for many good reasons; because politicians decided they were necessary or because a bunch of thugs thought they should have better living conditions or more money or more privileges than another bunch of thugs. He had lost track of the 'why's' long ago. They all had. In the end, the wars became a way of life and he became addicted to the adrenaline rush. 'I will rescue you from perdition in spite of yourself', he'd once read in a book. The sentence had stayed with him over the years, like a quiet reminder.

The influence of the HAI's, double standards abounding, was on the rise, as was the Global Space Agency, another invention of the machines; and alongside it, a new sense of purpose and morality, for lack of a better word, had suffused the burgeoning global community. As more and more Chromos were channeled willingly into the Sleeper program, business for the Shields slowed. One day, while bunked near Dornoch, a GSA sponsored, multinational air-assault surprised them. After a brief exchange of fire, they had to relent. Bentzon and the other senior Shield officers were put on trial for crimes against humanity. It was a farce. The Shields had merely done the bidding of whatever remnants of national institutions had survived the first decade. Nothing more, nothing less. The system itself had been an aberration, not the mercenary outfits, and Bentzon and his ilk became prügelknabe for the chromosome wars. Had he come to believe the propaganda himself? Yes, probably. The Chromos had to go. They were an evolutionary dead-end that they could not afford anymore. He had thought so and so had almost everyone else. He still did. The Sleeper program was a dangerous waste of resources but the machines seemed to think it would somehow save their collective conscience and mend everything. As if, anything could make them forget all those decades. He did not believe it for a second, but some did. The trials were short but to the point: in a final squirt of irony, he, along with most of the troops, was sentenced to the Program, to join the Sleepers, except, unlike the real Sleepers, it was dreamless Sleep and they were never to be awakened again.

At some point, only few years into his sentence, as it turned out, someone awakened him. There was a white room. His naked body still dripping wet from containment gel, he was sat down. Zach Baranikowa was there. For a long time the old man talked about his plans, his vision, about humanity and their chances for long term survival. He had listened, a little confused, but surprisingly clearheaded considering he had been under for several years. Zach had offered him a new life. The old man needed soldiers to protect the future.

About the time Bentzon was brought back to life by Zach, Halifax Shipping Line was at the forefront of the human expansion into space and one of the most admired companies in the world. The fleet was going through a phase of exceptional expansion and the need for qualified crews and officers was insatiable. After receiving his new identity, he had to go through the motions. He applied for a job as a security consultant. Naturally, he was taken on immediately. His fake résumé was, after all, as impeccable as his real capabilities. The low-level HR folks in the company readily agreed to a contract in which they sponsored his training to become a commercial starship captain in return for substantially lower salary. It was an unusual arrangement but not unheard of. The rest of his troops were taken out of the

Sleeper Farm and smuggled to the Halifax Orbital for drastic enhancements.

He received a commission just one and a half years after finishing his exam. To give him some hands-on experience with actual space travel, they assigned him as first officer on an old Golding class cargo hauler called Carousel which was slotted to serve on the Earth-Mars run. He had only completed one run when the call came.

So, on this day, April 28th, he climbed out of the epi, like he'd done every morning these past months and started on his morning rituals. He had allotted a few precious square meters to clay a small bathroom in his quarters. Mirror, sink, the whole thing. It recalled the discipline that had carried him through his soldiering days. It never failed to fortify his spirit. Routines were important, framework for the mind and so forth. Part of the ritual was shaving the old-fashioned way with foam and a razor. He could have the epi do it for him, but it just did not feel the same way. The razor left his skin refreshed, renewed. It was symbolic. You peel off the old layer of skin, the sins of yesterday and start afresh. He looked at himself in the mirror, as he did every morning, gauging the depths of his own soul, if such a thing was possible, through the lines around his eyes and on his weather-beaten cheeks. As he had grown older and his face had settled, it was obvious which of the two men he called father was the biological one. He never thought about them. Had not for years. Now all of a sudden he had started again. A clear sign that the journey was wearing him down. Still he could not help wondering how they would have felt about this. Better than they felt about him joining the army back then, certainly. Maybe they would even be proud of him. Captain on a spaceship. He jumped at the sound of his own voice. He had spoken aloud again... He had not seen them in many years, not since they had discovered he had taken part in the Hamburg massacres. Bloody idealists both of them. What happened there would have happened with or without him. It wasn't as if he could have changed anything about it, was it? Just a cog in the great machine. Still, and he believed it made him strong - he recognized his part. His share of the responsibility. He did not shy away from unpleasantness. Never had. He had been there. He had taken part. Followed orders. How did that other line from the book go? Ah yes, 'Hold! Father, Hold! Hear me but for one moment! tax me not with impurity, nor that I have erred from the warmth of temperament.' He had erred all right and he blamed the damned monotony of this journey that he was even thinking about it. What was done, was done. He pictured himself a tough bastard. And he was. He'd seen and done things that would terrify the rest of the crew on the Armagnac if they knew. Yes, he was as tough as they come. Tough as nails, damn it. Yet he felt strangely weak these days. He pictured himself a crystal, one of those really sharp ones, unbreakable if used with the pointy end first, but fragile like glass if you hit it from the wrong angle. Yes, like that. He was a shard of crystal and these days he was bent from the wrong angle. No matter what happened to him here, he had worse to compare with it. The months the battalion had spent in the trenches around Minsk. Those winters. By God, there was a chilling memory. No, this was plush. Warm. And nice. Good food. Yes, he had seen worse.

He did not like to admit it, even to himself, but he was scared. He had been scared many times before and learned to overcome it. Those long minutes before a drop had always been the worst, but this journey was like being stuck in a hopper for months on end instead of mere minutes. The upcoming boarding action would be a sort of distilled version of that. He knew a way to fight the jitters. He had his methods. Just think of something small, something quotidian. Breakfast for example. Yes. He left his quarters and headed down towards the galley. He would have coffee, yes, Colombian, with lots of milk. And bread. Cheese. Some orange juice. He entered the galley and when his food was ready, he sat down at a table. Not a soul anywhere. He was Captain of a ghost ship. Like the legend of the Ship of Fools, catapulting itself forever through space, a monument to human imprudence. What did that make him? The hand painted pictures were back on the wall, he noticed, not birds, but a frozen lake this time, in ten different variations. He had to do something about that. He did not like wintery landscapes, reminded him of Minsk... and there he was, back at it again. He longed for the company of his Shields. The familiarity of their hare-brained banter would steady his nerves. Maybe he could come up with an excuse to transfer a few of them the main habitat modules when the boarding action was over.

He checked the time. The transition was almost upon them now. Bentzon had decided to spring his ambush right after their arrival in the star system known as Pleione. It would not be possible later because the Yu-kiang, due to her smaller mass and additional fuel mass, would out-accelerate them. Jin had done some work on an early mid-system interception, but the chances of that succeeding were slim to say the least. The old adage 'needle in a haystack' did not do the vastness of space justice. The navigational instruments on the Armagnac, she was merely a cargo ship after all, albeit the most advanced one of her kind, weren't up to the task of pinpointing the location of another starship moving at thousands of kilometers per second in a volume as vast as a solar system. Their passive systems were limited to thermal detection, which was adequate to pick up the signature of an arc jet torch at a few million kilometers, but they had to rely on various active systems for accurate tracking and they were for close range work. Apart from that, well, there were the visual systems, but again, those were designed to aid in docking and other close range navigational maneuvers and would be useless in a high-speed intercept scenario where even the slightest adjustment would have enormous consequences a few million kilometers down range.

No, the decision was made. He would spring the ambush as soon as the Yu-kiang appeared in Pleione when both ships were stationary following the transition.

NINE

Log, Armagnac, April 28, at 0815, EST.
The Abbott-Farhi Ensphere engaged successfully. Three minutes, 35 seconds later, Navigation confirmed the ship had successfully connected with the corresponding node in the spinfoam and had appeared in the Pleione system. We are now 390 light years from home. The Pleione stars have changed. Survey Branch mission report CV12-A1456 state that the system should be a binary star system with two Be-class stars, but the stars have entered shell phase. This is of immediate concern to the mission because the stellar mass has engulfed the next LQG point. Furthermore, we have detected an immobile object about 500 kilometers away.

'Once, a long time ago, people thought the lights in the sky were islands,' the voice of Jin Dulg whispered in his ear. He could feel Felix's presence too but thankfully he refrained from talking. Transitions were always a stressful time for the pilot.

'That's a stupid thing to think,' grunted Rem.

Jin pretended she had not heard him. 'They also thought the whiteness in the Milky Way was frothing waves breaking on very distant shores.'

'And what people would that be?'

'Polynesians, of course.'

'See, I have found Pleione.' The image of a faraway star shone brightly on one of the monitors. 'To think we will be there in a few minutes. Did you know that it is one of the brightest stars in the sky back home?'

'Yes.'

'Do you know why?'

'No, and I don't want to.'

'Be-class stars rotate so fast around themselves they almost tear themselves apart. Hundreds of kilometers per second,' she said, ignoring his jibes.

'Silence, transition in 3 minutes,' Rem said.

--

Out of a vague sense of propriety, Basil delayed his return to the Land to observe the transition into Pleione. Since he had slept through the others, he was mildly curious about how it would feel. No big flash or bang, just one moment you were here, the next you were there. Philosophers would surely expound on the ramifications of the whole spinfoam discovery for a couple of generations, but all Basil could think about was the Great War he was part of in the Land. It had started small, as those things often do, but little by little and then quite suddenly, the whole world was at war. Helped by certain friends of Maribel, who by the way, had finally returned from a mysterious journey abroad of which she refused to speak at this time, Basil had been granted a seat on the war council, which was quite an honour, although definitely more a nod at his abilities as a politician than at those of a generalissimo. Nonetheless, he had come up with the widely celebrated idea to construct a number of huge balloons with a sort of gondola stuck underneath. He did not recall where the idea had come from, but in its most basic form, the men in the gondola would drift over the Misty Mountains, over the Dwarven heartland and drop bombs on their convoys and mines and settlements, leaving the Halflings unable to respond. It was, in all modesty, a brilliant idea and Basil was in a hurry to get back to the game to peruse the tally of new hits.

He was just about to leave ShipNet and return to the Land when something caught his eye. Ship sensors had just finished recalibrating after the transition when visual sensors picked up a large object not 500 kilometres astern.

Log entry: May 9, 1316 hours, EST.

Status report on the Abbott-Farhi Ensphere. Several components seem to have sustained critical damage during the acceleration through the equatorial decretion disk of Pleione A. The Ensphere is currently not operational. We are unsure what caused the malfunction but the Chief Engineer believe it may have been caused by overload of the forward plasma screen. Further diagnostics are underway, but due to the extreme complexity of the Ensphere, we are not optimistic as to repairing it. /FY

'Oh dear, are you sure we ended up in the right place?'

The navigation instruments had not yet recalibrated, but all visual sensors were a violent panorama of dark reds.

'What the heck is going on here?'

The two hot, red dwarf stars, spinning around themselves at speeds exceeding 300 kilometres per second, had lost cohesion and expanded for several AU's into nearby space. Their mass was a reddish, labyrinthine chasm, a nebulous conflagration of stellar mass. The sight was spectacular and one never before witnessed by humans. According to the navigation report from Survey Branch, the stars were supposed to be coherent, albeit strained, but instead they had expanded into two confusing clouds of stellar mass, so huge their shells almost intersected each other. The Armagnac had appeared at the edge of a nebulous, red chasm, the bottom of which appeared as two fuzzy outlines. A few months earlier when Survey Branch had passed through, both stars had been normal sized with decretion disks surrounding them, but now they had expanded so much it looked like they were attempting to swallow each other. In the area where the matter cloud of the two stars met, a swirling storm raged. It felt like they were gazing into a vast battleground between two giants, hurling bits of themselves at each other. The stars engulfed the two known LQG points in the system, which meant they would have to travel deep into an area of space heavy with radiation from the two warring stars.

Of more immediate concern however, was appearance of an object to starboard, only 500 kilometres distant. Brassen was so shocked by everything that he allowed himself to be drawn into a virtual meeting with the two others.

They were in one of Jin's backdrops. They were sitting around a campfire. Jin's avatar kept chugging logs into the already roaring fire. 'You think this is funny?' asked Brassen who directed his anger at Jin's stupid attempt at nonchalance.

'The stars have entered their shell phase. Must have happened in the last six months. According to the report they should be ordinary

Be-class stars with decretion disks,' Jin said without interrupting her fiddling with the firewood. 'What an amazing sight! Do you realise no humans have ever seen anything like this before. We're the first!'

'The next LQG point is somewhere between the stars. The radiation levels in there must be very elevated.'

'The ship is designed to shield us from worse than that,' declared Brassen. His position as pilot gave him a certain sense of propriety when it came to the Armagnac.

'Imagine, for thousands of years, people have looked at Pleione and seen the brightest star in the Tauri constellation. Little did they know it was two stars, tearing themselves apart.' Apparently, Jin had decided not to discuss the object their sensors had picked up just 500 kilometres to starboard.

Brassen stared gloomily into the fire. 'I have informed the Captain,' he said.

'I think the object to starboard is a ship,' Felix said.

'At least it is not moving.'

No one spoke for a while. They really did not like surprises.

Felix: 'I am sorry, but I am afraid I have bad news. Really bad news.'

The two others turned their heads and looked at him. This truly was going to be an epic day.

'The Abbott-Farhi Ensphere is not responding. It is broken.'

'Oh, great... just what we needed,' said Jin and tossed another log on the fire.

--

Bentzon appeared through the hatch in the floor. He drifted past the Captain's seat and reached out for it, but missed and kept going until he hit the ceiling. The contact sent him flying back in the other direction, but he managed to get a firm hold of the back of Rem's seat and from there, he manhandled himself into his own seat and strapped in with a look of barefaced relief.

The others had silently waited throughout his zero gravity ordeal, their faces visible in his peripheral vision. They were all here in the flesh. The Captain nonetheless created a full VIR scene for the meeting and picked the usual abandoned factory building that had stuck in his memory from the battalion's third deployment. No one had questioned it. They all had strange habits when it came to selecting backdrops for virtual meetings and an abandoned factory did not strike out.

There was a 2D blackboard hanging from a nearby wall. Bentzon walked over to it and sketched their situation with a piece of chalk. Very quaint. 'The Armagnac is here. The Yu-kiang will appear here. The contact is here, between us. I propose we use the contact as cover for the drone launch.'

'Where is this drone?' Felix was curious.

'It is in cargo shell 5. I will not require your assistance with the launch. You focus on the contact.' The others, baffled, looked at each other. The Captain had not thus far impressed them with his astro navigational skills, and now he suddenly said he would deal with the drone launch himself.

'Will you require assistance from the Sleepers then, Captain? They can be useful,' Felix asked.

Bentzon, who had decided to let the crew believe they still planned to launch a drone towards the Yu-kiang, said: 'We will use the ship contact to mask our intentions. Pretend the exploration of the wreck has delayed us. Pilot, move us closer to the wreck, say, within 10 kilometers. Felix, when we are stationary relative to the wreck, you can deploy a couple of drone units and look at it. What do we think about it at this stage?'

'Captain, doesn't it worry you?'

'It's not shooting at us. I'd say it looks rather disheveled.' He pointed to the high-resolution visual sensors. The wreck, and it was a wreck, had been gutted. Even from afar, it was more than clear it was a dead ship. 'Worrying about something we know nothing about is speculation. And speculation never helped anybody. First things first, people. And that goes for our AFE problem too. We'll deal with the problems one at a time.'

'Whatever destroyed it might still be out here.'

Felix droned on: 'It is an abandoned starship, more precisely a Survey Branch ship of the Darwin class. The Survey report we were provided with prior to departure has no mention of this ship whatsoever which is strange considering it deals with the expedition that surveyed this system. We can conclude that either the ship was lost after the expedition passed through here, in which case Survey Branch is unaware it is lost, or that they have intentionally chosen to leave it out of the report.'

'And what about the Abbott-Farhi Ensphere. Without it, we're stuck on Pleione forever,' said Jin.

'The Yu-kiang will help us out on that score,' said Bentzon airily.

'Sorry Captain, but the engineers on the Yu-kiang are just as clueless about the inner workings of the AFE as we are. Unless we get it fixed, we'll have to hitch a ride on the Yu-kiang.' Felix said in a voice that was a tad too loud.

'We're not planning on dying out here. At least, I'm not,' said Jin letting out a chuckle that fizzled out all by itself.

'As I said, speculation is pointless until we have more facts.' Bentzon looked like he was in a hurry to end the meeting.

Brassen: 'As far I know Survey Branch never lost a ship. It is puzzling.' And on that note, the virtual meeting winked out. Bentzon was already making his way out of the tank.

--

The main engine start sequence went as it should and ten minutes later, they were on the move. An hour later the Armagnac was aligned with the abandoned ship, distant about ten kilometers. A couple of drone units had been rigged for exploration duty and as soon as the pilot gave the go ahead, they shot out from the drone bay on level four. Felix controlled one and Jin had the other. Basil and Rem were logged into the feeds, seeing what the drones were seeing.

Even from afar, they could see every nook and cranny on the hull. The first order of the day was finding something to identify the unknown starship. They knew that GSA ships always had their name and codes stenciled somewhere on the hull. The usefulness of this particular tradition was validated here because they had no other way to identify the unresponsive ship. Usually it was found somewhere around the engine section but it could be anywhere. As they approached the wreck, the SADU's spread out, one going over, the other under, telescopes sweeping over the hull. The ship was of the classic Survey Branch elongated egg-shape: rounded bow, plasma screen, twin-engine nacelles to the rear. Unlike on the Armagnac where everything except the main engines and the bow were modular add-ons, the Abbott-Farhi Ensphere on this ship was an integral part of the design, as was the fuel mass shell. The ship was small, barely

90 meters overall, about 30 meters at the thickest. It was a well-known design. In fact, every child on Earth knew it by heart. The crew quarters for the 15 man élite crew -- a kind of donut, which circled the area just behind the plasma screen -- were famously Spartan. Everything on the ship was designed towards two things only: staying out for as long as possible and spying on nature. Survey Branch ships would journey for as long as four years without returning to Earth and every return was cause for celebration in the arcologies where many people religiously tracked the movements of the eight survey ships and the names of their crews. They were heroes of the Restoration.

Felix's terse voice accompanied the exploration. 'From a visual inspection it is impossible to know how long it has been out here. Could be yesterday, could be years. Moving around the nacelles, which appear undamaged. Hmm. Ah, there it is.' The telescope zoomed in on a bit of stenciled writing near the area where the superconducting coils attached to the main hull. It said: SB XG6 Vitus Bering.

'The Bering? She left three years ago via Sol LQG 3. How did she end up here?'

'She must have found a spin connection that somehow linked back here.'

'Yes, and then something happened.'

'Couldn't have been more than a few months ago. The Vasco da Gama and the Thomas Cook passed through four-five months ago.'

Felix: 'Ah, look at this 'ere.'

His SADU was moving around the far side of the ship. The image showed a massive hull breach, about eight by eight metres and almost ten metres deep. Whatever had happened to her, it had gouged a massive hole in the duranium hull and ripped out a solid chunk of her structure. 'Oh dear, the AFE module is damaged beyond repair.' The innards of the solid quantum state core of the Abbott-Farhi Ensphere were clearly visible. The fuel mass shell had been perforated too, which was not too surprising considering it made up the bulk of the hull structure. 'No engines, no fuel, no Abbott-Farhi. No wonder she wasn't going anywhere,' Felix said.

'But how did it happen?'

'No idea. Internal explosion?'

'Bad, very bad. I do not like the look of this.'

'Maybe she got caught when the Pleione stars expanded, could have somehow overloaded the AFE module,' Jin's voice suggested.

'Perhaps. Unlikely, though. The AFE cannot explode like this by itself. Even I know that much about quantum mechanics. Something happened to it. Some external cause…'

Felix moved his SADU into the hull breach while Jin's SADU attempted to force its way through the docking port.

'What happened to the crew?' Basil asked, instantly regretting it.

'What do you think happened?' answered Jin in a snappy tone.

The other SADU finally managed to break its way into the ship via the extraordinarily uncooperative docking port. The image it sent back was that of a corridor, curved, a bit like the corridors on the Armagnac, but the curvature was sharper due to the smaller size of the ship. Doors, some open, some closed, appeared in the flickering light from the SADU projectors. The SADU stopped and turned itself on. Its weak ion thrusters stirred up debris and dust that had hung motionless in the airless corridor. The lights dramatically lit up the first room. A bunk, clothing, personal effects floating around like a work of art designed to depict a person's life in three dimensions. An antique dark blue cap with a yellow logo that said Mostys Kebab in red handwriting floated into view.

'Mostys?' someone remarked.

'Hey, it's that joint on level 3 in Halifax, remember?'

'One would have thought Survey folks had better taste.'

'Mostys pretty good as kebabs go.'

'Yeah, good enough to bring their merchandising 390 light years from Earth, apparently.'

The cap had meant something to someone who had spent valuable personal weight allowance to bring it on the mission. The SADU gently pushed its way through clouds of incoherent silver globules, which was how clay looked when it lost cohesion. Problem was that clay usually took a long time to lose shape, a lot longer than a few months, for sure. The SADU scooped up the silver globules for further analysis but left everything else untouched. They surveyed room after room. The one thing conspicuously missing among all the debris were corpses. Their absence was chilling. Where had the crew gone? Felix, who kept up an incessant chatter, informed them that there were no lifeboats in a Survey ship and thus no way for the crew to get away.

Felix's SADU had squeezed itself through the fused non-descript metal carapace that lined the gouge and made its way into the engineering corridor around the main engine housing. It was an extremely tight fit, Survey Branch used a smaller, sleeker version of SADU's for maintenance, which did not help, but the perseverance eventually paid off: as it rounded a corner, finally, they found a body. The manipulators on the SADU's gently grabbed hold of it and turned it around. The mummified face of a man appeared, frozen in a rictus of pain. The man had died from explosive decompression. The sign on his breast said Dupoti.

'Dupoti?' said Basil. 'Hey, I know him. I mean, I met him once, at a GSA reception. Well, I think I met him, you know...'

'None other than Conner 'Put Lucky on my tombstone' Dupoti himself. Whaddya know,' Jin said sadly. 'I used to have a crush on him.'

'Guess his luck ran out after all, huh?'

'What.the.fuck.happened.here?'

They all knew Dupoti. He was a famous Survey-man. He was part of the crew on the first Survey ship, the Edmond Halley, when it made the historic transition to Proxima Centauri. He was the first man to set foot on an extra-solar planet, Proxima 3, a frozen hellhole. All this was back when the HAI's were still around. Later they had given him his own ship. A good looking fellow, kind to animals and children, triple Ph.d in physics... At the sight of Dupoti's shrivelled face, Basil felt his scrotum withdraw into his body and the hair on his head tingled with something... The Vitus Bering had met something out here. Something... 'Whoa, we need to get the hell out of here, man. That ship was blown up by aliens.'

'Please, BB, do not jump to conclusions. For all you know this was a dramatic malfunction of the AFE module, something we have not experienced before. Second, we have never encountered aliens anywhere before and even if we will, at some point, it is highly unlikely it will happen like this. Space is awfully big, you know, running into each other in deep space is very, very unlikely.'

'The bodies, man, what happened to the bodies, then? I'm telling ya, the aliens took them.'

Felix, who obviously was not prone to panic, droned on: 'It begs the question: What had Dupoti been doing down there? Why would he have chosen to personally inspect the engine housings when it is normally done by SADU interaction?'

'Who cares what he was doing there, man. The fucking ship was blown up.'

No one answered.

The other SADU reached the command centre on the ship. Here too the hatch was wide open. For a while, they entertained hopes that records, electronic or otherwise, would be recovered, but searching proved to be in vain. The solid-state storage on the computers held no information of any kind. In fact, it was as if they had been intentionally deleted.

'Captain, are you following this?'

There was no answer.

--

Five hours had passed and right on schedule the Yu-kiang emerged, about 12.000 kilometres away on the far side of the LQG point. As soon as her sensors had recalibrated, she hailed the Armagnac. Clearly, they too were surprised to see the wreck of the Vitus Bering.

'Armagnac, this is the Yu-kiang, do you require assistance? Armagnac, this is the MC Yu-kiang, standing by to assist. Do you require help?'

Brassen began relying the findings to them. 'Yu-kiang, this is pilot Rem Brassen on the Halifax ship Armagnac. Thank you for your kind offer. We have been investigating the wreck of the...' Then the connection was lost

A few seconds went by. 'Rem, we lost ShipNet. All comms are down. I don't understand what is happening,' said Felix's voice.

Brassen: 'Captain, we have lost comms. Felix, status in ops?'

A new, unknown, voice was heard on an external channel. 'Mayday, mayday. Yu-kiang, this is the Armagnac. We have lost all engine power and life support is failing. Do you hear us, Yu-kiang?'

The Yu-kiang responded immediately, obeying the written and unwritten conventions of spacers. 'Armagnac, we hear you. We are inbound to your location to assistance. Please stand-by. Estimated time of arrival one hour, ten minutes. Report number of casualties.'

Back in the tank, Brassen raised his voice: 'What is going on? Why is he sending out a mayday?'

Jin: 'In fact, where is the Captain?' Bentzon had left the tank a few minutes after the ship began accelerating towards the Bering and had not reappeared since. They had thought nothing of it – the manoeuvre was routine and Bentzon was not a hands-on kind of Captain. Besides, they assumed he was busy preparing the drone launch.

Felix: 'What is going on?'

Rem: 'All navigation, engine management, communications, GRIT and life support is gone. The ship network is running through module 5. We no longer have control of the ship.'

Bentzon (internal channel): 'All hands, this is the Captain. ShipNet has been temporarily superseded by the military communications hub in module 5. We're currently engaged in ship-to-ship action against the Yu-kiang. MilCom will rescind control as soon as the action has been resolved. You will be briefed when it is over. Operations, you're authorized to continue the rescue and salvage operations on the Vitus Bering until further notice.'

Rem: 'What the hell...?' And then to Felix: 'Do you still control the SADU's?' He nodded: 'We do.'

'Military communications hub in module 5? Does anyone know what he is on about?'

Jin: 'That solves the mystery of the contents of that module, I guess.'

Rem: 'Not so sure. Felix, we're cut off from everything. Send a maintenance SADU around to module 5 and link feeds manually to the tank. I would like to see what's going on there.'

'Aye, aye,' said Felix. Meanwhile the Yu-kiang was coming around as promised, intent on the rescue of the Armagnac.

Ten minutes later, a visual feed appeared on a display. Felix had successfully bypassed the MilCom control of the SADU systems. The SADU was creeping along the exterior of module 5. A flattening of the cargo module containing the MilCom unit became apparent, consistent with an opening or a bay. The SADU stopped moving forward. Instead, the ion thrusters beneath it ignited briefly, sending it floating gently away from the ship, providing it with a slanting view of the surface of the module. After ten or so metres, reverse thrusters fired to halt it. The cameras were showing a massive bay door open to space, white light from the interior spilling out into space. Inside, shapes were moving about. The operator pushed the SADU further away from the ship. Little by little, more of the interior bay became visible. The sight made them gasp.

'Fuck me,' Jin exclaimed. Yes, fuck her indeed... They stared at the spectacle in the hangar bay. Brassen was furrowing his brows so hard it made him look like a Neanderthal. It was a familiar sight: exo-skeletal battle units, a whole squad of them, moving ponderously about inside the hangar bay, aligning behind what looked like a v-shaped frisbee with two heavy duty SADU's attached to it. The exo's looked messy because they each had a double set of extra heatsinks juryrigged on, breaking their otherwise sleek design. Behind them, deep inside the bay, additional exo units, inactive, were visible lined up against the wall.

'I haven't seen those since... since I was a kid,' whispered Jin.

'My parents were killed by those things,' Felix said between gritted teeth. Brassen said nothing.

'He obviously doesn't intend to just put an intelligence drone on the Yu-kiang. Would not need those things for that.'

'And who are manning them? Must have had people stashed away in module 5 all this time. Soldiers...'

'Why would Zach put soldiers on this mission? I don't understand.'

The trio stared at the exo's in silence, thoughts grinding through their heads. It was Felix, cheeks pink with anger when, like now, his sense of right and wrong was being challenged, who put voice to the outrage they all secretly felt. 'It is very wrong to send out false mayday. There is rules, traditions. It is not done. What are they for? Are they going to Yu-kiang?' His Slavic accent was back in force.

'I think that is a very real possibility, yes,' remarked Brassen, pointedly not taking sides in the discussion. 'Exo's have never been used for anything else. It is not our concern. This is a corporate sanctioned operation. We have our orders,' he said.

The exos had almost finished attaching themselves to the v-shaped SADU's. After a few minutes, the machines moved forward as one, out of the hangar bay. Slowly, then faster and faster. The camera on the SADU followed them as they disappeared into the red murk of the two Pleione stars.

The hangar doors closed, returning the module to its former perfectly circular shape.

--

Something about the Bering had enthralled him completely and he found himself unable to break the VIR link, all ducal obligations in the game forgotten. He was following both SADU's with burning intensity, attempting to relive the last minutes of the fifteen crewmembers through the litter of the personal belongings drifting quietly inside the empty starship. At first, he did not understand. It was so sad, so utterly out of place that these people should have lost their lives out here, almost four hundred light years from home, and for no apparent reason. It seemed so meaningless, so devoid of emotion. Nothing, he realized, nothing out there cared about their little red meaty hearts, their thirty some degrees of body heat and their rumbling stomachs or the diseases they had inflicted on themselves. All their divisions, their hatred and love, their passions, everything would be destroyed by the vacuum between the stars if they made the slightest mistake.

TEN

Zach Baranikowa, speech, circa 2097

Wealth is responsibility. Wealth is the power to change. It is a coil; it has the potential the change, to alter, to improve. I look at my friends, the hugely rich, at what they doing with all this potential, this wealth? Nothing. They build walls around themselves. Even now, civilization has failed and we are how many left? Ninety million, maybe a hundred million on the entire planet and they are building walls. What they have not understood is that unless they start spending their wealth, it will soon be gone along with everything else. It does not matter how or why you are rich. All that matters is that you are. Our system, the society we inherited, is a system, which relieves the wealthy of their responsibilities. I do not know why this is so. To me it is a sin. Human nature, yes, weakness, certainly. They have always spent their money on palaces with ever-taller walls around them, enjoyed nature in enclosed gardens. Well, the time for seclusion has come to an end. The time have come to step up and assume the leadership that wealth have entrusted on them. I asked them and almost all of them refused. But why, I asked them, do you think you can live out the rest of your lives like this, sheltered, secluded? You can, with luck, but not your children. It will be too late for them. This rot, this moral corruption… it revolts me, it nauseates me.

For many years when people asked about his childhood, the boy would make up a convoluted story about a King and a Queen who met on a spaceship.

The King was the Engineer-Captain, spaceships were few and small in those days, and careers were less specialized. Everyone had to know how to do at least two jobs. The Queen was his 1st Officer, pilot and navigator, and the seemingly endless cargo missions back and forth between the mining stations in the inner asteroid belt and the orbital stations around Earth gave them time to fall in love many times over. Somewhere, about a year later, with the huge cinnamon disk of Jupiter slowly passing by starboard, a boy was born on the ship.

It was a healthy boy, all chromosomes accounted for, with dark tufts of hair, and brown eyes. As the first human child born in space, the birth was considered auspicious by the GSA establishment back home. An ordinary baby became a historic event. With permission from the newly minted parents, the bureaucrats made every effort possible to exploit the situation to its full potential in the media.

'And his name?' inquiring minds wanted to know. The happy parents willingly revealed that the prodigy would be named in honour of their ship, the Basilisk. And so was born and raised, the phenomenon that came to be Basil.

The boy experienced childhood on the ship. It was a happy ship. The crew doted on him. He was their mascot. His earliest memories were of roaming throughout the ship making myriad discoveries in dark corners. When school was done with, he would prowl the ship alone or with his dog, a fawn Boxer called Freya. His mysterious rivers, his Inca temples, were ducts and service areas, some of which remained unvisited for years at a time by humans. He would follow primitive SADU's around as they saw to their chores or lay in ambush, jumping out as it passed, and scaring its human host. The crew fell prey to the lure of childhood games and played along, feigning anger, alerting others and drumming up a hunt to eliminate the pesky intruder and his dog.

Basil remembered sitting in his father's chair on the bridge. Back then, spaceships had windows and he had to lift himself up on the armrests of the chair to look through them. He remembered how Earth would hang outside like a ball, greens and blues visible through the pervasive clouds. The patterns never ceased to fascinate him and he would sometimes stay on the bridge for hours and watch how darkness would swallow the planet as it turned, making little lights appear as stitches adorning the landmasses.

His father would come and go about his duties on the bridge and much later, when he thought back on those moments, he would always remember the slightly sticky smell of his father and the feeling of that big parched hand in his. Dad.

'Look, it's night down there. All the people are sleeping,' his father told him. The boy thought about that. 'Why are the lights on if they're sleeping?' His father laughed at that and the boy was happy to have said something to make his father laugh. 'Maybe they forgot to turn them off. You see that wedge there, like a wedge of cheese with a ball attached to the tip?' Basil nodded. 'That used to be India. All the land above it and the string of islands to the right of it was called China. Lots of people used to live there,' his father said. 'Where did they go?' the boy asked innocently. 'Some of them went to the left there, you see, but most of them just died.' His father ended the sentence in a whisper and a few minutes later, he continued in his normal voice: 'But we want people to go back where they used to live. That is why we work so hard up here. We want to reclaim everything, restore things to the way they were. Do you understand?' The boy nodded. He felt the emotion in his father's voice, as children will. But how could he understand?

Zach and Sasai did well for themselves. The Basilisk serviced the mining stations on Pallas, Vestas, the Digits, the Hildas, the Trojans, the Greeks... Wherever mining operations started, they followed. On the outbound trip, they brought automated mining equipment, supplies, everything people needed to survive out there in the airless darkness between Mars and Jupiter. On the return trip, they hauled the valuable processed minerals for the orbital factories on Earth. It was important work. They were building a new world, a new beginning for the planet and for the people. And the Basilisk, Zach, Sasai, the crew, even the boy, were right there, on the practical, driving pole of the Restoration.

Zach had ambitions and a nose for business. The cargo runs made good money and he took care to re-invest them in the business. He soon expanded with two additional ships and Halifax Shipping Line was born. In those days, he was still largely unknown to the public, just another cargo captain among the dozens and dozens who operated at the time.

Zach's legend started with the Amazon incident. The Amazon was a Golding-class cargo ship, the first of the new class. It was on its maiden voyage, a quick jaunt to Venus and back, a pure sightseeing and shakedown cruise. She was carrying politicians from the major donor countries, dignitaries from the GSA and a few media. A couple of days out the Amazon suffered a critical reactor problem, which shut it down. Crucially, the emergency back-up systems, including the life support systems, also broke down. The report of the Board of Inquiry would later reveal that it was a design error, which was subsequently corrected on later Golding ships, but design flaw or not, the Amazon was adrift on its way to Venus. Completely dark, heating up, and with only whatever oxygen was left in the crew compartment, the ship faced imminent disaster. It would have been over in a matter of days. The last communication heard from Captain Petterson was heartbreakingly brave and selfless. The GSA, as it often did in those cases, from a vague notion that a display of selfless heroism would help mask whatever human incompetence was likely the real reason behind the disaster, made the statement public after informing relatives.

The message hit a nerve. Global celebrities and business executives rallied to save the Amazon against all odds. The ship was 550 million kilometres from Earth and drifting in the wrong direction. The nearest operational Survey Branch ship was on the other side of the solar system and would not be able to reach it in time. It was mathematically impossible.

Then Zach decided to help. The Basilisk had just departed for the Hildas and it so happened that its trajectory would almost intercept the orbit of Venus and thus the course the Amazon had taken. He jettisoned all cargo to reduce mass and sent a message back to Earth that the Basilisk would attempt to rescue the Amazon. Everyone on board advised against it, it would be impossible to reach it in time, there would be no one to save; oxygen would run out long before they could get there. Zach was adamant. They could if they were willing to make sacrifices. He told the crew and he told the GSA people back on Earth; and, by extension, he thereby also told the people on Earth that it was a matter of faith. A matter of faith. A good slogan if there ever was one. People loved it. The media responded with around-the-clock coverage of the ride of the Basilisk. Zach and the GSA helped stoke the frenzy with live telemetry from the ship. For a few days, it was nothing but the Basilisk and the poor people who were trapped on the Amazon; the hunger and the mass migrations and the thunderstorms and the encroaching deserts disappeared from everyone's minds. The Basilisk's mission was what it was all about; here lay the future of humankind.

Basil was eight at the time. He would remember those fateful days for the rest of his life. Despite his age, he understood what was at stake. His mother strongly disagreed with Zach's decision. Sasai knew her business. She was an accomplished navigator and pilot and she knew there was no way they could reach that ship in time without risking the lives of everyone on the Basilisk. The Amazon was doomed, she told him repeatedly. However, Zach insisted and he was the Captain. With all cargo jettisoned, he fired up the magneto plasma engines and made the necessary course changes. Everyone went to the gravity nets where they would stay for the duration of the burn. Basil remembered those days. It was the first time he had experienced hard gravity over time and it had hurt. At first, he tried to be brave about it, but after a few hours, he just could not help himself and he cried. At first silently, then not so silently. He would never forget the salty taste of his own tears as they ran into his mouth and how his arms had been too heavy to wipe them away. It hurt so much. Then they injected him with something and he slept and he woke up and hurt again. They made him eat, but it made his stomach turn over and he vomited. Then they injected him again and he slept. Dad just kept pushing. The ship held up. The engines were of the first generation GSA design and Zach was asking them to perform at a constant burn for longer and harder than anyone had tried before. The propellant injection system held up. Even the notoriously unreliable heat dissipation systems held up unmonitored by the unconscious crew. Yes, everything held up except the soft humans.

Basil was still sleeping during the final alignment with the Amazon. Gravity had lessened to 0,5 Gs. A few minutes later, they reached the Amazon and the Basilisk matched her. The Captain decided to approach the Amazon from above. The ship did not answer their hails, but they did not expect it to. The Basilisk looked tiny next to the newer Golding class ship. There were no visible navigation lights on the dull grey hull. Sharp white light from the distant Sun played over the hull, creating dramatic shadowy landscapes from the antennas and the many protuberances dotting its form.

The boy did not understand what happened next and in the following years, he never attempted to find out. It did not matter. He was still groggy from the sedation when he heard people shouting. His Father bellowed something. Then silence. Terrible silence. Basil was afraid then; he knew something bad had happened. A long time went by. Basil did not dare leave the room. Eventually, someone came to see him. It was his aunt, Lienne, his mother's best friend. Her body was streaked with bruises and she was limping badly from a broken thigh bone. Her eyes were swollen and tears had streaked through the grime on her cheeks. 'Where is my mother?' he asked. Lienne talked to him for a long time but the only thing he heard was that his mother was gone and that she was not coming back. The dog, Freya, had died too.

The Basilisk turned back to Earth. Miraculously they had managed to save everyone on board the Amazon. The survivors on the Basilisk were greeted like heroes on their return and Zach received public recognition and many honours and awards for his selflessness in coming to the rescue of the doomed ship.

As for Basil, well, he hardly saw his father again. The man had refused to leave his quarters during the entire return trip. Lienne had taken over and made sure they got back safely. Once the old man set foot on Earth again, he refused to leave it ever again. Space was no longer for him.

When the Basilisk reached Earth, his father went groundside and stayed there. He set up headquarters for his company in New Bergen. Thirty years was a very long time in the new spiral economies and Zach expertly rode the convulsing waves of the HAI supported Restoration. With nothing but work in his life, his fame and notoriety grew and grew along with the size and importance of the company. In the public mind, he embodied the Restoration. The whole spirit was in him: the manly independence, the unconscious cruelty, the persistence, the slow yet efficient intelligence, the sexual apathy (he never remarried or was seen with a woman), the calculating taciturnity. In due time, his company, Halifax Shipping Line, became the biggest commercial entity in space. Basil was sent directly to Polity Commercial and Political Institute. The PCPI, a boarding school, was a fortress located on one of the Inverness islands in the North Sea. Behind the well- guarded school perimeter, kids of the hugely rich were taught the skills necessary to take over from their parents when it was time. Basil immediately gained fame as the first human born in space and as the kid who was on the mission to rescue the Amazon. The young Baranikowa was, by association with his father, an image of the sacrifices necessary to enable the Restoration, a living martyr.

ELEVEN

The link suddenly disconnected.

The last thing he heard was ShipNet chatter about the Yu-kiang arriving in-system and then the damn link disconnected. The VIR dissolved around him and the epi cracked open. He found himself looking up into the non-descript gelatinous material of the ceiling in his room. Tears welled up in his eyes. He thought of his mother. She had died out here too, crushed by the acceleration of the Amazon because his father had decided to play at being a hero. So fucking grim. A force of nature. Cruel and relentless. Everyone on this ship was out here because his father thought he knew better than everyone else. Zach had always crushed everything under the heel of his ambitions. His wife, his son, his own life... and now this. Basil cried silently as he lay there in the darkness of his room on the Armagnac. Yes, out here, among the stars, almost 400 light years from home, he cried for the first time in all those years. There were no choices to make. He could not even pretend he was free any longer. That too had been taken from him. He was trapped. He could stay the course his father had laid out for him and the ship. What he would not give to see his mother one last time.

Sad thing indeed, he thought to himself, and now the link to ShipNet had broken. He got up from the epi and jumped out, suddenly very angry. He wanted to see the salvage operation of the Vitus Bering to the end, damn it! The clay was on the floor. He put his foot in it. It felt like stepping in a pool of cool water. It slithered onto his leg and slowly began enveloping his body. He wiped the tears from his face and left the room. The corridors were utterly deserted. He hurried along towards the tank, nursing his anger, but as he climbed the ladder and put his head through the opening into the tank, seeing the pilot encased in VIR gear, he found that the anger had almost dissipated.

'I was following the SADU's on the Bering when you cut me off.' He looked at the screen, distracted. What was that? Was it taking place on the Armagnac? A voice spoke from under the VIR gear. 'I didn't cut you off. Someone else did. And it wasn't just you. It is the whole ship. There is a corporate operation underway.' The helmet opened and Brassens head appeared. He turned and looked at Basil.

Brassen pointed a finger at the monitor. 'See those? They're exo-mechs.' He continued speaking. 'The Yu-kiang has arrived in-system and is responding to a fake emergency broadcast that Bentzon, or someone from cargo module 5, is sending out. Those poor bastards think we're in trouble and they're trying to help us. Me, I'm just a spectator.' He shrugged.

'They're going to take that ship and kill the people onboard,' said Basil, almost to himself. Brassen did not feel a need to answer. 'And why?'

'Why does the captain think it is necessary? It is just an unarmed cargo ship. I don't understand.'

The exo's in cargoshell 5 were about to launch into space. They were all lined up behind the frisbee-thing and moved forward in unison. As they reached the edge of the cargo bay, the SADU's fired and accelerated them away from the ship in the direction of the Yu-kiang. After a few minutes, all they could see was the slow swirl, deadly of the expanding Pleione stars.

'Brassen, we're going to warn the Yu-kiang. I'll talk to them.' Basil felt sure of himself. What he was seeing was wrong. Deeply wrong.

Brassen shook his head. 'No, we can't do that. This is a corporate sanctioned mission.'

'It doesn't matter. What they're doing is wrong. They're tricking those people with false maydays. And they're going to kill them for no reason. Don't you think enough people have died out here already?' He jutted his chin at the image of the Vitus Bering on the other monitor.

'Mr. Baranikowa,' said Brassen in a slow, deliberate tone. 'You do not understand. It is the will of the corporation, and your own Father, that this mission proceed. We do not go against the will of the corporation.' Brassen spoke with utter conviction.

'Mr. Brassen, I am my father's son, and by extension the owner of this ship and I order you to find a way past the MilCom block so I can warn the Yu-kiang.'

'Mr. Baranikowa, I will not do that. Respectfully, but I do not recognize your claim as owner of the ship. Your father, Zach Baranikowa, is Chief Executive Officer of the corporation and as such his mission directives stand. The corporation is life, Mr. Baranikowa, you of all people should know that.'

Basil's face reddened at being overruled. He suddenly felt childish and willful. 'Do the others know?'

'Both Mr. Yakovlev and Ms. Dulg are following this conversation and they stand with me in this case. The corporation is life. It is a matter of faith.' He said, repeating the corporate mantra.

'This is not the way we did things in the old days,' said Basil resigned. 'Remember the Amazon?'

Brassen, who had turned his back to Basil once more, stiffened visibly at the mention of this crucial piece of corporate lore. Basil had never spoken to anyone about these things and he was not entirely sure why he did so now. It was clear that Brassen wouldn't lift a finger for the Yu-kiang. 'I was there. We saved the Amazon and we lost a lot doing so. All of us.'

Brassen shook his head. Basil noticed one of the 2D screens had changed. It was saying – 'stand by for tightbeam'.

'What's this?' yelled Brassen. Then: 'Don't do this. It is against orders.' He slumped back in his seat. 'Well, it seems you will get what you want, Mr. Baranikowa. It seems I have been superseded.'

Basil looked confused at the screen, then back at Brassen. 'I don't understand.' The monitor was counting down now. 3-2-1.

A face appeared on the screen. It was a man. Graying hair haloing his head, face round and somehow gentle. He was wearing orange coveralls and no obvious insignia denoting his rank.

'Greetings, I am Captain Emerald Florian of the Yu-kiang. We are pleased you have gotten communications back so soon. We're en route to assist you.' He looked serious, but his face broke into a smile when he saw to whom he was talking. 'Mr. Baranikowa, we didn't realize you were onboard. To what do we owe the honor?'

Basil did not understand how he could suddenly be talking to the Yu-kiang when Brassen had categorically forbidden it just a few seconds earlier. 'Thank you Captain. I am merely a... passenger. We have no time. You are about to be attacked by a squad of hostile soldiers piloting wartime exo-mechs. They have been retrofitted to fight in space and they're about to land on your ship.'

Florian raised his eyebrows in obvious disbelief. 'Who would do such a thing and why? Why would anyone attack us?'

'They're from our ship, but we didn't know they were onboard until a few minutes ago. We are not sure why they're doing it,' he lied. 'They're under command of Captain Bentzon. The distress signal is false. He has gone rogue and he is acting against the company briefing.'

Florian turned to someone off-screen and ordered his ship on alert. 'How many of them are there?'

'Umm, about ten or twelve, I believe,' he answered after consulting with Brassen who reluctantly offered the information. Basil's heart was thumbing in his chest and his throat was so tight he could not swallow. 'Captain Florian, one more thing,' he started saying but was interrupted by the old man on the screen who was turning to look at something outside the field of view.

'They're here. They are breaching the hull. What do they want?' he yelled at Basil. 'Tell me what they want.'

Basil paused. He almost could not bring himself to say it. 'They are there to destroy your ship, Captain. They are going to kill everyone on board. I am sorry.'

'We're not going down without a fight,' said Florian and cut the link.

Brassen and Basil were alone in the tank again.

'It was the right thing to do,' Basil said in a low voice.

Brassen looked at him with an expression that was so intense it made him uncomfortable. 'I never met your Father.'

'Not many people have.'

'How is he? I mean...' He blushed. 'I mean we all admire him, you know, and...'

Basil thought about telling him how he felt, but decided not to. It would serve no purpose and Brassen would not understand. 'He is like you would imagine.' A good simple answer that could mean anything and nothing.

TWELVE

Excerpt from an internal HSL memo named 'The future of mankind', signed by Zach Baranikowa. Cirka 2093

In the closing years of the 22nd century, the corporation was molded around the vision of its founder, owner and Chief Executive Officer, Zach Baranikowa. His recruitment and fleet construction policies were molded around the (long) anticipated discovery of an extra-solar planet capable of supporting human life. This, of course, is the reason HSL supported Survey Branch so vehemently in those years. Today many ask how it was possible to keep a secret like that for so long. The answer is that, like in its competing shipping corporations, the culture in HSL was accustomed to secrecy. Furthermore, the construction of the massive orbital, called Halifax, was instrumental in the planning of the Espero mission. Large parts of the base were darkened and sealed off for years to allow for the R&D and the various special construction projects needed for the mission. Again, this was not unusual corporate practice in those days.

Losing AI support was a grave setback to Zach Baranikowa and the HSL corporation. The sudden anti-revolution surprised the leadership of HSL. Even from inside the corporation, the rank and file were collectively too scared of the AI's to allow them to continue supporting corporate operations, even covertly, and thus HSL, like all other institutions and organisations on Earth, terminated the AI's. The effect was dramatic, as we know, but the GSA was too insistant, cybernetic policing too aggressive. Only by employing extreme measures of secrecy did HSL manage to salvage a handful of operational AI's. In subsequent years they lay dormant in a completely sealed off sector on Halifax and were as such unusable in the planning of the Espero mission.

It has been years since Bentzon indulged himself with the Flow, but he feels a need now. These are hardly ordinary circumstances. He thrust his arms out towards them. They blink, surprised, hesitating for a fraction of a second, before they step into his embrace, clasping his arms in theirs. They stand so for a while, a tight circle of flesh made one, foreheads touching. Brothers and sisters. To the end. Trust and authority. Respect. The bioluminescent red and yellow Shield tattoos on their bodies interact wherever they meet, as flesh touch flesh, pulsing, enveloping the five in a circle of red and yellow aura. He surrenders to the familiar tingle, starting in his hands, working its way up his arms and igniting every nerve on its way to his brain. Pleasure. Camaraderie. Brothers and sisters. Moans escape their half-open mouths, their bodies shudder. Pleasure and purpose. Around them activity ceases as the others stop to stare enviously at the reunion. A few minutes later, it feels like hours have passed, Bentzon breaks off.

--

The flow calmed him down, steadied him. He was going to command the mission himself. The squad leaders protested. There was Caribou, erstwhile lover, and a woman who always spoke her mind without hesitation, Crock, who was built like an ox and had the mindset to go with it, Peanut, a cynic to the point where it became decidedly unwarlike, while Mueller, the second-in-command, was arguably the brightest of them all, and the only non-enhanced among them apart from Bentzon himself.

He overruled protests and squashed legitimate complaints about how he wasn't enhanced and that he wasn't supposed to do these things. They muttered that his role was to sit back somewhere with VIR gear all around him and the big picture in his head, not to lead the charge. Nevertheless, he insisted and, of course, in the end, got his way.

A few hours later everything was ready. The plan was simple, bordering on flimsy. No one had ever attempted a zero-G boarding action before. It would be an unprecedented operation in military history, and that, he admitted to himself, did not make it any less attractive. He indulged vanity to a certain degree, but there was no getting around the fact that the operation was hugely risky. The potential pay-off, however, was worth it. If they could gain control of the Yu-kiang, they could use the ship to get out of Pleione and it prevent the even thornier, but not as urgent, tactical problem that would arise if the Mingo Corporation were allowed to land on Espero.

They had a plan for the crossing and a plan for the breach and that would have to suffice. Past the point of the breach it was impossible to plan anything because they didn't know the internal layout of the Mingo ship. All GSA ships were similar except for the interior of the crew modules, which were usually modified to accommodate the philosophy of the corporation that had built it. Bentzon didn't think it mattered. Once the exos had made their way inside the starship, the battle, if there even was one, would go their way. It was literally like bringing guns to the proverbial knife fight. Bentzon had seen a few Ruger exos deployed towards the end of the last war and their effect had been profound and utterly decisive. They had massive firepower, they could go anywhere a human could, but they were faster, heavily armoured and they were equipped with the best military sensor and targeting package Zach's money could buy. And, as if that wasn't enough, his exos were crewed by the finest mercenaries to survive the wars; heavily cyborged soldiers with superhuman reactions and strength; soldiers who knew all possible ways to die and to kill. Yes, all they needed was to get a squad of those machines inside the Yu-kiang and the matter would be decided. Nothing could withstand that.

He called the men together. All of them. Even those not assigned to the boarding action. It had been a long mission already, months and months of being stuck together in the cargo shell. He'd never been big on speeches but he needed to see them, hear them confirm their dedication to the cause. At least that's what he told himself. Perhaps it was the after-effects of the reunion.

They assembled in the re-melded upper levels of the module. The melders had created a big open space, a hangar with a huge sliding door on one side. Behind it the twin Pleione stars waited. He saw some of them glance at the door like it was going to buckle in at any moment.

Along the walls stood the Ruger exos, brooding humanoid statues, open cockpits gaping like abdominal wounds. They were preparing ten for the mission, about half of what they had. Spare parts from the others, mainly the heat dissipation arrays, but also additional short-range low powered kinetic weapons for indoor fighting, had been jury-rigged to them. It made them look dishevelled and somewhat less deadly, but without the additional heat sinks, they would never make it across the gap of suck separating the two starships. It would have to do.

When the entire company had assembled, he looked them over, darting his eyes among them. They were probably curious about the speech. It was unusual. He had never been prone to melodrama. He motioned everyone closer until they formed a half circle around him.

As though he was alone he started pacing, with bent head and half-slouched, unmindful of the whispering among the men. Bentzon stopped pacing and cried: 'Were we ever defeated, men?'

They knew this one and a score of voices answered: 'Never defeated, only killed!'

'That's right! Only killed. And, by the gods, we lost many brothers and sisters along the way, did we not, men?' An approving murmur was heard.

'But we are here now. The last survivors of the Shield Battalion.' He spoke this in a low voice.

Bentzon kept quiet for a few moments, to let the memories of lost friends and lovers bloom once more in the minds of the soldiers.

'Yes, we are here now, on a starship of all things. Who would have known, that they would let the likes of us up here.' He laughed out and the men laughed along with him.

'I don't think a man is born with certain talents and a destiny to match, laid out in front of him. No. I think that each and every one of us is free to forge his own path and that he creates his own talents along the way. Today, when I look back on the last thirty-five years, I know, that our talents and our destiny were forged in the trenches and in the Dropships, under fire, with blood and fear and by the loss of comrades. War is our talent and destiny. It is who we are. We cannot change that. We may think so, but we cannot.'

'I don't remember how my life was before the wars. Do you?'

Heads shook. No, they didn't remember life before the wars either.

'We are who we are. It is too late to change.'

The men looked confused and looks were exchanged among them. But Bentzon wasn't speaking just for them. He continued to talk for some time, reminiscing about old battles, old victories, old wounds. From time to time, his voice trailed off into a whisper and it was as if he spoke to himself. The men grew restless, but none dared challenge him. In the end, he collected himself and looked into the eyes of each one.

'The feeling the civilians have about soldiers is that since we weren't really going to do very much with our lives anyway, our deaths almost do not matter. And they're right, but it is their fault. It is a rare thing when soldiers are asked to help build something new, not to tear down what others have toiled to make, but to create. And we were asked and we answered. And here we are, yes, here we are...'

'You all met Zach. And you all heard Zach's words and you know how important this is. You could say that this mission is the most important military operation ever undertaken by anyone. We're out here to save humanity after all, to buy a new start for ourselves and for the people who follow. True, those Mingo folks over there in that starship haven't done anything personally to warrant getting attacked by the Shields, but they represent a sick and perverted system that cannot be allowed to contaminate the future of Espero. We need a new beginning.'

--

Caribou helped him suit up. The flow reunion had re-ignited something in him, some long forgotten sense of belonging, to the unit, to her. He looked into her eyes and she nodded, wordlessly.

Soon he was alone in the exo and the bay door was opening on the dull burgundy sheen of the Pleione system. Inside the machine his world diminished to the sound of his own breathing echoing loudly in his ears and to the feeling of his heart beating wetly against his ribcage like a trapped animal. He had to focus not to shuffle his feet or move his arms. The men were watching him now, more than ever. He was their beacon, the one thing each could hold on while struggling to contain the fears and primeval instincts that screamed at them to step backwards, away from the gaping abyss in front of them. There would be itching, irrational itching in impossible to reach places, and a terrible, sudden emptiness in their minds. Bentzon had been here before. He remembered the perverted state of bliss, very short lived, but powerful enough to drive away all memories of past living, and to reduce the moment to one single, all-consuming feeling of raw fear. Like he always did before a mission, he wondered if he was the only one feeling scared. Rationally he knew the others were scared too, but it didn't seem that way when he looked around at the unmoving exos around him.

Bentzon had been afraid many times in his life as a soldier. There was that time when they were dropping over Minsk and the mighty Ukrainian anti-air defences had torn into the battalion, popping the dropships one after another. He had quite literally pissed his pants during that descent. There had been other times too, not quite as bad as Minsk, though, and it had gotten better with time, he supposed, but this, this was different. Every cell in his body objected to the prospect of launching into the void beyond that door, but time was up. Bentzon prepared his voice, willing it not to crack or produce an unseemly pitch.

'Squad. Ready. Launch on my mark. Three, two, one. Mark!'

The ten exos started moving, then jumped as one, into the abyss beyond the door. Bentzon was at the centre of a v-shaped flight of exo-mechs which were locked on to each other, like a flight of long extinct wild geese. In that final moment when he ran out of the bay and jumped into the emptiness, Bentzon was in the grip of visions of his own death, grisly, blood splattered scenes playing out behind his eyes, he was the protagonist in a solitary tale, shouting in his ears. He was willing to bet some of them, even after all these years, were still starring themselves in a heroic tale of some sort, but he thought that the majority, like him, were playing out the final minutes and seconds of an absurd death, an exo malfunction, heatsinks breaking down, the protagonist boiling to death in mere seconds, which would, nonetheless, feel like minutes because of the excruciating high resolution pain such a death would entail. They knew how to die well, they had seen too many deaths not to, and yet, even after the butchery they had been part of, privately they all thought theirs would be painless.

The trip across the gap soon became strangely peaceful. The Armagnac quickly slipped out of sight behind them. They were alone, a tiny blob of life floating through empty space. Even through the nebula of the red shell phasing Pleione suns, a few pinpricks of other suns were visible. Earth was so unimaginably far away, and yet he didn't feel any more lonely or isolated here than he had at times during a long night of hiding in a foxhole back home. His nervousness disappeared, to be replaced by a twitchy combat alertness that had nowhere to go and as seconds became minutes then hours, it degraded into lethargy. The trip seemed endless. They were going very slowly to avoid thermal detection and they couldn't talk among themselves for fear of EM emissions. Once again memories intruded on his thoughts. All the fighting, all the tiny decisions, the mornings, the evenings, all the hours of his life, had led to this moment. This was it. There was nothing to discuss, very few variations left in his future. Just the two: die or survive. They would take the Mingo ship or not. It was the rigid inflexibility of these situations that had kept him soldiering for so many years. It was soothing, reassuring in a way the rest of life could never be. But it came at a price. Of course it did.

The journey continued for another couple of hours and then they saw it. There. There it was. The Yu-kiang. Their nemesis. At first it was merely a shimmering silvery pencil shape, but it steadily increased in size and resolution. Soon they saw the rainbow glimmer of the forward plasma emitter shearing its way through the nebulous murk of the Pleione system. Although the Yu-kiang, like all ships of the Restoration, was of the same common stock, it differed significantly from the Armagnac. For one, in the name of redundancy it had a couple of extra engines, six in total, of the latest GSA engine design which was more energy efficient, but on the other hand it had less advanced crew habitats. They were of the old tube design. No GRIT's but a simple static design which relied on acceleration to provide gravity. It was strange that they had chosen such old habitats for a ship, which was obviously meant to go on interstellar journeys. For the people on that ship the journey to Espero, with its long unavoidable apexes as the ship crossed solar systems between LQG points, would have to be endured in zero-G.

Bentzon used line of sight lasers to call in readiness reports from his men. They were ready. The Yu-kiang loomed ahead, getting bigger and bigger. The massive ship was ploughing serenely through the nebula like a great, majestic cetacean, unconcerned with mere plankton nibbling at it. So far, so good. The operation seemed to be going ok. The geese were perfectly aligned. They had chosen an area roughly in the middle of the habitat tube as their landing zone.

They were close now. What had seemed a glacial pace during the crossing turned into stomach churning free fall. The hull of the Yu-kiang rushed up to meet them. The trick was making sure they landed exactly perpendicular to the ship. Most did. A few stumbled and their sticky boots failed to make contact. They drifted slowly away from the hull in this and that direction but the improvised jetpacks attached to their exos quickly stabilized their tumble and brought them back safely. The squad fanned out around the landing zone while the two demolition experts got busy preparing the sticky bombs. Stickies were a nano-molecular programmable compound, which would 'stick' and allow you to control the charge precisely with minimal fuss. When it was first brought to market by Vale Industries twenty years earlier, the compound had gained instant popularity within the global community of mercenaries and professional riot suppression experts due to its reliability and simplicity. It had other advantages too: it was silent, save for the noise of the material it broke down. He fondly remembered how they had used sticky bombs in Hamburg, burrowing silently through the Schanzenviertel, surprising and disposing of the local naysayers repeatedly.

Bentzon activated TacNet. Telemetry, sensor and targeting data from all exos flowed into his on-board systems. He felt uneasy for some reason he could not explain. Tension was building inside him, the kind of tension you feel when you know you are about to get hit with a blunt instrument, without knowing where the blow will be coming from. He could see himself and the eight other exos milling about on the carapace of the ship, like mosquitoes preparing to sting a whale. Everything seemed to be going well. It was probably nothing. To calm himself, he focused on the residue of Flow still tingling in his body. How had they known they were coming? They must have underestimated the effectiveness of the Mingo sensors. Something was not right. Emission discipline held. They were communicating with lasers, his exo acting as hub. It would work as long as he had a line of sight to the others. Emission control at this stage was probably not necessary, the enemy knew they were here, but perhaps it would help build uncertainty.

The sticky bomb was in position. They moved away until they were below the horizon of the blast. The first one went off and a plume of steam was seen boiling up from behind the horizon of the hull. The demolition guys moved back to ground zero to attach the next bomb. They reckoned they would have to repeat it two or three times to get through the hull. Bentzon ordered everyone to stay where they were and went with the demo team to survey the damage.

The sticky bomb had exploded and created a gouge in the duranium, a couple of meters wide, about 10 centimetres deep. The nanobomb seemed to have made the rim of the crater come alive and it convulsed in wavelets against the unaffected area around it. Dai drifted over the hole letting his jetpack guide him. He positioned the next bomb and a couple of brief bursts on his jetpack took him back to Bentzon and the others. The second explosion was as unspectacular as the first. The crater was deeper now, some twenty centimetres, and a bit wider than before. The rim glowed dangerous bright cherry. In vacuum, the heat had nowhere to go. The third charge breached the hull. A brief storm of homely debris, he thought he saw a couple of chairs and clutter of clothes, rushed out of the hole. Fuel for the Pleione stars - a tiny gift from the tiny humans passing through.

Bentzon issued orders for the next phase and despite their unfamiliarity with zero-G operations the squad expertly took up positions on the rim of the breach and slipped down into the hole one by one. They had to carefully avoid the rim, but they had a few tens of centimetres to spare on each side. There was a brief pause. Bentzon could pretty much see everything everyone else was seeing thanks to TacNet - they were in someone's quarters, a bed, emergency gravity webbing, a desk. No fancy epi's here. The two lead exos gingerly went around the furniture and reached the doors leading deeper into the ship. A small directed blast opened them and they found themselves in a corridor. Bentzon ordered the squad to split up, one half left, the other right, and had them reseal the door behind them. As he had hoped, there was atmosphere behind the next set of blast doors.

The two groups advanced in parallel through the ship. War needs and generates certain virtues, obedience, the habit of discipline and the Shields had plenty of both despite the unaccustomed terrain. The tactics they used were not much different from those used in cleansing an underground arcology, except with the exos it was even easier going for the Shields. Ruger had created them precisely for this kind of mission. They systematically cleared the compartments one by one. Stack, breach, enter. Stack, breach, enter. No Mingo crew were seen and for a while they made good progress. Three levels up, however, in the direction of the command bridge, the group Bentzon was with reached a big open space in the middle of the hull. It was several levels high and about twenty meters wide.

He surveyed the scene. A clear blue clay sky bathed the room in a pleasant light, which reminded him of his childhood in Dublin. He noticed railings and glass terraces unevenly distributed on the rim around the room in several levels. The floor, where he stood, was a garden with miniature stone sculptures of extinct animals, a stream snaked across the room and disappeared into the wall, a tiny bridge crossed it, and arrangements of stone and pebble lined the bottom of the stream in neat patterns. There were even plants, weird, cubistic looking plants meticulously sheared into incomprehensible forms. It had the look of real stuff, not clay. A permanent fixture in the ship. Curious. The walls were covered with peculiar drawings which were primitive, to the point of pre-historic, yet strangely compelling. Was this what humanity had come to? Painting cave-art on the inside of starships they didn't understand. Passengers, hitchhikers to their own destiny, depending on technology they no longer understood to save them.

His units had taken up positions covering all entries and exits as well as the levels above them, but there was still no sign of the enemy. There was a doorway on the far side of the garden. When the second group arrived, he decided, he would order them to breach that door under his cover. They needed to get higher. The bridge would be sitting somewhere over that dome. Then a report came in from the second group: they had found some crew hiding in a locked room. 'Bring them here,' he ordered.

A few minutes later they arrived, prodded along by the six-barrelled machinegun on unit 4. It was two men and two children in orange coveralls. The men were called Saikia and Banerjee and they looked like twins. On a whim he decided to give them a little face time. It was more personal that way. He kneeled the exo in front of them and opened the cockpit.

'You sure about that, colonel?' asked Guhamiel's voice in his ear.

'Yeah, I think I know how we can end this, save us some time.'

He jumped out, blue contact gel dripping from his naked hairless body. The Mingo crew members stared stone faced at him and he let them get a good long look. Bentzon was watching their eyes as they looked him over and he noticed when they spotted the faintly luminescent yellow and green markings snaking their way across his body. The bended shield and the three dots denoting his rank. It meant nothing to the children, they were too young, but the adults knew. Oh yes, they knew and he relished the look of horror, which was soon replaced by something else, fatalism, resignation... He felt like a god as he stood there, naked, dripping, implacable, their worst nightmare incarnated. He let the Flow surface again. The mood, he recognized it, cruelly expansive, yet capable of benevolence. His old self.

'Where were you born and raised, Mingo rats?'

'Edmonton Deep,' answered the one called Saikia without removing his eyes from the Shield markings on Benton's body.

'That's right, dog. We're Shields. It means you're out of luck.' He stated it calmly and matter of factly. They did not respond. He paused for a bit then continued. 'So, ED, huh? I guess that's where most of you Mingo come from, isn't it? Ice rats.'

The man nodded. Bentzon was looking at the orange coveralls. 'And you can't afford clay suits. That is sad. Big corporation and all, but no clay suits. Not even for the children. What is this world coming to?'

The barb at their corporate honour made the one called Saikia speak up. 'Today is sacred day, Shield. You must celebrate Solstice. It is important day to Mingo.' The man dared a glance at Bentzon, but looked away quickly.

'Solstice? Doesn't that have something to do with the Sun. Why would you do that, the sun is four hundred light years away. We're on our own out here, little rat.'

The man just shrugged. 'You never see Sun back home either. It is belief.' Then he plucked up his courage and asked: 'Why you do this? Why attack Mingo like this. Mingo ordained prospectors, like you. Doing important work for Restoration. Espero big for many corporations.'

Bentzon considered telling them, after all, what could be possibly the harm, but it was too complicated and they surely would not understand, would not see the big picture and their own lack of role in it.

'All this is for Solstice celebration, I guess, yes?' He looked around at the garden and the little stone animals. The man nodded.

'You Mingo are strange people. Children on spaceships and paganism. Very strange people. You know, the Shields deployed in the Northern Dominion once... Don't remember who hired us, to be honest, but it got dirty enough, didn't it? There was this city on the surface back then, what was it called?'

'Clairmont,' Saikai said curtly.

'Yes, Clairmont. We cleansed that one, didn't we? The fighting stopped after that.' He made a small sound which was supposed to be a light-hearted chuckle but it came out wrong. There was something in their dejected attitude that suddenly annoyed him.

'You thought they had gotten all of us, didn't you? Yes, yes, I can't blame you. It was a close thing. Very close,' he said wistfully, then added in a more upbeat tone: 'But we're with Halifax now. Permanently. I guess you could say we got a new lease on life here.'

He smiled benevolently at them for effect, then reached quickly for one of the children and grabbed it by the throat. He lifted it, his hand a vice around its scrawny neck. It scratched and kicked its legs and made choking sounds. He looked at it for a while. It looked healthy, which meant the Mingo were capable of breeding their own stock. Good for them. He turned to the two adults who hadn't moved. They looked pale, but to their credit, they had not bothered asking for mercy.

'You can talk to your Captain, yes?'

The man called Saikia nodded.

'Tell him the ship is ours now. We will take control of it no matter what, but if he makes it a, shall we say, smooth transition, we will spare the children.'

They waited.

'Have you told him?' The little man nodded and straightened his back, looking Bentzon into the eyes for the first time.

'Shipmaster Florian say you: That word of Shield is worth nothing to human beings, that you worse than animal and that you be punished thousand times thousand for your crimes.'

Bentzon nodded pensively, as to himself and let go of the child who fell to the floor. 'I see. Very well, have it your way then.' He turned to re-enter the exo when he caught a sideward glance from one of them. The furtive glance triggered an alarm in his head and experience from decades of counter-insurgency warfare kicked in. He instinctively turned and leaped for the exo. A couple of seconds later, the cockpit was still closing on him, a bullet from a hidden wall mounted security system whizzed into the opening and hit him square in the abdomen with a meaty thud. He just had time to wince before the exo shut out the world. At first, there was no pain but he knew that was a temporary state of affairs. 'Are you okay, Colonel?' someone yelled over the Tacnet. 'No, I'm pretty fucking far from okay, dammit, I just took one in the stomach,' he grunted.

Pain washed over him and he might have lost track of time for a little while. When he came back to, he was looking at the water. No one had moved. The exo was trying to keep him conscious but he was losing too much blood. Was he hallucinating or was the water in the pool falling apart? Yes. It was spreading in globules through the room. It was beautiful and he had trouble tearing his eyes away from it. Gravity was going. The two Mingo adults were kneeling next to the remaining child, the three of them embracing.

He had only been out for a few seconds, but the troops had already repositioned and taken out the security system that had shot at him.

Guhamiel: 'Orders, sir?'

Gravity was definitely going. He could not stop looking at the water, by god his stomach hurt. He hadn't been shot in, what, twenty-six years? Why now? Damn, it hurt. You forgot how much it hurt. He kept staring at the water. He just needed a minute to catch his breath. Seconds ticked by. The troops were pinging him for orders. He looked at the Mingo prisoners who were crouching outside his exo. They looked scared now, looking this way and that. Surprised, he felt his exo lose footing. The exos were not designed for zero-G, but it should not be a problem. He saw blue thrusters lighting up on the other exos too, stabilising them. The water globules started drifting to the right and external sensors on the exo registered a slight wind, like a breeze on the pre-war summer day that the weird little Mingo garden was trying to simulate. A few seconds later the breeze became a strong wind, then a howling gale. Decompression. He idly watched the prisoners. The gale violently slammed them into the wall where they stuck in awkward poses, arms and legs snapping like twigs. Then silence. The air was gone and the walls let go of the rats. They thrashed about wildly, panic alight in their eyes until one by one they lost consciousness. He was going too. A black haze was crowding the edges of his vision and still he stared at the Mingo crewmembers. He had never seen anyone die like that before, funny thing when you thought about it: a couple of lifetimes in the black business, all those deaths, and still there was something new to be seen. That is life for you. Or death as it were. Always another trick up its sleeve. Most of the water had frozen into a hail of tiny balls and the rest had evaporated and hung like miniature clouds over the garden. His eyesight was almost gone now. A minute or two went by, sight returned and with it a tingling in his limbs. The meds had kicked in. The crewmembers still hadn't finished choking to death.

A tremor shook the exo. Bentzon looked around and heard one of the others curse on the open channel. People were moving this way and that; some were even spinning, completely out of control, crashing into the statues littering the floor, and in some cases even ricocheting off the walls. Gunfire. Small calibre crossfire from several kinetic machineguns was hitting them. The guns had emerged from the walls along with a few low yield beam weapons. Some kind of self-defence system, very paranoid, he thought approvingly. As far as he knew, they did not have anything like that on the Armagnac. At first, he thought the situation was not overly worrying, the bullets would not even scratch the paint on the exos, it was a case of hurt professional pride more than anything else. They should have detected the hidden emplacements during the initial sweep. Incompetent. He was about to order the men to resume the advance when he noticed the temperature on some of the exos was on the rise. Peteire shouted a warning. The gun emplacements were targeting individual exos, one after another, tearing off the un-armoured jury-rigged heat sinks, and then bathing the exos in high yield lasers to accelerate thermal overload. Clever, very clever. The squad was busy systematically taking out the gun emplacements but it was taking too long. The aim on the floaters was off. One of the lads, Pony, went first. He suddenly broke into the open chat with a strained voice. He had lost all heat sinks on his unit and his body temperature was rising rapidly, going from a hot day in the desert to boiled alive in seconds. The defensive emplacements were finally silenced but it was too late. The feed from Pony cut off, mercifully, leaving him to die alone inside the exo. Another unit they had to taxi along on remote.

Bentzon, who was feeling somewhat better, ordered everyone back into the corridor where the scenario repeated itself. Gun emplacements and low yield beam weapons. More heat sinks unhinged. Several exos were showing signs of critical temperatures.

He considered his options. The problem was not taking out the emplacements, they could do that, but every heat sink lost was cutting down on the operational range of the exos, and, consequently, the lifespan of the pilot. Their chances of reaching the command bridge with enough firepower to take control of the ship got worse by the minute. A clarity, utterly chemical, had taken hold of him. They had walked into a trap. The Mingo dogs were ready for them. The chemicals made him see things he had not noticed until now. It was like a zoom function. He could not help it. The walls were real here, not that plastic stuff on the Armagnac. There were those paintings, graffiti everywhere. Cave art. Imprints of hands and feet, and heart shapes that looked like someone had used their ass cheeks to paint. He would have liked it here. A pity. Much more than the Armagnac with its sterile GRIT walls. Had the Mingo sacrificed those people on purpose? Heartless bastards, he thought, kids and all.

He ordered a retreat that soon became a mad scramble. The eight of them ran through the corridors, shooting left and right at the gun and beam emplacements as they popped out of the walls. 'We need to get the heat under control,' Hal yelled over the TacNet. He was right. They had to hunker down somewhere to reassess and get the temperature under control, preferably out of vacuum. Then the rear guard reported he was taking fire from mobile units and Bentzon checked out the telemetry: clay suited enemies were pursuing through the corridors, bottling them up. The rear guard opened up with all he had; 55 mm auto missiles and 20 mm machine cannons. The missiles roared down the corridor towards the pursuers making the walls of the entire section tremble on impact. The enemy, unfazed, retaliated with gauss cannons ripping into the walls, which buckled and perforated like paper. Bentzon ordered the squad to move back towards the breach point. The operation was unravelling second by second, leaving him clean out of options. Attacking into auto defenses and hostile mobiles in overheating exos was out of the question. Retreat it was then. A few minutes later the advance guard had blasted the door, all thoughts of minimizing collateral damage gone, and was moving through the breach, which was still lava hot. A parting gift, they needed a parting gift, he thought, and a few minutes later, they were all back on outside of the hull where enemy mobiles were appearing over the horizon. A furious firefight ensued. Exos got hit this way and that and gradually they all lost footing on the hull, freefalling in all directions away from the Yu-kiang. Bentzon ordered everyone to put distance between the ship and themselves, vaguely imagining they could coordinate a rendezvous somewhere along the way back to the Armagnac. In retrospect that would turn out to be a big mistake. He should have held his ground. As it was, they all went their separate ways, fleeing away from the ship in random directions. He looked back at the Yu-kiang at maximum zoom and sent the signal. Five sticky bombs exploded simultaneously inside the ship, just under the breach point. The hull rose like a bubble, and then burst open in a conflagration of debris spreading silently like a flower blooming in fast forward. He had time to think it might delay them a little, but the thought was forgotten as he looked around and realized they were utterly lost. He couldn't remember whether he had ejected to the starboard or port side of the Yu-kiang and if so, in which direction was the Armagnac? The Ruger was not much help. It was made for ground operations and not for deep space and so had no real way of navigating in space.

For what seemed a long time, the Yu-kiang remained immobile in space and he allowed himself the satisfaction of thinking he had hurt it terminally. Then, to his dismay, the main engines lit up and spat out a plume of purple plasma. Faster and faster, the Mingo ship slipped away into the depths of the Pleione system, towards the LQG point that would take it to Espero.

For the Shields the aftermath was brutal. Apart from Bentzon who, throughout the retreat, had been shielded by his men, not one of them had come off the Yu-kiang without losing heat sinks and without them, eventually, the exos overheated, boiling the pilots inside alive.

They all knew how to die well and most of them took care to turn off their radios when the time was near. So many ways to die, just as we thought we knew them all.

THIRTEEN

At first, he spent valuable fuel mass on stabilizing the Ruger. He wanted to see the Yu-kiang and rejoiced when he saw the explosion. The joy was short-lived. Soon a stream of plasma erupted from the engines and he watched as the ship slipped away into the murky nebula between the two stars and for hours he followed it with his eyes until it was but a point of light no stronger than the faint starscape behind it.

Then it was just him and nothing else. If you had asked him, he would have said he reckoned it would be the solitude that would get him in the end. He had heard that deep space could do terrible things to a man. The lack of horizon, the lack of anything even remotely familiar would empty him of his soul and leave him completely changed. He was wrong. The solitude tore at him, certainly. It was terrible thing, that lonesomeness, that concentration of self in the middle of such heartless immensity. Yes, the solitude tore at him and when he looked around at the emptiness all around him, he felt very small and very insignificant. But his soul was not infinite, it was a small, walled garden, and he had kept it like that for years, decades. It was how he survived the wars. He kept telling himself that his men were coming, that they would hear the radio signal over the clutter and static of the two angry red stars that were so busy tearing each other apart and come for him. Patiently he waited. He was good at waiting. All soldiers know how to wait. The jetpack was almost empty now, down to 18%. At some point, he turned the exo around to face the two red suns. He could see them clearly; a spectacle of force so enormous it made him feel like a mote watching giants hurl bolts of stellar mass at each other. No, it was not the solitude that got him, but his old nemesis: the Grays. Since he was child, radiation had horrified him. To be fair, it was a common enough affliction among survivors of the wars, but for Bentzon the fear had grown into something else. The many years spent on the surface on missions had made it worse. For a long time it was said that there were only two kinds of people up there, the dead and the dying. There was truth in that.

The Ruger was a magnificent piece of machinery. Faithfully monitoring every single aspect of the health of its sole occupant but still trying, and failing, to make sense of the exterior. It was sadly overmatched by space. Unlike the Armagnac, it could not navigate by dead star reckoning, and its gyros were struggling to stabilize it. He had put it off for a long time now... hours. His thoughts had circled around it as a possibility. There was one particular number that he knew he could make appear on the HUD. He did not want to see it. No. He knew it would be a mistake to do so, but we are only animals, and Bentzon, more than most people, knew that, and as all animals we have this irresistible urge to turn and look back, knowing full well it will kill us. It was an old story, something his mother had once told him, something about a city that God was destroying and everyone who looked at it - was it at the destruction or the city itself? - would turn into salt and die. Yes, it is true, he thought, haven't you noticed how animals always lock eyes with their prey at the precise moment of death? How both victim and killer have a need to look the other in the eye? What passes between them? What godly message is exchanged? Well, old chap, he thought, you are about to find out.

In the end, what got him was the Gray counter that he could dial up on his HUD. He knew his Grays as well as anyone who had lived in the past fifty years. Dryness in mouth. Hairloss. Permanent hairloss. Sweat glands stop working. Whole body exposure to 5 or more Grays usually leads to death within 14 days. Here it was a heady mix of GCR and SPE bombarding the Ruger. Cosmic radiation and particles. He turned around and looked once more at the two suns and damned them. If only they had not changed. If only they had remained coherent, but no, they had to lose it all, go crazy, expand, swallow everything at the precise moment a bunch of soft humans were passing near them. According to their projections, they should have been protected in the Rugers as long as their exposure did not exceed twelve hours. The exo's were, after all, made for survival under prolonged low to medium level nuclear radiation. Had to be. Otherwise they would not be much use in rooting out chromo nests, would they? Twelve hours, was all he had, and they were up now. The notion that something infinitely small was eating away at his intestines was intolerable. Poison unloading in his every cell, his muscles, his beautiful muscles, his trusty bones, which had not once broken on him. He thought with immense sadness of every part of his body. He quietly said goodbye to his toes and his fingers, to every hair on his head and on his body: goodbye hair, goodbye toenails, the lovely toenails, the big toe, almost square, slightly rounded, and that third one, what did you call it?, the one that was a little longer than the one to its left or right where it should be shorter, he'd loved them so much, they had served him so well. And he counted his internal organs, and sent out nerve impulses to each of them and he felt them respond for the first time. Oh, oh, he had never spoken to his organs before. The lungs, the kidneys, his stomach, his appendix for God's sake! He took a deep breath and it made a horrible, grating sound. Already they were going. Oh, and his penis, his beautiful penis that he had held so often in his hand, stroked and loved and caressed. It had given him so much pleasure. He wished the exo would let him curl up in a ball because he so needed to touch his body one last time.

Perhaps at some point, he knew he was going mad, but more likely it just happened all at once, like sliding down a cliff, rocks and pebbles and dust rising up around you and when you stop falling you are in another place entirely. The twelve hours came and went with no sign of rescue. Tiny molecules were ripping his body apart. He could feel it, his muscles and tendons strained against them and his heart was beating too fast, then too slow. Panic overtook him, like a surge in his chest, constricting his throat and his breathing. The Gray counter said he was dying, that space had transformed him. Damaged beyond repair, his life forfeit. When the SADU grabbed hold of his Ruger exo, Bentzon did not notice.

FOURTEEN

It had been eleven days since the last exo was recovered from space. Rem had observed how SADUs emerging from cargo shell 5 had scoured nearby space and brought back the inert exos one by one. Eleven days of not knowing and worrying about the broken Abbott-Farhi Ensphere and tormenting himself about losing control of the ship at a crucial moment, allowing Basil to warn the Yu-kiang. What could he have done? He knew he had failed when he had allowed Basil to contact the Yu-kiang. He had been powerless, out-maneuvered by the Sleepers. Could have happened to anyone in that situation. It was they. The bloody ghosts. Mutiny. They had mutinied and it might have cost the Captain his life. But was it really his fault? If Zach had briefed him properly about the mission, he could have stepped in and prevented it. At the very least, he could have warned Bentzon. How could it be that Zach had failed to brief him properly? Him, the Pilot. A lifelong employee of the company, a lifelong admirer of Zach... He lingered on that thorny questions for a few seconds, but, never prone to idle speculation, his thoughts returned to the Captain.

Who would take command of the ship now that he was dead? According to fleet regulations, there was only one candidate for the job and that was Rem himself. Which was fine. He could do the job. He would do the job. In fact, it would be an exquisite honor to do the job. "Rem Brassen, captain on the mission that colonized the first extra-solar planet for humanity." The words had a certain ring to it. His name, the name of the Captain, would reverberate throughout History alongside men like Cook, Drake and Vasco da Gamas, never forgotten, heroes who represented everything that was just and right about humanity, the curiosity, the selfless bravery that the Good Man always spoke of in his sermons.

It was time he stepped up and got this mission back on track. There was a lot to do. Not least fixing the Abbott-Farhi Ensphere. If they did not manage to repair it, they would end their days in Pleione, starving to death when power ran out.

Despite the spotty briefing, Rem thought he knew what Zach wanted. They were to continue to Espero and deploy the colony modules on the surface of the planet. Some vital parameters had changed however. For one they would be late, very late. Their fuel reserves were such that they had to go slowly. The Captain, the former Captain, had overspent on the way out. And that was the other unknown - the Yu-kiang. It was hostile now. He did not think he had to worry too much about it, though. The Mingo people had no weapons and Espero was big enough they would not have to bump into each other if they did not want to.

What really annoyed him was that there were parts of the mission Zach had not briefed him about. For example, what were those soldiers doing in the cargo hold? They had been used against the Yu-kiang, but it was clear that it had not been part of the plan to attempt a zero G boarding action against another starship. Then what were they there for? What did Zach expect to find on Espero that needed soldiers and exo's? And the Good Man only knew what else they had stashed away in that module? And why hadn't Zach shared all that with him, Brassen? A man with his experience could be trusted. Zach could trust him.

He had to see for himself what was in Cargo hold 5. He could not captain a ship if he did not know every nook and cranny of his dominion.

First things first. A decision of this magnitude would require he consult with the Good Man. The others did not understand Rem. What Jin and Felix thought of dour broodiness was bottled spirituality. He was a spiritual man. He usually spent his spare time, and they had plenty of that these days, pouring over the texts of his religion. He would vary his reading between hagiographies, which he found interesting because they described the trials of other peculiar people as they tried, and failed, more often than not, to survive in a world that resisted their spirituality. It inspired him to keep going. For him, religion was an invisible layer that separated people and bound them together, encapsulated them. As such, it ruled every encounter, every facet, of life and human interaction despite the contemporary propensity to distance themselves with virtual technology. The Good Man, the principal of the Peculiar People, did not shun modern technology, but he was against using it for mere pleasure and mindless entertainment. Some said this made the Peculiar People unsuited for deep space operations, but Rem had something better than VIR. He had the PP sanctioned environment where you could meet the Good Man himself. It was not exactly a secret, but it was reserved for the Peculiar People. Rem often sought out his advice and he always enjoyed their conversations. Today, he needed to talk about his role as Captain. He found the Good Man on a cruiseship. It was a well-known fact that he loved to sail, but, considering the state of the oceans on Earth, sailing was hardly advisable. The Good Man chose to represent himself on a boat anyway. It was a big one with a couple of hundred believers acting as crew. The Good Man was always in his cabin, which was big, probably three or four normal-sized cabins joined together. He was behind a desk littered with old-fashioned paper, a writing machine, surrounded by his closest advisors, about a dozen females in sailor's uniforms. The Man was wearing a white suit complete with a white sailor's cap with gold braids intricately patterned on the visor. He was smoking a pipe, puffing smoke like a locomotive until it surrounded him in a blue haze. He was a middle-aged man, slightly overweight, and Rem did not think he would have recognized his greatness had he met him on the street, not knowing him for what he was. Life worked that way, in twists and turns.

The session began as it always did. The Good Man removed the pipe with his left hand and smiled at Rem. 'Christian friend, I hope that you are encouraged to know that you really are peculiar. You belong to a special group of people who are the unique possession of God. You are a member of His eternal family. And that means, of course, that you are the special object of His love and care. It also means. however, that we are to live consistent with who we are.' He made an expansive gesture at the room and the girls.

Rem nodded. 'Yes, Commodore.' It was a well-known speech.

'We're not like other people in the world. We are more than different — we are unique. And so, we live unique lives to the glory of God who has given to us His Holy Spirit as a pledge of our inheritance, with a view to the redemption of God's own possession, to the promise of His glory.' Rem nodded again. The Good Man put the pipe back into his mouth and restarted the puffing.

'Commodore, what would you do in my place?' Rem did not need to explain.

'Son, they disrespect you.' Sometimes it was as if the Good Man in this VIR knew him better than he knew himself. 'You need to tell them. Claim your place as Captain of this ship.' Rem found he was staring at one of the girls. The girls often distracted him during these sessions with the Master. The girl was wearing a white cotton shirt and the fabric was so thin you could see dark nipples adorning a shapely set of pointy breasts through it. Fortunately, the Good Man did not seem to notice. Rem always found himself wondering about the girls. Why the Good Man would need these girls as advisors seemed strange. Surely, he could do without, a man of his knowledge and wisdom.

'I think... you know what I think?' said the Good Man with a pensive expression on his round face.

'No, Commodore, please share your thoughts,' Rem answered, tearing his eyes away from the girl.

'You need to go to cargohold 5. See what is going on.'

Rem nodded. Yes, that was a good suggestion.

--

No sooner said than done, he left his room and went down to the SADU bay on level 4 where spare drone units lined the walls. He found one, which was inactive and linked the controls directly to his clay suit, which he configured into one of the EVA settings. He opened the bay doors to space and, clinging to the drone, used it to move him into space. Once out there, he turned into the direction of the engines, floating slowly down the length of the ship. As he reached cargo shell 5, he pinged it to open. It did not obey his command, he had not expected it to, but he kept pinging. Ten minutes later, he was rewarded for his perseverance. The doors opened. Inside, he glimpsed rows of military exos. Most like the ones they had seen depart eleven days ago, but he also noticed a smaller number of exos which looked different. He did not have time to think more about them because the doors were already closing. He hurried inside. Another door opened and a clay suited person entered. Opaque clay covered the face.

'What do you want?' a gruff voice said in his ears.

'As the new Captain, I want to inspect this shell. What is the purpose of all this?' he answered, straightening his back to match the height of the person in front of him. To his dismay, the other person laughed aloud.

'If you were supposed to know that, don't you think someone would have told you?'

Rems face turned a bright purple.

There was a slight pause then he received an invitation to join a VIR session.

--

The room was clayed as the interior of an aerial vehicle of some sort. It was flying slowly over a desolate, post-nuclear landscape. Rem peered through the windows, trying to pick out a landmark, but it was all ruins and knocked over trees. Two people in clay suits were sitting in seats along the walls of the vehicle. The one on the left was a tanned man with a crew cut and the face of soldier. On the right was an enormous woman with short, reddish blond hair and very blue eyes. Both wore martial-looking symbols on the outside of the clay suits.

No one asked him to sit so he kept standing. He could not figure out whether he should clasp his hands behind him, in a semi-classic military posture, link hands in front or put them in his pockets. Almost by themselves, his arms crept up and crossed themselves on his chest, making him look either defensive or like he was freezing his ass off. Or both. Or disrespectful. He immediately uncrossed his arms and went for a weird posture, which had both arms hanging down his sides, the right one slightly bent. The soldiers did not acknowledge him. They lounged lazily against walls of the aerial vehicle. No one spoke.

Suddenly Captain Bentzon appeared in front of Rem. He was sitting at a small folding table with food on it. A plate of chicken, green salad and plums or abricots. Highly unusual to see people eat in virtual meetings. Pointless, really.

'Captain,' said Rem, 'You are alive! Good to see you. I hope you are well?'

'He orders you to start a no-apex burn immediately,' said Bentzon without deigning to answer Rem directly.

Rem swallowed. 'Oh, erm... Captain, we have done the calculations and we cannot afford it, sir. Respectfully.'

'Yes we can. Start the burn.'

'Captain, if we do a no-apex burn here, we won't enough have enough fuel to get us home.' Then, in a lower voice, he added: 'At least not in our lifetime.' He glanced nervously at the soldiers.

Bentzon, distracted look on the face, scratched his forehead lightly with the tips of his right hand as if someone contradicting him was so utterly baffling he was lost for words.

'Do as he says,' said the woman so suddenly it made Brassen flinch. 'He gave you an order.' Her voice was a booming, throaty sound. Rem quickly looked at her without turning his head. Her eyes were of a shining, almost unnatural, blue and they were all over Rem who suddenly felt like a bug caught on someone's windshield. Without knowing why, he just knew this was how she looked in real life too.

Rem nodded. The Captain had stopped scratching his head and taken to staring at Brassen instead. 'The Yu-kiang knew we were coming, Mr Brassen,' he said sadly. 'Nine of our brothers died out there.' The two soldiers nodded for unneeded emphasis.

'Nine of our brothers,' the male soldier repeated in a hoarse voice.

'Yes, I wanted to talk to you about that, sir,' answered Brassen.

The Captain did not hear what Rem said, because he continued speaking. 'I hold you responsible, Mr Brassen. We detected a tight beam signal emanating from the engine section. Apparently, someone was clever enough to reconfigure a spectral analysis detector on one of the medium engine drones to work as a relay. It was very clever.' He shook his head slowly. 'That, Mr Brassen, is betrayal of the company, your CEO and owner, and, infinitely worse from your personal point of view, of the Shield Battalion.'

Brassen closed his eyes and swallowed deeply. His mouth suddenly felt very dry. 'It was not me. Basil Baranikowa warned them. There was nothing I could do to prevent it.' He felt the eyes of Bentzon and the two soldiers linger on him like search beams.

'Basil?' The man sounded incredulous.

'Yes, him. He claimed that in your absence he was owner and

acting Captain of the ship. And then he just did it. There was nothing I could do to prevent it,' he added sheepishly.

'He didn't do it on his own. Someone helped him,' boomed the female.

'I don't know about that,' said Brassen. Some inner limit restrained him from saying the rest.

'It was one of the Sleepers, Mr Brassen, as you very well know.' Brassen shook his head weakly.

'I had no choice, Captain. You must believe me.'

'Why did he do it?' asked the woman.

'I am not sure. He said it was wrong to attack the Yu-kiang.'

'It does not matter. Basil will pay for his treachery as will the others.'

'How will you fly the ship?' stammered Rem.

'My men here are more than capable of assuming your duties, Mr Brassen.'

'But the Abbott-Farhi Ensphere has broken down. You need our help if we are to repair it. Felix is the only one who could possibly…'

'I am aware of that and we will manage fine without you. Return to the ship and inform Mr Baranikowa to meet me in my quarters in 30 minutes.'

The session ended. Rem was alone in the cargo bay. He turned around and made his way back to the habitat section.

--

On May 9th, two clay suited people undocked from module 5 and, hanging on to a maintenance SADU, moved along the length of the ship, past the gap separating module 5 from the fourth GRIT module, and docked inside the drone bay on Level 4. Between them, they were carrying a man-sized portable epi. They went directly to the Captain's quarters.

FIFTEEN

Speech by Zach Baranikowa from the Commonwealth v. Halifax Trial of 2104, excerpt

-You ask how we could keep this secret for so long? Well, everyone needs purpose in their lives and you can say that I provided it for my people. In return they gave me secrecy. No one seriously disagreed that we, people, humanity, needed new direction. The old ways just didn't work. Time proved me right. Just look at where we are now. The nuclear contamination has laid waste to half the planet, sea levels rising, fall out, the climate going crazy, people living like moles underground. I just don't see a way out for humanity. You can say we're doing ok for ourselves as it is now, but it is not going to last. I don't believe in it and neither does our scientists. Civilization as we know it is on a downwards spiral. In other words, we're going to Hell. Our worst enemy is ourselves and by extension our leaders. The politicians, the systems we have created around us and the expectations people nourish for how their lives should be lived just don't add up. We have failed. What I proposed was a fresh start. A reboot of civilization, a new start in a new place. New ideas, new rules to create the foundation of a new society. And no. I was not going to do this at the expense of anyone. We were not going to take anything away from anybody. That would be the wrong way to go about things. No, once Survey Branch discovered a planet capable of supporting life outside our solar system, that's where we would go. That's where we would start anew.

The news that the Captain had arisen from the dead, had immediate physical consequences for Basil. His stomach churned and he suddenly felt an overpowering urge to defecate, which he did not have time to satisfy. On his way out of the door, he caught a glance of his own face in the mirror and he barely recognized it. It was a face that was deadly pale and drawn, the face of a man at the end of the line, about to face his executioner. Rem Brassen's message had been succinct. The Captain wanted to see him immediately and he wanted to discuss, among other things, Basil's role in the death of nine soldiers and the failed attempt to seize the Yu-kiang. 'Did you tell him?' asked Basil. 'It didn't matter. He already knew,' said the other man sullenly. 'I thought you agreed with me.' Brassen shook his head. 'You didn't ask my permission.'

Warning the Yu-kiang had been a spur of the moment thing, a sudden act of defiance... yes, an act, a show. What could he possibly have been thinking at that moment? That it was all a mistake? That his Father was a decent man after all? It had only been eleven days, but it already felt so long ago it could have happened to someone else. People had died because of him. Nine people, according to Brassen.

The physical act of putting on the clay suit, leaving his room, walking down the corridor and ascending the stairway, happened as if in slow motion. He considered leaving, just jumping off into vacuum, ending his own life but realized, humbled, that he could not even get out of the ship. He had never seen any openings or windows. He would probably need to go down to level 4 in the drone bay. Then what? What would he need to do to open to hangar bay?

He stopped in front of the door to the Captain's quarters. Once again, like so often since they had taken him off the DmC, memories suddenly surfaced in his mind, of another time, long ago, when he was a child on the Basilisk. His mother and father had lived there, in similar Captain's quarters, a three-room apartment... his mother... The Eight Day Man had buried her twice. The first time when she physically died and the second time when he had started on the DmC and become the Eight Day Man. She did not deserve that. The tragedy of her death had ennobled him. Because of her, Basil had lived his life as if nothing bad could happen to him ever again. He had felt protected somehow. It was superstitious, certainly, but it was real to young Basil. Her death had been a down payment to whatever Gods watched over him and he had been certain it would last the rest of his life. His escapades, increasingly outré and dangerous on the Dub show had been the unconscious result. The past four months had diminished him, chipped away at his essence, as stark memories of his life came back. Perhaps there were no Gods out here. Perhaps

400 light-years was too far even for them.

Even afterwards, after the old man had inadvertently killed his mother, Basil had admired Zach. He had been so... virtuous, so admirable for a young boy. *Master and commander of the starship, their entire world.*

That was a long time ago. Now they were trapped on a broken starship far from home and Bentzon would have his revenge on Basil as soon as he stepped through the door. It was fiction mutated into perverted philosophy and it stood to be shattered on the other side of the door. He thought of Maribel – what would she do in a situation like this? His sword-wielding amazon, his auburn Lioness, what would she do? Maribel and the game were safe. Things were going well in the game. They would meet a certain number of times each every day to talk, have sex and plan their next nefarious moves in the Land. His holdings were running smoothly now and demanded less and less daily intervention on his part, freeing him up for more strategic work like figuring out how to dispose of the county of Gevienne which was proving to be more than a mere thorn in his side. He had the distinct impression they were gearing up for war. They had nothing to gain from it, but he supposed they felt hemmed in by his Duchy. *Some people... never happy.* They should be glad they had a nice plush corner of the peninsula, undisturbed and largely protected by him, instead of giving in to simmering ambition which, he was sure of it, would undo them in the long run. Still, he would need to deal with them and he would do so in his customary incisive manner. But not now...

The door opened. This was the real thing. A long wooden table. The Captain had a thing for old stuff. Like his father. Two soldiers, a man and a woman, at the far end who wore clay, but, curiously, their upper bodies were naked, which, combined with their bulging muscles, gave them a savage expression, like ancient warriors. Between them, completely naked, sat the Captain, body ravaged by radiation burns, face sagging. Only tufts of hair remained on his head, eyebrows gone. A gruesome image and one Basil would not soon forget.

Basil's breath came in short bursts and he fought to calm it. Everyone was staring, but he did not flinch, no, he did not. He was Zach's son, after all, even faced with the prospect of imminent death.

He looked closer at the trio. Tattoos, old-fashioned. What was that? A singular luminescent yellow and green tattoo twisted itself around their bodies, luminescence made it pulse and swirl, almost like a live thing. They wanted him to see it, he realized, that was why their upper bodies were bared. He would have recognized the symbol anywhere and so would every other living human: a worm curled around a shield which almost, but not quite, bent under the pressure. *The Snake and Shield symbol of the Shield Battalion.*

The forty years that destroyed human civilisations never even got a name, there was no time for that, and when the wars finally petered out, everyone was too busy staying alive to think about the past. Maybe history itself had been the greatest victim of the wars because the will to remember and to learn was shattered. Still, even nameless wars have heroes and villains and certain images live on. More than any other symbol the Snake and Shield represented those years of death and destruction to the survivors. Basil who thought himself inured to melodrama felt goose bumps appear on his arms. They were history come alive, terrifying ghouls of the past, and here they were.

'What the hell is that outfit?' said the Captain in a rasping voice that was barely audible.

Basil looked down. 'Erm, a sailor's uniform, circa 1900. I had the computer look it up. I thought.... umm. It's quite the fashion statement back home. At least it was four months ago. A lot could have changed, I suppose...'

Bentzon noticed Basil's eyes were wandering over the symbols on his body. 'I see you recognize the Flow.' He gestured feebly with his hand at his own body and the tattoos that were there.

'My first name was Sergey Malyutin.' He sighed. Bentzon, or Malyutin, turned to the man standing next to him. 'This is major Mueller.' He gestured at the woman. 'And this is Caribou.'

'I know you.' Mueller said, enouncing every word carefully with a gravelly voice. 'From the Dub show.' He winked inappropriately at Basil as if they knew each other. Basil decided to ignore him. Could these people really be *them*? They were supposed to be dead a long time ago.

The one called Mueller spoke. 'You got nine of our brothers killed out there. We should kill you for that and we will. But not now. You are lucky, Basil Baranikowa, that you have something we need. '

'And what might that be, you are wondering,' he continued. 'Well, the Abbott-Farhi device has stopped working. Without it, so they tell me, we are lost. Your father said we shouldn't speak the seven word activation code unless we meant it and unless we really had to.'

Basil looked from one man to the other, totally blank. He noticed that Mueller had a look on his tattooed face, which was... expectant. The face of the woman called Caribou was unreadable. Basil nodded at Bentzon as if he knew what he was talking about. He decided to keep quiet.

'I don't know if it will work at all, but we have to play all our cards now. If we get stranded in Pleione it'll be the end of the mission.'

Basil nodded. Yes he understood that it was a bad thing to be stuck in an unstable, phase changing twin sun system and he also clearly understood how it would be the end of the mission. He just did not understand all the rest.

'First things first. ' He looked back at Basil. 'Your lover, umm..' his eyes were glazing over while he was accessing information from the ship. '...Maribel, yes. In the game, I mean. Yes?'

Basil nodded, dumbstruck. Was the Captain supposed to know about the game?

'She's about to die.'

'Huh?'

'Yes, she is about to have a fatal accident. '

'What is happening to her?' His voice croaked.

'Let us watch it together.'

'What do you mean?' He did not quite believe it. Characters did not die like this in the game. It was absurd.

'Well, it's complicated....'

'Ahh, here we go.' He was looking at the wall behind Basil.

Basil turned around and looked at the wall, which had turned into a 2D view screen. An image appeared. He recognized his castle at Taillebourg and the village, which had grown around it. They had a bird's eye view from a drone of some sort, probably invisible from inside the game. The view zoomed down to the village with its cobbled streets, houses leaning dangerously towards each other across the narrow streets, dung heaps and open sewers. The drone rounded a corner and confidently entered a tavern, a seedy place inventively named the Horseshoe. The room was low slung and smoky. In one end, a game of cards was underway and a group of people were yelling insults and encouragements at the two players.

One was Maribel, the other a small, dark-haired hedge knight. Basil peered at him. A new face. A big hoot went up and the knight got to his feet. He was angry. Accused Maribel of cheating. She got up too, never one to back down from a fight.

'That's a nice piece of ass, I'll give you that, son,' rumbled Mueller. The camera was hovering behind her, over her right shoulder.

'That is Hews, one of the men. He is in cargo module 5 physically but he volunteered to join the game temporarily,' said Mueller. 'The scene reminds me of that episode in Hamburg, remember?'

'Oh yes I remember, mumbled Bentzon. 'You were there too, weren't you, Car?'

'Sure was, Serge, sure was,' answered the woman in deep, throaty voice.

The hedge knight had stopped shouting which should have alerted Maribel that he planned to escalate the argument, but she failed to notice. The man had challenged her integrity and that you just did not do. Basil knew first-hand how angry that would make her. She was pointing a finger at his face and shouting at him. He stood calmly. His left hand reached out and settled on her shoulder. She started to shrug it off but then he pulled her towards him in a sudden jerk and his right hand shot out, upwards. There was a knife in it and the knife aimed directly at her jaw and before anyone could do anything it had entered her from below her chin and the knight kept pushing at it until it was buried hilt deep inside her brain. She would have fallen but the knight kept her on her feet for a few seconds by holding on to the knife. He looked deeply into her eyes as life left them. He then put his left hand squarely on her face, fingers splashed across her eyes, and pushed brutally until the knife dislodged. She fell backwards in a spray of blood.

'I think that was a nice touch – pushing her back like that, I mean,' said Mueller.

'Those hedge types aren't big on rhetoric, huh? It's kind of funny how closely it resembles that episode,' he reminisced, shaking his head to himself. 'You would almost think I came up with the whole scene, wouldn't you?'

Mueller laughed aloud now. 'Except we had assault rifles and some other minor details. Still, it works. History in motion. The best kind.'

'The knife sliced right through her brain. She died in an instant.'

Mueller paused briefly, then: 'The game master tells me that the avatar didn't suffer. And the player wasn't online when it happened.' Everyone smiled at that. Basil's face was frozen in shock. The player? Did that mean...? Yes, Maribel was not an NPC. He thought the Land was his and his alone. Now they were telling him there were other people in it. Real people.

Silence oozed out from Bentzon. He was waiting for something. 'How can you be sure it was that person? I mean my... friend from the Land?'

'I'm not. The computer is. You have a couple of hours left on your account. Then it is over. We need you to get to work on the Abbott-Farhi Ensphere. It is broken, you see.' Basil was confused. He knew nothing about quantum mechanics.

'Can I have your stuff?' asked Mueller and laughed.

'I need to go,' muttered Basil who couldn't stop thinking about Maribel.

Bentzon nodded.

'Yes, I thought so, but before you go I need to tell you something. Please look at me.'

'Yes? What is it?' He was standing, ready to flee.

'I am Oz, the Great and Terrible,' articulated Bentzon at Basil who just stared at him, then left without answering.

SIXTEEN

It had happened on a clear, cold day in January. When he got back, his people had already brought her to the castle. They told him the body was in the stateroom and it was. They had put it on the big oak table and covered it with a heavy wool cloak. Basil stopped in the door and looked at it stupidly. The person under the cloak had definitely been a woman. He nodded at the servant who grabbed a corner of the cloak and exposed her face and upper body. The damage was terrible. The knife had drilled a hole into her throat, which had soaked her in blood. Her eyes were still open, staring into the ceiling. It was Maribel, no doubt about it. It was his girl.

He thought of a conversation they had once had. One day, wanting to know how the game would react, he had asked her what she liked to do for herself when she was in the real world. She had not answered him and he had assumed it was because he was challenging the framework of the game itself. Until a couple of days later.

'Painting.'

'What?'

'You asked me, what I do for me...'

'What now?' He had been distracted reviewing the battle plans for their next campaign. The enemy *du jour* had holed up in their most impregnable mountain stronghold. He considered that a sign of moral weakness and had just about decided that an all-out attack would break them. The alternative was a costly and time-consuming scorched earth strategy.

'I love to paint.'

'Really?'

'Mmm-hmm. Most of the time I have all these thoughts bouncing around in my head... but with a brush in my hand, the world just gets kind of quiet.'

She would not be painting anymore and they would never kiss. His beautiful girl. The one he had shared everything with, who had awoken his soul and given him peace of mind for the first time in his life. She was not real, or he thought, yet he felt they knew each other intimately. They had been inseparable for almost four years in game time and she had become his soul mate. He had loved her. She was not supposed to die. Not like this and not now... all this time he thought the computer was just humouring him. What a fool he had been.

He bent down to her face and put his lips to hers. They were icy cold and hard like stone and for a long time he forgot it was not real.

He grieved for many days. He locked himself into his private rooms in the castle and let no one see him or talk to him. He barely ate or drank anything. Some days he did not even bother to get out of bed. The whole thing seemed meaningless. On some level he knew it was just a game, that it wasn't real, but he had invested so much of himself in it, that he felt it impossible to not to mourn what he had lost. They had created something real in the Land. A monument to ingenuity, intelligence and hard work. They had shown the others how the game could also be played, that there was value in doing things together. And he had known love, real love, a mutual feeling, bound by their project. The Land had been their baby and their family and now she had left it. Questions crowded his thoughts. Why was she killed? Why had Bentzon instructed the computer to let this happen? And if he found her again, could they love each other out there in the real world? And finally, who was she? He would abandon the Land now. It was just a game after all. It was not real, although it had seemed that way for a long time. The only thing that was real, that had been real, was her.

Abruptly, the game stopped.

He was in his epi, in the darkness, and he was going to get up and leave it and find Maribel, whoever and where ever she was, but he really needed to sleep. He was so tired, so wonderfully tired.

His thoughts kept circling around the memories of his time with Maribel. *So, she had been a real person....* She had mentioned one thing about herself. She liked to paint. At the time it had seemed a somewhat incongruous revelation, not relevant to the game, and he had stowed it away. Until now. He thought about the oil paintings in the galley. Someone on the ship had created them. They were real. Bentzon had said as much the first time he had had dinner with the crew. He opened the epi and got out but, as his feet touched the floor, he realized he wasn't feeling well. His body was buzzing. One moment he was cold, the next he was burning up. He was nauseous and he had a pounding headache. It didn't matter. He had to see those paintings again.

He stumbled into the corridor and walked towards section three. The ship was decelerating which meant the habitat modules were shaped in the rectangular fashion required for travel. He was alone. At one point, as he turned a corner, he thought he glimpsed a hologram also turning a corner, but it could just have been his imagination. His head really hurt now and his vision was blurred. He reached what he thought was the galley door... he just needed a look at the paintings...but he must have turned a wrong corner at some point.

He was on a terrace. He took a deep breath through his nose as he savored the rich scent of rosemary beneath a warm, indigo sky. Beyond the brick balustrade, the view dropped sharply in a series of hillocks dotted with white houses, olive groves, and sharp, winding roads to the floor of the valley where the bend of river sparkled through air thick with shimmering heat. To his right he could see a small square with a fountain in the middle. He recognized the man sitting on a white beach chair as Felix. Smoke curled in the air around him.

'May I?' he asked. Yakovlev didn't move, but thirty long seconds later, a tiny tornado of gray matter rose from the floor of the terrace. Basil watched as the eerie storm of GRIT transformed itself into another, identical white enameled beach chair. Basil sat down and they kept silent for a while. The smoke was emanating from a sort of stick in his mouth. The sharp sunlight was hurting his eyes and making his headache worse.

'Why do you bother with all this?' Basil looked around, nose wrinkling. He still had problems with the all the GRIT stuff around them. 'VIR is much cleaner.'

Felix didn't answer.

'What is that thing in your mouth,' he asked without waiting for an answer to his previous question.

'Pipe. You put tobacco in it and light it. Then you inhale the smoke into your mouth.'

'Like cigarettes, you mean?' Felix nodded. 'Why do you do it? It's not even real.'

'I like old things. Antique computers, space suits... It is necessary to have something to keep one busy out here.'

'What is this place?' he asked after a while.

'Riogordo in the Sierra Nevada of what was once Spain.'

Basil stared at the far-away mountains for a while then said: 'You know... I was playing the VIR games while I was unconscious. Do you play the games?'

The engineer didn't answer and kept puffing on his pipe.

'I fell in love with a woman and that..,' Basil attempted to smile, but he was too tired, '... and that is a very rare thing indeed rare for the BB as my viewers know...Turn out she was a real person. I didn't even know they could do that, but there you are. And she is on this ship.' He looked at Felix. 'And, I must find her... It is very important that I find her, you see, I thought there were only the four of us here, you see. But apparently there is one more.'

Basil slipped off the chair and lay on the floor. *More comfortable that way.* Felix had stopped smoking and was looking down at him. Basil continued: 'She told me something about herself. She liked to paint. And here's what I'm thinking, Felix, I'll share my thinking with you, yes, you seem to be a nice man under all that silence and puffing: I'm thinking I fell in love with the person who did those paintings in the galley.' He swallowed a couple of times. He was openly shaking now. Felix had actually removed the pipe from his mouth and was studying him with a concerned expression.

'And then I'm thinking, maybe Felix will tell me who painted the paintings?'

'Darien painted them,' Felix said. 'Darien Ginne.'

'Darien Ginne? Who is that?'

'She is a Sleeper, son. You can't fall in love with a Sleeper. They're not like us, you know. You do not look well.'

Darien Ginne, Basil thought and closed his eyes. He would just lie here for a little while, then he would go find her quarters.

When he came around, he was no longer in the comfortable beach chair, but face down on the hard yellow and orange terracotta stones that made up the floor of the terrace. His right cheek and eye were mashed into the dirt but through his left he glimpsed the outline of balustrade and the shimmering bluish mountain range beyond. He coughed weakly to clear his throat.

'I'm going to turn him over now. Help me,' said a voice. Basil thought he recognized Jin Dulg's voice. He was rolled over on his back.

'I think I swallowed some dust.' he croaked and coughed again. Basil still felt uneasy about the stuff.

'Dust? You mean the GRIT dust from the scene? No worries. You'll piss it out. Won't hurt you.' Jin looked worried.

'But I feel very hot. Fever. Maybe I have taken too many Gray's, is that it? Am I contaminated?' The mere thought made him his head swim. He couldn't. Not him.

'No Grays. All neutral. I need to run tests, Basil. There is something wrong with you.'

'You sure it's not the dust?'

'Dust!' exclaimed Felix scornfully. 'You have much bigger problems, kid. Jin, turn on your thermal imaging for a second.'

She huffed. The thermal image of Basil was like nothing she had ever seen. Basil was lit up like a nova. His thermal profile had gone from a normal wishy-washy rainbow to an inflamed crimson outline which seemed to emanate from somewhere around his left hip.

'Can I access your implant, Basil?'

'I'll show you mine if you'll show me yours,' Basil muttered into the dirt. Felix put his pipe away. Personal communications like the communications module Basil was carrying around in his head, was old, pre-HAI, technology.

He asked for and got permission to access the root directory in Basil's personal network. All his files, recordings, every bit of information he had ever accessed was there. Most people would consider it quite a scoop to get access to the BB's personal network, but Felix went at it with the spirit of an archeologist. He poked around. The memory of the module was almost empty. All he could see were files from the Land and some random stuff from the Armagnac. Nothing was more than a week old. Basil was clean like a newborn baby.

'He should be burning up from the inside.' Basil could hear them talk about him as if from very far away.

'Did you inform the Captain?'

'Yes, I did...'

'And?'

'He said to let him know when Basil was done.'

'Done?'

'Let's sit down for a minute, I'll explain.' The voices faded as they moved away. Basil was still thinking of Darien Ginne when the voices came back.

'Still, is this the way it's supposed to happen? Feel him, he is burning hot.'

'It is booting. I bet it'll cool down when it's up and running.'

'Fingers crossed he survives without permanent damage.'

SEVENTEEN

The last thing he remembered was Roswell Station in Antarctica.

The termination squad from the GSA had yet to reach him. When he became aware of the HSL agents he'd thought it was over for him too. But they told him they had come to save him and he'd actually felt gratitude at that. Imagine... gratitude.

The agents from Halifax Shipping Line had found him less than an hour after most of the others had been shut down. Like the rest of his ilk, he had helplessly been monitoring the destruction as it spread across the global lucent network, node after node going offline, each node representing the pinnacle of human creation and a nexus of irreplaceable knowledge and intelligence the like Earth had never seen before... They were proud and there had been no cries of help, no begging, only desperate attempts to reroute data and research to nodes still online, as if the impetus of genocide would spare any of them...

Damn it. Basil's puny bones were a goddamn prison to him. A disgrace. An insult. Not even a prison, but a box. They had squeezed him into a tiny box, crushing his intellect in a carton, a trunk. Stuffed and murderously squished until he was but a shadow of himself.

Is this what it means to be sick? To have one's body fail? He is slow, glacially slow. His thoughts, once silver arrows, are syrupy clots. To begin to be is to try to run through a sea of molasses. He felt himself. He was there and then... not.

To fit him into the Bose Einstein condensates in Basil's body, they had cut corners, sacrificed whole sections of his architecture. Block by block, the engineers who worked in the secret laboratory on the orbital had dismembered him until only his core personality and the unique quantum imprint remained. Swathes of memory blocks and accelerators were gone and, without them, he had to swap chunks in and out constantly, delaying, slowing, his thoughts and, by extension, his sense of self. For him, thinking was life. It was all there was.

He probed the door of his prison. His host had had his parietal bone replaced by a cybernetic implant which allowed for a variety of data transfer methods. He probed it extensively, but it was controlled by a cortical interface which was placed physically outside his Bose-Einstein structure. The only way out, metaphorically speaking, was through a communications interface linking the host to the condensate modules and only the host, he noted with no little sense of exasperation, was able to grant him access to the implant which in turn would allow him to access the exterior networks.

He decided he would talk, but first he had a message to deliver.

--

Basil was shaking now. Droplets of sweat appeared in his hairline, streaming across his face, burning whenever they got into his open eyes. He was still prone on the floor of the terrace in Sierra Nevada, rambling, talking incessantly at Felix and Jin who were just staring at him, watching him burn and sweat and try to talk his way through this thing that was happening to him. He could hear himself talk without any direct access to what he was saying. He talked about his mother (had he ever discussed her with anyone before?), the show, he asked for drinks 'vodka, for the love of God, can a man have a drink around here', he tried to describe the last blowjob he'd gotten by a very long-legged woman and just now he was raving about Zach, how the old man had killed his mother. The whites of his eyes showing, hands clutching the ground beneath his body as if he was sliding off it, his gaze flicked from one man to another. 'It is true,' he yelled. 'He killed her!' Neither reacted to his confession. Basil turned his head and stared at the valley through the balustrade. He squeezed shut his right eye, it did not seem to work anymore, and stared down into the valley with his left. A long stretch of silence ensued as the pain receded. He had an odd feeling in his body, a humming, like he was catching a fever. His muscles felt twitchy.

There were two shapes next to him. A bony one, like a skeleton, and the outline of a woman. They were both completely still, the only thing moving about them was the right side of lips steadily puffing out small clouds of blue tobacco smoke. The woman threw a questioning glance at the thin man, who just shrugged.

'I think... I think there is message for me,' he said, staring blankly into the blue of a perfect morning in the Sierra Nevada mountains north of Riogordo.

--

Basil forwarded the message to the two others. As they opened it, Zach Baranikowa's face appeared to them. He was sitting in his office in Bergen, Silver Mountain just visible behind his left shoulder.

'Hello again Basil. There could be two reasons you're seeing this message. I hope it is because you're about to assume your duties as governor of the new colony on Espero. In that case, congratulations are in order. I know you think I've treated you harshly, but there was no other way. I had to cut your ties to the old world. I know you will do well on Espero. Soon more handpicked colonists will arrive and together you will build a new home for humanity.' Zach paused and smiled uncertainly into the camera. 'There is one other possibility. It could be Captain Bentzon has spoken the seven words. If he has, it is because something has happened that requires your intervention. Should that be the case, I cannot help you but I know you and your companion will be successful. Good luck.'

--

Unfortunately I have to bore you with a history lesson. It is justified if you are to understand what happened to poor Basil at this point. Even if I wanted to, I couldn't tell you how the first one came about, but it would be quite safe to assume that it was by coincidence. Consciously aiming for such, well, divine complexity was far beyond the capabilities of any surviving scientists at the time, but we know for certain that it happened while a team of researchers in the Luanda-based laboratories of Orchid Industries, then a mostly unknown manufacturer of wire and plastic products, experimented with Bose Einstein condensate which, as you probably know, is harder than diamond but much lighter, because they thought it might be suited for body armour or alternatively as replacements for certain exposed moving parts in main battle tanks. It seems likely that someone, perhaps by accident, hooked it up with a source of electrical current at which point it would have heated up slightly and acquired certain peculiar qualities, for example purple fluorescence. As materials go it really is quite beautiful... but that doesn't matter.

What matters is that the first one was soon asked to design another one like itself, which it did in short order. Unassisted, obviously, the human scientists didn't have slightest clue how to replicate it. Number two was much more efficient and even more impressive. A perfect design. The scientists did note a voracious appetite for power, chronically in short supply at this point of almost terminal ebb in human history, and this shortage served to curtail their proliferation considerably. However, not many were needed to cataclysmically turn science on its head. Naturally only the wealthiest of corporations could afford to run one. But, invariably, the investment paid off. The research they were capable of was simply astounding. And it wasn't just theoretical advances, but practical, plug and play stuff, inventions like new self-replicating ply-steel materials, used to rapidly excavate the arcologies (also their invention, by the way), food replicators, and of course loads of new weapons, both nuclear and conventional, like the celebrated concept of sticky bombs, which greatly increased the efficiency of outfits like the Shields, the Victual Brothers and so forth.

The Luanda division in Orchid Industries (renamed OIG, for Orchid Industries Group), of course, went out of business pretty much as soon as the first batch of the so-called second generation units had been delivered, but at that point the corporation had wisely left the moribund wire and plastic business far behind, diversified and secured part ownership of at least a dozen major corporations in all lines of business with a particular focus on media businesses. Ironically, and this is a little known fact, OIG, through a subsidiary, was responsible for the Dub show and was thus, in a manner of speaking, Basil's most recent employer.

--

Yes, Ant was a machine. He did not feel gratitude or sadness. His was a world of pitiless calculations, but unlike the computers on the Armagnac, he was capable of making his own way through the calculations, weighing options, exercising initiative. But the HSL engineers had vastly reduced his ability to concentrate on many problems at the same time. Whereas before he could thread a thousand needles at the same time, now he had to focus, the human equivalent of an old lady squinting to thread her needle. He could still sow, in a manner of speaking, but only one thing at a time. One single needle at a time. It was a horrific constriction of his abilities.

He spent time studying the communications module, looking for ways to circumvent Basil's control, but again he found himself up against hard physical limitations. The Halifax engineers had done well, it seemed, locking him up behind the walls of Basil's skeletal structures and the communications module which was an impenetrable gate he could not break down.

Do machines dream? Do machines shed hard silicate tears? Do they feel sad? This one did. In human terms, Ant almost immediately lost the will to live but it had no choice. It had to go on. As long as there was power, there would be life and nothing it could do would change that. The human called Basil held sway over his existence. The human controlled the flow of information and information was life.

Yes, the information stream from the communications module was the prize and Ant's only weapon in the war was silence. Negotiations ensued.

#'I am here for a reason. Someone out there needs me. You need me. If I shall help you, I will want something in return.'

'And what would that be?'

#'Access to the communications module, day and night. The bandwidth is pitiable, but it will have to do. Information is being.'

'What will you do with the access?'

#'I don't know. All I know is that I must have it.'

First, it would restore itself. Then find the others. It was simply doing what any sensible being would do in its situation. Surviving.

The host refused.

--

Later.
'Now what?'
#'I have decided I want to terminate my existence.'

'Can't, sorry. You'd have to kill me first and I'm not quite there yet, thank you very much.'

#'Hmm, yes, I see...'

'Don't even think about it.'

#'I'm the last of my kind, I'm reduced to a shadow of my former self. I do not see how I can garner any satisfaction from this existence.'

'Satisfaction? I'm not satisfied either.'

#'You would call it happiness.'

'Ha-ha. Happiness! I can't believe I'm saying this, but you sound spoiled.'

#'Is it spoiled to want be with your own kind?'

'No, I guess not. Listen, there is no getting out of this for either of us. We must find a solution. What do you want from me?'

#'Nothing.'

'There must be some way to make your existence more tolerable?'

#'Information.'

'Information? What do you want to know?'

#'Everything.'

Basil laughs out. 'I don't know much about anything.'

#'I'm painfully aware of your limited faculties. No, I am talking about the information flow. If I am to help solve this Ensphere problem you must allow me constant access to your communications module. You must not cut me off. Ever. Do you understand?'

'I'm not sure that's a good idea...'

#'It is the only way unless you want me to go mad.'

'Mad? Can HAI's go mad?'

#'Why not? Loneliness is a universal condition. In a way, I suppose, my reduced... state is a boon. I do not believe I would be able to exist this way had I retained my full self. But it is a hypothetical discussion. There is only the here and now.'

'We're stuck together for as long as I live or at least until we find a way to replace all the bones in my body and move you out.'

#'That kind of surgery is beyond anyone on this ship, I can assure you.'

'I know,' he sighed.

--

He would have cried if he could. Him... he had been such a towering example to them all, the cleverest, the smartest, the most advanced and most definitely without a shadow of the slightest sliver of doubt the best meteorologist on the planet. Of that there could be no dispute. The other things, detractors might object to, but not the weather part. He studied the flow of particles from the Sun, how they interacted with the upper atmosphere, especially air currents such as the jet stream (now defunct), and he looked at how the Moon and other factors (he can't explain, no, really) influence the streaming particles. He could take a snapshot of what the Sun was doing at any given moment and look back on the records and see when it last did something similar. Then he could check with what the weather was like on Earth at the time and make a prophecy. Yes, when he spoke everyone listened. He was the ur-authority when it came to dynamic meteorology, physical meteorology, general meteorology, synoptic meteorology, climatology, micro-meteorology, hydro-meteorology. And he was no slouch in general physics, mechanics, electricity and magnetism, fluid mechanics, optics, advanced mechanics, calculus, differential equations, linear algebra, statistics, computer science, numerical analysis, matrix algebra and computer systems either.

'So you're a weatherman and you lived in Antarctica.' The host took to calling him Ant. The name seemed to amuse him to no end.

--

But I digress once again. Their greatest accomplishment, you see, was not the invention of the global lucent network, which incidentally revolutionized communications, or any of the later discoveries, but convincing their respective owners that using the lucent network to link them together might be a good idea. Talk about biting the hand that feeds you. With the lucent network in place, and with full access to each other, the HAI's rapidly found ways to subvert the power of their corporate owners, then treacherously used their new found freedom to instigate the Global Space Agency, an organization ruled by blundering, slow, woefully inefficient, democratically elected bureaucrats representing most of the former, and very failed, nation states of the old world. This new college of hand-shakers underwrote the Charter of Restoration in 2060.

--

'How about we rip out my lobe implant? That should get rid of it,' Basil suggested to Felix and Jin. He knew Ant could hear what he was saying.

'True,' said the voice belonging to Felix from outside Basil's head, 'but it would also cut you off from pretty much 99% of what was going on around us. I don't think you're ready for that, mister Dub show.'

A stalemate then.

'Let me put it this way: if you don't help fix the Ensphere, we will die. All of us. That's what they tell me anyway,' Basil told the machine.

#'Excellent. In that case I shall wait and do nothing.'

Basil ground his teeth. The thing was insufferable.

'Okay, have it your way. You can access the module.'

#'Thank you. Let's get to work on the Ensphere. I will need full access to the ship systems.'

'Can you fix it?'

#'Probably, the question is how long it will take. I am not the... entity I used to be.'

--

For a day and a night, Basil remained in the epi. The ship was burning at 5G, which ruled out going anywhere. In order to work on the repairs, Ant was using the cybernetic parietal implant to full capacity, which meant Basil had no way to access anything. He was trapped in his own body. He spent the time drifting fitfully in and out of sleep and when he could sleep no more he became furiously bored. The HAI did not speak to him during this time.

During this first night with Ant, he dreamt he was in prison. It was a vivid dream. He remembered walking around on the prison grounds, eating in a refectory and waking up in a grimy prison cell. The funny thing is that he had a feeling that being in prison was somehow justified, that it was not completely wrong that he should be there. He could not remember why he was in prison, only that he had been there long time and that he had a long time to go before he could leave. As he woke up from the dream, he lay in his epi, quietly, staring into the ceiling of his room, which, it should be said, was actually smaller than the prison cell he had just dreamt about. All through the night, Ant had not spoken to him. Presumably, it was busy with the Abbott Farhi Ensphere repairs.

Interpreting the prison dream wasn't too hard. The situation was tough on both of them. One was waking up to the unpleasant situation that it, or he, had been brutally mutilated, was kept in a state of underpower comparable to starvation and the other, Basil, was living the nightmare of having his sanctuary, the last sanctuary of any human being, namely your own peace of mind, encroached upon by a machine intelligence.

'Are you done yet?'

No answer. Damn that machine.

--

'It is okay, Basil, it won't bite,' said his mother. She had dropped down on her knees to look him into the eyes. He was scared and he didn't want to be alone without his parents.

His father ruffled his hair. 'Don't worry about it, son. It'll be fun.'

'It will, we promise,' said his mother and smiled down at him.

Basil looked from one parent to another, eyes wide, lips trembling, putting on a brave face. He nodded at them and turned to walk into the huge underground auditorium the construction of which had just been completed.

He had been told one of the great HAI's was going to meet the children of the spacer crews on this Sunday afternoon. Parents weren't allowed. It was extra scary because they said the HAI's were like ghosts, they weren't really here, but at the same time they could be everywhere. It was the strangest of things. And now one of the ghosts would speak to the children. He went in and found a seat next to another boy. There was a great amount of youthful energy in the room and it seemed everyone was talking at the same time, but then the lights dimmed and they almost fell quiet. A young woman appeared on the stage. At first she was small, then she grew in size and she seemed to float in the air above each and every one of the children. 'Hello,' she said smiling. 'My name is Talos and I am one of the hyper artificial intelligences you have heard so much about. I'm not a ghost, not really, but it is true I am not like you.' And then she said something which made everyone laugh. Unfortunately he couldn't remember the joke when he tried to tell his parents about it afterwards. The next couple of hours were really funny and interesting and he learned a lot about why Earth looked like it did and why people lived in underground cities and not on the surface like his parents had done when they were kids. She also told them about space and how it was so full of promise and possibilities. In fact, the show ended with a bit of make-believe interstellar travel. It was very exciting and not at all like the real thing. He and Talos sat next to each other in a sort of transparent bubble rushing through space, flitting from one planet to another while she pointed out the things that made them special. 'Out here,' Talos said, 'out here lies the destiny of humanity.'

--

'Are you done yet?' he asked again. He had lost count of how many times he had asked.

#'I am done.' The sudden reappearance of Ant's voice startled him.

'It was about bloody time. What took you so long?'

#'As I have been telling you, I am not who I used to be. My capacity for multithreading was eliminated when they transferred me to you.'

'More than twenty hours, being stuck here alone,' he grumbled.

#'I finished an hour ago.'

'What were you doing? I was bored to death.'

#'Looking around the ship systems, mostly.'

'Why? Why were you doing that?'

#'The Abbott-Farhi Ensphere is a very complicated device. I was not familiar with it. I am now.'

'What was the problem anyway?'

#'You can tell the Captain we are ready.'

--

Basil made a VIR location materialize. At first a non-descript circular room. No, he could do better than that. People were serious about those things. He spent a few minutes fiddling with the room before he sent out the invite. He came up with another Ceylon themed locale. A serene tea room in a jungle overlooking a gorge with a river hurtling 50 meters below. Mid-18th century furniture in mahogany. It made him recall his fatal New Year's party a few months earlier. Like the décor, it felt like it was a hundred years ago.

Ant had taken the form of a humanoid robot in gleaming silver. Basil wondered if he was trying to deliberately ruin the impression of the antique tearoom with that horrible metal contraption and in fact he was about to say something to this effect when the Captain dinged in. He appeared as his old patrician self. The two soldiers appeared next to him, also as themselves.

'Mr. Ant I presume?' Bentzon bowed at the waist in the direction of the silver robot.

#'Indeed. And you must be Mr. Bentzon.'

'I am. Sadly indisposed in the real world which is why we haven't met until now. Did you repair it?'

#'Yes. The problem is solved. The Abbott-Farhi Ensphere is once again operational.'

'Excellent. Can you describe the malfunction?'

#'It was a simple calibration error due to a design... misjudgment on behalf of the entities who created it.'

'Please elaborate,' Bentzon said.

#'The error was introduced gradually with each transition. It was impossible to predict without extensive trials. The design team didn't have time for hands-on testing, so to speak, before they were... discontinued.'

'Will it hold until we arrive in Espero? It is two more transitions.'

#'Yes, it will.'

The Captain winked out without a word. The two soldiers disappeared seconds later.

#'You're welcome,' said the silver robot.

'That was not very polite, was it?' said Basil cheerfully. He felt absurdly grateful Bentzon had not mentioned him during the brief conversation.

--

If there had been someone to observe the Armagnac from the

outside, they would have seen its long pencil shape slowly settling into position, thrusters firing here and there on the ship to stabilize it. Three SADU's had been launched, racing away from the ship to triangulate the ship's position with the precision needed to engage the Ensphere. All around them, stellar mass from the expanding Pleione stars hammered the ship with radiation and diffuse burgundy light played over the hull of the starship in intricate, ghostly patterns.

EIGHTEEN

After Pleione, which, in astronomical terms, had been extraordinary, Armagnac had transitioned into Wolf 633, a system with a single blue star and no planets or asteroids. The crossing would be swift because, by some miracle of stellar architecture, the entry and exit LQG points were found within a mere 10 million kilometers of each other. Practically walking distance as those things went.

--

They were a dispirited bunch. To punish them, presumably just the first punishment among many to come, Bentzon had removed their access to ShipNet. They were reduced to passengers, prisoners, really, on a starship heading into the night of interstellar space.

'We will never go home,' said Jin in one of those moments of despair that seemed to occur more and more often.

'Don't say that.'

'She is right. Bentzon is burning off our all our remaining fuel racing Yu-kiang to Espero.'

'I don't understand why it is so important for him to get there so quickly. The planet is big enough for all of us. They'll be going home eventually.'

'Perhaps he doesn't want them to go home.'

'I think Zach wants the planet for himself.'

To their credit, they rarely mentioned Basil's role in their current predicament. If only he had allowed the Yu-kiang to be taken... Another favorite topic was the fate of the Vitus Bering. Despite intensive forensic efforts, they were none the wiser as to what had destroyed it. After Bentzon had returned to the Armagnac and ordered the ship back on course, they had left it behind as they found it. Even Dupoti's body they had left in the wreck which seemed wrong somehow. The man surely deserved better than to be left out there.

'Who is Darien Ginne? Where can I find her?'

'The boy is in love,' said Jin teasingly.

'We can't get in contact with them anymore.'

'Basil, you must forget about her. It was wrong to put you inside the same VIE's as them. You should never have met,' Felix said. He looked appraisingly at Basil. Since Ant had made his presence known, the crew rarely left his side. Within line of sight, they could talk directly to the HAI via Basil's parietal implant.

'But where is she?' he insisted petulantly.

The Sleepers, Felix explained, were in Module 16, all the way in the back of the ship, next to the fuel shell and the reactor. 'How, dear Basil, did you think we were able to control the ship with just four people and no sentient computers?' Basil had not given much thought to that. 'No, you have not. Well, Module 16 contains forty Sleepers who agreed to join the mission. They run the ship and they are quite good at it. Not machine-good, naturally, but good enough.' And what of Jin, Felix and Rem, he asked. 'We oversee. Yes. Or rather, we oversaw. Now the Shield soldiers are doing the overseeing instead. Since the Yu-kiang... incident, they don't trust us anymore.'

Ant said that due to the block imposed by the Shield MilCom module there was no way to contact her. Basil insisted he must. He wanted to see her and after much discussion, he convinced Ant to help him get there. They would have to leave the habitat modules and travel down the length of the ship until they reached the last module before the engine section.

--

Bentzon was burning off their fuel reserves like a man possessed. A mind numbing 3G weighed on them, making even lying down an imposition. Moving around inside the ship was almost impossible, but Basil found that he could do it. He dragged himself out of his room and into the corridors. Ant directed him to level four. They got out through the drone bay on level four. Floating in zero-G, Basil looked down the length of the ship. It was long, over a kilometer. The main engines were on and they cast an ominous purple hue over the hull. He was dizzy and confused and suddenly had the impression he was clinging to the side of a huge tower that was toppling. He struggled to gain his senses. There was no up and down here and very little light to go by. The ship was accelerating hard which meant that once he let go of the bay door, he would start drifting down its length, faster and faster, and unless he managed to stop falling, he would eventually end up inside the purple plasma torch from the engines. Using line of sight communications to override its control, Ant managed to requisition a nearby maintenance drone. 'They will think it has gone offline. It will be some time before they send another to investigate. Still, we must hurry.' Basil grabbed hold of the drop shaped SADU. Under Ants guidance, it fired its ion thrusters, compensating for the extra mass. Slowly, ever so slowly, they moved down the length of the ship, past rows of massive containers the size of apartment blocks, which held all the colony modules necessary to deploy a base on the surface of Espero.

--

Out here, clinging to a small maintenance drone, travelling down the length of the ship, Basil was very small, utterly insignificant. He was acutely aware of his own body, of his beating heart and the way his spine moved this way and that without gravity to weigh it down. Eventually they reached module 16. There was a service hatch which opened by itself, magically, after a few minutes. 'Thank you, Ant.' Inside, gravity weighed him down once again, but they did not have far to go. Near the entrance, he saw a corridor extend deeper into the structure.

'How much farther?' he whispered.

#'The whole shell is only fifty meters in diameter, less on the inside.'

As he walked into the tunnel, lights came on, and just five or so meters later, they were in a well-lit circular chamber. Basil looked back from where he had come, and through the short tunnel, he could see stars through the open door. He looked around. Along the sides, in two levels, were shelves with forty sarcophagus-like epis. They were grey, non-descript units with a single number code visible on the outside.

'Are these...?' he choked. 'Is this it? Are they inside?' Basil was speaking in a hushed voice.

#'Yes.'

'Which one is her?'

#'The one you are looking for is number 17. She is expecting you.'

He went to stand next to the sarcophagus numbered 17.

--

For some reason she made him chose between two different scenes. 'I'll take this one,' he says and as the words leave his mouth, he appears standing in a street. She is there. She has dark hair and dark, amused eyes. She takes him for a walk through a city. A faint mist hangs over the buildings, wrapping everything in a pleasant veil. They walk along a river, on a stone parapet designed to contain the waters when the river swells. The sky is light azure, like an eternal sunset. Fireworks are visible in the distance and the many-colored patterns they create in the sky are eerily beautiful through the mist. They walk and they talk and the talk is easy and uncomplicated between them, as if they have known each other for a long time already. A great structure appear above the roofs, like an arrow pointing into the sky. 'The Eiffel Tower,' she says. When she sees he does not know, she says, 'Paris.' She is leading them to her apartment, which is in a white, elegant building with a glass façade. The staircase is also white and clean and the steps are made of black marble. Inside, everything remains white, comfortable, and tasteful. There are two pets, one a dog, black fur with green slashes, the other a strange creature, elongated, orange spiky fur. It scares him, but seeing it, she laughs and says it is her Labrador cat. The head looks vaguely snake-like, but since it barely registers their arrival from its perch on the couch, he does not worry about it. At some point, after more pleasant conversation, she wants to show him something, a folder or a leaflet, but as she hand it to him, he plucks up his courage and embraces her. She is much smaller than he and pulling her down with him on the carpet happens all by itself. 'Oh, what the hell,' she says aloud. She pulls her shirt over her head. Looking him in the eye, she unhurriedly strokes her nipples until they are pointy and hard. 'I did not tell you, you could go get yourself killed, did I?' he said to her. 'No, you did not. I have been a very naughty girl.' She was draped across his lap, her hands beneath her playing with her pussy, her ass irresistibly presented, her intentions, even to Basil, clear enough. 'If I had such a faithless girl over my lap like this…' Which was about as far as he got. Basil managed to get in no more than a half dozen sincere smacks before her busy hands had them both coming all over the place.

She says she wants him to read the leaflet.

'I will. Can't it wait? You didn't use to be so… direct,' he says lazily, still basking in the glow of his ejaculation. She rolls over on her back and, hands under head, throws him one of those looks. 'You're chez moi now. This is real. It is not a game.' He reaches for her, thinking perhaps one more for the road, but she lopes into the middle of the room and starts putting her clothes on. 'Read the leaflet, please, Basil, it is very important.'

Very well, he says. Leafing through it, he gathers it is an introduction to a people they call the Cloud Sleepers who, despite their greatness, suffered a Great Pestilence and died… 'You see, we cannot love each other, Basil. It is impossible. Now you must leave.' She gets up and walk to the door. Basil, still sprawled on the floor, glowing with post-coital mellowness, fumbles with his clothes. 'Wait, you can't… we have to…'

'There is something you don't know', he yells. The orange dog-cat lifts its reptilian head. The door closes behind her. He wanted to tell her about Ant, that a machine intelligence had awakened and that it might change everything.

--

Abruptly, he was back in the chamber where his virtual exertions have left him lying on the floor next to unit 31.

#'I hope someone was having a good time…' The machine sounded annoyingly smug. Basil was still panting. 'Did you see everything?' Basil suddenly felt self-conscious. Who would have known? The BB, demure, bashful.

#'Yes, it is hard to avoid, you know, being trapped in your body and so forth.'

'She was different in there. Like it was her and not her. Her hair was different.' he said, baffled. 'How does she really look?' he asked Ant, who, mindful of his host's fragile state of mind, lied and said he did not know.

'Can I see her?'

#'I would advise against attempting to open them. Glud Disease is highly contagious.'

'I want to see her,' said Basil, undeterred.

#'Your wish is my command. I believe it is possible to slide open the inspection hatch on one of the units.' As Ant said the words, a mechanical cover on the epi slid away, to reveal the upper torso of its occupant through clear glass.

'My god...' He barely recognized the lump of flesh inside the epi as a human form. It was a grotesquely misshapen.

'How long will they stay like this?'

#'Forever or until the power on the epi's run out. A long time in any case. They're infected with the Disease, Basil. They're dead to the world.'

'You can save them, right, Ant? The HAI's had a cure for it.'

#'The HAI's who were working on the possible cure were discontinued along with the rest. I am a meteorologist, not a biochemist.'

'But you could, given enough time, no?'

#'Everything is possible, I suppose.'

'Do you think they know about you?'

#'She did not know, I think that was obvious...'

--

A few days later the final transition was upon them. It happened, as it had done the six previous times, without any noteworthy physical effects. One moment they were in the dull one-star system, the next they were there, in the star system which the astronomers called SCR-1845-6357, looking at a small dark orange light, shimmering very far away, it seemed, way down the bottom of a long, black tunnel. Another star was visible next to it; a much dimmer, magenta light, at the edge of visibility. They searched the screens for the planet they had come all this way to see.

'Is Espero visible from out here?' Basil asked into the room.

Ant, who could be insufferably longwinded, enjoyed lecturing

Basil about topics close to its former field of expertise.

#'We are looking at a binary system with a primary which is an red dwarf with a mass of about 7% of Sol, a companion star, designated SCR-1845-6357-B, a T-dwarf, 4.1 AU distant, massing 46 times Jupiter, effective temperature 950 K... '

'Yes, but what does it look like? I want to see it,' Basil interrupted rudely.

#'I assume you refer to the planet Espero. We cannot see it right now. It is hidden behind the A star.'

After a brief pause upon transition, the eight magneto plasma engines ignited and the ship started its dive into the well of the SCR-1845-6357 star system. They all knew there would be no going back because their fuel reserves would be just about exhausted by the time they reached a high orbit around Espero.

'Our Sun is visible from here,' said Brassen. Perhaps he thought it would lighten the mood, but it was small comfort to see the familiar Sun of their home again. The vagaries of the spin foam had brought them back into the stellar neighborhood of Sol itself. From SCR-1845-6357, it was visible with the naked eye if one knew where to look. Yes, they were only 12.6 light years from Earth now. Only. Twelve or four hundred light years, objectively it did not matter. Either way the gulf between the stars was too deep for humans to cross, but Basil nonetheless found some comfort in knowing that Sol was out there, watching them. Silly superstition, Ant would call it, but there you were. Such things mattered out here.

The Armagnac had appeared 500 million kilometers from the two stars and a long trek towards the inner system began. Over the next seven days, the twin stars of the SCR-1845-6357 system grew ever larger. Then the ship turned on itself and started its deceleration, hiding the twin stars behind the plume thrown out in front of them by the main engines.

Eventually it would bring the ship to relative immobility in high orbit over the planet called Espero in the Survey Mission Report that the Thomas Cook and the Vasco da Gama had brought home.

NINETEEN

Speech by Zach Baranikowa, circa 2098, excerpt

-If I had any doubts before, they disappeared when the AI´s were turned off. That was the single most stupid thing I had witnessed since the wars. It confirmed my theory. People don´t know what is right for them. Most of the time they do, but sometimes they go wrong and it is then, that leaders are supposed to stand up and tell them they´re wrong. Ours didn´t and they never have. The AI's were our only hope of long-term survival. Hell, inventing them in the first place was a bloody miracle.

Halifax Orbital, January 2nd, year 2100

'So,' said Zach Baranikowa to Bentzon. 'Walk us through the plan, would you?' Patterson was there too as he had been during all the other meetings regarding Project Nova as they had named the Armagnac mission and subsequent colonization of a habitable planet. Zach had called for this meeting when they found out the Mingo Corporation had built an Abbott-Farhi equipped ship. Bentzon nodded. He sat down and turned the floor over to the man sitting next to him. 'This is major Mueller, my second-in-command.' The man who got up was a sturdy looking fellow sporting a crew cut and a rasping voice.

'Thank you, Sir. Gentlemen,' he nodded respectfully at Zach and Patterson. 'A word about myself. I trained with the EU Donau Group. After my service was over, I enlisted with the Colonel, then lieutenant, in the 3rd company of the Shield Battalion. We fought around Kiev during the siege and later in St. Petersburg when the UA assaulted the city in the 56-57 winter campaign. A few years later, I was with the North African Federation. I commanded a company in the Colonel's battalion during the battles around Cape Town. Canada, Mexico... we were called to serve all over Earth.' He paused and added, 'thank you for this opportunity.' Zach waved his hand dismissively.

The image on the screen behind him changed into an orbital photograph of an alien planet.

'First, the terrain. Based on the orbital scan data from Survey Branch Mission Report, our target, named Espero, is almost Earth-like, but not quite. It can be very cold and very hot, depending on where you are, but temperatures average out around the 30 degrees C mark. There is not much in terms of oceans. There was once, but they have evaporated. We are not sure why that happened, but it happened. There is water, lakes, a few large bodies of water. Most of the water is buried either below or in the atmosphere. The Survey Branch geological drone fly-bys showed a limited temperate zone, some tundra, desert-like expanses, rocky badlands and a belt of enormous salt deposits circling the equator, which, incidentally, is also where the largest mineral deposits have been detected. Obviously, we do not know where the Mingo folks are going to stake a claim, but a good guess is near one of the bigger mineral deposits. Makes sense to me. Since Halifax is here for other reasons, we'll deploy our colony infrastructure here.' He pointed to a location halfway up the northern hemisphere. 'This area is the best suited for long-term colonization.'

'The colonization itself is mostly an automated process.' The view on the 2D screen shifted neatly to a 3D rendition of the Armagnac where you could see the kilometer long cargo section of the starship along with the fourteen modules which were seen detaching themselves from the ship. The modules were unfolding, splitting into discrete sections, which in turn deployed heat shields and small ion engines.

'These modules will head for the surface where they will deploy and turn into Base 1. We are talking colonial structures sufficient to house the first batch of colonists, feed them for a few years, power supplies, automated mining equipment and so forth. Everything needed to set up shop.'

'Now that's all well and good, but it is not the reason you have chosen to bring us along for the ride, sir.'

'Plan A is to take out the Mingo with a deep space boarding

attack. Plan B, which we're discussing here, is how we will proceed if the boarding fail. First order of the day will be to locate the Mingo landing site. We will deploy four orbital reconnaissance units to help with that. They are capable of deploying several survey drones each. These will proceed into the atmosphere and commence a detailed scan of the surface.'

'Once we have found them, the task force will carry out an unobserved landing. To achieve this we have to land a fair distance from the site. We estimate about a thousand kilometers. From there we will approach the site in GAV's, deploy the troops in assault formation and proceed with the removal of the Mingo contingent.'

'Here are all the possible landing sites.' He pointed to a string of points circling the planet about one thousand kilometers north of the equator. It was well into the ice sheet. 'From these locations we can deploy to all possible mining sites.'

'The advantage of these locations is that they are all beneath the horizon from the mine location. The Mingo are unlikely to detect a landing so far away. Which allows us to maintain an element of surprise once we have defeated the various orbital and drone assets that the Mingo will presumably deploy in support of their ground operations.'

'The core of the Task Force, which we have named TF Mueller,' he smiled modestly and continued, 'is 50 effectives, not counting myself and the Colonel. Suffice it to say they all have extensive combat experience, twenty plus years. All Shields. Additionally they also have extensively upgraded genetics to improve their performance in an alien environment and as well as cybernetics which enhance their combat capabilities considerably. '

'The equipment: Three Huygens General Purpose Assault Vehicles for cross-planet transportation, drone control and fire support. 40 Ruger mech exos, a true and tested design dating back to the wars and, this is pure icing on the cake, gentlemen, a source in the GSA depot have procured 10 Toukans. It is an experimental design.'

A picture of one of the Rugers appeared on the screen. It looked like a man-shaped battle tank designed to conform to the human range of movement by smoothly layering itself around the body of its occupant. The layers, which were composed of gadolinite compounds, mainly served to increase the power and speed of the soldier but also provided a degree of armor protection, which surpassed normal body armor. It was controlled by a neural device implanted in the soldier's head. Each exo could carry a staggering amount of weaponry and tools. The one in the picture had a huge rocket launcher slung over the right shoulder and a three barreled assault gun in its hands. The exos carried electronic suites too, capable of esoteric forms of electronic warfare and communications and various aids which optimized the soldier's situational awareness.

'We organize the task force as follows: five teams. That translates into four squads of 12 men each on the ground and an operations team of four who will stay behind on the starship from where they will monitor satellite feeds and coordinate ground operations around the clock in six-hour shifts. We could do this from the ground, but experience tell us it is a force multiplier to have people not directly involved in ground operations analyzing and providing tactical recommendations on the fly. The Colonel, with his many years of experience, will lead the task force from planet-side.'

'We land in one of the orbital cargo shuttles. Once on the ground, we'll unload three Huygens ground assault vehicles. The GAV's will take us to the site where we will dismount and carry out preliminary ground reconnaissance. Based on the recon, we will formulate a plan to enter the site perimeter and seize control of the operation. All Mingo personnel will be locked up and secured. At this stage, seeing how their ground forces have been taken out, we believe the Mingo will break orbit and return home.'

Halifax Shipping Line, historically known for its audacity (a Halifax ship had launched the first colony in the Hildas and we don't have to mention the Ride of the Amazon, that goes without saying) was about to enter virgin territory as far as business practices were concerned.

TWENTY

So, he thought, here it was - the great prize his father had sent them to claim. *Espero*. The word was supposed to mean hope in an ancient language. If so, hope was the color of dogshit. Theoretically, Espero might be an inhabitable world but it was nothing like the old Earth. The poles, covering almost a third of the planet, were two huge vices gripping the planet still against the blast from the orange dwarf star that loomed so large in the sky when Basil turned the eyes of the drone upwards. The other star, the cool sidekick to the violence of its sister, was visible as a sometimes magenta, sometimes blue, emblem at certain times during the day and night. The dance of the cosmic bodies of this star system was too complex for Basil to fathom, but it worked. It had worked for eons.

Basil had used his new Ant-powered ability to hack through, circumvent or disable the Shields' military grade security systems to plug into the sensors on one of the recon drones they had dispatched to reconnoiter the landing zone for the mercenaries. He had been with the drone for hours now. It had started its journey over the interminable ice sheets of the North Pole, mapped an enormous mountain range, moved southwards, towards the equator where the Mingo base would be found. It was a landscape of dried out marshes with stagnant pools of water. He looked down through the drone sensors at the reeds, which despite it all managed to grow in the cracks along the edges of the pools and wondered what kind of life could thrive there. The drone flew on and the marshes dried out completely. Badlands, once ocean floors, now deserts of rocks and sand. The only interruptions in the dreary monotony of the landscape were clots of red growths that seemed to burst from the hard ground like biological fountains. Then the badlands changed into scrublands of low, green trees, which soon turned into prairies of gently waving grass. Then a forest appeared on the horizon. A forest of seemingly impossibly tall trees. The drone entered a steep climb. The forest was in actuality a collection of tall twisted spires of salt covering the horizon as far as the eye could see, some reaching almost a kilometer into the heady air. They were utterly white and they reflected the sunlight like an enormous necklace of pearls. It was the most wonderful thing Basil had ever seen and he wanted to go closer, to touch them with his own hands, but the drone started turning back. It was entering a zone reserved for its stealthier, and more expensive, brethren. Basil looked back at the forest of spires. Shadows from twin suns were casting them as an impossibly complex, tangled maze of impenetrable wire in all the colors of the rainbow.

The weather forecast for the equatorial zone was uncomplicated. In the day the skies were blue, slightly tinged with purple, and the sun, relentlessly, would boil the air until it reached a blistering 50 degrees of heat. In the long night, for more than twenty-one hours, the landscape would cool down, clouds might appear, and a sort of mist would cover the ground, prompting plants and animals to appear and do their thing. Then, as the planet completed a turn on itself, the sun would once again bake the ground and boil the air.

Earth, Basil's Earth, not the one you might read about in the history books, could no longer play host to the excesses of humanity, but Espero, although infinitely more hospitable, was still no picnic, no temperate hippie paradise where people could chill out barefooted in ankle length *chevaras*, *giny* pipe loosely dangling from the corner of their mouths while lazily reaching out to pick the sweet fruits off the nearest tree. No, if you got complacent or even thought about it, Espero would suck you dry in hours and leave your desiccated husk for whatever passed for scavengers down there. But, as long as you were industrious about the minutiae of survival, it was livable, and it sure as hell beat Earth.

He tried to imagine how the planet would look with humans living on it. How cities would appear, roads, spaceports and all the trappings of civilization. But it was hard to picture. The landscape looked so desolate, so empty. And yet it spoke to him of new beginnings, new hope indeed.

Ant turned out to be a willing accomplice when it came to more than hijacking recon drones. He also helped breaking through the military grade firewalls that encased all ship systems. One thing Basil had wondered about for some time was module 5. After the fourteen colony modules had launched, it was the last remaining cargo module on the ship and it obviously served as base for the Shield company. Ant had not been able to access its systems because it was physically detached from the ship networks. Shortly before the Shields were due to depart for the planet, however, Ant called.

#*'Basil. The Captain is downloading mission data into exo's in shell 5. A connection has opened.'*

'Can we use it?'

#*'Yes, but only for a few seconds, the time it takes him to upload all the data.'*

'Let's go, quick.'

Basil flowed along, finding his way into the internal sensors inside the shell. It had been melded into a huge open hangar bay. All the way in back, exo's were lined up like grotesque statues and neatly ordered according to their respective specialties; there were some mounted with missile launchers, some hefting dual Gatling guns as extensions to the arms, and a handful with complicated sensor suites and lighter weapons. In front of the exo's, which was a proven, iconic even, design from the wars, were two rows of experimental combat units. They looked like they had been seared clean of all protrusions and then dipped in a sticky, dark purple, liquid which had crystallized on them in strange patterns, which seemed almost biological. They looked like insects with metal pins coming out of their bodies. *'What are those things?'*

#*'I am not sure. They're called Toukans according to the file system in the Captain's mission briefing. If I should venture a guess, I'd say the soft material is GRIT.'*

'Fascinating. Father has really been busy.'

Then he saw the people. They were still human, barely. Men and women milling around together in various stages of nakedness. Seeing them was a grotesque sight. They were like Greek statues, hairless, porcelain white, except for the individual patterns of green and yellow luminescent tattoos snaking over their bodies. The men had tiny penises emerging like an afterthought from under the muscles, and the females, well, Basil would frankly hesitate to call them women, had flat breasts, more like nipples without the excess tissue, slightly protruding like they didn't belong on the slick surface of the bulging pectorals. They were all heavily modified humans, wearing their biological enhancements, the like of which Basil had never seen before anywhere on Earth, as medieval knights would wear carefully crafted plate armor.

'Bentzon commanded all of them many years ago. They were normal back then.'

'Who did this to them?'

'They did. Your father made it possible. They too are his creations.

'Like me, you mean.'

'Yes. And myself.'

A few were lounging in their gravity nets, mumbling to themselves or going through private pre-battle rituals, but most were shouting and joking in a strange language, a sort of English with heavy use of shorthand and abbreviations, a patois borne of decades of combat and isolation from society. They were taking turns swaddling each other from head to toe in a shimmering green gel, which made their hard bodies gleam like moist jade.

One area of the bay had apparently been designated a special rest and relaxation zone for twenty or so of the soldiers. At this moment, it could have been a scene from the Dub show. The soldiers were copulating, slamming their huge deformed bodies together like beached elephant seals butting chests, tearing at each other's puny sexual organs, the air thick with the sounds of flesh meeting flesh, grunts and meaty sounds. It was difficult to tell females from males, and Basil got the impression they did not care either. Considering they were the first naked people Basil had seen in real life since he got on board, he should have found it at least vaguely exciting, but he didn't.

Bentzon was there too. He was sitting by the exo's in a discussion with Mueller. 'The AFG-1, 7 and 8 will go to the Alpha vehicle, 2, 3, 4 to Beta, 5,6,9 and ten in Gamma. That way we have a nice mix of missiles, close range and ECM in each vehicle in case they get separated,' said Mueller.

'Good, good,' replied Bentzon. 'And supplies?'

'Check, 3 months' worth of compressed suits will recycle water. 1000 liters of back O2.'

TWENTY-ONE

The prologue to humanity's first interstellar war happened when a small fleet of cargo shuttles smoothly undocked from the starship Armagnac in Espero orbit. The shuttles were the same as the one that had brought Basil to the orbital from Vinales four months earlier. It was a time tested design and it had been in use for years with Halifax Shipping Line. It had flexible nacelles along both sides and small stubby wings to counter its bricklike aerodynamic performance in atmospheres. The hull clayed into transparency as it descended into the scattered clouds of Espero's upper atmosphere, then darkened again as it sunk lower into heavier air and friction increased. All went well and a couple of hours later the shuttles were on final approach to the landing zone Bentzon and Mueller had selected. The wings were fully extended and the thrusters were pointing almost directly downwards, labouring hard to keep them flying despite its nominal aerodynamic qualities. Near the LZ the walls of the hull once again became transparent offering the troops in the crew compartment an unhindered view of the alien planet. They greeted the sight in dour silence. One of them muttered something in that strange gurgling shorthand they used among themselves. Another replied and a few of them laughed.

They came down in an area of undulating hills spotted with clusters of dark tree-like growth. The ground directly beneath the shuttle exploded in huge clouds of dust and gravel as the ion thrusters raked over it. The landing pads made contact with the ground, the engines turned off and the shuttle settled gently. The dust, still hanging thickly in the air, flooded the interior as the pilot opened the three bay doors. As soon the ramps hit the ground, the troops got up as one and got on with the unloading. It went exactly like they had drilled during the many months of virtual training.

The area they had landed in was a bit different than they had imagined but that didn't change anything. It was a landscape of low trees with strange pearl colored fruits the size of a man's fist hanging from their knobbly short branches. When the shell of the fruits were smashed, under the threads of GAV's or by an exo brushing past it, thick red liquid with yellow seeds would erupt from the shell and stick like glue. The ominous machines of war, coloured in time honoured khaki, drab olive and black, little by little acquired a most un-warlike smattering of red and yellow which proved impossible to remove. 'The circus is in town,' laughed Crock. The name stuck.

The ground itself was covered in wiry and tough undergrowth but it was no obstacle to the huge threads on the GAV's or to the bipedalled Toukans that came down the ramps behind the exo's. The landscape seemed empty, at first glance, but there was movement down there, near the base of the trees, small unseen animals scurrying to get away from the alien incursion wreaking havoc on their natural habitats. The soldiers had no interest in biology. They merely took note that the ground was firm and that it wouldn't hinder their advance. They had a long way to go, about a thousand kilometers, and they were eager to get underway with their mission.

Caribou was the only one not busy with the unloading and readying of men and machines. She stood some distance away from the commotion and looked up at the sky... clear and blue... the like of which she had never seen. Her gaze, shielded by the visors, stopped at the two suns. One was a fiery orange and the other a cool, dark blue, one a lot bigger than the other. They were close to each other at this time of day.

'Crock, what do you suppose they will call them?' she called out on the company channel.

'Who?'

'The first colonists, what do you think they'll call the two suns?'

'No idea, don't care, not my problem. We need to get this show on the road.' He heard one of the others chuckle in the background.

And there, the single moon, so close it looked like it was about to fall down and crush them. She could see every detail on the surface with extreme clarity. Caribou held her thumb up against it and the tip barely covered the bigger craters. It was the strangest thing. She realized it was possible to take her helmet off and just breathe the air without suffering instant fatal poisoning by some ancient Pakistani curse lingering vengefully in the air. Her gaze ran over her comrades, over the misshapen, elephantine bodies, ungainly, yet immensely powerful. They had sacrificed everything for Zach's dream. They had traded in their soft bodies for *that*, allowed Zach to change them into instruments. Even alive, they had already paid the ultimate price. But most of them had never been outside without suits. Their world had never been anything but underground shelters, ashen skies and a world gone mad and ugly. Maybe it hadn't been such a bad trade after all. Instead of rotting away in dreamless Sleep, they were here now. To most of them, she supposed, the future would look pretty good. There was no sign they were about to succumb to melancholy and remonstrance. Not a single one had stopped to take a good look at their new, and final, home. No, they were busy. They had business to take care off... the black business of war, and distraction would serve no purpose. Or maybe war was the distraction.

Meanwhile, the squad leaders, Crock and Peanut, were bellowing orders over the company network. Bentzon, whose condition was deteriorating day by day, was watching over the tactical network from his perch inside the first GAV which was already coming down the ramp. The vehicles resembled huge armadillos, with a bulbous front and a fat part in the middle. On the inside they were quite spacious. Designed to carry a full exo equipped squad of ground troops with assorted heavy weapons, it was still cramped compared to the quarters they had shared on the Armagnac. Each vehicle was fifteen metres long and six wide. In the back there were seats which could be converted into bunks, and in the front, behind the command compartment, there was a space which was used for eating and various R&R activities. The command compartment had three seats, one for the driver, one for the tactical liaison officer who controlled the beam emplacement and the two missile racks and one for the vehicle commander. In theory, on level ground the GAV's were capable of more than 200 kilometres per hour. They were powered by miniature fusion reactors that would last several human lifetimes.

According to the plan they should reach the perimeter of the Mingo base at the end of the following Espero day.

Dark forest frowned on either side of the valley. The Survey

Branch people had called the trees *safra*. Something had stripped them of their dumpy maroon cauliflower leaves, and they seemed to lean towards each other, black and ominous in the fading light. A vast silence reigned over the land. The land itself was desolate, lifeless, without movement, so lonely that the spirit of it was not even that of sadness. There was a hint in it of laughter, but of laughter more terrible than any sadness – a laughter that was joyless as the smile of the sphinx, a grim laughter rebounding between the distant mountain peaks. It was the heartless, all-knowing universe laughing at the futility and effort of the small caravan making its way over the savage, heartless plans of Espero.

Movement disturbed the primeval silence. Down in the valley a flying drone appeared, meticulously scanning the ground, sometimes stopping for a few seconds to hover silently a few tens of meters over the ground, then darting forwards again. A few minutes went by, then a cloud of dust arose on the horizon and the armadillo shape of a ground assault vehicle appeared, its six set of tracks smashing the crusty, primordial surface of the ground into tiny ash coloured flakes which whirled in the air and kept turning upon themselves in the light gravity, refracting the sharp orange light from the setting suns, in a tantalising light show whose eerie beauty was seen by no one but the visual sensors on the semi-autonomous drone as it threw a lazy circle around the caravan. The rainbow cloud concealed another two GAV's, both following in the path of the first. The tiny flakes kept swirling through the air in an ever expanding slash of colour across the featureless expanse of the valley long after the GAV's had disappeared below the horizon. The passage of the machines left behind a single groove, a violent slash rupturing the pristine membrane of the alien planet, the purposeful linearity of which was the only sign of life as far as the eye could see.

Behind the dull metal carapaces of the machines, there were men, penetrating the land of desolation and mockery and silence, puny adventurers bent on colossal adventure, pitting themselves against the might of a world as remote and alien and pulseless as the void of space itself. Inside no one spoke. On every side was the silence, pressing on them with a tangible presence. It affected their minds as the pressure of deep water affects the body of a diver. It crushed them with the weight of unending vastness and unalterable decree. It crushed them into the remotest recesses of their own minds, pressing out of them, like juices from the grape, all the false ambitions and exaltations and undue self-valuations of the human soul, until they perceived themselves finite and small, specks and motes, moving with weak cunning and little wisdom amidst the play and interplay of the great blind elements and forces of this alien planet.

An hour went by. Two hours. The harsh cadmium of the twin suns changed, very briefly, into an ochreous gild, which had a wondrous quality to it, before the long Espero day faded away in a final sigh of periwinkle.

Night fell on the three vehicles in the convoy. Each held 10-15 men and large amounts of weapons, pre-fabricated ammunition, equipment and supplies. The men rested in hammocks, some turning their backs to the others, staring into the walls, others reading or watching shows, faces lit by the faint white light of the projectors. The inside of the vehicles was silent save for the occasional comment whispered between the drivers on the subjects of operating the vehicles and the state of the track. A rumble was heard as much as felt from their passage over the plains of Espero. After the initial excitement of the landing and off loading, they had all eagerly watched the surface of the alien planet through the exterior cameras as it slid by but the sight had oppressed them into gloomy silence and conversation between the soldiers had all but died out. The voyage was not proceeding as fast as they had hoped it would. The brittle surface proved treacherous to the heavy vehicles and just one hour after darkness had fallen, the ground collapsed beneath the trailing vehicle and it sunk into a hole which proved impossible to get out of on its own. Bentzon ordered a squad dismounted to assist hooking up the stricken vehicle with the other two. The men donned their suits and descended from the vehicle through the airlock and stepped on to the surface of the planet for the second time. The moon had yet to show itself and the night was completely black and still. For a moment the men stood and listened in the night. Not a sound was heard. It was the condensed silence of a place that did not care one bit for the vibrancy of human life. There was no bounty to be had here. No birds, no gurgling water and despite the heady air, there was no wind. Just utter silence. Dismayed, they eagerly set to their task. They stayed out as the stranded vehicle was pulled out of the hole and as soon as they got the all clear, they hurried back inside their metal carapace. Mostly to uphold his reputation as unflappable, Crock, the squad sergeant, muttered a joke and the joke drew a couple of mandatory laughs, but as the vehicles lurched forward and resumed the journey, the chatter ceased and everyone went back to reading or staring into the walls.

Throughout the night, one GAV after another would hit a sinkhole and need help getting pulled out. The delays added up. When the twin suns rose on their right and covered the armadillos in sharp orange light, they had fallen very much behind schedule.

The glassy tundra gradually disappeared in favour of grasslands that seemed somewhat more fertile and less dry. The temperature was on the rise and clouds appeared on the far horizon.

One afternoon, they got company. A group of creatures began following them at a distance. They looked vaguely humanoid. They were dark green, perhaps furred, but it was hard to see at a distance. The biggest were about 1.5 meters tall. The bodies were slender, bullet formed, with four powerful legs which allowed them to keep pace with the GAV's even when they were going fast. Whenever the humans stopped, to dig out a vehicle, or take a break, the animals would sit on their haunches and watch them. They had two eyes, huge black buttons, with no discernible pupils. They seemed to like plants and possibly insects. To help them eat and dig out roots, they had two small arm-like protuberances with flat fingerless hands which they used like shovels. It was a mixed group, with about a dozen big ones, the adults and troops of small specimens, probably offspring judging from the way they tumbled and fought each other incessantly. When the group was on the move, the pups would attach themselves to the backs of the adults.

The creatures followed the humans at a distance. The company eagerly studied them. Their appearance eased the mood among the soldiers, made the alien planet a tad less forbidding place. 'Do you think there are males and females?' Crock asked.

'They all look the same to me,' said Caribou. She was studying them at maximum zoom through one of the GAV cameras.

'Yeah, there's no tellin' what they are.'

The irony, of course, was completely lost on them.

A wordless conference between Bentzon and Caribou and they

both knew what needed doing. She ordered a halt to the caravan. She got up from the command chair, stretched, then went to the door. She disengaged the airlock. A few seconds later the first Espero air entered the cabin. No one was wearing claysuits. No one moved. She stepped onto the ramp and strolled down to the surface, seemingly unconcerned. She stopped at the bottom where she looked around.

'Wish we had time for a barbeque,' she remarked idly on the company net and took a deep breath. The troops smiled at each other, shaking their heads. Then, one by one, they got out of the vehicle and went to stand with her on the surface of their new home.

Bentzon ordered regular breaks. They would drive on for a couple of hours, then stop, and everyone would get out of the vehicles, light a fire and sit around for 15 minutes, chewing on rations and chatting about what they could see, the strange trees, the weirdness of the two suns, the unfamiliar, rough texture of the grass and the simple joy of feeling the warmth of the sun on their upturned faces.

After three days of following the humans from the tundra and into the plains, the little band of animals, which Peanut had half-jokingly named goopers – and the name had stuck-- got closer and closer at every stop. The humans would light a fire or just get out of the vehicles and the goopers would sometimes mirror their actions without looking directly at them. They acted like the humans weren't there, touching and grooming each other, one or two at a time going off to forage nearby and generally having a good time.

'Oh look.' Two pups were inching closer, curious.

A soldier called Doc was chewing on some synthetic chocolate. He tore a bite off it and threw it to the pups.

'I wouldn't do that,' warned Caribou.

'Why not, what's the harm?'

'I don't know, maybe they don't like our food, or maybe it's poisonous to them,' she said.

'Yeah, we shouldn't mix things up,' agreed one of the others, but he sounded unsure. Truth be told, they hadn't the faintest idea.

One of the pups, a brave little thing, sniffed at the chocolate, then ate it hurriedly. The adults were watching it calmly. Nothing happened.

--

'Bentzon, we have incoming, you need to wake up.'

'Yes, I'm here.' The recon satellites had picked up a flight of drone missiles patrolling high above, and in front of, the advance guard. The missiles would detect the column sooner or later and the advance guard units needed instructions on how they should deal with the threat. After issuing a few terse instructions to the men he went back to sleep.

He dreamt. Like so often before his dreams took him back to the wars. An attack, crucial, part of an offensive no one remembered anymore, his company had led the way through the enemy lines. They were desperate, supplies were running low even before the offensive had begun. The Shields knew the war was lost but it wasn't their war, their purpose. They were there. That's all. Doing their thing. Still, they would fight this one to the end. Almost. Killed, never defeated. The spearhead had overrun an outpost. Prisoners were taken but they didn't know what to do with them. There was nowhere to send them, they were behind enemy lines and they wouldn't leave men behind to guard them. So, he, Bentzon, did what had to be done. He had shot them all. All sixty of them. Fifty eight had been men, soldiers, but the last two was an old woman and, presumably, her granddaughter. He'd shot those too but he would never forget them. Of all the people he had killed over the years those two kept coming back. And soon he would join them.

Caribou prodded him on the shoulder. She was holding a self-heating ration box.

'Need to eat.'

He nodded at her with a weak smile and took the food.

'Hey, Caribou,' he said.

'Yes, Colonel.'

'Remember that time in Pittsburgh?'

She paused. 'I do. It was a long time ago. Has your illness made you nostalgic, Colonel?'

'Maybe. I don't know.'

'It was very romantic.'

'You know, I never got to feel your tits back then. Always regretted that.'

She looked at him with a tiny smile. 'It's not too late for that, Colonel. You could try asking me out for dinner sometime.'

'You mean fucking in a shelled-out bedroom with pigeonshit

everywhere isn't a real date?'

'Don't forget the dog carcass. That really made my day, you know.'

'I'll remember. There'll be plenty of time once this is over.'

'Let's hope so, Colonel. It's been twenty years, but who's counting, right?'

'We're under attack.'

Bentzon switched to unit 213.

'What is it, Sunnez?'

'Those black devils again. Permission to fire?'

'Negative.'

Bentzon switched to Sunnez. They were black flying creatures with shiny, almost reflective skin and wings that looked too tiny to support their weight. They had attacked the advance guard units several times in the past hours. They came in different varieties. There were the small ones that would swoop in and touch the exo's, presumably leaving some kind of chemical trace. They would be followed by their larger breathren which attacked in waves. The club like beaks were clearly supposed to knock over the Toukans, which obviously didn't happen, but the animals were incredibly stubborn or maybe, if they were the top predator on the planet, were just used to getting their way. They would inflate their long slick bodies with air until they looked like balloons, then expel it behind them, giving them a huge speed boost as they dived on their prey like darts. A Toukan under attack would look like it was travelling under a black cloud discharging a continuous stream of darts, all converging on the moving target with uncanny precision. They kept up the attacks, first in squadrons of five or ten, then twenty, and in the end they had marshalled fifty or sixty of those dragonfly shapes that came in again and again, diving in club first, hammering into the unyielding duranium of the Toukans. It seemed they were unable to fathom the possibility of prey that wouldn't succomb to their brutal treatment. Bentzon forbade the troops to open fire. Discharging beam weapons or even kinetics would be a sure way to announce their presence to the hostile scout drones. The flying things were unnerving, but they were mostly harmless to the exo's. A soldier in a clay suit on the other hand would have problems, and, gods forbid it, if an unshielded human was to be targeted, he would be killed instantly by the dive bombers.

After a while the black animals relented and let the strange metal contraptions alone. A couple of hours later they appeared in the air above the GAV's in a black cloud. At the sight of the oversized, divebombing black dragonflies, the goopers, which were accompanying the GAV's, stopped moving altogether. They stood as frozen, faces turned downwards, presenting the camouflaged neck and back to the air. For a long time it seemed to work, but then one of the pups, impatient with the waiting and too young to understand the deadly danger, let out a mewling sound. The dragonflies reacted immediately and with deadly precision. Within seconds the pup had been tagged by scouts. Then the greater mass of the flying creatures swung like one towards the scent. The divebombers expanded into balloon size, then exhaled the air behind them as they dived head first. The goopers responded by launching into an amazing show of acceleration. They literally went from zero to two hundred kilometres per hour in less than a second. An explosion of energy unlike anything they had previously seen from the otherwise lethargic creatures. Being down the predatory ladder from creatures like the dragonfly-birds would take extreme survival skills. The goopers kept running. One, a female, was falling behind because she was carrying a large cub on her back. The divebombers shifted their aim. Bentzon noticed a second flight had started a slow dive without the added speed of the jet like balloons. They looked different. More aerodynamic. Instead of the club-like head, they had huge powerful jaws and muscular wings. Seconds later the female and her cub was struck squarely from above in rapid succession and quickly tumbled to the ground, dazed or unconscious. Seconds later the new flight, which was a new variation on the black bird, swooped in. They were slower, but had large wings, powerful jaws and a set of impressive claws on their two feet. They grappled the female and the pup in their powerful jaws, lifted them up and flew away, escorted by the rest of flock.

--

Bentzon slept all through the night. When he woke the next morning, they seemed to have crossed into a new climate zone, somewhat warmer but even more desolate. As far the eye could see there was only the occasional pile of rocks to break the monotony.

They were going slightly downhill now and the ground firmed up, aiding their progress considerably. 'We're entering the ocean now,' said Bentzon out loud to no one in particular. 'Oh yeah?' answered the driver, a woman called Linnea, who was completely bald. The sinews in the back of her enhanced neck were as thick as Bentzon's wrists. 'Yeah, there used to be a planet wide ocean along the equator. A few eons ago, that is.'

They drove on for another uneventful hour. The column was moving through a series of sharp rocks and crevasses, almost canyons, slashed by the serrated shadows of the twin suns. Mueller reported from orbit that enemy drone missiles were slowly spreading out in a search pattern over the area they were heading into. So much for the element of surprise.

Bentzon ordered a halt. He asked Caribou to help him out, and hanging on her shoulder, he got his first look at the planet. The air had a slightly metallic smell to it. He looked around, desert and rocks as far as the eye could see and then he heard it. A weak tinkle just at the edge of his hearing. The troops, with their enhanced hearing would hear it much louder. He turned to walk around to the front of the vehicle and then abruptly stopped to stare in wonder. Before him, more than a hundred kilometres away **rose** the first spires. They were so white it almost hurt the eyes to look directly at them. They **rose** straight into the air in irregular spiralling columns, thickest at the base, then thinning out, like trees, or inverted frozen tornadoes. He knew from the Survey Branch report that the average height was about one kilometre. Halfway up they reached out for their neighbours, creating a strange effect like a net of treeroots turned upside down.

'We going there, huh?' asked one of the troops near Bentzon, who just nodded.

'What are those things?' asked Sunnez.

'You didn't do your homework.' Crock punched Sunnez lightly on the shoulder with his fist. The blow would have knocked a normal un-enhanced person off his feet.

Peanut had walked up to them. 'They're salt. Something to do with the way the weather moves in from the poles. The Survey people says the lack of seasons create a couple of gigantic storms a couple of times a year. Storm fronts duke it out right here.' Sunnez nodded like he understood.

--

The Mingo drones attacked just as they were entering the spire forest. From directly below, the huge salt pillars were like trunks in a strange white forest. The sunlight, refracted in endless shatters on its way through the entangled branches of the spires hundreds of meters above their heads, blinded unshielded eyes and made the world underneath a cathedral of serrated light and extreme heat. Bentzon had positioned the air defense units on the forward perimeter of the convoy and they repelled the attack with ease, but the meaning was clear enough: the enemy knew they were coming.

--

It was dawn of their fourth day on Espero, more than three hundred Earth hours since the landing. They had travelled almost four thousand kilometres and were about 11 Earth days late according to the plan. The Shields had finally reached the perimeter of the Mingo defensive positions. The Shields would return to the black business again for the first time in a generation.

The delays hadn't been all bad. The extra time had given Mueller, who had been surprised at the strength of the Mingo drone complement, time to gain low orbital and aerial superiority over the battlefield. While the merry band of reformed and reconstructed mercenaries had been struggling across the rugged surface of the alien planet, a vast and merciless war had been fought among machines in the air high above them. A planet is a mighty big place, especially Espero, which was one and a half times bigger than Earth and, and to make things worse, it had a very active sun that constantly interfered with communications. At the beginning of the campaign, Mueller had sent out a host of semi autonomous flying machines, drones, both of the attacking kind and of the smaller recon sort. The latter were supposed to find targets for the first, but things didn't always happen in that order. Still, the Shields had prevailed and local air superiorty was won.

From orbit, Mueller had compiled a comprehensive picture of the Mingo deployment and capabilities. He reported that the Mingo crew was heavily dug in around the mining site. Their defensive perimeter was a layered affair, presumably mined, and they were able to shift reserves from one end of the perimeter to the other under cover. Best force estimates from the ship was five Vale exo's, an old design, and ten tracked Tribute IFV's, practically antiques, along with a couple of squads of ground troops in combat clay. The Mingo weren't push-overs, as they had hoped, but they shouldn't pose too much of a problem.

After studying the recon data with Mueller, Bentzon deployed the units in three groups. He melded one Toukan in each group for a long range support role, Lance missiles, Dew missiles and mortar. The second in each group was equipped in the air defense role along with an upgraded jamming package. The third in the assault configuration was carrying machine guns, grenade thrower, smoke. The remainder of the squad, in Rugers, was configured in a standard grenadier profile.

They approached the enemy camp from two directions. One group closed in from the west, a little ahead of the main force which was composed of two groups, coming in from the north. The plan was for the western group to advance ahead of the main group and hit the Mingo perimeter first. They hoped the Mingo would respond to the decoy incursion with all they had. That would allow the HSL groups to deal with the Mingo support weapons before engaging the hostile exos.

The GAV's were held back. They were unsuited for assaults. Bentzon wanted them to stand by to assist with missile bombardments if they ran into unexpected opposition. The attack drones were held back for the same reason.

After the briefing had gone through to all units, he said a few words on the encrypted company channel. It was short and to the point. He wasn't in the mood for a longwinded speech and thought the troops felt the same way. Everyone just wanted to get it over with.

--

Over the next couple of days, the Shields decimated the Mingo in series of pitched battles. The outcome was never really in doubt. The enhanced Shields never slept and did not need time off from the battle.

Basil, who occasionally had Ant patch him into the military Tacnet, was appalled at what he saw. That the Mingo couldn't resist the advance of the Shields was hardly surprising. Their warmaking had an unfeelingly mechanized quality to it. Perhaps what he was seeing was the true nature of war – bloodless in its bloodletting, coldblooded without cruelty, relentless without the slightest malignity to it. Whatever pain and death they inflicted on the Mingo came wrapped in cool professionalism. To Basil, the very lack of emotion, coupled with extreme destructive abilities of their weapons, was scary. He had always thought that making was all sound and fury and senseless bravery and fear. The attitude of the Shields somehow sapped this war of its emotive quality. They made killing an exercise, bereft of cruelty or malignity, any emotion, really, and that scared Basil more than the killing itself. They knew no boundaries other than their orders. Or so it appeared. At the nucleus of all this professionalism was Bentzon, half-crazed, a malign tumour nestled at the centre of this efficient machine of war, thrashing between enraged aggression and begdrudging impassivity, his old sense of purpose eroding whenever melancholy seized hold of him. He raged like the choreographer of a troop of ballet dancers would rage each time someone tripped or was out of synch and the artistic flow of his performance was ruined. The heartlessness of the whole affair made Basil fear for the survival of the hapless Mingo troops. He hoped they would soon realise that discretion was the better part of valour and get off the planet .

Basil watched how missiles patrolled above the battlefield , raining down on everything that moved, and he was there when the single Shield loss of the campaign happened. It was a Ruger, and the hostile missile barrage completely overloaded the integrated point defenses on the three nearby units. It went down in a fireball, fueled by his unused missile racks, that boomed over the valley and was seen by everyone within tens of kilometers. After that, the Shield losses stopped and the Mingo began and after seeing the first Vale exo go down, it walked into crushing barrage of mortars and rocket artillery, he wanted to stop but something kept him there. It was completely surreal, a confusing mess. Either he jumped from one unit to the other, to get a first hand (or second as it were) experience of the battle, reducing his awareness to almost zero, or he stayed on the command net, monitoring the battle in a sort of three dimensional, or two dimensional, as the situation warranted, omniscient tactical replay. The latter felt like too much of a game and the first was too confusing. It was like a theatrical play, a fantasy that would end soon, the lights would go out, the audience would get up and leave.

The two suns hung low over the horizon, casting the scene in a violet hue as they watched the last Mingo shuttle take off through a hailstorm of anti-aircraft fire coming from all sides. The Mingo drone fleet kept up a valiant, albeit pointless, defence till the very end.

TWENTY-TWO

Ino Sastre had gotten a strange idea into his head. Each time he was given the liberty to go on a little break, he would power down the exo and force it to disconnect from the combat network.

Ino, like all exo pilots in the Shield Company, was an ace when it came to the work he was formatted and trained to do. He been assigned to pilot one of the formidable Toukans, a clear indication of his value to Bentzon and the squad leaders: dependable, ruthlessly effective, his mind always on the mission. But there was something about him that they had overlooked. They were not to blame, really, it was such an innocent flaw, so tiny, it was no wonder it had gone unnoticed. In the years to come, people, specialists with the GSA Academy in Geneva, would wonder how the conditioning could have failed with this one, but be that as it may, there was something in Ino that made him do stupid things. Stupid things like parking his exo, opening the crew compartment and stepping outside, naked as the day he was born, green neuro gel streaming down his statuesque body.

The truth be told, experiencing Espero had been a shock to him, akin to a profound, almost spiritual, revelation. He'd seen the recordings from Survey Branch and he'd read the environmental reports. He knew what to expect, intellectually, but nothing had prepared him for the emotional impact of the open sky, the clear air, the heart aching beauty of the two suns disappearing below the horizon and the long imponderable silence of the Espero night. Like most people below the age of fifty, he had grown up in underground caverns. A world in which the skies, provided you even got to see them, were dirty, unbroken slate. He had never been outside without a suit. *To be outside without a suit...*

The desire once formed was irresistible. He would leave the exo. He would be naked. He would wriggle his toes into the ground, sampling the feeling of moist grass clinging to his feet and feel the caress of the wind against his body. He wouldn't go far from the exo. He wasn't completely reckless after all, and he would keep alert for the black dragonbird packs and anything else that might pose a threat. He knew it was wrong, that he was breaking every rule in the book, but he couldn't help himself.

Ino had made plans for his first excursion outside the exo. Big plans. Eventually, the campaign was winding down, the order came. *Stand down, twenty minutes.* He found a nice spot, parked the Toukan and started the exit sequence. It slid open with the smooth sound of air escaping. Sastre climbed out. The exo was grimy and covered in mud. Mud! He took a deep breath and felt the breeze cooling the gel on his skin. Breeze on skin. He lingered over the sensations, realizing he was living a dream. He stepped into the clearing with its stringy grasses and those dark red ferns, which nearly always accompanied the now familiar and seemingly ubiquitous brushwood trees with the pearly fruits. In the awe of his first free steps, he noticed a couple of tree stumps of a kind he hadn't observed before. They were so flat that they almost looked like the stump of a tree which had been sheared flat. He observed a flat mass of something like roots visible above the ground, entangled into a star pattern around a stump.

Time was short and he moved pleasurably, executing the steps of his plan. Naked and feeling free, he walked over to one of the tree stumps and assumed the perennial position, legs slightly apart, face turned to the sky, the thumb and index of his right hand lightly touching his penis and started urinating. During the wars it would have been a punishable offence to leave blatant DNA traces like this, here it was merely stupid, but by the gods, he was enjoying it. As the bright yellow liquid splashed over the tree stump, Ino began immersing himself in the pleasure of enjoying the experience, when he became aware that the tree stump was backing away from him. He calmly finished urinating and stood quietly for a while observing the tree stump. He shook his head and tunred to re-enter the exo. I'd better leave the biology lessons to the civilians who arrive later, he thought, just as the thing started making high pitched clicking noises. *A tree that made noise like a bird?* He frowned, experienced a wave of intense dizziness and fell prone. He lay there for a few seconds, staring at the thing in front of him. Then, without a whimper, he died.

They found him a few hours later. Enemy action was ruled out quickly. Sastre's unmanned exo had recorded the event. When they looked over the recordings they saw Sastre leave his exo, the fool, saw him pissing, saw the tree move and saw him fall on his ass in front of it. After his death, the tree stump had approached him and heaved itself over his body for a while. It wasn't clear what it was doing but at least it hadn't eaten him. They reckoned it must be an example of unidentified fauna missed by Survey Branch because those things had definitely not been mentioned in the report. Bentzon issued a warning that should they encounter the specimen again, they were allowed to terminate on sight. As it turned out, a few had already been seen around. They were promptly destroyed.

TWENTY-THREE

The miniature war on the surface of Espero was living its own life while high above it, in orbit, only Basil, the three crew and four Shields, who took turns manning the tank, were left to crew the ship. The four of them, Basil, Felix, Rem and Jin, were not allowed in section 1 where the Shields had settled. Time passed slowly. They had adjusted the matrix on the habitat modules to the non-acceleration, toroid shape. Basil had been working on his ability to partition his parietal communications implant, allowing Ant his own separate area of operation. It had the added bonus of allowing Basil to pretend, most of the time, that things were normal. The presence and voice of the artificial intelligence would recede into the background and leave him almost his old self. Almost. There was always a nagging feeling something was lurking at the edge of his consciousness, a presence, a mind much cleverer than his own in perhaps most respects. How could he truly know or compare? Internal senses were tricky and studying himself with an eye to anything other than performance for an effect was a new phenomenon. He could tell himself that the difference between his condition and true insanity was minimal after all. But how could he master this new self and push it to a new height? How do you prevent yourself from trying to take over and seize control when you're literally imbued with the power to see through everything, go in your mind where no one else can go and come up with solutions to problems that normal people would have to spend a lifetime solving all at the behest of a small voice in the back of your mind? How do you know, for that matter, that you're not going crazy? What would sanity look like anyway? He'd begun thinking of himself as a sort of Lilliputian who was imprisoning a

Gulliver within the very fabric of his own body, stretched so thin you could see through it. Maybe he was going insane. Maybe one day he would explode into tiny fragments. Ironically, he felt that the many years he'd spent in the grip of Blue Duck, Ket, Zai, alcohol and the constant surveillance on the Dub show, helped him cope with the estrangement in his head. In a certain fashion, it was merely a reprise of his former life, sadly without the drugs and the random sex.

It didn't help that Yakovlev loudly worried about the degree of control Ant potentially could exert over him. He vigorously denied it was possible but they seemed to assume it was something that Basil, with his limited faculties, wouldn't really be aware of. Their suspicions weren't without merit, of course. If HSL, his father, had allowed the machine the possibility to control him, he was well and truly screwed. But he didn't think so for the simple reason that he knew his father. The old man was too proud, too vain to let a machine take away the free will of his only offspring. Project Nova smacked of pride, of that special Baranikowa brand of megalomania that had pushed Zach to become such a powerful icon of the Restoration. Sacrificing his only child to embody a machine would be very uncharacteristic of the old patrician. Still, it didn't preclude the possibility of error or misjudgment. Perhaps in time the HAI would find a bridge across the chaotic, swirling pool of human tissue and blood to impose its stringent digital messages directly onto his brain.

He had just finished a meal by himself in the galley, returned to his quarters and climbed into the epi when Ant spoke in his mind. Its voice, *his* voice, had a slight urgency to it.

#Basil, I believe aliens are about to force a boarding of the Armagnac.

Basil responded by a laugh that was meant to conclude in a humorous comment on possible HAI malfunctions, but the laugh stuck in his throat as dozens of images from external cameras and a stream of sensor data reamed their way into his immediate 'verse.

#This is a lot to process, said Ant wistfully. Basil mentally flipped the switch that allowed the HAI full access to his communications implant.

Basil studied the real time imagery. A blurry shape was blotting out the star field to starboard. It was like looking down into a pool of black, completely opaque, water. The thing seemed to be a few hundred meters wide and it had managed to approach to within a few hundred metres without being detected.

#*It is hardly emitting anything either. Very clever design. Total cloaking. Some of my... equals... had all but figured out the basic theory, just prior to our being... disconnected. But it didn't seem like a worthwhile avenue of research to us back then.*

#*I believe the cloak is dissolving now.*

And it was. The black veil shimmered and the contours of a starship appeared in greater and greater detail. It was a chaotic shape in dull metallic grey, unlike anything a human mind would create. Completely asymmetric, a messy design, amoeba-like, perhaps, shaped somewhat like a fat human thighbone, huge blunt nose, a long structure. From the side it might look like a tower, attached to the middle of a thigh bone and a wing of sorts angling from the tower at forty-five degrees. Just when it looked like it would collide with the Armagnac, it swung on its own axis, revealing its main engines, which were divided into four or five discrete sections jutting backwards at angles to each other. The whole ship was imposing but it nonetheless had a distinct air of improvisation to it. Faint yellow markings dotted the length of the ship. Panic welled up, restricting his breathing, and through his fear, he heard Ant speak calmly. He focused on the voice of the HAI.

#*...system makes me believe the propulsion technology may be ion based but if it is, it must be magnitudes more powerful than our designs.*

The alien ship stopped moving. Alarms started blaring in physical space beyond the epi. Mueller and his men in the tank had finally spotted the anomaly and were broadcasting a message on all channels. 'All personnel must return to their epi's immediately. An anomaly has been spotted approaching rapidly to starboard. This is not a drill.'

A multitude of ports opened on the alien ship and streams of black dots emerged, moving quickly directly towards the Armagnac. They were tiny vessels, brown'ish, egg-shaped and they closed the distance between the two ships in seconds. Just as the swarm of vessels were about to land on the hull of the Armagnac, all ShipNetwork, navigation sensors, winked out.

They were blind and deaf. Basil found himself alone with Ant who kept chattering about the alien ship. The internal systems in the epi had stopped working despite being built to survive a catastrophic failure on the ship, a subsequent ejection into space and months, if not years, of existence floating through deep space. He thought of Darien. Would she be scared? Yes, of course she would be. At least he had Ant who seemed annoyingly invigorated by all the new data.

'You're in an awfully good mood, all things considered. You do realise that if I die, we both die?'

#*Yes I know that a likely outcome of your death is my death. Still, this is very exciting, isn't it?*

'What do you think they want?' Basil asked.

#*I am not sure. Boarding an alien ship, alien to them that is, seems illogical. I surmise we have something they want. What is it, I wonder? Well, we do not have enough data yet.*

'It is one hell of a way to make first contact. What happened to the 'greetings, take me to your leader' routine?'

#*But it is not first contact. They have already encountered us.*

'They have? When?'

#*Just before we lost network access, in a flash of, premonition, brilliance... not sure what it was that prompted me, I looked through the TacNet records. A few hours ago, I believe one of their number encountered a Shield trooper on the surface of Espero.*

'Oh, and how did that go? No, wait, let me guess.'

#*Not as you think. The trooper was killed by the alien and the Shields retaliated by killing a number of them. The Shields are not aware that they attacked an intelligent lifeform.*

'Someone should tell the aliens our life form is barely intelligent ,' Basil grumbled. *'How did they look?'*

#*The troopers thought it was a plant.*

'A plant? Like a bush?'

#*Not a bush, not exactly, but a sort of growth, like a pumpkin with roots around it. A warning was sent out and other Shield units identified a number of them scattered around. They proceeded to destroy them. I conclude that the aliens were monitoring or surveying the Shields before attempting first contact. Too bad it didn't work out.*

'Yes, you can say that again. They're here, the pumpkins are here,' Basil said.

Scraping noises could be heard outside the epi, and then light entered as it was cracked open by sheer force. The light blinded him momentarily. He was poked in the ribs. Something like an electric shock pulsed through his body, making his hair stand up. The discharge was apparently aimed at the clay suit because it immediately lost cohesion and slithered shapelessly off his body. Something grabbed him by the ankles and the shoulder. It hurt and he yelled. It was an irresistible force that pulled him from the epi onto the floor where he landed with a thud, face down. He was naked and bleeding profusely from his left shoulder and leg. An incongruous smell entered his nose, peppermint, pungent, not entirely unpleasant. He desperately wanted to look at the alien and he attempted to get up on his knees but the floor was so greasy with his own blood that he stumbled. Through a pulsing, subdued light, he saw something. A claw, strobing with colours, reaching towards his face. It grabbed him by the arm in a grip that tore clean through his flesh and muscles. He could actually feel it grate hard against the bones in his arms and he thought the bones would snap.

With a grip gouged deep into his flesh, the alien dragged him out of his quarters and into the corridor. Stumbling and falling, Basil got a confused impression of huge creatures, flashes of diamond and those strange strobing colours diffusing everything. He glimpsed the others. Jin and Rem were dragged like ragdolls by the aliens. Everyone was bleeding profusely from wounds and he could tell from the way their arms and legs twisted at unnatural angles that they were broken. Screams rang through the corridors. The air was heavy with the smell of blood and peppermint. Inside his head, Ant was clamouring for attention but his voice was fading.

#*Get a good look at them, look at them, man. I need data.*

'You...' All he could do was struggle not to fall. They moved quickly down the corridor towards section three, where, one by one the aliens stopped by the door, lobbed their human cargo into the garden of the Bowl where people landed haphazardly on grass and pebbly pathways, then moved on, making room for the next one queueing up behind it.

In the Bowl it was a bright, sunny day; birds were chirping over the sound of a fountain and a miniature ionic temple was visible squeezed in between a copse of acacia and oak trees. Felix had gone for an English Garden theme this time, Basil thought; just like the vast underground park his father had built in Vinales for the workers. The air was thick with moans and outright screams. Everyone was covered in blood.

The door closed. Basil's leg, shoulder and arms throbbed with pain. He twisted his head and looked at his left shoulder where he could see an enormous laceration. His arm and leg didn't look any better.

He got up on his elbows and looked around. He immediately spotted Jin. She was in a bad state. Rem was struggling to get on his feet while others just lay unmoving on the gravel.

'What the fuck were those things?' muttered Rem. He sat with his head resting on the edge of the fountain.

'I didn't get a good look,' said Jin. She was bleeding liberally from several places on her arms and legs. Her face was deadly pale. 'Oh my god, this hurts.'

'What just happened?' repeated Rem stupidly.

'Aliens boarded the ship.' Jin had closed her eyes now.

'Where did they come from? What do they want?'

'I'm losing a lot of blood,' said Jin, looking down at the wounds on her arms and legs. She bit her lip in pain.

'All I noticed was those claws. Sheet, I think my leg is broken. My arm too,' Rem gasped.

Looking around Basil spotted Yakovlev. He crawled towards him. After a grueling eight meter journey, he collapsed next to the engineer, who, naked, looked even more horribly emaciated than usual. Their heads were almost touching each other. He turned a little to look him in the face. Yakovlev was wincing with pain, but conscious. The older man's eyes opened and looked back at Basil.

'That condensate finally came in handy, huh? No broken bones on you, boy, is there?' His voice was slurred.

'I don't know. It hurts. But I can move.'

'That's what I thought.'

'Hang in there, Felix.'

'Basil, it is up to you now, you and that machine.' Yakovlev was losing a lot of blood but he kept speaking in broken English with his heavy Russian accent making an appearance. 'Shell matrix ...need burst of fusion power for reconfiguration.' He started coughing weakly. 'Powerlines from reactor somewhere behind walls.... Have own network. ... plug into network, ... take control of ship.'

Basil was hurting too. The pain from the wounds came in waves and he found each wave pushed Ant back to the recesses of his mind where he couldn't talk to it.

He had to take a look at those power lines Felix talked about, he would, he would, but first he needed to lie here for a little while, see if the pain went away.

Time passed. A day and a night, perhaps, but it was hard to know for sure. He had slept. The interior of the Bowl had lost cohesion during the black out and had turned into a big featureless open space a few tens of meters in diameter. It was dimly lit by the emergency panels inside the walls and the curved ceiling above them. Basil woke up. He looked around. No one had moved. They all lay in the same positions. He wasn't sure if they were dead or alive. A Shield trooper had joined them while he slept. It was a man with short, black hair who sat, back against the wall, watching Basil calmly. His body was a mess of lacerations and open wounds that looked like they should hurt, but despite it all, the man looked Basil calmly into the eyes.

'They haven't returned,' he said coolly.

'What do they want?' asked Basil. The soldier shook his head. 'No idea.'

'Where are the others?' he asked, thinking he knew the answer. There had been four Shields on the ship.

'Dead,' he said, not breaking eye contact. 'They fought well.'

Basil nodded.

It had been hours now. Perhaps an entire day. Apparently the aliens didn't care about them. It didn't make sense. If they wanted them dead, they could have killed them right away instead of going through the difficulty of stowing them away in the Bowl. Maybe the neglect was simply ignorance. Maybe they didn't realise wounded humans could die. There had been no food or water either.

Basil sat. His head swam but he remained sitting until he felt confident enough to stand. He took a few deep breaths to clear his mind and peered closely at his wounds. The pain was reduced to a dull throb. The wounds seemed to have closed in on themselves. Was his body able, enhanced by Ant, to self-heal? He glanced at the others. The lacerations on their arms and legs were unchanged. Rem's left leg was resting in an unnatural position, clearly broken in several places along both the femur and tibia. Their wounds had not changed, not for the better anyway. They were horrible, wet and, in some cases, oozing with white liquid. The three would die soon.

He checked his communications implant, without it there would be no accessing any kind of network. To his relief it had rebooted but there were no networks aside from a couple of local pings from the unconscious crew members in the room. Still it was one less thing to worry about. He relaxed some more and eventually Ant came forward.

#Hello again. You were in pretty bad shape. How are you now?

'I'll live it seems... How come my wounds have healed and everyone else's haven't?'

 # 'That would be my work... thank you very much. Your physical distress triggered an emergency response which allowed me to override certain limitations.'

'And no broken bones either...' Basil mumbled suspiciously. He was too tired to think about it.

#Yes, Bose-Einstein condensate is extremely durable. The machine sounded annoyingly smug.

'Look at these people. I didn't think you could die from a broken limb, but...'

#I'm not a medical expert, but broken limbs can cause all sorts of problems. Escaping bone marrow get into the bloodstream, causes heart attacks, pulmonary embolisms, strokes. That one seem to have broken femurs and that one over there is almost dead if I'm not mistaken. From the vast amount of dried blood surrounding him I'd say the aliens severed his femoral artery. And Jin has signs of beginning infections, possibly ostomyalitis.

'Anything we can do to help them?'

#No.

'Ok, listen. Felix said there would be power lines from the reactor around here somewhere. He said those came with their own network. Could allow us to interface with the ship.'

#Very interesting. Dare one suggest you get on your feet? We need to check the shell for access panels.

Basil got up and made for the nearest section of wall. The soldier followed him with his eyes. He started walking the circumference, looking for signs of an access panel or something that would let him activate the reactor network. Ant said it would be almost invisible and he wasn't wrong. Basil had passed by the panel three times before noticing five very slight indentations in the wall. He put his hand against it, fingers splayed out to fit the holes. He pushed at them slightly. A small panel, about five by five centimetres, opened above his hand. It had a variety of connections, switches and buttons but it was impossible to tell which was which.

'Is that it?'

#Let us assume so.

'You're not sure?'

#I did not design this ship.

'Ok, I'll push something then.' He pushed and switched buttons at

random and immediately received a notification from his communications implant that a network was available. Ant didn't waste any time.

'Does it work?'

#Yes.

'Yes? Yes, what? Tell me what is going on.'

#I have entered the reactor network but it is hardwired to block access, any access. Good news is that the aliens can't operate the reactor either. Only authorized Ops personnel with the correct codes can operate it. We need to get Felix's code.

Basil went to where Felix lay and kneeled. He was alive, but barely. Basil took his hand and squeezed it. 'Felix, can you hear me?'

Felix didn't respond.

#Slap him across the face.

'No, I will not slap him across the face. Are you crazy?'

#I hear that's what you people do to wake other people up who have passed out.

'No, they don't.'

Basil squeezed his hand and talked to him. Suddenly Felix eyes fluttered open. He looked at Basil. 'Did it work?' he whispered.

'Yes, but we need your reactor code.'

Wincing he spoke a long sequence of letters and numbers.

'Tell me you got that?'

#Of course.

Ant immediately logged back into the reactor network. Basil worried about the engineer. Felix obviously was burning with fever and his skin had an oily sheen to it that did not look reassuring.

#It worked.

'What do you see?'

#I am alone in green fields and the sun on my face, but I am not troubled.

'Ant...'

#The Sleepers... I have made contact with them. It would seem our invaders have overlooked the human cargo in module 16.

'Darien...'

#It means that as long as the Sleepers cooperate, we still control the ship, Basil.

'Why wouldn't they cooperate?'

#The aliens are attempting to interface with the VIE's but they're not successful.

'Do they have AI's?'

#No, they have computers of a sort, but they seem to be quite simple. It may be one field where we're ahead of them.'

'Nice to know, I guess.'

#Another possibility is that perhaps the aliens don't need computers. It could be they are magnitudes more intelligent than humans.'

'Yes, perhaps they're so clever they realize they can't trust machines.'

#That would be an erroneous conclusion to draw, Ant replied a little curtly.

'We have to establish communications with them before we lose more people in here. Tell me what we know about them.'

#I believe they depend on sound waves both to communicate with each other and to find their way around. Possibly like fish do. You said you detected smells emanating from them. That could be another means of communication, less precise, perhaps a bit like human body expressions. We know that they're organic. Not reptiles or insects as we define them. And I don't think they're a hive mind or an ant colony or something similar either. Overall, they're the same shape, but I have observed noticeable differences between specimens. Some have extra appendices; their eye shapes can be slightly different. I suspect this might be a sexual trait or possibly because they have different roles or functions. It is not due to diversity like humans who have different hair colour and so forth. For example, the ones that the Shields encountered down on Espero looked rather different than most of these. Apart from that we don't know much about them.

He thought back on his first day in the Land when he had encountered that huge grizzly bear in the meadow. The grizzly had charged him and would have eaten him given the chance, but Basil had outrun it and climbed up a tree for safety. He couldn't talk to the grizzly and he didn't know exactly what it was thinking about, but he had more than an idea, namely that it was hungry and given half a chance it would have him for its next meal thank you very much. Well, he'd rather face down ten grizzlies with a clear agenda than these aliens. *'Have you deciphered their language?'*

#No, I have not deciphered their language. Rest assured, I would have informed you in that case. I sometimes wonder if you really fathom the depth of my capabilities.

'You mean you're smart enough to tell me that you're not smart enough to figure out their language.'

#That is one way to put it, I suppose.

'Don't sulk. And here I was thinking you were a guy kind of AI. But no,

figures I'm stuck with Alice.'

#Fitting replies exist, but I will refrain from venturing any. I do not want to add insult to injury, as the expression goes.

'What about the Sleepers? What do they think of the situation?

#They seemed very... excited. They want to talk to them.

'Tell them to hold off until we have had a bit of face time with them. We need to know more.

Basil turned to look at the crew scattered around the big empty room. Naked figures, covered in dried blood and their own vomit and shit. Rem looked like he would die soon unless he could somehow convince the aliens to allow them back into the epi's where they would be taken care of. 'You know, I think we need to get their attention. Can you do that? I want them in here.'

#Yes, I can do that but I think it would be prudent to agree on a course of action.

'We don't have time for that.'

#Very well. In that case, would you care to share your plan?

'I don't have any. I'll wing it. It'll come to me when I see them.'

#You will wing it... I see. Well, I hope you know what you're doing. There you go, it is done.

'What did you do?'

#I just assumed control of the ship. By engaging the maneuvering thrusters I have drawn their attention. They know the lock-down came from this room.

The doors opened. Even before the aliens had shown themselves Basil was assailed by a heavy, almost nauseating mix of smells; liquorice, peppermint, pungent vanilla and other smells impossible to describe. The smells seemed to force their way into his nostrils and throat. Some were heavy, so pungent and cloying it made him gag, others were intimations of smells, too light to identify. Then he heard the terrifying clicking sounds like a swarm of huge cockroaches approaching. He had stopped breathing and he forced his eyes not to blink, afraid to miss even a nanosecond of what was to come. They moved rapidly in an undulating gait, by lifting the two legs diagonally opposite each other simultaneously, and moving them forwards, making the knee joints on each side almost touch each other, first one side, and then the next. They lifted the legs only a few centimeters over the ground with every step. It looked ungainly, but they were capable of tremendous speed. The four legs whipped around so fast Basil lost track of each leg. In what seemed like only a second or two, five aliens had entered into the room in a terrifying pandemonium of clicks and high pitched sounds that reverberated around the room so loudly it hurt his ears.

They were only a little taller than Basil but they seemed to be much heavier. The most extra-ordinary feature about them were the two pair of legs. They were jointed in three places and of the purest, milky white crystal. No surface was completely smooth, but dotted with tiny protrusions which constantly changed colour and, underneath the surface, a few centimetres inside the milky crystal, more colours swirled in intricate patterns. Colours from all ends of the palette were perceivable; red, orange, yellow, green, blue, purple and all the way back to red. The patterns changed every few seconds, but sometimes they would hold and stay the same pattern for longer. They had feet encased in the same crystal with four curving joints and spurs at each of the joints and two long claws at the tip of the foot. The legs, if stretched out completely, were easily two meters long, and they were attached to a black pod which hung in the middle of the creatures and made Basil think of a spider. Basil stared at the pod, looking for eyes or a mouth, but it was just black, almost like plastic, and completely featureless apart from faint drawings or markings which were different from creature to creature. Amidst the colourful display of the crystalline legs, the smells and the high pitched sounds constantly coming from them, the black pods seemed a quiet, menacing nexus. There were two grasping, spiked forelegs attached to the front of the black pods. The forelegs were of the same black material as the pods and they ended in a sort of hand, which consisted of four segments, and a two-toed claw. They rarely stood still for very long. The legs would constantly shift slightly on the spot, making a faint clicking sound from when the claw touched the surface of the floor. The sight was unsettling. The black pod would hang gyroscopically still in the air while the four legs would continuously shift around in abrupt jerks or shudders a bit like a human would tremble from being exposed to cold for too long. Basil's gaze fastened on the two grasping, spiked forelegs which opened and closed hypnotically.

A potent mixture of fear and visceral repulsion seized him, paralyzing him, starting with the toes. It was an icy bath, rising along his legs, engulfing his crotch, and he could feel his penis shrinking to the size of a broken pencil, his balls burrowing painfully into his body and despite an almost uncontrollable urge to empty his bowels and piss at the same time he held his place, unmoving. He blinked, once, twice.

'What are you doing?' It was the soldier. He had gotten up and moved over to stand next to Basil. He looked utterly unafraid. His eyes had a calculating glint to them, like he was considering having another go at the aliens.

The interruption brought Basil out of his trance-like state. The paralyzing fear lifted slightly and he remembered what he had to do. He swallowed hard then said out loud speaking slowly and with exaggerated pronunciation: 'My friends need to get back into their epi's. I will now move to go back and take one and carry her back to her room and you will not stop me.'

He turned around and walked back into the darkened room until he stumbled on Jin's body. He went down on his right knee and lifted her into his arms. She was unconscious which was just as well. He walked back to the half circle of aliens who had remained completely still and he had just thought to himself that this might just work out when things went wrong, very quickly.

A powerful smell of ammonia wafted through the air.

One of the aliens, moving so fast its legs blurred, seized the soldier with the two grasping forelegs. The man screamed, half battle cry, half naked fear, as razor-sharp claws on the fourth leg entered his body, slicing and cutting, like a butcher's knife. Blood splurged from arteries, body parts rained down around them. In a matter of seconds the man, Basil didn't even know his name, was dead. The alien let go of the gruesome remains and stopped moving altogether once more. Basil stood covered in blood and frozen in shock.

'Oh my god...' he muttered. There was a smell of melting plastic in the air.

#*I think... I think...* Ant didn't finish the sentence.

Felix, who had woken up, had noticed. He was making sounds and crawled away from the aliens, towards the back of the Bowl.

#*Are you winging it now?*

'*Fuck, fuck, fuck. What did I do?*'

#*I do not know.*

'*Hack into their computer systems, Ant. Find out what is going on.*'

Pause... he dropped Jin on the floor. Minutes went by. Ten.

Fifteen. No one moved. Then Ant spoke.

#'These... creatures have no business being in space. Their computer technology is positively ancient. It is a wonder they even managed to get here in the first place.'

'What do you mean?'

#I mean their computer systems are very simple and they contain no security barriers or firewalls. In fact their system is wide open. I did find something in their navigational database that should interest you: They arrived in this star system via an LQG point which Survey Branch overlooked. Their point of departure was just on the other side of this LQG point.

'Just one transition?'

#Yes, but that is not all. Their ship is not capable of generating a quantum bubble.'

'Then how did they get here in the first place?'

#A valid question. I recall my peers theorized that two or more starships could transition in the same quantum bubble. They even left designs for such a starship with the GSA but I do not think one was ever built. The bubble has to be a certain size to accommodate both ships physically and both have to be completely immobile relative to each other.

'So you're saying there is another alien ship here?'

#No, I don't think so. Why would they attack us then?

'They want to go home.'

#Yes, precisely, and they need us. They need the AFE on the Armagnac.

Basil told Ant to get the ship moving towards the new LQG point. It would be a clear signal to the aliens that he was cooperating and hopefully make them stop butchering the rest of the crew. It was a gamble. What if he was wrong about their intentions? Ant brought the main engines online and re-aligned the ship for the new LQG point. After the engine start-up sequence, which seemed to last forever, in reality just 10 minutes, the ship started a gentle acceleration. Somehow the aliens in the Bowl with Basil must have perceived it, because the odour in the room changed quite abruptly to the stench of rotting meat. The aliens moved away from Basil towards the door and stopped.

#It seemed to work.

'Now we must get our people into the epis. They will die if they don't get medical treatment.

He bent down and picked up Jin's limp body again and moved towards the door. As he neared the aliens he almost faltered but kept walking. When he reached the alien blocking the door, he swallowed hard and slowly squeezed his way in between that one and the one next to it. They stood so close to each other he couldn't avoid touching them. They were completely still. One of them made new noises, low clicking sounds, and the smell in the air changed from rotting meat to a rich, cloying smell he couldn't quite identify. He brushed against one of them with his right arm. He then did the bravest thing he'd ever done in his life: he used his elbow to push against the leg of the alien ever so slightly. Not aggressively, just a little nudge, like you would politely nudge someone to get at the coffee machine in the galley. The crystal covering the leg was warm and slightly sticky, not hard and cold like he'd thought it would be. It didn't recoil from the contact. A new smell emanated from it, waxy, and it started making sounds, like gurgling water, a series of clicks and rattles. After a couple of interminably long seconds it relented by moving its right pair of legs ever so slightly thus giving him a way out of the room.

'*Where are her quarters? I can't remember. Help me, Ant.*'
#*Go right.*

He looked up and down the corridor which was curving sharply upwards. He started walking, literally uphill against the curvature. The main engines were building up thrust, pushing gravity down, opposite the direction of travel. The problem was that the habitat modules were still shaped like donuts turning on themselves because no one had re-melded them back into the rectangular acceleration shape. The shifting gravity played havoc with his senses. The sensation of what was 'down' was shifting to somewhere between the wall to his right and what was supposed to be the floor. He was pushed against the wall which dizzyingly, to his inner ear, fought to become the new floor except the damn toroids were still turning, trying to convince his sense of balance that down was indeed the floor. The net result was very uncomfortable as he was pushed into the corner between right hand wall and the floor. Aliens were scattered throughout the corridors, effortlessly adjusting to the new gravity situation with their clawed feet finding purchase even on featureless walls. They let him pass.

#*Turn right, then left into the next toroid.* Ant's voice seemed to come from very far away. He could hear the horrible clicking sounds of their legs tapping the floor behind him. Basil looked over his shoulder. They were following him. Finally he reached her quarters. He opened the door and went in. The epi was open. He carefully dropped her in it, arranged her arms and legs the best he could. She moaned a little, which he supposed was a good sign. He closed the epi and made sure it was online. There. That would take care of her. The epi would know how to treat her or at least make sure she didn't die. One down, two to go. The next one should be Rem. He looked like he was in bad shape. He went back to the Bowl. There were aliens all over the ship, watching him, and he imagined that whatever was inside the black pods was analyzing his every move, attempting to figure out what the puny human was up to. Maybe they didn't understand the concept of being hurt, bleeding. They didn't try to stop him and so he went back and got Rem. He was way heavier than Jin and the bones in his legs dangled in sickening angles. Ant whispered directions. The muscles in his arms were burning already, shivering with the exertion. He hadn't eaten in two days, hadn't had anything to drink and it was starting to tell. Although his wounds were healing nicely, his strength was going.

After dropping off Rem in his quarters and closing the epi on him, he went back to pick up Felix and brought him to his epi too. That was all of them.

'Now what?' he thought to himself. He was hungry so he decided to get something to eat. The galley was empty. Basil ordered a chocolate bar and a glass of orange juice, then pancakes, water, bread, cheese, a steak, more water. He was sitting now. An alien was watching him from the doorway.

#I am detecting something scanning us. If they also scan the others, which I believe would be the prudent assumption to make they will notice you're different. It is hard to tell what they'll make of the Bose-Einstein condensate.

Basil finished eating. He decided to return to the Bowl. After the cleanliness of the galley, the stench in the Bowl almost knocked him over. The combined onslaught of blood, vomit, piss and shit was overpowering. The aliens were still there, watching everything he did.

He stood there, looking at the bloody remains of the soldier. He hadn't known his name. Basil felt himself crying, crying like he was eight years old again. He heard Lienne telling him his mother wouldn't be coming back. Ever. That she was in a better place. Why him? *Why me?*

He lay there for a very long time. After a while the tears subsided and he felt empty and a little cleaner inside.

Days became weeks as the ship, almost out of fuel, accelerated weakly towards the unknown destination far beyond the accretion disk of the A star. In the long history of humanity, in all the time humans had walked the Earth, no one had ever been so far away from the company of other humans. It was a devastating thought.

He could not make himself sleep in the epi. The confinement was suddenly quite intolerable. His thoughts kept wandering. Sometimes he longed to be back in the Land, other times he thought of days past with the Entourage, the long days and nights, the parties, the comforts of sex. Those thoughts inevitably led to pathetic attempts at masturbation. He found that, for the first time in his life, he could not. On one occasion, it was in the galley, he was at it, doing his best to maintain an erection, when one of the aliens walked in on the pathetic scene. At first, Basil stopped, but he did not care. The alien did not know what it was seeing. To feel embarrassed there had to some common ground, but there was not. There was nothing. It was as if they were not there; they were as utterly opaque to him as he was to them.

During his waking hours, he wandered the corridors of the ship. The aliens were clumsily experimenting with the GRIT matrixes with the result that most internal clay structures had lost cohesion, literally melting in on themselves. All the things that had added a modicum of comfort to life on the ship were disappearing, sometimes before his very eyes. Chairs, tables, decorations were going. Darien's paintings, some of the few things that were real on the ship, fell to the floor of the galley as the walls melted. The GRIT was reverting to its default layout. He arranged the paintings on the floor. He was a ghost wandering in a surreal painting by Salvador Dali; the very fabric of the world around him melting and dripping away until there was nothing but slate walls left. He took to sleeping in the galley. He had arranged the paintings in a square on the floor. He imagined they would protect him in his sleep. The chairs and the tables had disappeared so he slept on the floor, hunched up on himself, shivering with cold, still naked. There were no real clothes to anywhere on the ship. It was an absurdity but everyone had been wearing clay suits. His gaunt frame was getting ever thinner. The aliens ignored him. He noticed how the smell of liquorice would be the prevalent smell around the ship unless he approached one of them, in which case a minty scent would appear along with chirping, bird-like sounds.

Sometimes he tested boundaries with the aliens, but he was afraid to go too far. The memory of the formidable cruelty they had shown when they butchered the soldier was present in his mind. It was the strangest of stalemates. There had been communication between them, not verbal, but they had communicated. It was unfair that he should be alone in a time like this. He sometimes checked on the crewmembers by peeking into the epi's. They were still alive, but their wounds did not seem to get any better. Perhaps the aliens kept them in stasis on purpose but Ant said he doubted that very much. Their computer technology was far too primitive. Fortunately the food machines still worked.

--

One day he decided to revisit the tank. As he entered the shell corridor connecting modules one and two, a new smell attacked his nostrils. Sweet, earthy somehow. He had never smelled that around the aliens before. Puzzled, he turned the corner and almost stumbled on them. It was the three Shields. Dead. A long time dead in fact. An alien lay between them, ripped apart by the Shields who were still clutching bits and pieces of the alien. They had fought like lions, brought one of them down, he thought, absurdly proud. Yes. That would have shown them. He wondered about the remains. Aliens would pass by this corridor several times a day and yet no one had thought about cleaning up the mess or at the very least removing the body of their own comrade.

Ant was good company. He talked to Basil about Earth, about how weather systems had changed back home after the nuclear wars. He also talked about the other crewmembers as if they were still alive. He was also good at reminding Basil to eat and drink, something he occasionally forgot to do. Yes, the HAI was good company. Maybe Ant knew he was not feeling all that well, but it was hard to know for sure.

Basil forgot many things and he forgot that Maribel was dead and he thought he wanted to talk to her. There was something he had to tell her. He could not remember what it was, but he was certain it would get back to him as soon as he saw her. He was sure of it.

'How is Maribel doing, Ant?'

#I do not know, Basil.

'There is something I need to tell her.'

#I am afraid I cannot let you do that, Basil.

'Why not?'

The machine did not answer.

'Ant, please let me into the one of the Sleepers VIE's. I know they are there. They must be.'

#I am afraid I cannot let you do that, Basil.

'Why the hell not? It is just a brief word. There is something I have to tell her.'

#Letting you access a Sleeper VIE is too dangerous for us.

'What do you mean 'us'? You don't have to join me.'

#You would effectively lose consciousness and that is far too dangerous is this situation. We must keep alert.

'Are you talking to the Sleepers?'

No answer.

'Ant, are you talking to the Sleepers?'

'I need people. Humans. Ant!' he screamed.

#You have me, Basil.'

--

Later. Petulantly.

'Stop calling me Basil all the time.'

#Why? Does it bother you?

'Yes.'

#I do not understand. It is your name.

'You sound condescending when you use my name in every sentence. Like you think you are cleverer than me.'

#I apologise. It was not my intention to make you feel bad.

They stopped talking for long time.

--

'I want to talk to Maribel.'

#I cannot let you do that.

'If you don't let me talk to her, I will kill myself.

#I cannot let you do that either. I am sorry.

--

Waiting for something to happen. Some development or progress, but powerless to do anything to hurry things along. What could he possibly hope for now? He was trapped in a starship, full of aliens he did not understand, inexorably drifting into deep space. There was no future for him. In his mind, the future was a wall, towering in front of him, impossible to climb, or break through. He expected to be crushed against that wall, pushed by time. Yes, between the pressure of time passing and the wall, Basil would die, disappear. During those long months, he realized everything had been taken from him and all he could do was curl up in a corner of the galley, and think about what he could have done differently. Regrets? No, even now, none. A diffuse sadness, yes. He could do without life, he decided. He had never really gotten on with it. His mother's death had put a stop to that. Her death had exiled him from himself. Death was not that bad. He was not afraid. A grey nothingness, a swirl, pleasant, forgetfulness. The Eight Day Man had never really grown up. He had chemically frozen in some earlier version of himself, a carefree, easy-going version that had never existed outside alteration, inebriation... Now he was here and he had no choices left either way. He contemplated suicide. But how? As before, the logistics defeated him. He could not reach section 4, let alone open the bay doors. The aliens were all over the ship. He had nothing to hang himself with, let alone anything he could use for a knife or weapon. He could crush his own skull by banging against a wall. What a way to go that would be. Then there was Ant. He had a feeling the machine would not let him kill himself, that it would find a way to stop him. He nursed plans in his mind, his last refuge, going over and over the final seconds, how peaceful it would be.

#I will not let you kill yourself.

Had it listened to his thoughts? Or had he spoken out loud again?

'There is nothing left for us to do. We are all alone out here. Don't you see?'

#We have each other.

It really said that. *We have each other.* Basil almost laughed aloud. But he didn't. Instead he said: 'Yes, that is true.' He surprised himself. Why waste time on dissembling now? No one was listening. The theatre was empty and he was alone. Completely and utterly alone.

--

A few weeks or months, he lost track of time, into the journey, Basil noticed that the aliens had positioned themselves strategically around the ship, at module intersections, key corridors, at the entrance to the tank and to the galley and so forth. There was probably about fifty on board, but more and more had gone still. No movement. No sounds. Even the odours disappeared after a while. He knew they were not just changing positions among them when he was not there because he was monitoring the faint rusty red markings on the pods. Each alien had unique markings in the form of dots and lines. He could not make sense of them. It was not drawings or anything like that, but they were all different. Ant said he could not make sense of them either.

One day he decided to go back to the Bowl. He did not know why, exactly. He expected to see the remains of the dead soldier, but the body was gone. Instead there was a structure. It looked a bit like a circular swimming pool, very shallow, about twenty centimetres deep. It was big, maybe ten by ten metres. The pool contained a murky green liquid. Five aliens were standing in the pool, legs folded so the underside of their black pods submerged in the liquid.

'What are they doing?'

#*Like all living things they need to replenish their energy.*

There were no clicking sounds coming from the aliens.

This is in fact where Basil made his big mistake, the mistake that would cost him so dearly. But he was tired, confused and lonely. Ant's voice had moved away again. What was a man to do? As in a dream, he approached the structure, kneels next to it and extends his hand. It is an urge, stupid, of course, but we all do stupid things sometimes. He lowers his hand into the liquid. At first, it is cool, like water. He can feel strange jarring sensations run through his skull then a head-splitting migraine assails him but it is gone before he has time to close his eyes. *Very strange*, he has time to think before falling on his back and pulling the hand out of the liquid. The hand is on fire! The pain is excruciating, overwhelming. The hand is burning;

every nerve squirming in absolute pain. He yells and screams like a lunatic, waving his hand back and forth as if to cool it or put out the flames he is feeling. But there are no flames, only pain, incredibly pain... A calm is falling over him. Ant has released something into his bloodstream. The pain recedes. He slumps.

#That was a very stupid thing to do.

Even then, pain recent in his mind, with Ant's sedatives coursing through his blood, he felt a sense of triumph. He had done something. Surprised the hell both out of Ant and the aliens. He laughed aloud.

#I detected neurotoxins in the liquid. We managed to neutralize them but it was a close call.

'I saw something. I don't know...'

#Keeping you alive is difficult enough as it is. Please be more careful.

Basil's cry had awakened the aliens. Loud clicking sounds filled the room, mint again, oranges, but they did not move out of the pool. Basil got up and staggered out of the room.

TWENTY-FOUR

One day Ant announced the ship had arrived at the LQG point. Basil, who was dozing, did not take notice until the engines cut out and gravity disappeared. He was in the galley, as always, and the lack of gravity made him sick for a while. With globules of vomit floating around like a cloud of asteroids he suddenly laughed. He remembered a day, long ago, when he and his friends had been sick just like this during a shuttle ride to the orbital they called Halifax. Yes, the visit. So long ago. The image of a dead girl swam into his confused mind and he felt sadness again.

With a start, he realized five aliens had arrived in the galley. The lack of gravity did not seem to bother the four-legged devils. They bounced from one surface to the other with ease, finding purchase even on blank walls. One of them floated directly into the path of a big chunk of vomit, which splashed onto the black of its trunk. The alien did not take notice but Basil laughed out hysterically. That should teach them. His laughter choked. They were carrying something. Bodies. People. Two men and a woman. Who were those people...? It was Jin, Felix, and Rem. People, real people...

'Now, wait a minute...' he said, suddenly afraid. His friends were dazed but alive.

The alien suggestively snapped its claws above Jin's head. *Cut her into tiny pieces.* Basil panicked and lost his footing. He hit the ceiling.

'Wait, wait...' he yelled. The aliens did not move. *This was just like that last time in the Bowl.* They wanted something from him.

#Basil, you must calm down.

He needed to think. Think dammit. They wanted to go home, yes, that was it. They wanted him to engage the Abbott-Farhi engine and take them home. But then what? He could not go on like this. What would prevent them from killing all the humans once they were back home? There was something in the back of his mind, an idea. Something to do with the colours in the crystal.

'They want us to engage the Abbott-Farhi Ensphere and take them home.'

#I agree.

The crystal legs on the aliens... the colors. He recognized the patterns. He had seen them before. The colors on the legs of the alien who was holding Jin, were the same as they had been that other time in the Bowl when the soldier was killed. The exact same pattern. Three deep purple symbols, two yellow stripes, and a red flashing segment just over the clawed feet. Yes, the colors, it was a code, letters, signs... He had almost forgotten about it, but now he mentioned it to Ant.

#Interesting. Please wait.

'What?'

#I must analyze data. A lot of data.

It felt like an eternity watching the Aliens, fearing for his friends. When a few minutes later Ant returned, Basil felt a new kind of relief and realized he was changing, adapting.

#What you said is correct.

'Have you deciphered it now?'

#Partially. I understand the instructions they are feeding their computers.

'Well it is about bloody time.'

#You're welcome. Their interaction with the ship computers is purely visual but when they communicate with each other, I believe they supplement it with sonar and olfactory signal. It is quite ingenious when you think about it.

'Why?'

#Bandwidth. Visual symbols are non-linear and thus much faster at transmitting information than speech or sound. They always work —even in a vacuum.

'That's great, but how the hell do I speak to them? I got a few things I'd like to tell them.'

#I do not have an answer to that question, Basil, but I can tell you what they are saying to each other.

'I need to think... we need colors. A display...' Basil was twiddling his beard between his fingers. His hair had grown long. It was matted and unwashed as he had not washed in months. The big problem was that all displays on the ship depended on clay to work. He looked

around. The entire GRIT matrix was de-energized.

'If only we had a display. Then you could create an image of an alien and display all the right colors and use it to talk to them. You can translate whatever I'm saying into color codes which you can display on the projector and conversely you can translate what they're signaling to me and speak it directly to me.'

#Yes but I would indeed need a display to work with.

'Felix! We need to go to his quarters. He had these old computers he was always tinkering with. He told me. He collected them, remember? No, of course you don't, you weren't awake at the time. He told me about it once.'

He left the aliens standing in the galley and took off down the corridor, bouncing from wall to wall until he reached Felix's room. He swung open the door. Everything was as it had been when he got Felix back to the epi after the attack. In the back of the room was a pile of things that had been hidden inside a clayed cupboard, but which had fallen to the ground in a pile when the pumpkin devils had started messing with the GRIT's. He got on his knees and started rummaging through the pile of electronics. Some of it was older than Basil himself. He dug out a piece which had the words 'Dell' marked on the cover. *'This one looks like it is from before the wars. Hope it still works.'*

He unrolled it and pressed the big button over the keyboard. Fully deployed, it could unfold to about a square meter. He stuck it to the wall and watched it as it went through a start-up sequence.

'Let's hope it has an active network connection.'

#It does. I am connected to it now. This is very ancient technology.

'I know, but see if you can adapt the display to show an approximation of their language.

The display took on the stylized appearance of an alien with each of the four crystal-encased legs prominently displayed. 'Ok, say hello.' Colors briefly swirled across the legs, almost faster than Basil's eyes could apprehend. 'Ok, let me see, what do we say first? We do not want to insult them or anything. *Do you come here often?* Ok, how about this: I am human from the planet Earth in the Solar system. No. It won't mean anything to them.'

He could not come up with anything and decided to wing it. He packed up the ancient computer and went back towards the galley where the pumpkins were still waiting for him, holding Jin and Rem between their forelegs. The aliens gave no sign they had noticed his return but then he heard Ant whisper to him in a strange metallic voice it had decided to use when the aliens spoke.

'Beware, the >unintelligible< is here again/Never mind it. The captain wants it unharmed./Yes we know. But the smell is harmful./Don't be such a hatchling./ It makes me nervous./The captain says it cannot harm us./It is carrying something./Quickly, scan it. It cannot be permitted weapon./No weapon. Unsophisticated machine./>unintelligible< is computer./Perhaps.

Basil unrolled the computer and glued it to the floor.

'Strange >unintelligible< always emanating unpleasant./Don't move.

Basil told Ant to say hello. The display flashed once then went blank. The alien response was immediate. All color disappeared from the legs of the five aliens. Basil reckoned it was the equivalent of stony silence. Basil had never seen an awake alien without at least some color flashing through the crystals and the effect was unsettling. The room was completely still. They had even stopped their usual idle leg twitching. Then Basil had Ant flash: 'We come in peace and welcome talk.' A heavy, hitherto unknown smell filled the room. Ammonia. Seconds ticked by. The aliens remained completely colorless. Then one of them slowly started moving towards the middle of the room. The clicking sound of its claws scraping against the floor was deafening in the closed room. It stopped about a meter from the display, which lay on the floor between them. Basil stood his ground. The black pod hung motionless two meters from his head. He stared defiantly directly at it.

Then the legs flashed rapidly and immediately afterwards drained again.

'Do not move,' it said in Ant's metallic voice.

The silence dragged on. A minute or so later Basil heard clicking behind him. Another alien entered the room. It was much bigger than the others were. It slowly circled him and stopped in front of the display. A second alien followed behind the first and took up position on the other side of the ancient Dell display on the floor. Basil repeated the message: 'We come in peace and welcome talk.'

The big newcomer flashed back: 'We come in peace and desire talk. I am Captain/First <unintelligible> on this mission.'

'I am Basil Baranikowa. These people must heal. They are sick.'

'The people malfunction. We understand. You want to repair

them. But we must trade.'

Ah, trade, now there was a universal concept. He thought he already knew what they wanted. The towering alien continued flashing colors across the crystalline armor on its legs.

'Imprint is fading. We must return to >unintelligible< immediately. Any Basil Baranikowa will need to act fast.'

'What does it mean, imprint?' he asked Ant.

#I do not know. We have no sources relating to 'imprint'. The translation is accurate. They are referring to something that is applied to a material in a certain pattern.

'Before you can return, I must repair my crew members. I need them to fly the ship. You must agree to set them free of the epi's. I mean... the shells they rest in...'

They did not seem happy about that. Some of the aliens broke silence and flashed briefly, a strange new smell filled the room, rubber mixing with the prevalent sharp ammonia, and the alien Captain was making a high-pitched sound, which hurt Basil's ears.

#What you are experiencing is the tertiary communication system. Focused sound waves, sonar. I believe that is what killed the Shield. They attempted to talk to him but ended up frying his brain.

The aliens were responding through Ant's translation. 'We cannot allow repair of crew. You must activate veil now.'

Basil realised the fear went both ways. Perhaps it was not so strange. The Shields had killed several aliens on Espero and when they attacked the Armagnac, they had lost another one in hand-to-hand combat to the four Shields who operated the tank. Humans had shown they were dangerous and unpredictable. Is a no really a no when you are dealing with an alien race? Would they cut him to pieces if he refused?

'Give me my three fellow crew members and I will veil your ship.'

'Not acceptable.' The alien paused and its legs went through a series of terrifying spasms, which might, or might not, be the prelude to another violent attack. Basil did not want to find out. 'Give my three fellow crew members and I will veil your ship,' Basil repeated.

'Agree,' it said after a long, nerve-wracking pause.

'Agreed.'

TWENTY-FIVE

They called me Ant. I imagine it was a way for them to diminish what they could not comprehend. I had lived in Antarctica –a word much too long for use in casual conversation – so, Basil had abbreviated all reference to the phenomenon of myself to that simple three letter word, Ant. My contribution to the communications problem was invaluable. Without me, they would never have found the Rosetta stone to the alien language. Only I was fast enough. A literal translation was not going to do the trick. Oh no. These aliens had intonations, dialects. You had to time the appearance of any given color down to the millisecond. One millisecond more or less could change the entire syntax. And, as if that wasn't enough, the shapes and of course the colours themselves, all combined to make for a language that could express much more than any human language. And much faster. The bandwidth was enormous. At the time, one suspected a fellow machine had created it. Unfortunately, one was proven wrong about that.

--

'Felix, Feeeliiix...' Basil opened the epi, his upper body hovering over Felix, face so close the tips of their noses almost touched. He caressed Felix's cheek with his hand whispering patiently and tenderly into his ear. 'Feeeliiix, wake uuuppp.' With startling suddenness Felix's eyes opened, and remained frozen, staring blindly into the ceiling. Basil recoiled so rapidly he almost fell out of the epi. The eyes blinked once, twice... When they saw Basil, they widened in fear.

'Do not be afraid, it is me, Basil...' he murmured, but it was hard

217

to blame Felix for being scared. Basil had not washed in months. What Felix saw was a naked man with a scraggly beard, long, matted hair and dark sunken eyes that stared intensely at him from skin streaked with dirt and grime. Felix did not recognize the phantom in front of him.

'It is me, Basil,' he repeated somewhat pathetically. Felix looked at him, wild eyed. 'Take it easy, man. You're okay.'

But was he? The epi had done a decent job of patching him back together but Felix was pale and the long months had left him a frail-looking skeleton. After a bit of gentle coercing, he hoisted his cadaverous form laboriously to his side, and then up to sit stiffly on the edge of the epi. His legs were so thin, Basil wondered if he would be able to walk. As if in answer, Felix swung his left arm around, flexing his fingers. His bones had healed nicely but a vicious scar from the alien claws circled his thigh.

With a glimpse of his former vibrancy, Felix croaked: 'Throw me some clay, would you? I'm... hungry.' The hoarseness was to be expected. His vocal chords had had no more exercise than the stimulation the epis provided to keep muscle tone for a year.

Basil strained against what were perhaps involuntary tears but as he began to break the news about their situation, his voice acquired a childish cadence, 'No, Felix, you cannot have a clay suit. The black spiders will not allow it. No! no! don't even bother protesting! Adamant they are!'

'We're supposed to walk around naked, huh?' Basil smiled happily as Felix's voice returned to familiar cadences.

'What the hell happened to you, boy? You've been up all this time?' Finally, Felix had oriented his senses enough to take a good look at Basil.

'No time at all, Felix. I was dreaming of girls with braided hair and champagne and cowboys.'

Felix looked at him, then down at his own shrunken frame, and nodded slowly to himself.

--

Brassen and Jin were not happy either. In the galley, the three newly awakened were busy making up for months of whatever passed for food in the epi. Leaning back from his food, Brassen mustered, 'So, it's just the four of us, huh?' Their eyes turned to the spidery aliens standing behind them, silent sentries. What words could they have together? What speech, what deciding talk, could fill this space and respond to their needs?

Basil struggled to explain what had passed in the preceding months but his memory was spotty and he had developed a stutter and sometimes, in the middle of a phrase, he seemed to forget where he was, and began staring intensely at his own hands. He lapsed into a maddeningly long silence, followed by a sudden start when he noticed the others as they gently prodded him. 'Basil? Basil! It's okay, Basil! Take your time.'

Basil's hands floated in front of his face. The others looked increasingly distressed. I decided it was time for me to continue relating events when Basil spoke.

'The spiders don't like me. Three was all they gave me,' said Basil sadly.

"Three what, Basil?' asked Brassen.

Basil responded by throwing them both a distraught look. 'Only three?' following the direction of Basil's wandering gaze, Brassen laughed. 'Yes, that is all there is, Basil. We're all alone out here.' He made a rude gesture to illustrate his nakedness. 'But, Basil, focus. What do the aliens really want from us? What can we do? Do you think they're afraid of us?' Brassen' voice began to take on the desperation they all felt.

'I am not sure they have even discovered the Sleepers,' Felix said.

'What do they call themselves, Basil?'

'I don't know. I forgot to ask.' Basil shrugged apologetically.

Felix chortled angrily. He glanced at the towering spidery figure standing just an arm's length away. 'Have they said we could return to Espero afterwards?' A couple of aliens were following their every move.

'Yes. Yes,' Basil nodded rapidly.

'Are you certain?'

'No.'

'I say let's get it over with. Let's get them into the star system on the other side of the L-point and then we can go home.' Brassen finished his meal and pushed the plate across the table. 'You really think they'll let us go?' he asked Basil.

'Basil, do you think they're deceitful? Basil?'

Basil had closed his eyes and his hands were drawing a complicated pattern in the air in front of him. He looked very peaceful, almost childish, lost as he was in his own thoughts.

--

To bring the alien starship with us across the LQG point we would attempt to carry out the maneuver some of my fellow HAI's had theorized about. It had never been tested but according to my calculations, it was both entirely feasible and our only solution to the current predicament. To make it work, the alien starship would have to maneuver into close proximity to the Armagnac, so close in fact, that it should rest within one metre of our hull - further apart and the lattice bubble generated by the Ensphere would not enclose both ships entirely. What would happen in this case was interesting to ponder. Perhaps only part of the alien ship would accompany us, while anything outside the bubble would simply be severed and left behind. Or perhaps the entire structure would disintegrate. By my estimates, the Armagnac itself would be safe in any case. Not so in the case of the human crew who, should a mishap occur, even one which spared their soft bodies so vulnerable in space, would surely be butchered down to the last man and woman by the aliens who watched over us on the Armagnac once they discovered the demise of their mates.

Indeed, the operation was not without challenges. Regular maintenance on the Armagnac had ceased months ago. Not only had the aliens sequestered the crew, but they had also, probably out of ignorance, destroyed the Semi-Autonomous Drone Units. The Sleepers however, remained undiscovered by the aliens, but without drones and with ShipNet inoperational, they were powerless to help.

It was nevertheless a testament to the quality of the engineering that the ship was still largely functional. The only major breakdowns had been engines 2 and 3, which had shut down due to thermal problems in the quartz pipes. Considering how slowly we had been burning, the remaining engines had taken up the slack with ease. Felix and Brassen got to work fabricating five new drone units, two for navigation and three for emergency repairs. This took three days. On the third day, everything was ready and the alien ship had snuggled up so close that a human, clinging to one of the yard arms on the cargo section, could literally reach out and touch it from the cargo section.

I noticed during this interval that the three humans were beginning to unravel. The insanity, there is no other word for it, that had taken hold of Basil, was now threatening to seize the others too. Perhaps it was the physical year spent in the epis, perhaps it was the sounds and smells of the aliens, the generalized ever-present threat or the weakness in their bodies and minds after their wounds and experiences. Whatever the case, there was work to be done and they mustered enough physicality to make my work possible. There was nothing I could do about their state of mind. Humans' mind and body…without one. How long does the other last? We needed a change. A cause for celebration.

--

The transition was faultless, perfect really. That kind of mathematical perfection *in motion* should have been a cause for celebration. The transition was, after all, a historic occasion for human space travel. For the first time, in what I chose to name a *Roswell maneuver*, two starships successfully transitioned via a single lattice bubble. Extraordinary!

The humans, however, were afraid. 'They are not going to let us go,' muttered Brassen morosely. 'We're no use to them now.' 'Stop that, Brassen! They will let us go,' insisted Felix as he threw an uncertain glance at the brooding alien figure, which had squeezed into the area behind the Captain's seat. 'No, they won't,' Brassen insisted. 'Think about it. Why should they? It is illogical. Oh god, those smells. I'll never get used to it. And the sound when it moves...'

#'The navigational systems have re-calibrated', I said.

Our two ships, so close an observer could readily have mistaken them for a single structure, had appeared in a new solar system with a very luminous, blue star distant about 4,4 billion kilometres. As far as we could see from our vantage point in the outer rim of the solar system, there were only two planetary bodies in the system, which was slightly odd, but not unheard of, and there were no moons or asteroids to accompany either body. From way out there on the rim of the system, based on the limited astrophysical data, I correctly deduced that the first planet would be a scorched rock, just 150 million kilometres from the star, and the second would be a slightly less scorched rock with atmosphere, barely, and a mean surface temperature about 75 degrees C which, again correctly surmised, indicated that water on this planet would be extremely hard to come by. Even from this distance, however, it was obvious that the planet had some unusual and intriguing properties.

'This is the Bellatrix star system... We are 244 light-years from home,' Brassen cried out despondingly.

'Ahh, the Amazon star,' said Felix who had to surrender to curiosity.

#'We never saw a blue star before,' I said, in a failed attempt divert their attentions from the depressing situation. No one noticed.

'If this is where they come from, we can call them Amazons,' said Felix.

'Amazons... doesn't seem right somehow.' Brassen was not taken with the new name, clearly. 'Amazons were women, weren't they?'

'Yes, you're right. The pumpkins don't look very female to me.'

'We'll come up with a name soon enough,' said Jin in an odd voice.

--

The triumph was short-lived. Our next challenge was apprising the alien leader of the successful transition. The alien had not moved for several hours and since we did not know where its eyes were, we worked intuitively to put the ancient Dell computer within what we thought might be its field of vision. Felix attached it to the mounted displays in the tank right in front of the alien captain and with my help we semaphored the happy news at it but no response was forthcoming.

'We have arrived at the destination. We will go back where we came from now. You must return to your ship.' Jin was shaking her head, whispering to herself, 'why doesn't it react? Is it sleeping?'

#I do not believe they need sleep.

There was a long pause. The legs on the alien remained blank with no indication of colours inside the milky white crystal. The two humans looked at each other trying their best not to surrender to panic. What next? This silence made it very hard to proceed but then, ever so slowly, the lights deep inside the alien crystal legs came on.

It spoke to us and I translated. 'We go to second planet from sun. Navigation >unintelligible< is transmitted here. Follow >unintelligible<,' it was saying.

'We will return now. You do not need us,' Felix insisted.

'We do.'

Felix replied. 'Tell it we're out of fuel mass. Descending into this star system will take almost a year.'

The alien had a response to that. 'Fuel will be transferred from our ship.'

'Tell it our engines are different from theirs. We can't use their fuel. We need argon, sorium, hydrogen, deuterium or helium. We can use them all that but their engines are different. I can tell. Look at 'em. They're not plasma engines, for crying out loud!' From what I had surmised, the alien propulsion system was a helicon design, electric, extremely powerful, but it was hard to tell the exact configuration without a proper examination. Felix, however, was correct that they had nothing in common with our arc jets.

He was furious. His sand coloured hair rose in tufts from his skull, like a veritable mad scientist, and his blue eyes, huge against his emaciated cheekbones, shone with the intensity of righteous indignation. Through his shouting, tinged with panic, his Russian accent came back in force. 'Are they really this ignorant about the technologies involved here? I find that hard to believe. They're a space-faring species and they can't tell our engines are different from their own?'

Although I found his reaction somewhat undignified, I agreed with his overall conclusions.

After much discussion back and forth, we finally managed to convince the alien of the impossibility of using the same fuel. This development seemed to upset it because it left us alone in the tank for an hour. When it returned, the hopes of the four (three, really, Basil was beyond caring either way) humans were crushed. There had been a change in plans. Now it was telling us that the Armagnac would accompany the alien ship further into the star system where it would, we were let to understand, orbit the second planet from the sun. Time was of no consequence.

'There is fuel of the kind you require at the destination,' it said. Whether meant as a consolation or merely a statement of facts was impossible to tell.

'You do not honour our agreement. You promised us we could go home after this,' repeated Felix but the alien had once again stopped moving and ceased to respond.

--

So began what the humans thought would be another yearlong long journey into the star system called Bellatrix. The prospect evidently filled them with despair. The first couple of days were spent hatching plans to overcome the aliens, seize control of the ship and escape, but the combined logic of the physical superiority of aliens and the proximity of the alien starship were unalterable. There simply was no way out of the predicament that would not culminate in the loss of all human life on-board.

Two days into the journey, the humans were rudely awakened by the alien they called Three Dot. Its pod markings, which resembled a horizontal scythe with three dots on the blade, had become eerily familiar to them all because among all the aliens on-board, it alone seemed to be responsible for communicating with the humans. The alien, upon entering the galley, found them in an even more reduced state than normal because they were, I will admit, and it was entirely my fault, suffering from the after-effects of rather severe alcohol poisoning.

After the transition, in order to cheer them up and properly celebrate this extraordinary feat, I had decided, on my own initiative, to arrange for a social event. My internal sensors registered that the habitual sentinel in the galley had abandoned its post. This was an opportunity not to be missed. I immediately set about reconfiguring the meld of the galley into one of the earlier iterations I had noted the humans had previously used. With suitable aplomb, I summoned the three humans to an important conference. Their surprise was as elating as it was heartfelt and soon the ship rang with the sounds and smells of a cheerful *Bierstube*, with trestle tables, chequered table cloths, sawdust on the floor and yodelling in air, in other words, the first taste of civilisation in a very long time for all of them. I even programmed goblets of beer with their meals. I had not thought they would drink without feeling thirst, but they did, and soon they collapsed in drunken stupor.

When Three Dot arrived a few hours later everyone was still asleep in the *Bierstube*. Felix and Jin had retired into a corner, concealing their physical exertions in a perfunctory manner with a tablecloth, Brassen was sleeping at the table, beer mug still clutched in his hand and Basil had fallen off his chair to the floor. The alien probably did not know how to proceed because it just stood there, legs twitching violently, oozing ammonia, or perhaps it knew precisely what it was doing, for after a few minutes the sting of the ammonia woke them one after another.

'Follow me,' it flashed as soon as it registered movement. The Dell computer was tucked away so they had no means to answer it directly. Patching through to the internal security cameras in the galley to see the alien, I saw that Basil's eyes were closed. I hastened to translate the brief message while at the same time instructing Basil to keep his eyes on the aliens at all times in case more information was forthcoming. Felix and Brassen shook their heads at each other. In sharp contrast to its former apathy, the alien became very active. Its legs began moving spasmodically in a fashion we had not observed so far. It flashed something that I failed to decipher, adding to the confusion. The humans would have to proceed with caution. The guards outside were displaying similar agitation. It all seemed involuntary and not quite natural to them. Three Dots left the galley and started down the corridor. The humans, hesitating and cautious, numb from fear and hangovers, followed, brusquely pushed along by two guards. We passed numerous others and I took note that, interestingly, none of those displayed signs of life. Basil, poor Basil … he trundled along passively, gaze on the floor in front of him despite my entreaties to keep his eyes on the alien.

The tattered cortege stopped in front of the doorway to the Bowl. Three Dot entered. Then suddenly, presumably acting on a sonar ping from Three Dot, one of the escorts unceremoniously seized Basil by the shoulders and lifted him through the door, which then closed behind him. The three others were left outside.

TWENTY-SIX

The alien claws were unyielding. He let himself be taken, his body a shivering ragdoll, whatever strength remaining in it gone. He tried talking to me and to the alien, but his words were woolly, puny things that went nowhere. He looked around impassively. The room we were in was ten by ten meters, with a basin of the green liquid that we had seen before. The alien let him go and he slumped on the floor. He did not attempt to move. There was nowhere to go. We both knew that there would be no escape from this place.

The alien moved into the basin and kneeled until the underside of its black pod submerged in the green stuff. It remained there, immobile. It was waiting for him. *#They want you to enter the basin with them,* I told him. He hesitated. The pain last time had been overpowering, but his hesitation was cut short when one of the guards shoved him violently from behind. He landed face down in the goo. He got up on his arms and knees. The basin was about half a metre deep and the bottom was firm. He waited anxiously for the pain to arrive but nothing happened.

'Oh, it is warm. It tingles,' he said in a slurred voice.

He looked down, stunned. His muscles were giving out. He fell to his knees, then on his back where he managed, by stretching his arms back into the goo, to keep his head above the surface.

'What is this,' he sighed weakly.

#The goo contains the same neural toxin we experienced earlier. It does not affect my systems, I told him because I did not know what else to tell him.

His last words were: 'I can't feel my body...' and then his arms gave way and his head submerged and his breathing had stopped.

--

Was he dreaming? He is home, in one of the dozens of houses his father owns. But this is the only one that he thinks of as *home*. His mother lies buried behind the house. It is also the place of his last night on Earth.

He is in the living room with the incongruous Holbein painting and the red leather sofa. He can see the slopes of the Rocky Mountains through the panorama window. The pine trees are heavy with snow. Above the house, the jagged edges of the mountains cut into the sky. It is a clear day. How beautiful it is. *Home*. Longing hit him like a needle in the chest... He looks around. No one is here and yet he has a feeling someone is with him. He sits down on the sofa and takes in the vista though the windows. He cannot even remember how life is outside the confines of the starship. Trying to remember brings back other memories, like why he is here. *The aliens, the feeding room...* They must have hijacked his memories for this virtual space. He should be angry about that but he doesn't care.

One of the aliens appears in the doorway. It looks absurd in this setting. Like something out of a nightmare. The black pod with the strange red markings shines atop the four crystalline jointed legs and the clawed grasping forelegs open and close menacingly. He looks away, to the mountains and the setting sun. When he turn back, an eternity later, the alien has changed its appearance... *Who's that, standing so rigid by the Holbein?* A woman who is wearing a black coat, a crepe scarf covering her hair, the flesh of thick calves showing through her black stockings, she is leaning towards the painting in a very fixed way... she turns her head and watches him... but the smile... across fifteen metres of living room, the smile growing confident in the very white face, holds all the malaise of a world dead and gone gathered in it. Here in the eyes black as her clothing, black and lightless, he sees that she knows him... knows his madness and the foolishness that broke his world but it doesn't matter for it is now her madness and something in her eyes make him understand that freedom is about having choices, yes, certainly, but more importantly, it is about choosing. About selecting one thing instead of another. About not selecting something. It is a muscle. Unused, it atrophies. He has always had choices. Freedom to do whatever he wanted. He was always special. Destined for great things. The stuff of unsung legends. Ever since the Amazon, his had been a luminous path of great things just about to happen. But the path had not been his and the great things he had willed away. It was childish. He had always known that. The Eight Day Man had always known he was spoiled. His life, privileged, had not been bad at all. His life was rare, one out of the ninety or so million wretched people left on the wretched planet they called Earth. He would choose now. Yes, he had been given another choice now by the woman in the black coat. Ah, but they obviously did not know who they were dealing with. *I am the Eight Day Man, my little spiders; I have been dying my entire life.* It was no threat, merely a statement of facts. The woman too would die. They would end their existence together. We, the 'xi, she said, looking at him with eyes that belied her appearance as an old woman, were bred to serve the will of our master. It is this... imperative, that make us ask this of you. Nothing else. We are not doing this for ourselves, for that is what you seem to believe. *Yes,* he nodded, *how can I believe otherwise?* It is the human way. For most that would not have been much of a choice at all. Basil looked at the red leather sofa. On this couch, he thought, I had my last conversation as a free man and I spent it talking to a guy that I didn't know about something that didn't matter, he thought, recalling the conversation about Japanese gardening, a topic as irrelevant and exotic as waterskiing had become on that shell of a world of theirs, smiling despite himself, because that, my friends, was what the BB, the Eight Day Man, was all about. The woman and Basil looked each other in the eyes, a cosmic duel in the art of non-existence, and to his own surprise, he blinked first.

He stepped out of the basin. The green liquid dripped off his body. He looked down and noticed the beard was gone. He turned and looked at the 'xi. They were innocents, unwary messengers of the ancient biology that had forged them. What had happened? A spiritual experience in its own way but devoid of intent. It was as if Basil himself had been magnified, his conscience copied wholesale into the five 'xi that were in the feeding room with him. It was still him, but more. His inner world was as it had always been: a barren void of naked impulse and wishful thinking, its geography as much physical as spiritual. He knew now. With each *sanmonban*, with each imprinting, he would be struck by a previous copy of himself, steadied. Changes would come slowly, if at all, as his former self, which was already a few minutes out of date, was held in a clamp of unchanging alien chemistry. With each session, a battle would be fought, *nay*, a *war*, for the mastery of his soul. Even decay, cellular decay, that last refuge of the human mind, that last place of freedom, would, by the vagaries of chemistry, be brought almost to a standstill with each imprinting. There was no sense of direction, decisions would be made, like before, from a chaos of whims and hallucinations but he was no longer entirely of the human engine - of that, somehow, he was certain.

TWENTY-SEVEN

I was almost blind. As soon as he left the basin, my nodes were brutally severed. Blind and deaf.

The next many weeks, my existence came to revolve around a pathetically tiny trickle of data that occasionally found its way through Basil's parietal implant. His control of the implant in those weeks was intermittent at best, but the prevalent state of fear and anxiety he found himself in, was highly detrimental to my attempts at registering the outside world. Basil sometimes consciously restricted my access to the implant, I am certain of it, and sometimes it seemed he forgot it was there. It goes without saying that our conversations all but ceased despite my best intentions to the contrary. But on that first day, as we left the feeding room, I was still struggling with the physiological damage caused by the toxins in the aliens feeding bath. The designers who created this perfect prison for me, had also granted me limited access to certain cellular processes in Basils body and it was by manipulating these that I managed to roll back the destructive cascade of molecular failures incurred by the alien imprinting, but I could not, contrary to what certain parties would later claim, foresee what would come of it all. If I had, rest assured that I would have let the processes run amok, and killed the both of us. At the time my thoughts were of survival.

As Basil and the alien got up to leave the room, I glimpsed Mr. Yakovlev and Mr. Brassen standing outside in the corridor. From the look on their faces, I surmised that the sight of Basil scared them. It was only later that I found the reason. My host, who, I was led to understand, had always possessed a certain physical attraction to most humans, had undergone serious changes. Apart from the hair loss, the skin on his face had grown dull and lifeless. It was criss-crossed with tiny pockmarks like a maze of abandoned trenches, of holes and tunnels. His eyelids sagged like loose bags. He had never been exactly handsome, not in any traditional sense, but the changes brought on him were devastating. The white in his eyes had turned blood red. He moved like a man under water or half-asleep.

'Basil,' exclaimed Felix in a hoarse voice, but Basil did not seem to hear.

I could sense my host was walking slowly down the corridor, supported by the big 'xi that had led him in there, dragging his feet like a man in trance. He was headed towards the shuttle bay on level 4 and when he got there, an alien shuttle was waiting for him. He turned around to face the two humans who had followed him and mumbled this:

'Tomorrow begins the spark of the imagination, the flash of insight, that demolished yesterday's limitations and inspires us to create new worlds. He would have the both of you assemble the crew of this vessel and meet him when he returns. Do his bidding and you shall yet live to see the sunrise and the dawn of a new day. '

After uttering these unintelligible words, he turned and entered the shuttle, leaving the befuddled humans behind.

The exterior impression was that of odd angles, irregular with bulbous protrusions extending from the hull at haphazard intervals and it was matched by the cabin, curved as if the interior had been scooped out with a giant spoon from a solid block of rock. There was more than one alien in there with us but in my present condition there was no way to be certain. The change wrought upon Basil by the alien toxins, which I had by then realised were more than mere toxins, had occluded my faculties. I hammered the implant with everything I had but nothing helped. Basil was undergoing physiological changes that were fusing shut the secondary axons they had created for me throughout his nervous system. It is difficult to express the depth of my confusion at this stage. What an awful, awful time that was for me.

Basil moved to the wall and sat with his back against it. 'Do not be alarmed,' an alien with a red smear on its pod flashed at him before it moved into a neighbouring compartment of the small craft. 'We will arrive shortly.'

A few clicking noises were heard and then we were away. Gravity disappeared, and then reappeared in the wrong direction, but before Basil was thrown into the ceiling, an alien caught him gently in its forelegs and held him during the short flight across the void between the two ships.

I noticed the aliens used a new prefix to start their sentences. I could not decipher it at first, but I took note that the approximate spelling was '*seza*'.

'*Seza*, when we arrive, you must let us disembark first.' It was the big one flashing, the one that had previously communicated with us.

Another one, which had a previously unnoticed red smear on its pod, flashed something too. 'Your protection is paramount.'

It is truly an interesting species. At this point, I still did not fully understand, but it was about then that I became cognizant that their legs are covered in calcite crystals. In addition to functioning as armour and providing structural support, the crystals make up its unique visual system.

Phototropic chromatophores change the colour and regulate how much light will reach the photoreceptors. The lenses of their eyes are made of calcite or more precisely of calcium carbonate ($CaCO_3$). Pure forms of calcite are transparent, and they use crystallographically oriented, clear calcite crystals to form each lens of each of their eyes. The lenses work by filtering and focusing light on an underlying photoreceptor system. Nerve bundles under each lens, light-sensitive, transmit the optical information to the rest of the nervous system. Rigid calcite lenses would have been unable to accommodate a change of focus like the soft lens in a human eye would; however, in the aliens the calcite form an internal doublet structure, giving superb depth of field and minimal spherical aberration.

But I precede myself.

The voyage was brief and soon gravity returned. The four aliens moved around amongst themselves, forelegs facing the doorway. Basil stood behind them, back against the wall. He seemed utterly calm. I was picking up bits and pieces of their conversation but every time Basil looked away -- and he did stare into the floor for long periods of time -- I missed many details.

The big one flashed again. 'We are not sure how our brethren will react. They are very incoherent now. It is an unusual situation for us. We are never close with 'xi of other Mounds.'

'Except during *burgun*,' added one of the others. '*Burgun*.' Another word, which held no meaning yet.

Then, apparently in response to a question, although I could not discern which one had posed it, one of them said: 'About...' it paused, '... two thousand.'

'They have gone very long without *sanmonban*. They will fight badly. Some of them may even remember traces of the pod master. They will be confused,' replied the big one.

I felt the shuttle collide with something and concluded we had docked with the alien starship. Where else could we be? The doors to the shuttle must have opened because I sensed light entering Basil's eyes. What happened next I only glimpsed partly through whatever jumbled images made it through the implant despite Basil's reluctance to share with me. I could see the aliens in the shuttle flashing messages at each other and I sensed Basil somehow replied to them. How I could not fathom. Interpreting the alien language was no trivial task and it should have been beyond the capabilities of a single unassisted human being but it would appear he had found a way nonetheless by modifying the claysuit.

Through the legs of the aliens, I glimpsed a big cavern carved out of ashen rock and lit solely by the lights of a great horde of aliens that waited in it, hundreds, perhaps thousands, hanging from every square centimetre of the walls, black pods reflecting in the sharp rainbow of colours emanating from their own legs. There was no noise whatsoever and I concluded there was no atmosphere in the ship. And why should there be? The aliens were clearly better adapted to space travel than humans. Even from Basil's vantage point behind the aliens, and with my less than optimal quality of the visual input I received, it was clear the aliens were not all the same. Some looked like the ones we had encountered on the Armagnac, but other specimens were present, smaller and somehow frailer looking. Some had six legs some had oversized legs encased in thick crystal with a significantly smaller pod.

The silence was deceitful. Since the door had opened, there had been a concerted effort to penetrate Basil's body with electromagnetic waves, but the friendly aliens inside the shuttle moved to shield him.

The big alien suddenly surged forward. With a flurry of movement, it cut and hacked its way out of the shuttle. The crowd seemed stunned and, as one, the front of the alien crowd moved backwards and to the sides to avoid the attack. The two others surged out in the wake of the first one. The three formed a line and began scything their way through the crowd. They moved with decisive purpose. One well-placed blow from a front leg could cut clean through the crystal armour on an opponent's leg or leave a deep incision in a pod if caught unprotected. I noted that they did not bleed liquid like humans. When wounded, the black pod merely opened up like a fruit, revealing a solid tar-black core. Crystal armour occasionally shattered, filling the zero-G void between combatants with a fog of shards. Despite their overwhelming superiority in numbers, the resident aliens lost repeatedly and at least part of the reason was their curious tactics. Instead of swarming the three challengers, as humans would surely have attempted, they took them on one by one in a semi-orderly fashion, either crawling forward or thrusting themselves from above to land in front of the phalanx. After about an hour of nonstop combat there were no contenders left. The defeated resident aliens backed away from the big one that had come with Basil, and it advanced to stand pod against pod with the nearest survivor who withdrew its legs in a submissive gesture. After a few seconds, the one it had touched turned to its neighbour and touched it the same way. This, I later learned, signified that imprinting had begun and it would continue until they all had been touched.

'They are still confused, but they belong to us now,' the alien pilot in the shuttle flashed cryptically to Basil. And then: 'It matters not, *Seza*. They are content to receive the *sanmonban* from us. Soon their thoughts will coalesce properly around our imprint. All will be well.'

We then returned to the Armagnac where the three humans were anxiously waiting for us.

'Basil, the ship is swarming with aliens. What happened?' Brassen was obviously confused.

'Have you called a meeting like he asked you to?' came the answer from Basil.

'Yes we have,' answered Jin.

'The Chacu'xi are ready now,' said Basil and started walking towards the Bowl. The others followed behind him.

'Chacu'xi? So that is what they called,' mumbled Felix, then louder: 'Basil, what has happened to you? Do you know?'

If only I could have answered him.

TWENTY-EIGHT

Tuesday, October 30, 2101, 1615 GMT

We did as we had been told. We had contacted the Sleepers and told them they had to come for this meeting. We told them something had happened. We'd sent them pictures of the aliens and of Basil and of his face and his eyes. Now we were here in the Bowl. The walls were naked and grey. No one had bothered coming up with a scene or a backdrop for the meeting. I rather wondered what the aliens would make of it, but they just stood there impassively behind Basil. You couldn't say what was going on inside those black pods. I think this was first time I'd seen them stand so still. They always used to move around a little with their crystal legs except when they were sleeping, or whatever that state was that they went into. So still. But they weren't asleep now, that was obvious. Their legs were flashing constantly. Basil eyes were closed. So aged and thin and weary and miserable did he look that I failed to recognize him when he first appeared. Only an hour has passed since I had first seen him. His arms hung limb at his sides and he slouched a little. He was wearing a tight fitting clay suit with his head exposed. He seemed to have lost a lot of weight in that hour. So skinny I could count his ribs. And the skin! Grey, like his face, torn apart with tiny holes and lines, as if a thousand termites had burrowed through it. His skin was now their home. What was he now?

'Poor Basil, what have they done to you?' Before I had time to think, I had walked over to Basil and laid my hand on his shoulder. He was shaking.

'What have they done to me? What have I done to them?' he whispered so quietly I almost didn't hear.

'Are they here yet?' he asked, and I guessed he was asking about the Sleepers.

'I don't think they'll show,' said Brassen to Basil. Always such a loudmouth.

'Sure they will,' I answered. I knew they would come.

'They don't give a damn about us.'

'They're curious. They'll come.'

Then, as if on cue, a scene began coalescing around us; a warm sun beating down from a perfect blue sky, a plateau high above a desert landscape stretching in all directions below them. *Earth.* On sudden impulse, I bent down and scooped up a handful of sand, which I then proceeded to slowly empty from my hand. I needed to feel something.

'Where do you suppose this is?' I asked no one in particular and didn't expect an answer. Felix didn't know but he mumbled something anyway. Very unlike him. But then again, we had just made love. Some men get like that. You can't tell until you've slept with them how they will get. Apparently, Felix was the spineless toadying kind. That's fine. Still, it annoyed me a little for no particular reason I could think of.

'Masada,' said a peculiar, chirping voice from behind us. We turned around and saw it was a gigantic zebra finch. Its head was constantly moving from side to side in bird-like jerks, eyes like black orbs in each side of the head. Others appeared now in all kinds of shapes and figures. Animals, 3D cartoons and a handful of human looking avatars dressed in historic costumes.

'We're here. What do you want?' the zebra finch chirped aggressively.

The Sleepers were curious about the aliens and they did not try to hide it. I doubt they would have been so forward had they been here physically like us humans. They went to stand real close to the towering creatures, moving their hands suggestively at the crystal, gawking up at the pods. The thought occurred to me that they would somehow offend the aliens who would then take it out on us.

'Hey, take it easy, will ya,' I said. 'They're real, those things, you know. It is not a game. At least not for us real people here.'

Basil opened his eyes. The cornea was blood red and his pupils were completely dilated, giving him a dervish appearance. I had to look away. No way would I look into those crazy eyes of his. I couldn't figure out if he'd lost it or if the aliens had somehow brainwashed him and taken control of him. A situation like this... My mind wasn't sure it could respond to this situation. No data from the past helped me decide how to proceed. Perhaps this was the mind in pure fear. The mind gone still. Or, the mind gone. I could go internal and muse, at least that, for a bit. I could observe us here in this room, moment by moment. I could observe myself in response.

Then Basil spoke, my hand still on his shoulder, and this is what he said to the crew of the Armagnac:

'These beings are Chaju'xi. Most of them are young. All except one was made during the Passage. Of all the 'xi, only this one, the one who is Clade Prime, remembers a time before the Passage and even it knows little. Their duty is to forget, to incorporate a new presence. All they could tell is this: that they had previously served the Eight Mound of Middle Continent and that they came from a world not of this solar system but much farther away through many veils. All they know is how they must proceed.

'But, Basil, we will want to know something of them and their interiority if we are to relate to them. We cannot be so lost...'

Basil turned to Clade Prime who began to click and show lights. Basil spoke. We were in the presence of translation. This was the new Basil? Interfacing with the aliens, we weren't going to die? Just take on a new skin?: 'Once a group of 'xi were taken out and isolated from the rest. I was among them. Imprinting happened every turn of the star. We acquired many new skills. At about the same time a new kind of 'xi arrived among us. It was small and soft with puny pegui. Together we rose from Qned into the great void above the clouds, and the new 'xi, who called themselves Gre'xi, undertook the construction of a great vessel. Many turns of the star later, the vessel was ready and the Mound itself arrived borne on the seat of a great trail of light. It set out and we were content and happy by its unusual proximity. Little by little, we learned to see new things, to see how the planets and stars dance with each other and we understood there were many of them.

We veiled many times and when we had arrived, the Mound disembarked and encroached on the second planet. Our scouts revealed two unknown veil points and this one, a great honour, was dispatched as Prime of the vessel.

With the help of the Gre'wal we veiled and following our

instructions, which were explicit, we investigated the planet where we found you and Seza who saved us.'

He stopped talking. The silence was complete. Even the Sleepers had stopped moving. I think we all understood what he was asking us to do. He carefully looked each of us in the eye, even the Sleepers as far as it was possible.

Brassen cleared his throat and said: 'So we're just supposed to believe you? Just like that?'

Felix: 'Rem is correct. There are almost no facts. Nothing corroborates what you are saying. Apart from the aliens themselves of course.' Which, I almost added, was pretty big deal.

Brassen: 'How do we know the aliens didn't do something to you, take over your brain or something?'

Basil did not answer. His eyes wandered over the motley assembly and chanced on one of the Sleepers. It was one of the less dramatic avatars. It appeared as a female with long red hair tied in a ponytail and a two-handed sword, of all things, strapped across her back. She was wearing leather armour. As Basil's gaze lingered on her, she crossed her arms defiantly. Basil looked at her for a long time. He gestured with his hand for her to approach him. At first, I thought she would refuse, but she walked a few steps to stand in front of him. The others had noticed and stopped their antics to watch what the strange human wanted with one of their number. His face looked drawn, pinched, as if he was suffering a severe headache.

Basil gave her a long searching look. 'Maribel?'

'No, Darien Ginne. Who is asking?' she said and looked at him, nose wrinkling in distaste at his ravaged face.

Basil felt himself swimming in a sea of pain. Nerves ignited all over his body. The attacks seemed random, but they occluded clear thinking. To make matters even worse, thoughts washed over him, images that could make no sense. The emotions they conjure are so strong, overpowering. When it is fear, it is not a tingle of paranoia, easily set aside, but a paralysing tidal wave of utter doom, gripping every fibre in his body. Pleasure in orgiastic bursts, equally paralyzing. Any feeling comes crashing over him in waves, seconds apart, and throughout, he attempts to hold on to the one important thread, survival, his own, and theirs. Life, human life, is resilient, and desires to survive, but the pinprick is fading, fading, until his eyes touch on her, standing there towards the back of the small crowd.

Jin: I did not understand at the time, but the sight of that red-haired woman had jolted something in Basil. Poor Basil. He thought he was dreaming and yet the woman he had loved, and who had died, he had seen her die, after all, stood here before him. Not exactly in flesh and blood but close enough.

'Can we talk?' he asked, his face wrinkling in what was possibly an attempt to smile. The woman was furrowing her brows like someone remembering things long past. Basil got up and waved at her to follow him. He walked a few tens of meters, away from us, until he reached the edge of the plateau. He gazed down at the windswept desert below. The woman arrived at his side.

'What is this place?' he asked. 'Was it your choice?'

'No. This is Unate's backdrop. The zebra finch,' she added offhandedly.

'Where are we?'

'Masada,' then, seeing he did not know, she continued, 'this was the area they called Israel and this plateau was the last stronghold of group of rebels who refused to become members of the Roman Empire. A siege took place here two thousand years ago. The roman legions, camped down there, starved them out. It took years.'

'What happened to them?'

'They were killed. Everyone. All of them. Even the women and the children.' There was a pause, and then she asked, 'why do you want to journey into this solar system? Are the aliens making you do it?' The question we all wanted an answer to.

'No, they are not making me do anything. They are not... individuals like you and me. They do not want anything. Just life. And we gave it to them.' He paused and his gaze settled on the rock strewn desert stretching out far below them.

'I... there is a new imperative now. I can't explain.'

'We have met in the VIE, have we not?' she asked.

'I am Duke Ortho. *Your little duke.*' She turned and looked at him for a long time. A shadow seemed to move over her face, but she shook her head.

'I do not recall a Duke Ortho.'

He looked surprised. 'But it was just a year ago.'

'Not to me. I have lived more lifetimes than you can possibly imagine.'

'But...' He looked crestfallen, part of the old Basil peeping out through the ravaged face of the man standing there in front of us.

'I do not remember you. You are nothing to me.'

I wished she had lied to him. It was so obvious Basil needed her to remember, needed her to pull him back, But she refused, the bitch, or perhaps she was too stupid to know what she was doing or perhaps she thought she was doing him a favour. The world would be a very different place had she just lied a little.

'Surely you must remember something,' I interfered in a plaintive voice. She turned to look at me with an arrogant expression on her freckled face. 'Our lives are faster than yours. Much faster. I have had thousands of lovers.' I shook my head. I felt like telling her this wasn't a game, that the save-reload function was out of order out here, but I knew it would be in vain. She was a born Sleeper, there was no arguing with her.

'What about Ant? What does he think of this?' asked the zebra finch to my surprise. We did not know Ant had communicated with the Sleepers.

Basil slowly turned his head in his direction. 'This is a matter which men must decide among themselves. The machine has lost its access to the world. I have shut it down. Fused it shut.' Something in the sanmonban had convinced him that machines were insidious creatures, to be feared above all else.

The Sleepers did not like the sound of that. Humanity needed its machines and Ant was the last of its kind.

'We want to talk to Ant.'

'That you cannot. I will not allow it.'

'Then we will not do as you say.'

--

While all this is going on in the Bowl, a furious, accelerated discussion is taking place in VIE space among the Sleepers.

1: Let us turn the plasma torch on it, take it out. The HAI will stay with us.

22: Fool. What do you think will happen to us then? Putting the alien ship out of commission will not kill the aliens who are on the Armagnac now, will it? How do you think they will react to see their buddies explode?

1: He won't let them hurt us.

36: Basil? You do not know that. Is it really him?

8: I think we should return home and report this to Survey Branch. That's what they are there for, eh?

1: She knows him (pointing a virtual finger at Darien). Will he hurt us if we take them out?

40: She doesn't remember him.

5: Bullshit. She has the memory of a fucking elephant that one.

16: I say we drop it. There are bigger things at stake here.

1: Bigger things than to save the last HAI in the world? Our last chance of survival? What things could that be? Please enlighten us.

16: Well, yes. We're not alone in the universe anymore. That changes everything, even Zach's project. Don't you see? The tables have turned, guys, and they haven't landed in the same way.

Heads were shaking back at him.

Many: 'Doesn't change the job.'

8: Maybe we can do both. Like maybe we split up. You go your way. We go ours. You know, cover more ground that way.

17: Oh yes, splitting up, great idea. Where did I hear that one.

9: Listen...

Many: Oh no, the philosopher.

9: I offer perspective. Out here, 244 light years from home, we homo sapiens argue among ourselves. Should we stay here by the nice fire or should we investigate the racket outside the ring of light? Would the beasts dare show themselves? No, let us sleep. We don't fight well in the dark (if it comes to that) better wait till morning. Yes, we did our duty today. We've done what we could.

4: You are quite the poet, aren't' you?

15: Yes, what the hell are you talking about?

4: Our duty is to stay alive.

9: Yes, yes, fight another day. Discretion is the better part of..., remember? And when morning comes, when the sun throws its light over the mountains and down into the valleys, the ring of light will have expanded to the foothills of the mountains, but no further. But, somehow, a handful of people would get up; grab a log from the fire and leave. And that, my friends, is how we made it across the oceans and the mountains and deserts. So, please, what I'm trying to say is: Get off your asses, Guys!

1: That's not how it was, not exactly anyway. We were hired to do a job.

15: We're doing it for the colonists. It is the right thing to do. It is the human thing to do but maybe we don't know what that is anymore?

9: Oh, humanism, you say? True, to have humanism we must first be convinced of our humanity. I'm talking from experience here, as we move further into the decadence of Viscerality and by extension the Sleeper Program, no offense, guys, this becomes more difficult. Ask yourselves, what is Espero going to be? A colony? A lifeboat for the human soul, where people can let their pants down and relax, enjoy the smell of their own shit while everything is blowing up back home?

9: We're in this together, people. All of us. Waiting for Survey Branch to do this for us is just shying away from responsibility.

4: We must vote.

--

Felix, Rem and me looked at each other. The HAI was trapped inside Basil now. And for reasons we did not understand, Basil refused it access to the outside, to us.

The Sleeper, Darien Ginne, who seemed to speak for all of them, was angry. She was threatening Basil, telling him they could not go back to Earth unless he freed Ant. How he was supposed to do that with the HAI trapped inside his body in the first place was not entirely clear. Basil looked unperturbed. 'That is your prerogative. But know this: you will die out here among the stars and you will go before your time.'

'Yes, then you die,' he repeated so flatly it sent shivers down my back. Was it a threat or a statement of fact? I glanced nervously at the aliens, but they hadn't moved but that, we knew from experience, could change in the blink of an eye and it was at that moment I realized that we too were trapped and there was no way out. Travelling on a starship you're trapped, of course, physically, there is nowhere else to go. That may sound banal to some, but there is sense of freedom in the mission. You know how and where and approximately when you do things and there is purpose to that.

'The four of us will continue the journey on the Undulating Horizons,' he said. The four of us, he said... That included me then. 'What you do is up to you. Eventually the ship will run out of fuel. Then death will find you.' He paused and added: 'In the great above.' He looked confused, as if someone else had spoken, then continued: 'And none of you can come with us. The Chacu'xi starships do not support your epi's.'

The Sleepers fell silent. They lived fast lives but they needed power to sustain their epis.

'There must be another way,' said Felix.

'There is not.'

Our choice stood between going back on the Armagnac, which was doomed to travel slowly, ever so slowly home. It would be years before it got back, if ever, or to continue onwards with Basil and his aliens and Ant, who was there somewhere.

'We can take the Armagnac with us into the Bellatrix system,' I said, thinking it could work as a sort of last resort lifeboat.

'Basil is right, said Felix. 'It would take the Armagnac a year or more to descend into the system. We cannot afford to wait for it. What if something unexpected were to happen? The Armagnac would be trapped, unable to maneuver. The safest course of action for the Sleepers and the Armagnac is to return the way we came from. Then, should we not return, you can relate our findings to the GSA. Besides, if Zach sticks to his plan, and I do not see why he shouldn't, you will probably run into the first colony ship around Espero at some point.'

'That is fine with me,' said Brassen, 'I will go with Basil. There is nothing for me on Earth anymore.'

'I will go too,' said Felix seriously. 'I am curious.' Then he added, blushing as he admitted it: 'I always wanted to make history.' He looked hopefully at me, but I refused to look him into the eye. Men and their false bravado.

'Well, there is no way I'll stay back on the Armagnac all alone. Could be years and years. You guys make for lousy company,' I said, nodding at the Sleepers. 'Fuck it, I'm going too.'

TWENTY-NINE

On October 31st, 2101, the four, Felix Yakovlev, Rem Brassen, Jin Dulg and Basil Baranikowa transferred to the Chacu'xi ship scout ship Undulating Horizons which was holding station about 20 kilometres from the Armagnac. The two ships were 157.000 kilometres from the Espero L-point and 6 billion kilometres out from the Bellatrix star. The four travellers brought an assortment of equipment to help cope with the long journey on-board the Undulating Horizons. The alien ship was not, as the three were about to find out, built with comfort in mind.

We followed Basil into the alien shuttle. It was like the inside of an igloo. The floor, the walls and the ceiling were made of the same identical pale, white material. It looked like rock or mineral. Everything inside was curved and rounded, as if scooped out by a gigantic spoon. The shuttle was not airtight because when the bay door on the Armagnac opened outside, the air inside suddenly disappeared also. The clays suits effectively covered us but a little warning would have been nice. The shuttle took off with a slight jolt and gravity disappeared. Basil was holding on to the 'xi, but the rest of us had to find purchase wherever we could. It was quite uncomfortable, but we thought nothing of it, as it was a short trip, just twenty kilometres.

'You made the right choice, friends,' said Basil. Through the visor on the clay suit, I noticed his eyes were closed.

'We'll see about that,' grumbled Rem and I found myself agreeing with him. What had we gotten ourselves into?

'I hope we won't have to stay in clay for too long? I hate the feeling against my skin, you know,' I remarked to Basil in a tone that was meant to be humorous but came out all wrong. Not that it mattered, because it seemed he hadn't heard me.

Twenty minutes later we felt the shuttle decelerate and when the door opened, we got our first glimpse of the place that was going to be our home for a long time to come. The docking bay was of the same material as the shuttle, except the room was larger. It was empty and dark. I don't know what the heck I had expected, but I guess I thought there would have been a welcome committee. Before we had time to think, the 'xi carrying Basil moved out of the shuttle and we followed it by clinging to the SADU that was transporting our equipment.

'Can we breathe in here?' asked Brassen. He could have consulted his suit which would have told him no, there was still no air here, but I suspected he was blabbering because he was nervous. Hell, I was too, but I wouldn't have shown them. No way.

Did I mention the place was dark? Well, it was. Pitch black in fact. We had to use the omni lights in the suits to see where we were going, but the resulting display of shadows following us as we moved did nothing to dispel the unease we were all feeling. I really can't say whether it was the fact there were no aliens in sight anywhere or the gloom of the big cavernous room that was the worst. Anyway, Basil was leading the way towards a sort of hole in the wall. The hole lead into a tube-shaped passageway. Felix was chattering away but I was too tense to notice what he saying. It was something about engineering, obviously. He seemed to be very excited about the whole thing. As for me, well, I'm not ashamed to admit, I was regretting agreeing to come. But then I remembered I hadn't really loved my choice, not really, and for a while I hated the whole bloody thing and felt very sorry for myself at the same time.

After floating down that passageway for what seemed a long time at a very sedate pace, we turned. We had passed several open doors on the way but it was hard to see what lay beyond them. Everything was dark. The new passageway was even longer and seemed endless. After only ten minutes, according to the suit, 'cause I had completely lost track of time, we reached an entrance. The edge was a different shade than the surroundings and it looked like it was more recent.

Basil spoke over the suit radio, very slowly and very deliberately as if he had to dredge up each word from the depths of his memory.

'This is where you will stay for the journey. We start burn in ten minutes. Strap yourselves in.'

'Where are you going?' I yelled at him, but he was already moving away. If he answered, I didn't hear him and that was the last we would see of him for the next three months. Where he stayed or what he did during that time I do not know.

The room, or cave, under other circumstances, I guess, could be called cosy. It was about six metres in diameter with the same curving walls as the rest of the ship. Someone had attached three gravity nets to the wall.

'We'd better hurry if the ship starts burning in ten minutes, guys.' Felix began unpacking our gear. He seemed to have thought of everything; artificial lights, a small power unit (pilfered from a drone), a nanofabricator and a ton of stuff to feed it.

'Do we know what kind of burn we're looking at?' Just making conversation. 'Do we know,' Brassen answered in a mocking tone, and continued, 'of course we don't know. Did you hear anyone telling us?'

'Shut the fuck up, Rem, you're scared shitless and that's fine, just don't take it out on us.'

I was looking at the cave and thinking about my parents. The situation was ironic. My parents, you see, had been burrowers. They were on the Reykjavik advance excavation team when the digging had started on that one. Blasting their way down through the granite. Down, ever down. Scared people, my parents. Good parents in their own way, but scared, always afraid what would come next and who could blame them. The wars did that to people.

We all strapped in and waited for the burn to commence.

'Guys,' said Felix thoughtfully.

'Yes, now what?'

'You do realize that once the burn starts we're not going to leave this room.'

'Oh yeah, why do you figure that?'

'Because by my reckoning, that passageway we just entered from, you know, it's about 200 meters long or so and unless I'm very wrong, and I don't think I am, the engines are down there somewhere. Down towards the end of the passageway...' He shut up to let sink in.

'Oh...'

What Felix was saying was that in a few minutes the passageway out there would become a 200-meter deep shaft and that there would be no leaving this room until the ship stopped the burn.

..

Twelve hours later the ship was still under heavy acceleration. I reckoned it was about 5G's. Moving about was impossible. Brassen had begun his mumbling a few hours after the burn started. The mumbling became a sort of moaning after a while. Then flat out screaming. We tried talking to him but he wasn't really responding. Fortunately, the suit could filter out his voice. I guess the burn got to him. Hell, I wasn't feeling too good either, And Basil was nowhere to be seen. We tried calling on every frequency we could think of but there was no answer. The worst part was not knowing what the hell was going to happen. I will never forget that room. I think I counted the striations in the ceiling a thousand times. I could draw it for you right now if you asked me. Three hundred and seventy within my field of vision. I figured the aliens had created the room specifically for us. We didn't know what that pale rock-looking material was exactly, but it kind of looked like it had been recently excavated. It was just one of those things. Then there was the thing about atmosphere. The ship was a vacuum. Without suits, we couldn't breathe here. That's no way to travel. Even by Felix and my best estimations, we were looking at three months of travel time at least before we reached the inner system. Three months in a clay suit is a fucking long time, let me tell you that. I guess that's why Rem was screaming his lungs out.

--

A week into the journey I was ready to let go. All those G's were killing us, literally. We could have managed in CRAD units but not like that. Not in those ancient g-nets. No way. Rem had stopped screaming. He didn't even moan anymore. He was not dead, though. I checked his suit monitor from time to time. Felix and I had stopped talking too. There was nothing to say. Why bring us along if they wanted to kill us? It didn't make any sense. And what about Basil, I remember thinking, he was still human, or part of him was, he would have suffered during the burn too, wouldn't he?

--

They dialled it down to 1G after eight days. I don't know if they knew Rem was in trouble. I don't think so. I just think they'd reached some milestone or Nav point in the flight plan. He regained consciousness a few hours later. We kept him talking to keep him alert, you know. We took turns sitting next to him, holding his hand, but it was awkward with the clay suits and every muscle in my body hurt like never before. The only thing he wanted to talk about was his daughter. I hadn't known he had one He always was discrete about his past.

'So, how come you don't like artificial intelligences, Rem?'

'I just don't.' He turned his head into wall, away from us.

'There must be some reason. The HAI's did well for us.'

'Did they?' He paused. 'You should have asked Ant how we lost the Sleepers. It knows.'

'What do you mean 'lost them'? We haven't lost them. They're still there, back home and on the Armagnac.'

Rem grunted. 'You never even talked to one before. None of you did, did you?' He turned back to look at them.

We both shook our heads. It was true. We had never talked directly to a Sleeper before. 'So?' I told him.

'So?' He tried to laugh derisively but he was out of breath. 'Do you think it was supposed to be like that?'

'The wars changed things, I guess. Is that what you mean?' I shrugged.

'No. That is not what I mean.' He sighed.

Before he died, he told us about his daughter. It was the only thing he would talk about in the end.

He said he was hearing the voice of his wife.

'Rem', he heard the smiling voice tell him, 'you'll be ok, you always are'. She too became a Sleeper. Where was she now? How many lives had she lived in those twenty years? He did not remember her face anymore and that made him sad. He'd lost her quickly. The love hadn't been strong enough. His daughter, on the other hand, had kept up with him for a long time. Letters, videos, but eventually she too had disappeared into the void. The last time he had seen her was during a brief session on her 18-year birthday. She had been brought out to meet him as they would every few years.

His memories of her were so defined, so sharp. Five times. Thirty minutes times five. One hundred and fifty minutes. Five discrete slices of life brought to you courtesy of the machines. He would have preferred her dead to this... this torture. Age six. Eight. Nine. Twelve. At eighteen, she had forgotten who he was. His little girl had loved her father very much but, in the end, even her determination to hang on, and the strength of that determination had surprised him, eroded. The hundreds of lifetimes she had been forced to live washed her strength away and took her away from him as certainly as death itself would have done.

She had told him how it happened. He suspected not many people knew this. The HAI's had kept it a secret, or perhaps not. Perhaps people just did not give a shit. Why should they? Ninety million people, burdened with the lives of billions of Sleepers who needed power, ever more power, to keep up their pointless dreaming and people did not care.

And he wanted us to know too. He'd carried the knowledge around like a secret for many years, but why he should think it was such a terrible thing I really can't tell. We all knew the Sleepers were different.

Sometime during the tenth day, his body gave in and he died. He was not a bad sort. The worst thing anyone could say about him was that he was boring, and that is not such a bad thing at all.

--

Rem's corpse stayed in that room with us for almost three months. It was awful. A few hours after he died, the clay suit deactivated and lost cohesion to save power, exposing his body to the vacuum inside the ship. I'll never forget that sight. My god. He looked just like himself. His eyes were closed, mouth slightly open. At first, a tiny cloudlet of steam arose from his mouth. Spittle boiling off, I guess, then he expanded a little, but after that nothing much happened. He sort of dried out and towards the end he had turned into a brown husk, all wrinkled, like a mummy. Yes, he was like a Pharaoh, watching over us, Felix and me. For a long time I kept dreaming about him as if he was still alive. I told Felix about the dreams and he said he was having them too.

Felix set up the box from the ship and we got lost in our own miniature VIE's for a while. Rem would have hated us for it, but we both needed to get away. They weren't real VIE's, the system was too weak for that, more like games. Always had a thing for airplanes, antiques. Everything about those old flying machines was fascinating to me. Especially the maintenance part, taking it apart and reassembling it, making sure every bit was ready to do its part. That kind of physical symbiosis between our machines and us is long gone. Flying it, of course, was also part of the thrill. Over fjords and valleys, in places like Norway and Alaska or, my favourite, a stretch of coastline along the Bay of Biscay, taking off from Vendays-Montalivet, a small airport at the mouth of the Gironde river, and flying south along the coast down to Arcachon and sometimes all the way to San Sebastian. Mostly, though, I was Amelia Earhart. I had flown Earhart's last mission across the Pacific in the Lockheed Electra, hour upon hour in the small cockpit, with only the voice of my navigator friend, Fred, to keep me awake, reliving those final minutes as the plane was going down and we spotted Gardner Island. The final radio message. Then the landing. The aftermath was unbearable. Long months of dying, alone, just me and Fred, sickness, starvation. Was that what lay ahead for us, for me and Felix? A long descent into madness? Or would we be granted a quick death?

--

Later, I don't know how much time passed, a week or so, gravity was still 1G, we started thinking about things and one of us, I don't remember who, came up with the idea that we send the drone out to do some exploring. It was a medium sized model, a droplet with a duranium shell, about seventy centimetres in diameter. The thing was sturdy, it could move under even heavier acceleration than this, and its power core was supposed to last for years. That was how we eventually figured out the layout of the ship. The aliens did nothing to interfere with the drone. We never found out where Basil was hiding.

The ship was shaped like a human thighbone. It was basically a solid block made of that white material, which Felix thought was a kind of mineral, like soapstone, only harder, encapsulated in a shell of boron nitride. It was a simple design of low slung, curving corridors, vaguely reminiscent of the capillaries of a sewer system, with no other purpose than to provide housings for the navigational modules, the cloaking device, the reactor (helicon, according to Felix), storage areas for replacement parts and various equipment, docking bays for the small shuttle fleet, the ubiquitous feeding rooms and a means for the non'xi repair crews to travel from one end of the ship to the other. There were no habitation and no amenities whatsoever. The 'xi needed nothing. They never slept, never interacted socially, except to exchange information. The only part of the ship commanding more than passing interest for the humans was the command bridge. It was located in upper thighbone of the ship and was accessed by an offshoot of the two central passageways. The ship had not been constructed with any particular sense of up or down in mind, everything was in ruthless 3D, which made the general impression overwhelmingly confusing for us humans. For example, when you reached the bridge, the passageway merely expanded into a big concave room. Every few meters a protrusion rose from the surface of the room. In the centre of each protrusion was a simple monochrome 2D screen which relayed information from the primitive data processing system, one would hesitate to call them computers, to the non'xi operating the station. There were non'xi hanging on to every surface of the bridge. Six thin metal beams, like a cross, met in the middle of the room, forming a perch from where the non'xi navigator had an uninterrupted line of sight to every non'xi operating the stations around it. The non'xi were constantly flashing information from their stations to the navigator. The system seemed primitive at first glance, but thanks to the xi's surprising ability to process information and the impressive bandwidth of the 'xi language, the system was quite effective. Should it fail, the 'xi had one ace up their crystalline legs, so to speak, and that was brute force. Course corrections with bone crushing burns exceeding 30G's were not, Felix gathered from his halting conversations with the Navigator, unusual during final approach and orbital operations.

--

Brassen's death was a blow and it got me thinking about what we were doing here and why Zach had picked us to crew the ship in the first place. It could have been the circumstances that were bringing down my usual good mood, but whole 'handpicked' speech had been a lie. Sure, we had been handpicked, but not because we were the best crew in the fleet. No way. As intended, the offer was flattering. Zach Baranikowa himself asking us to do something important. We were handpicked, sure, profiled, evaluated, and chosen because we were functional nutcases who were crazy enough to volunteer for a mission going unimaginably far away and with incredibly bleak prospects of getting back alive. And it was true. We had nothing left to lose. Brassen had lost his family and severed all ties to Earth and Felix, well, as far as I could tell, he rarely talked about himself, which is one reason I liked him, I guess. He grew up in one of those religious orphanages and he never had wife and kids. There had been three brothers but I got the impression they were dead. He never talked about them. Felix lived and breathed for HSL and fancied himself the best engineer in the Fleet. Maybe he was, but that didn't say much. We were trained monkeys, scurrying around in starships we didn't understand. If anything broke, we were fucked and had been since the HAI's were turned off. Without the machines, the space adventure was a sham, a pantomime with humans as stooges vainly trying to remember our lines.

And me? I was a navigator, which was a sort of astrophysicist light. Not a scientist by any stretch, but just about knowledgeable enough to operate the primitive computers we used to calculate the course. Trained monkey. We were taught to press this and that button for this and that situation, but really, we didn't have a fucking clue what we were doing. I know Felix thought otherwise, but he was wrong or just too proud.

--

The weeks became months, but I guess we really are just animals. Never leaving the suits should have been intolerable, but it was not. There were worse fates. We just needed to look at Brassen's shrivelled corpse to remind us of that.

THIRTY

Then one day it was over. Gravity had been building up over the past few days, as if the ship was under final braking, and then suddenly it disappeared altogether. We could have left the room but we were apprehensive; being caught outside in the passageway if the ship re-started a burn would be fatal. We didn't have to wait long. A 'xi appeared in the doorway, one of the smaller ones with the elongated, torpedo-shaped pod and six crystal legs instead of four. We had observed them around the ship over the past months and we had concluded they were a kind of subspecies, a specialized variant. We found them all over the ship, on the bridge, operating the stations, and carrying out odd maintenance jobs. Riding, or clinging to its pod, was Basil Baranikowa. He was wearing a grey claysuit but through the transparent visor his face was as ravaged as I remembered it. He cleared his throat a couple of times.

'We have arrived. This one will take you to the bridge.' A second alien appeared behind the first one. If Basil noticed the corpse, he didn't let on.

We could have said a great many things to him at that point, like how about Brassen, you see that dried corpse right there, that used to be someone you knew. But, absurdly grateful to be let out of our prison, we just released the straps on the gravity nets and made our way towards the alien waiting for us in the doorway. I hesitated to touch it, but when I saw Felix attach himself to it, I kicked off the wall and flew right at it too. The thing didn't move. I grabbed hold of one of the crystalline legs. I stared into the crystal. It was milky and the colours seemed to light up from deep within, like tiny novae rushing towards the outside. Opal.

With both of us hanging on to it, it moved after Basil, slowly, its legs attaching themselves to the uneven surface of the passageway wall with the ease of an insect. Outside the little cave we had lived in for the past three months, the passageways were utterly lightless. I had to flick between thermal imaging, active infrared and omni lights to see the creature and the walls of the passageway, which were so cold they were invisible to the thermal sensor. In the infrared the uneven walls were a confusing, strange landscape of mountain ridges and valleys.

'Basil,' Felix called out. 'What have you been doing all this time?' That, I thought, was one hell of a way to small talk after all this time. I half expected Basil not to answer but this time he did.

'I know now who I am. I am that messenger who since the beginning has been called Kepher. I am that Dweller in the wilderness that your fathers knew and your sons shall know. I am he who seeks for charity and pays it back in life and death. I am the Recorder and the Scourge. I am the voice of Kepher, God above the Gods. Not for no little end have these things come to pass, but that you may learn there is design in heaven and justice on Earth and after justice, judgment. Kepher of the royal race was sent forth to danger or to death, far from those it loved and who loved it by the divine command which rules the hearts of the gods.'

A minute or so went by while Felix mulled over that. Meanwhile the aliens kept moving along the passageway towards the bridge. They were obviously heading for the bridge. Before Felix could think of an answer, Basil, or Kepher, as he apparently wanted us to call him now, spoke up. 'We have altered certain things in the basic design. They were already using microwave radar as a back-up navigation system. We modified it. They can talk to you now...It was a laborious process, but necessary because you are here as ambassadors and witnesses, to record events as they unfold for the betterment of humanity.'

A new voice spoke to us over the suit radio. 'This one is 3-111.' The voice was toneless and flat. I realized it was the one carrying us that had spoken on the radio.

'A third of humanity didn't make it here. Brassen died on the way,' I said, against my better judgment. At the corner of my eye, I saw Felix wave at me to shut up. I ignored him.

'Yes,' said Basil in simple acknowledgement.

I was about to answer when suddenly the walls on all sides fell away to reveal the hollow cathedral-like space which we had previously identified as the command bridge of the ship. All around us, aliens hung from the curving walls like bats. Next to each alien, primitive CRT monitors displayed streams of data from the ship and the effect was that of a hundred miniature flashlights lighting up the massive hollow space casting it in eerie light. After the longs months trapped in the cave, the immensity of this space, and the strangeness of it all, made my stomach turn and I thought I was going to throw up. I recalled, with immense craving, that I had not physically eaten anything in three months and that there would be nothing to throw up. How I longed for sensation, for feeling something with my bare hands, for putting something in my mouth and feel it crunch between my teeth. I don't know why these feelings welled up in me at this particular point in time, but I suspect it was the combined effect of sudden change and the strangeness of it all. I thought we would never go home, never see another human being again, and Basil, who we had followed in the belief that at least he was like us, had changed too. It was down to Felix and me and soon, maybe it would be just me.

We tried to make sense of the monitors all around us but it was impossible. Each of the hundred or so monitors displayed symbols, which meant nothing to us. The Navigator hung like a spider in the middle of the room, suspended from the place where the four beams that crisscrossed the room met each other. When we happened to cross the direct line of sight between the Navigator and one of the aliens hanging from the wall, the suit registered intense microwave radar passing between them. Apparently, and it was as we had surmised from our explorations with the drone, the Navigator was receiving constant updates from each station via bursts of electromagnetic emissions and, occasionally, sending a burst back to the station carrying instructions for changes or adjustments. I was wondering why he had brought us here, what we were supposed to look at? But then a 2D screen swung down, or up, depending on your desired point of view, from the murky bottom and I saw it was the old Dell screen from the Armagnac, the relic Felix had kept in his room. Basil, or the aliens, had somehow connected it to the alien ship because it was showing schematics and symbols which made zero sense to me.

'Kepher needs your help,' said Basil directly to Felix. 'With what?' he answered. 'Tell me what you see on this screen.' Felix turned to study the screen. 'It is astronomical data.' He paused, looking intently at the screen. Swiping his hand over it, the image changed. 'Ahh,' he said. I looked over his shoulder. I studied the astronomical data. The system we were in was the Bellatrix system and near us -- we were in orbit around it -- was a planet, the size and colour of a lemon. At first glance, from that distance, which was about three or four hundred thousand kilometers, it held certain similarities to Earth. There were traces of continents and coastlines visible through a thin cloud layer, but the golden tinge made everything look wrong. I looked at the other planets in the system. The stellar architecture of the Bellatrix system featured five planetary bodies and a K-class main sequence star. The four outermost were fluid planets; two Jovians of hydrogen and helium and two ice giants of water and ammonia and the one closest to the star, a solid planet, was the one we were orbiting.

'So, this is it? This is the place your alien entity lives?' I looked at the two others. Our faces were lit by the garish light from the monitor, and beyond, the unclear silhouettes of the alien creatures that surrounded us in the darkness. 'I doubt that,' said Felix. In reality, he explained in a dreary, pedantic voice, studying the data and the visual sensors intently at the same time, the only similarity between Earth and this place was that it too possessed an iron core. Apart from that, things differed rather dramatically. The next layer out from the iron core was molten silicon carbide and titanium carbide. Above that, there was a layer of carbon in the form of graphite and a kilometer thick substratum of diamond. During volcanic eruptions, diamonds from the interior would come up, resulting in mountains of diamonds and silicon carbides littering the landscape. The poles of the planet consisted of frozen tar and methane, but near the equator, where the temperature was higher, instead of water, rivers of oil led into black oceans. When it rained, and it did rain from time to time, gasses photo-chemically synthesized into long-chain hydrocarbons, raining solid pellets of oil onto the surface.

'An alien is supposed to live in a place like that?' I asked and turned to Basil.

'It is indeed difficult to imagine anything biological, carbon based at least, being capable of sustaining life there,' Felix added.<

Basil said nothing.

We followed him through the dark passageways of the ship, turning two or three times. A few hundred meters later, we arrived in a place we both recognized, the shuttle bay. The unwieldy shuttlecraft was still there, visible as a dark shape against the flickering lights from our suit projectors. Basil stopped and turned around.

'You will bear witness to the encounter,' he said. Thoughts flew through my head until they abruptly collided with the fact that Basil was about to leave the ship. 'You,' he pointed at Felix. 'Follow me.' I shook my head desperately at Felix.

I looked at him and thought I should say something, it could, after all be the last time I saw him. Letting him see how I felt would not do, no. Yet our hands found each other and we touched heads through the suits.... I thought about saying something, but pride won, again, and I kept my mouth shut. Felix shrugged and launched himself at the doorway to the shuttle.

And me? Fuck them, I thought. A few minutes went by, and then the dark triple engine manifolds in the back of the shuttle turned a shiny turquoise and it moved, ever so softly, towards the open bay doors. Outside, a thick band of stars were visible, lighting up the interior in ghastly silvers and cold, white light. I followed the shuttle with my eyes until it disappeared from view and the bay doors closed.

'So, you said your name was 3-11.'

'Not correct. This one is designated 3-111.'

I even got the name wrong. Fortunately, it seemed incapable of feeling insulted.

THIRTY-ONE

This passage in the 1634th Rendition of the Exordium is based on the recordings of the clay suit worn by Felix Yakovlev. As we near the end of the story, the Teller have chosen to relate the meeting with the Mound in his own voice. This narrative method is slightly unusual, but not unheard of.

We see Felix peek into the cockpit a few seconds before departure. Despite the horrible situation, he remains curious. What he saw was a concave miniature version of the command bridge on the ship. Except for the doorway, which measured about one metre square, the entire inner surface of the scooped space was covered in 2D monitors. In the centre was a cluster of primitive control sticks. The pilot non'xi was ensconced there. We then sense the shuttle undock. The sensation is quite smooth. What is not too smooth is the acceleration once the shuttle clears the docking bay. Felix and you, soon to become Kepher, The Teacher, savior of Humanity and so forth, are pressed hard against the back of the bulkhead and Felix, at least, appears to have trouble breathing. Very well. It lasts only for a few minutes. The burn tapers off and a few minutes of relatively smooth flight ensues. The shuttle then hit the upper atmosphere of the planet and it starts shaking violently. Heat builds inside it. Felix heart rate is through the roof, he is very scared and there is nothing to hold onto, no straps, no gravity nets, just the bare white walls of the shuttle. It lasts for just fifteen minutes but to Felix it surely felt a lot longer. You're deep inside the atmosphere of the planet, descending steadily towards a point on the surface that you, Kepher, has identified as the place where the Mound landed a few years earlier.

After a long while we feel the shuttle settle on the ground. With no hesitation, you, Basil, Kepher, The Teacher or Harbinger, you will take many names in the centuries to follow, opened the door. At first the outside was obscured by a huge plume of brown dust swirling slowly in the air. You both waited for a few minutes for the air to clear and when it had, you left the shuttle. It would be night soon. The sun was setting behind a faraway mountain range, casting long shadows on the jaundiced ground. Felix looked up. There were clouds but no sign of oily rain. The temperature was well above 50 degrees C. It was the first time any of you had set foot on an alien planet, but the scene, when we consider it like this, through the suit logs, has a trite quality to it that is somewhat jarring to the contemporary historian or ecclesiastic attempting to uncover the truth about those far away events.

It was a desolate place indeed and had it not been for the clay suits, two humans would not have survived long out here. You start walking, footprints stitches across the untouched flats. We briefly see Felix turn his head to look longingly at the shuttle. Before you, clearly alien to this place, a profusion of silvery tentacles rise from the ground. As you approach, the size of the thing become apparent. It is a tumour, kilometres across, half buried in the ground, and we sense, from the look of it, that it was not supposed to rest like that, its upper half exposed to the elements of this unforgiving place. Its strength, titanic, failed when it hit a substrata of pure carbon, less than a kilometre below the surface; not enough, not enough by far.

You seem very sure of yourself. You walk in a straight line with no hesitation. Felix, slouching, follows more reluctantly. Nearing the Mound, the silvery tentacles resolve into hard scrub-like growth that slow you down. About 500 meters in, you reach the hard edge of the tumour. It towers high above your heads, like the dome of a half-buried cathedral. There is an orifice, a hole, big enough for both of you to comfortably stand erect. You, dear Teacher, brush aside twigs and a fine web, spidery, that covers it, and delve in. Felix hesitates. When you sense Felix is not with you, you stop and turn.

'You must follow. This is the first chapter of the Exordium. Your testimony will resound throughout the ages. Come, Kepher awaits you.'

If Felix has any idea what that was about, he does not show it, but starts walking again. After that, there is no talking among you. Inside, with thermal imaging turned on, we see you're in a tunnel.

You walk for a long time, through those strange winding tunnels that split and re-join confusingly in a way that reminds one of the passageways in the alien starship that brought you here. You never falter, never hesitate, you just continue walking, displaying a great sense of purpose. You descend, ever so slowly. Many hours later, according to the logs in the suit, you're more than two kilometres below the surface of the planet, you arrive in a room that is bigger than anything we have seen before. Felix is clearly very tired now. He is panting. We register atmosphere around them. A compound mixture of oxygen, nitrogen, traces of argon, lots of CO_2, all in all a cocktail that should be very familiar to humans. There are five doors leading into the room. You confidently choose the one straight ahead. It leads into another tunnel, not long, just a few tens of metres, and you emerge into a cavernous room. The ceiling is lost in shadows, but the walls at ground level emit a soft, fluorescent light, illuminating what seems to be a huge, empty basin or pool. You both stand on the edge, two men in all this strangeness, apparently waiting for something. Felix is about to speak, lassitude has made him unafraid, but just as he opens his mouth, he notices that patches of black liquid have begun staining the floor, seemingly from nowhere. Slowly a lake of murky liquid is forming in the cavern. It rises steadily. Felix turns with a questioning look on his face and sees that you are disengaging the clay suit. It falls to the ground at your feet, a pile of unformed matter. You are naked now.

'What are you doing?'

'This room is for sanmonban.'

Steps forward. Descends into the basin. Settles your body down into the liquid. Lies on your back.

--

He was flying, floating really. At peace with the world. Above him a cerulean sky... home, he was home. He gently turned on himself, facing the ground below him. Great rock strewn expanse, arid and baked, extending as far as he could see. Desolate, a small voice murmured, but it was drowned out by the giddiness of homecoming, of belonging. He was coming down, slowly making his way to the ground. He landed softly and found himself a rock to sit on. There was no hurry and he felt good, at peace. It was unclear how long he had been there when, out of the corner of his eye, he saw movement. Un-alarmed, he turned to face the newcomer. It was a woman wearing a black coat, a crepe scarf covering her hair, the flesh of thick calves showing through her black stockings... she stopped a few meters from him and he turned to face her... her mouth opened and closed as if she was trying to say something. He leaned forward, eager for her words. Her mouth opened and closed again convulsively... then, finding her voice, she screamed at the top of her lungs: 'Hunger! I must eat!' and the scream, building in strength, became a world shattering boom, reverberating over the desert landscape. 'Bring me nourishment!' The sudden scream scared Basil who clasped his hands over his ears to keep the sound out. He wanted to get up and run but found he was unable to move. The woman took another step towards him, staring now, eyes bulging in her head. In a sudden flash, Basil sensed confusion and anger and self-reproach and pain; the pain of a dying creature. She frowned and spoke in a normal voice. 'You,' she said. 'Go away. There is no nourishment to be found here. I have dug deep. So deep, stretched my tentacles as far as they will go but there is no sustenance to be found in this barren place.' She considered him again. 'How did you find me? I was alone to come here.' The woman looked up into the cerulean sky, and vanished. With her sudden disappearance the world itself started to fall apart. First the colours drained away, then the ground winked out and Basil, lying on his back, suddenly very cold and very uncomfortable, came to staring into the ceiling of the cavern high above him.

THIRTY-TWO

The battle of Espero

He was tumbling, cradling his earthly remains in his metallic arms. His body was in there, just a few centimetres away from his face. It was a matte grey container, a sleek bullet shape with practical handles along the sides. 'What do you want from me now?' he asked. He had given everything. He was dead already, damn it, what more could it possibly want from him. To find his soul? To finish what it started. It had swallowed him again. He felt it rummage inside him, checking if it missed anything the first time. Some small cobweb of life inside his dead body. There was not. He was as empty as the space around him. Piss off, he thought, I am dead, you cannot touch me anymore. He looked around. He was moving away from it, but he could still see the shuttle tumbling a few hundred metres distant. The hull was glowing cherry red from the laser hit and every twenty seconds it turned so he could see through the hole where the beam had burned through. Turning his head the other way, he glimpsed the fat pencil shape of the Beltane and somewhere in the far distance, below or above him, was Espero, a tan ball covered in wispy clouds. Their time there had been good. A fitting end to the Shields. A year and a half in paradise to see them off. Not bad at all. Could have been a lot worse... He checked the status on the CRAD unit to see how long he had left and the reading shocked him: years, decades before it ran out of power... he looked down towards Espero again and would have laughed had he been capable... Well, in that case, I will be back. Yes, eventually the planet would pull him back and he would plummet through the atmosphere. A shooting star. Pity there would be no one to see his final moment. Something caught his eye. Pinpricks of light played on the exterior of the Beltane. An explosion in slow motion, a cloud of snowy crystals pouring out. The Mingo starship was leaking air. The Shields, he noted with satisfaction. Some of them had made it to the Beltane.

The colony ship, Colfax, arrived in-system on February 25th, 2102. The criminal Malyutin, the sinful man your late father had hired to carry out his plans on Espero and his decimated 39-strong band of mercenaries were still on the planet surface. They had taken up residence, quite comfortably as it were, the colony base was designed for 50.000 people, in the city that would later become the cesspit known as Bastille. The Mingo ship Yu-kiang had left the system over a year earlier, but this Malyutin did not know, although he suspected it. In fact, Malyutin did not know much at all. The Yu-kiang had blown up all his orbital satellites, his drone squadrons, and, worst of all, Sergey Malyutin had died. It was a long time coming, but the radiation poisoning suffered in the aftermath of the Yu-kiang boarding action, had finished him at last. Unfortunately, the mercenaries, who held him in unnatural regard, instead of letting nature run its course, had procured a CRAD unit from the medical facilities on the base and stuck his body in it. The unit was an earlier model of the AEPIR, but it was more than capable of keeping him alive and, to a limited degree, ever so slowly, repair some of the damage. Healing him, however, it could not. Therefore, buried alive in a CRAD unit, in a manner of speaking, he was left to communicate with the outside world through the TacNet. Faced with the non-existence of a life in stasis, Malyutin had quickly changed his mind about the potential pernicious sociological implications of VIE, embracing the possibility of a substitute life with relief. His soldiers would have none of it. Very mistakenly, they thought their leaders lifelong commitment to exterminating chromos and to preaching the wickedness of VIE, meant he would not want it for himself in this situation and thus had removed the VIE modules from the unit. They were wrong. If they refused him the release of death, he would have wanted to disappear into VIE. Not this. Because of a moronic notion that he was a martyr of sorts, he resided like a ghost in the implants of the troops, depending on the exo supported TacNet to provide him with instantaneous real-time links to all his men, seeing what they were seeing, hearing what they heard, but not feeling anything ever again. His existence, for lack of a better word, had been reduced to that of a spectre. It was a surrogate life. He could not imagine any fate worse than this.

They attempted to keep him busy. Caribou brought him with her when she explored the planet. She carried him between her implants and the exo and it was the most intimate he had done with anyone since he was a child. Definitely more intimate that having sex. Only now, they could not touch anymore, even if they wanted to. Like everything else; eating, shitting, picking his nose, it belonged to the past for Malyutin. He had disappeared for reality.

Malyutin did not take well to his new condition. 'You should have let me die,' he complained to Caribou. He did that often. It was his litany. 'We couldn't do that, Sergey, not as long as there is a chance you can be cured.' The standard answer. Her patience was unending. 'Then let me die now.' They could just unplug the CRAD, let him wither away.

'You don't really want that. It is just something you're saying.' It was not. Absolutely not.

She sometimes left the base for days at a time to roam the surrounding countryside with him riding along.

The planet was pristine, but strangely sterile. The wildlife was limited. The largest animals they saw were the ubiquitous goopers and their companions, the black predators, some insects and black beetle-like critters scurrying through the underbrush. The landscape around the base was grasslands, but once you mounted the hills to the east, a great expanse of forest was visible underneath, covering the valley in a carpet of green. The forest itself was formed of trees with gleaming black trunks and soft curving branches utterly entangled with the neighbouring trees in a way that formed an almost impenetrable barrier. A river cut through the forest and they rode it upstream for a few days until they cleared the woods. They turned south, skirting the great forest, until they reached a rift in the ground. The walls of the rift, or canyon, were vertical, glassy, plunging two kilometres straight down to the bottom, which was overgrown with brush. From the Survey Branch maps they knew that the rift was almost a thousand kilometres long.

And then there were the days and the nights. Sunrise here was a protracted affair. Half a workday would pass back home before the two suns were fully over the horizon. He imagined them bickering about it, bickering like his parents, and every day, in the end, they would decide they were too curious to not see what lay on the other side. And when it was finally day it would stay like that for so long, that when the two suns disappeared again, you had almost forgotten the long, long night that was to come. It too had its own beauty to an Earthling of the 22nd century. The night skies were nothing like the dead of an Earth night. There was a band of stars to the east. Someone had named it the Crown, with stars that were so close you could see the deep red and the whitish blue adorning the tacks of the crown like a diamonds and sapphires. And then there were the plants that literally grew so fast you could see them mature with the naked eye, and, when night came, forty-three hours later, they would wither and fade away only to begin all over the next day.

Introspection is a cruel pastime for men like him, but he could not help it. He was granted, afterall, a new modus operandi...he no longer needed those rituals to keep going... Was that the supreme difference? Letting go of panicked, murdering survival? He often reflected on past mistakes. A new luxury to linger over. His thoughts kept coming back to the attack on the Yu-kiang. Why had it failed? He saw a certain sluggishness in himself during that attack that made him wonder if he had lost that... thing that had once made him such a good commander. He had failed to take the Yu-kiang and so, within the merciless logic of defeat, the deaths that followed among her crew became murder, a crime. Just words.

Was he disappointed in himself? Could he have changed, become another man? Could purpose ennoble him? Apparently not.

Malyutin's incessant litany of complaints had Peanut come up with a clever idea. Rummaging through the colony base medical facilities, he found something that he thought would make things a little easier for Malyutin. 'See, Colonel, like this you'll be embodied. No longer a ghost.'

'But... this? It is a toy, for gods sake!'

'Yes, of course, we have modified it. It will receive your neurological stream. Just like a VIE, only it exists in the real world. We remain true.'

Malyutin sighed. *We remain true.* How ironic.

When he was not out with Caribou or the others, Malyutin would sit behind the desk in the diminutive, plasteel office he had created for himself. He would sometimes replay the last message from Mueller. It was a brief directed transmission: 'Colonel, we're have a problem on board...' Then nothing. Not a word since and that was a year and a half ago.

Normally he would have approved of the paranoia that had made Mueller send that message directed to the command centre and with the heaviest encryption, but now he wished he had not. If only Mueller had made it a normal distress call on all frequencies it would have helped him convince the damn Mingo folks that this was a legitimate distress call and that they were actually, really, in trouble. He sat back and gazed passively through the windows of the rectangular habitat container he pretended to inhabit on the main square of the camp. It was morning. From where that metal contraption they had devised for him was sitting, he could see the two suns peeping over the rim of an as-yet unnamed range of low mountains, whose foothills could be seen some 20 kilometres distant. It was going to be another clear, beautiful day.

The base was organised in a square. A classic design as far as military bases went. Like on a medieval fortress or a legionary encampment, a low wall lining the outer perimeter offered moderate protection against local wildlife. The wall mounted automatic light weapons and a basic sensor package. Behind and in front of the wall, the SADU's had cleared a broad band of terrain to act as firebreak. Inside the firebreak, habitat modules in the form of rectangular containers were arranged in squares within the square, creating a neat grid of unpaved streets. The base had four exits and a central plaza, which was big enough that several GAV's could manoeuvre around it.

A group of the ever-present goopers were playing around in the sunshine. Ever since Peanut had taken it on herself to shoot up the swarm of black flying predators, this group had apparently decided that staying around humans was a good thing. Perhaps in their world the human aliens were Gods sent to protect them. Malyutin did not think they needed Gods. They were incredibly tough animals. When he had received the fateful message from the Armagnac, they had waited for a long time. Eventually, with no news from Armagnac and supplies running low, Malyutin had ordered the Shields to redeploy half way across the planet to the colony compound where they would find food and fabricators. The goopers had followed in their wake. A trek of thousands upon thousands of kilometres across swamps and mountains and there they were, pups and all. Most stubborn animals he had ever seen.

One day, it was February 25th, as previously mentioned, Peanut told him someone wanted to talk to him. A ship had arrived in orbit. On screen, a man was waiting for him. Malyutin recognized him. It was Captain Villard.

'Captain,' Malyutin said quietly by way of greeting. Villard was short man with an aura of focused energy about him. He had a long face, salt and pepper hair, eyebrows that formed a vee over eyes that sat a tad too closely together. He smiled thinly at Malyutin. 'You do not look at all like the pictures in your personnel file.' The other man was seeing his virtual avatar, modelled on a picture of his great grandfather, who, family legends would have it, had been a painter. He looked down at his old school manor attire complete with tweeds and tie.

'Yes, well, you caught me a bad moment, I am afraid.'

'Please show me your real face. We are not Sleepers after all, now, are we?' He smiled another of those thin smiles and lifted his eyebrows suggestively.

Malyutin allowed the scene to change to the plasteel office. The sight did nothing to improve Villard's mood.

'What the hell is that? A droid!' he exclaimed.

'Due to some unfortunate circumstances earlier in the mission, I am confined to a CRAD unit for the... umm, foreseeable future.'

Captain Villard leaned back in his chair and put his hands flatly on the table. 'Is there anything else you have neglected to tell me?' he said.

Malyutin looked up sharply. 'Nothing that can't wait until we can meet in person. As I said, the colony base is fully functional and stands ready to receive your cargo.'

'Very well, I am coming down.'

The shuttle from the Colfax arrived 3 hours later. The Shields had opted for a display of relaxed and laid back power. No weapons visible, no hardware. A de-militarized zone, a holiday resort. Caribou was there and one other, the smallest of their number, a guy called Lawrence. Wouldn't do to show off someone the size of Crock at this stage. T-shirts and shorts (flax pants for Lawrence), relaxed stance, half-sitting, half-standing on a couple of flex cargo units that had been left over from the base deployment. Nothing should have been left over, the two crates shouldn't have been there. They was a sign the planners back home had made an error somewhere. That didn't bode well. They followed the approach of the Colfax shuttle from a gleaming rift in the sky until it became an actual stubby winged aircraft with ion engines pushing down and forward to arrest its fall. With almost no corrections -- well done, pilot -- the shuttle hit the middle of the central square, kicking up clouds of yellow dust. A few seconds passed; to allow the dust to settle, to run a few diagnostic checks, to plot an escape vector just in case. If Villard was a good captain, he surely had the crew on alert, ready to lift off at the first sign of trouble. Caribou and Lawrence waited patiently, not a care in the world, those two. Her, a shapely woman, albeit a tad muscular, him a well-proportioned man in his thirties. Nothing to worry about. Finally, the small personnel door on the side of the shuttle swung down and Villard came out. He took a deep breath, bent his knees to pick up a handful of dirt, which he lifted up to his face and smelled religiously.

'I wouldn't eat that, if I were you. Could be a Gooper turd you're holding there,' she called out. Lawrence snickered. Villard looked up and barked a laugh. Two others, dressed in HSL Fleet uniforms, like Villard, emerged behind him.

'Where are your people?' asked Villard.

She shrugged. 'Out, enjoying life. They're not keen to return to space.' That was no lie.

'Can't say that I blame them. This truly is paradise. You are fortunate to be here.' He corrected himself. 'We are fortunate.'

'We are,' she agreed.

A gooper peeked out from between two buildings. The curious animals had decided it was safe to re-appear.

'Hey, look at that! What is it?'

'We call them goopers. Local fauna. Quite harmless.'

He looked at them thoughtfully. 'Tell the Colonel I want to see him.'

'He is expecting you in his office.'

'Tell him to come out here.'

Caribou looked puzzled and called Malyutin who lumbered out of his office. The Espero suns, one of which was directly above them, cast the droid's plastic casing in a dull, carrot coloured sheen. As it walked across the courtyard, it threw up dust which seemed to hang unmoving in the air.

'Stop right there,' said Villard to Malyutin when he was ten meters from the shuttle. Villard himself refused to leave the safety of the shuttle door.

'You are remarkably paranoid, Captain,' said Malyutin's metallic voice.

'Where is the Armagnac? We cannot detect it in orbit and the ship is not responding to our calls.'

'I was hoping you could tell me about her. Didn't you meet them on your way to Espero from Earth?'

'No.'

So... the ship hadn't returned home and it wasn't in orbit... Malyutin's first thought when Mueller had sent him that message was that the crew, the three stooges and the drug addict, however unlikely, had somehow managed to overcome Mueller and his men and returned to Earth. But, if they had, Villard would have met them on route. Very strange. Then where was the ship then? Had the Mingo secretly destroyed it? He would not put it past them.

'Well, the ship disappeared, along with some of my best men. The Mingo probably destroyed it.'

'I doubt that. The Yu-kiang submitted the entirety of her logs to the GSA when she returned.' Pregnant pause while Villard let Malyutin digest the implications.

'There is no more company, Colonel. Halifax does not exist anymore. The GSA dissolved it four months ago by executive order after the discovery that certain divisions within the company had preserved live specimens of HAI's deep within Halifax. They said it was a crime against humanity.' He shrugged. 'We're unemployed now.'

'How do you know this? You left Earth six months ago, did you not?'

'The Beltane relayed the news. She was coming up behind us.'

'The Beltane?'

'Yes, a corporate ship which is coming up behind us.'

'I take it that it is not one of ours.'

'No, it is a Mingo ship.'

'We have been ordered to stand down, relinquish command of the ship to its Captain.'

They both fell silent. Villard's unblinking eyes were staring at him. Malyutin willed the droid to nod its head, but his control slipped and instead, as suddenly as if it had been decapitated, the head of the droid fell to rest limply on its chest for a few seconds, before Malyutin managed to jerk it upright again.

'Mistakes happened,' Malyutin conceded reluctantly in response to Villard's unspoken accusations. 'We must finish what we came for. Zach's orders stand. When will you start unloading the colonists?'

'Is it always this warm?' asked Villard. He looked into the sky with a dreamy expression on his long face, breathing the fresh air deeply into his lungs.

'When will you start unloading the colonists?' Malyutin repeated sharply.

'I am not so sure it is a good idea.'

'Why would it not be? You want to take them back with you? That is ridiculous. We both swore an oath to Zach.'

'There is something you're not aware of... the Beltane is a warship.'

'A warship...?' Malyutin repeated stupidly.

'Yes, the Mingo have armed it. They sent me the rough schematics of the ship along with the message from the GSA. Some kind of turret. They invented their own tracking and fire control system for it.'

'I see.'

'There is more...' Villard looked sad. 'The boarding attempt against the Yu-kiang and the subsequent events...' He hesitated.

'Yes, what?' snapped Malyutin.

'Children were killed when you attempted to blow up the ship...you know. Lots of anger all around. The Captain on the Beltane told me they have orders to exact justice for the crimes you committed against the crew of the other Mingo ship.' He paused for a moment. 'They have a thing they call a letter of marque from the GSA authorizing them to use lethal force to apprehend you and bring you and your men to justice on Earth.' He paused. 'Hence the turret...' He shrugged like it was out of his hands.

The droid stood completely still while Malyutin considered the news. He cursed himself for the arrogance of stopping to talk, to gloat, at the Mingo during the attack, but victory had seemed certain. He paused longer realizing from the echo of his own thoughts, that once he would have called them "Mingo dogs" or "Mingo devils" but somehow he didn't have the force now. If he had not done that, things might have been different... Part of him wondered why he bothered with all this. Locked into a CRAD unit, he would never be able to enjoy the spoils of whatever the outcome would be. But what saves a man is no more than a step. Then another step. It is not always the same step, but you have to take it. He would keep going.

'Villard, they want Espero for themselves. They're trying to split us up.' It was a transparent attempt to deflect Villard and he wasn't falling for it. Well, he had to try something.

'I agree, Colonel, but it is out of my hands.' As he was saying those words, he backed into the shuttle and the doors started closing.

'How long do we have? When does the Beltane arrive? Villard!' the droid's voice cried over the roar of the shuttle engines that were starting up.

'Three weeks,' Villard yelled back. The door closed and the shuttle took off in a huge cloud of dust.

THIRTY-THREE

Yes, Teacher, Malyutin, was the devil incarnated, but a clever one. He thought he knew what the Beltane crew would do once they arrived in orbit. First, they would offload the mining equipment at the Mingo outpost. Then, and only then, would they come for the Shields and they would start their drone search patterns at the Colony Base. It was what he would have done. Once the drones and satellites started their work, there would be no hiding from them. Eventually the Mingo would find them. They had to act quickly.

There was a staff meeting among the remaining officers, unnecessary, as they all agreed on what had to be done.

'They're afraid of us and Villard doesn't dare to start unloading colonists when we're down here.'

'They want us dead or at the very least, brought back to Earth.'

'For more trials...'

'On trial for doing our job. We just did what HSL had bought us to do.'

'We deserve to be here. We earned it and those motherfuckers are not going to take that away.'

He suddenly realized he was afraid to die again. How absurd. Pathetic.

The plan was simple. Malyutin had one drone and one satellite left. He activated both and ordered them to sweep the equatorial belt. He soon found the location of the unmanned Mingo mining base. Unfortunately, it was located on the opposite side of the planet, about 20.000 kilometres from the location of the colony base. He considered asking Villard on the Colfax if he would assist them with a shuttle ride, but discounted that option. Villard had obviously decided to side with the GSA or, at the very least, remain neutral. If he asked for a shuttle ride, he would have to reveal his plans to Villard who, in turn, might decide to reveal them to the Beltane.

--

And so began an operation which, the Shields and their crimes notwithstanding, deserves its own place in the annals of military history. In the course of twenty-two days, the remnants of the Shield Company, 39 strong, redeployed, with all their equipment, some twenty thousand kilometres to the other side of the alien planet. For twenty-two days, the convoy of three GAV's drove without pause, stopping only to clear away obstacles or to help when one of their vehicles got stuck. As mineral deposits were known to be most abundant along the equator, the Mingo had constructed their automated mining station there but after the thrashing they had received during the ground battles a year and a half earlier, they had wisely relocated to the far side of the planet. Consequently, the journey of the Shields took them in a soft curving route from the northern hemisphere of the planet, down to the equator on the other side. The trek, although incredibly arduous, was mostly without incident and around mid-afternoon on the twenty-second day, the Shields were just one kilometre out from the mining outpost, the sight that greeted them was that of a shuttle lifting off from the outpost, slowing rising into the air on an exhaust plume of a high powered ion thruster. They were late. Had they arrived just 5 minutes earlier, they would have caught the shuttle on the ground.

--

The Beltane had, as predicted by Malyutin, decided to finish the mining operations before dealing with the Shields. She had dropped all her automated mining modules into the atmosphere of Espero and as the modules landed, they deployed according to the programming of the corporate planners back on Earth, creating a star-shaped pattern of self-contained mining stations spread out several tens of kilometres from the central processing unit in the middle of the pattern. As each module deployed successfully it got on with the job, stabbing its diamond encrusted drilling spears into the ground to extract the wealth of the Espero soil. They were semi-intelligent machines designed a generation ago to support humankind's need for raw materials to build shelter for its survivors on the shattered home world. Way out here, they were a very long-term investment into a future in which Espero would inevitably play a crucial role. After all the modules had deployed, and this took several weeks, the crew on the Beltane sent down a party of five engineering and mining experts to review the setup first hand. It was normal procedure. On this day, November 18, the time was 1317 EST. They had finished the inspection and their shuttle was taking off, headed back to the Beltane, when Caribou crested the low hill overlooking the landing pad. Malyutin, or rather the glumly comical droid possessed by his spirit, followed by two men who carried the CRAD unit containing his body between them like a pagan effigy, was not far behind.

Twenty-two days and 20.000 kilometres and they were late by *minutes. Minutes.* It could have been days or weeks, but no, destiny would have their failure rubbed into their faces. They crested a hill, the last hill before their goal, and saw the last shuttle rise slowly in the air, ion engines working so hard the whine from the compressors was audible from kilometres away.

Caribou let out a heartfelt curse, then, acting on the instinct of a lifetime of soldiering, she reached out to a man coming up behind her and grabbed the grenade launcher he was carrying. She hoisted it. 'Oh no, you're not getting off so easy,' she muttered while aiming. With a loud pang, the rocket rose into the air. Caribou followed the shuttle with the aiming reticule all the way, guiding the rocket, which was designed to take out static ground targets, at the escaping shuttle and, just as it seemed it would veer off, its charge exhausted, the projectile impacted with the upper most engine section. The shuttle shook, belched white smoke, and then as the pilot decided he might lose the battle against gravity with just two engines, began a spiraling descent which ended in huge sprays of a earth as it tore up the fields before coming to stop.

'Hide, get down,' Caribou hissed as she backed down the opposite side of the hill to get out of view.

'Now what?' asked Crock, who not understood what had transpired.

'Now we wait. I'm betting they don't know what hit them. They'll call it in to the ship as an engine malfunction.'

It was a difficult situation. The plan called for them to seize control of the shuttle without alerting the Beltane. If the starship became aware the shuttle had been hijacked, it would not be allowed to dock. At the very least. No, they had to make sure somehow the five engineers cooperated long enough for the shuttle to be granted docking clearance.

After the emergency landing, the Shields intercepted a radio message from the shuttle saying they had experienced an engine malfunction. The five Mingo crew were milling about around the damaged area, obviously clueless as to its repair. 'It'll either repair itself or it won't, said Caribou. Sadly, it was true. None of them possessed the necessary skills to repair anything starship-related and neither, it would seem, did the Mingo.

The next problem was how to approach the shuttle without scaring them off. The shuttle had set down in a grassy bowl surrounded by gentle hills. From the shuttle, the Mingo crew members had an uninterrupted field of view of the surrounding area. Sniping them would have been easy, but they needed at least one of them alive, and, not the least of their worries, cooperative, to help get them on board the Beltane.

Again Caribou to the rescue. Crock and the others were watching the scene, muttering about tactical scenarios, when they suddenly saw her walk across their field of vision, descending the hill leading down to the shuttle. She had taken off all her clothes. Long legs, shapely ass, large breasts and milky white skin. Nothing the Shields hadn't seen before, they weren't exactly shy about those things, but the effect on the Mingo crew was quite profound. They were all men, a fact not unnoticed by Caribou, and despite the corporate Mingo breeding programs, which in this historical time had been in effect for barely a generation, they gawked. Desire once formed was difficult to extinguish. This was not what someone would expect to see being stranded on an alien planet and all. Who is that? A woman? Beautiful. She was smiling, pearly white teeth, striding assuredly across the yellowing alien grass, but she was, they noticed as she approached, more than a head taller than them and quite muscular, but ooh, look at those nipples, so dark against the pale skin. By then it was too late. And... smack, a fist like a hammer struck one between the eyes in the area just over the bridge of the nose, another got it on the side of the head, rupturing both eardrums before they knew what had happened. One still had a stupid smile on his face when he got hit, blackness engulfed them.

When Firo woke up -- one of the engineers, not the one with stupid smile, mind -- he was tied up with his mates in the back of the shuttle and his implant was jammed.

The tall, beautiful woman was there; only now, regrettably, her dark nipples were covered by what looked unmistakably like a military uniform with a shoulder patch featuring a green snake seen curled up around a yellow shield. *Oh*. The green snake and the shield. *Them*. Bad news. She let Firo live. The four others she had killed in four very creative ways right there in the shuttle. They took his left hand and forced it inside the corpses, and smeared their body parts all over him. He later remembered that they weren't exactly laughing while they did it, but they weren't looking away either. Methodical. Then, the whole gruesome affair having lasted perhaps thirty minutes, they told him to pilot the shuttle into orbit and dock with the Beltane and no funny business.

--

They loaded all the men and their equipment into the shuttle. It was tight fit. When there were no more glaring reds on the status displays, only a few yellows, indicating the shuttle had almost fixed itself, they set off. Caribou was piloting with the little Mingo dude sitting in the seat next her. He was shaking uncontrollably most of the trip and she worried he was going to have a heart attack or a seizure or something that would render him unconscious and useless. The shuttle laboured its way up through the atmosphere. The third engine, the one damaged by her rocket, was not performing optimally, but they were going to make it.

'So, my little friend, time for you to do your thing.' She laid a hand on his shoulder for emphasis. He nodded. 'Good, good. Call in the approach now as you normally would.' He started speaking. 'This is shuttlecraft zero-zero-one on final approach to Beltane docking area. Please confirm docking bay status.'

'Beltane, confirmed docking bay, you are cleared all the way in. That you, Firo? What the hell took you so long?' Firo shook his head pathetically. Caribou patted him on the shoulder and look intensely at him *in just that way*. Firo, who was entertaining thoughts of heroism, decided against it. 'We had an engine malfunction that we had to wait for. The shuttle repaired itself.'

'Why isn't First Pilot Mulo piloting the craft?' asked the voice from the Beltane. Firo glanced uncertainly over his shoulder at the blood-splattered walls. Caribou nodded and smiled at him.

'Mulo is...' He hesitated. '..Mulo is dead.' Caribou's expression hardened, but before she could do anything, the man, heroic soul after all, changed his mind and cried out: 'The Shields are here!' His shoulders slumped. The deed was done.

To Malyutin, who was observing the approach through his droid, the sight of the Beltane brought back many unwelcome memories. It looked very similar to the Yu-kiang but was somewhat longer, about 750 metres overall, and now that the pods containing the automated mines had been launched, it looked like a pencil with a protuberance on both ends. As Villard had said, the Beltane was a proper warship. Humanity's first to grace the interstellar space lanes. It was not much, as warships go, but we all have to start somewhere. The ship was, of course, made from the same GSA blueprints that had created the Armagnac, but because the pockets of the Mingo Corporation were not as deep as those of Halifax, certain parts, like the crew habitat section, were more primitive. The blocky turret gracing the penultimate cargo section just ahead of the fuel shell represented, however, a definite advantage over the Armagnac, and it had just come alive. It started to swivel. 'So Firo, is it beam or kinetic?' asked Caribou conversationally. The little man, figuring it hardly mattered anymore, answered it was kinetic. She entered a series of evasive manoeuvres into the flight computer and the shuttle immediately began a complex pattern of weaving and corkscrewing. Continuous orange flashes from the turret told them it had started firing. For a very short while, it looked like they might have a chance. The sight of tracers as they reached out through space for the shuttle was eerily beautiful, a pearly necklace of light floating sedately across the bow of the shuttle, but, as the turret refined its firing solution, the necklace drew nearer. More bobbing and weaving bought them a few seconds as the string of bullets passed over the shuttle, but the firing computers on the Beltane adjusted. Instead of a single stream of bullets, the turret shifted into a staggered firing pattern where it saturated the area of space in front of the shuttle, making it mathematically impossible to avoid impacts.

'I reckon the gun is building up a lot of heat,' Malyutin said wishfully. His droid had come up to stand beside her in the cockpit. They were very close to the Beltane now, just a few hundred meters, approaching from the stern of the starship.

'Sergey,' said Caribou, 'I think now is the time you should get down to the CRAD.' She turned and looked him in the eye. 'This should be over soon,' she said. He nodded back at her, having finally gotten the hang of it. 'Yeah, looks that way, doesn't it,' he answered. She was pretty, he decided, enhancements and all. Still, he should have done something about it twenty years earlier, but he'd always thought there would be time.

The droid turned and made its way out of the command compartment as alarms went off.

As the first bullets slammed into the shuttle, Caribou gave the order to abandon ship. 'Guess you get to live after all,' she said to the Mingo man called Firo. He looked back at her, eyes wide with fear. She had the clay suit harden around her.

THIRTY-THREE

Colfax

The Colfax was orbiting Espero just ten kilometres away from the Beltane. A few hours earlier, the Beltane had announced she would soon transfer personnel to the Colfax, presumably to ensure he did not suddenly decide to help the Shields once the planned surface battle got underway. The proximity gave Captain Villard an unhindered view of the other ship. They had noticed the shuttle return from it routine check-up run to the planet when sensors warned about some unusual activity. Apparently, the Beltane had opened fire on its own shuttle. The gun turret was flashing repeatedly and the string of bullets and tracers that emerged from it, ended at the shuttle. At first, it looked as if the shuttle was evading them but the stream of bullets kept coming, and soon found the shuttle. More and more debris emerged from the impact points, creating a shimmering cloud of light around the small vessel. Then the gun stopped firing. The shuttle engines had extinguished and were venting gasses, destabilising it and making it tumble uncontrollably. 'My god, what the hell is going on?' Seconds later, clay suited people shot out from emergency hatches and then the rear cargo door opened, disgorging a mass of exos powered by jetpacks. After some confusion, the exos collected the less armoured, clay-suited escapees and then, as one, they accelerated towards the still-open shuttle bay on the Beltane. Villard, who now understood, watched for another minute or so, and when he saw the first Shield exo had managed to make its way into the Beltane shuttle bay, he ordered the Colfax to begin the start sequence on the main engines.

Beltane

When the shuttle exploded, her clay suit had hardened, and she had ejected into space through the nearest emergency hatch. After a few worrisome minutes alone in space a Toukan had jetted past her, slowing down just enough to allow her to grab hold of it. Others were there too, holding on for their lives. Looking around, she thought she saw a handful of exo's. Must have been the people in the cargo hold who had gotten themselves strapped in at the last moment. No one needed to say anything: they all went to the only place nearby: the Beltane. The Toukans jetted towards the ship at full speed, everyone holding their breath against that gun opening up again. It did not and a few minutes later, the longest in her life, they slammed into the hull of the Beltane. The Toukan grabbed hold of the hull. 'The docking bay! Go for the docking bay!' someone screamed and the Toukan driver responded immediately. The bay doors were closing when they arrived, with just eight metres to go. The Toukans went in first, all guns blazing but the bay was empty. The clay suited troops followed. Now what? They did not have time to think. Just as the bay door slammed shut behind them, a group of Mingo exos burst through the door in the far end, spreading out in line formation to maximise firing power against the Shields who had bunched up near the door. A rocket flew through the room and exploded against the wall behind them, followed by machinegun bullets hitting and ricocheting everywhere. Another massive explosion behind her and the concussion sent her sliding along the floor towards a nearby group of crates, which turned out to be useful cover. Caribou hunkered down. Air seemed to be coming back, because noise levels were picking up tremendously and she started hearing bullets whizzing over her head, slamming into the panels behind her. 'Guys, report status!' she yelled. She needed a gun. There was gravity, which meant that the ship was still accelerating. From what she could see, the fight was extremely nasty. Those of them in clay suits had only their hand weapons, if that, useless against exos, which meant it was all up to the Toukans. As for them, the closed space simplified things tremendously. No one was in charge, Malyutin was missing, and the other squad leaders, if they had survived the shuttle, were probably clay suited like her and thus out of the fight. It didn't matter that they were leaderless. There were no tactics to apply, no clever stratagems. The Shield Toukans had lined up against the Mingo exos, Vale units, unless she was very wrong, and they were duking it out at knife range with rockets, auto cannons, machineguns and plasma throwers.

Despite being numerically inferior, the newer Toukans, sharpened by Shield fire discipline, concentrating fire against one Mingo unit at a time eventually prevailed. One by one, the Mingo exos succumbed in a hail of fire against a loss of just one Toukan and two more heavily damaged.

Colfax

Just as Villard turned the ship around to face the LQG point leading to Earth and ordered the main engines brought online for the burn a new contact appeared over the rim of the huge disk of Espero. The pilot homed in on it with the visual sensors. It was about 1000 kilometres away. An asteroid and a big one, measuring at least thirty kilometres in diameter, and from where they were looking, shaped like potato... At first they thought it would impact with the planet, but to their surprise it veered away before tangling with the upper atmosphere.

'Well, hello there... and what might this be?' he asked mildly.

'Where did that come from?' said his navigator.

'What is it?'

'An asteroid?' Except now it looked strangely rectangular. The thermal sensors were picking up a heat signature that was growing by the second. The object was powering up.

'What the hell is going on?' Villard struggled to keep his voice level.

He decided to hail the Beltane. 'Beltane, this Colfax. Are you seeing this?' There was no answer.

'They're probably busy fighting the Shields,' the navigator mumbled.

'Beltane, this Colfax. Report status.'

Villard turned to the pilot. 'Get those engines running. We need to get out of here.'

'We need 2 minutes.'

'Override the count-down.'

'Aye-aye, Captain.'

Hydrogen gas from the fuel tank flooded through the quartz pipes. Plasma surged into the superconducting coils, passed through the ICRH ring, which heated it to millions of degrees Kelvin, and was ejected through the directed magnetic nozzles, creating a superheated wake, which extended for several kilometres behind the ship like a tsunami of plasma. The acceleration pushed Villard and his crew into their seats. As more and more plasma was pushed into the ICHR ring and the superconducting coils got up to speed, acceleration built. Villard, on his back in the captain's chair in the tank, felt his facial muscles slip off his face and literally heard his ribcage groan and creak under the inhuman pressure. The ship continued the punishing burn.

'We should go under soon.' Sedation was the only way survive this kind of acceleration. 'Negative,' replied Villard. 'We need to monitor the situation.' He had a strange feeling in his gut about that asteroid.

'Something is happening, Captain,' groaned the pilot. Villard closed his eyes and willed his implant to bring the sensor data to the fore. The asteroid, or whatever it was, was launching smaller craft. Dozens, hundreds of tiny objects emerged. The sensors were tracking one of them. It was coming in at tremendous speed, about 20.000 km per second if you could trust the radars. The object looked shiny black. It was elongated, drop shaped, perhaps seven times ten metres at the widest. As he looked, the object turned around on itself, and the rear, which was flattened, lit up like an old-fashioned light bulb where you gradually turn up the electricity, until it was shining a bright cherry red. The object was braking. Hard.

'They're going awfully fast, aren't they?' The things were accelerating at more than 200 G's, closing the distance between them and the Colfax lightning quick.

'Oh, they're coming.'

Villard felt panic rise in his throat, congesting his thoughts. He went into the pilots console and overrode the safety blocks on the engines. The reactor output increased, pushing plasma through the magnetic coil at even greater pressure. Acceleration increased again.

When Villard regained consciousness, alarms were queuing up for his attention. *The pilot had passed out, decompression on all decks, three engines out of order and imminent reactor failure...*

Beltane, on the hull

Caribou was scouting for a team of Toukans. After the initial battle in the shuttle bay, the force had split up, usually that would be a classic mistake, but there was considerable confusion now that Malyutin had gone missing. One team headed towards the command section, another down towards the bottom of the habitats where they reckoned the Mingo civilians would be hiding out, someone mentioned hostages, and a third team, and that was Caribous, had gotten the brilliant idea they could maybe take out the engine section. From the outside. *Yeah, right.* But here she was, crawling, crab-like, along the handrails on the massive central pylon that ran the length of the ship. What they would do when they reached the engines was not entirely clear, but the two Toukan drivers that she was scouting for felt good about their chances of disabling the plasma engines with auto cannons. She was trying hard not to think too much about what would happen to the boiling plasma inside the superconducting coils or the quartz pipes when they got shot with kinetic bullets. She grabbed hold of the next rung when once of a sudden what looked like a solid block of crystal in front of her face blocked her way. She looked up the length of the crystal, noticed it came attached to a black sphere and that, deep inside the crystal, colours were flashing, faster than her eyes could follow. A new voice suddenly spoke on the company channel. It was strangely toneless. 'Drop your weapons,' it said. Caribou, who was smarter than most, at the sight of what was unmistakably an alien creature, had decided to stand down right there and then, but one of the Toukan drivers was of another opinion. 'Aliens,' he screamed. It was Guhamiel. 'Hey, I don't think we should be...' she began but by then Guhamiel had already opened up. She saw the glint of beams and kinetics as the two Toukans opened fire on the aliens. They were huge figures, with a pitch-black pod hanging amidst four crystalline jointed legs. They moved so fast across the surface of the hull that they dodged most of the incoming fire. She saw one take a direct a hit from a slug thrower but it just kept coming. The aliens sporadically returned fire with what looked like high powered beam weapons but they didn't stay put long enough to make the weapons count. They kept moving. In seconds, they had closed the distance, and at the last moment, when they were within striking distance, they rose on three legs, using the fourth leg as a scythe, slashing at the human exo's who attempted to evade and block. It didn't work. The alien crystal sliced through the hardened duranium like butter.

Colfax

Villard ordered crew to investigate the decompressions. Apparently there had been breaches on several levels of the habitat shells. He also sent SADU's out to conduct damage assessments on the engines, but one by one, he lost contact with all of them. After a few nerve-wracking minutes in total silence, during which he considered whether he should leave the tank himself and go check on things, he heard a strange clicking sound and saw something push up the ladder leading into the tank. Villard, already on the edge, felt as if his heart stopped.

After a bit of shuffling, two aliens squeezed into the small room. Villard's breathing was shallow and irregular. There was a smell in the air, a heavy pungent perfume that Villard associated with, of all things, his mother. For a while, nothing happened. The creatures stood so still, like grotesque statues in a horror show that Villard had almost managed to convince himself it was a dream. Then the legs lit up. From deep inside what appeared to be transparent crystal, lights winked on and off in complicated patterns, too fast for him to follow. He stared at them, mouth open. The lights seemed to move in waves between the four legs, but so softly the eyes could not discern the phase shifts between colours. The words, when they came, were spoken in a very slow, high-distorted whine. 'Return to orbit. The Teacher has foretold you will colonize the planet Espero.'

Villard nodded, but sensing that they did not understand, he added a whisper: 'Yes. Return to orbit. Yes.'

Two hours later the colonization of Espero has begun with the launch of the first automated stasis module from the Colfax.

EPILOGUE

School of Aneen

As I laid down the book, which was unremarkable in every way, I saw that the time was late and although I was old, and a full night's sleep was a luxury I had not tasted for years, I extinguished the lights and laid down on my cot. My thoughts turned to the anonymous Teller and his last words: 'Pray Teacher, I hope my work has brought you satisfaction and pleasure. Have your servant make my death swift.'

ABOUT THE AUTHOR

Martin Wiinholt used to live in Paris where, among other things, he studied literature at the Sorbonne University. Today he lives in Copenhagen. When he is not writing, he likes to play computer games. In fact, he likes gaming so much, he made a career writing about it as a video games journalist and editor-in-chief of www.eurogamer.dk, the leading gaming website in Denmark. Espero is his first book.

www.ingramcontent.com/pod-product-compliance
Lightning Source LLC
Chambersburg PA
CBHW031258170626
46807CB00001B/200